FROM DARKNESS INTO LOVE

A SMALL TOWN SECOND CHANCE MYSTERY ROMANCE

HOPE & HEARTS FROM SWAN HARBOR
BOOK 1

SOPHIE BARTOW

CONTENTS

My street team;
The Wall-Giennie Wicks-Delaney,
Connector Inspector- Linda Hagerty
Reactor Inspector-Jami Fenton
Plot Crew – Maggie Grimes
Sign Crew- Kate Semenyuk

My family, who allow me to spend so much of my time in Swan Harbor.

Inspiration began,
when a lost girl fell for a lost boy

Two Hearts Press
An imprint of LLIPSS, INC.
Copyright © 2022 by *Sophie Bartow*

Amazon Paperback ASIN: B09Z9ZXR5H

Regular paperback ISBN: 978-1-965510-00-1
Large Print Paperback: 978-1-965510-03-2
Regular Print Hardback: 978-1-965510-21-6
Large Print Hardback: 978-1-965510-06-3

The book was updated, and new content was added in June 2024.
Cover Design by Kate Semenyuk

SOME RESIDENTS OF SWAN HARBOR

Jessica Prince: She is a trained social worker and returns to town after two years away. Jessie is the sister to Dylan. Her parents and brother, James, were killed when she was fourteen.

Cameron Hunter: He is an architect with HCI. Cam has been in love with Jessie for years.

Mary Hunter: A Psychiatrist at Swan Harbor General Hospital. Married to **Clint Hunter** and mother to sons **Cameron** and **Grayson**.

Clint Hunter: Owner of Hunter Construction (HCI). Married to **Mary Hunter** and father to **Grayson** and **Cameron**.

Grayson Hunter: Engineer at Hunter Construction. His story is told in The Memory of Love. His story is told in **The Memory of Love.**

Sadie Martin: She is an accountant and has been best friends with Jessie since they were in kindergarten. She lives and works in Augusta, Maine but is spending the summer in town.

Dylan Prince: He is a Deputy for the Swan Harbor Sheri!'s Department Sheri! and married to **Molly Barnes Prince**. Dylan is the brother of **Jessie**. Their story is told in **The Innocence of Love.**

Molly Barnes Prince: She teaches "first grade at Swan Harbor Elementary School and is married to **Dylan Prince**.

Catherine Gold: She was Jessie's ice skating coach in the early years.

Catherine also dated Dylan before he married Molly. She currently works at Swan Harbor General Hospital.

Eden Fowler: She has just finished her studies at Swan Harbor University and is dating Cameron. Eden is the daughter of Aaron, the Chief of Police. Her story is told in **The Forgiveness of Love.**

Hayden Patterson: He came to live with Danny and Sally when he was eleven, and his parents were killed. He just graduated from Swan Harbor High School.

Tyler James: He is a singer who went to school with Jessie and Sadie. His story is told in **The Christmas Love Song.**

Sally Miller Patterson: Owner of Sally's Diner, the place to see and be seen in Swan Harbor. Sally is married to **Daniel Patterson** and mother to **Christian** and **Tracey.** Her story is told in **Welcome to Swan Harbor.**

Danny Patterson: Married to Sally and the head of neurology at Swan Harbor General Hospital. He's the father to **Christian** and **Tracey**.

Welcome to Swan Harbor

A Haven of Hope for Lost Hearts.

The heart wants what the heart wants.

ONE
PRESENT DAY

Swan Harbor
June 4
7:00 a.m.

Princess,

Cameron Hunter stared out over the beach and watched Jessie. Her red-gold hair blew around her shoulders. Her stride was just as smooth as when she'd skated competitively, and, as it had for years, seeing her caused his heart to trip.

What did that mean? He'd given her everything he had to offer, and yet...

But did you? Did you really?

He brushed back his hair and took another drink of coffee. For the last few nights, he'd struggled to sleep. Waking early each morning, he'd taken a thermos and made his way to the cliff. Located on the edge of his parent's property, it jutted out over the water. During the day, it was the perfect place to think—and at night, the stars were bright.

Jessie stopped and kicked at something in the sand. When she picked it up and stuck it into her pocket, he grinned. It reminded him of other times when she'd done the same thing.

Suddenly, she looked up. Their eyes met across the distance. His heart stopped, and he almost turned his back on her. Except, he couldn't. The connection that had always pulled them together was still there.

What are you going to do about it?

Nothing. He wasn't going to do anything. That was how she wanted it. Right?

Cam took a step toward the path, and once again met Jessie's gaze, lifting his thermos to salute her in greeting. Then he started down the cliff, hoping to escape the feelings seeing her elicited.

When he reached the house, his brother Gray was standing over the coffee pot, watching it boil.

"Why didn't you make coffee?"

"I did."

Gray slanted him a look. "But you didn't share."

"Are you going to tell mom on me?"

"It would be a waste of time."

"Oh?"

"You are the baby, after all."

Cam ignored Gray and settled at the table with one of the last pastries. He'd thought when she was out of sight, she wouldn't be at the forefront of his mind. Unfortunately, it didn't work like that.

"Want more?" Gray asked once the coffee was brewed.

"Nah, I'm good."

Gray settled at the table across from him. The look in his brother's steely blue eyes made him uncomfortable.

"What?"

"You know what."

He did but wasn't ready to acknowledge that.

"I thought you were going to Boston for a few days."

"Changing the subject doesn't change what I'm thinking about," Gray grunted. "I think you know what."

"Maybe," Cam sighed. "I'm just not—"

"—Ready," Gray muttered. "I've heard that a time or two lately."

"It's still true."

"What about—?"

"Don't bring her into it," Cam shut him down. "I can't."

"Love doesn't work like that."

Cam laughed. "Oh? How would you know? Are you in love?"

"No, I'm just…"

"You know what mom would say, don't you?"

"She would say the same thing to you," Gray returned. "Listen to your heart—it always knows."

But did it really? If someone had asked him that same question three years, hell, even four years ago. He would have agreed. Until she…

"Is that what you're doing?"

"Low blow."

Cam studied Gray for a few seconds, then came back with, "I didn't mean it to be one. Is there a problem between you and—?"

"I don't know what's going on," Gray cut him off. "I'm hoping to figure that out on this trip."

"And if you don't?"

Gray shrugged. "I'll deal with it then."

He wanted to say, 'It seems we're both having issues.' Except, if he did so, it could lead to assumptions. Ones he wasn't ready to explain.

Gray pushed back his chair and gave him a pointed look. "While you might want to think our situations are similar, they aren't. Think about that while you're at the wedding and everyone is there. I'll see you in a few days."

Cam waved his brother off and pushed his 'what if' thoughts away. He needed to run an errand while he tried to come up with a plan.

Those thoughts propelled him in and out of the shower and toward town. One of his best friends was getting married, and he needed to pick up several things.

Sally's Diner
June 4
12:00 p.m.

"Here you go, Jess." Sally, the diner's owner, set a plate of fries and a milkshake in front of her. "Enjoy."

Jessie inhaled the greasy smell of the fries and sighed with contentment. "I've missed these."

"Is that all you missed?"

It was a question meant to trap her. That was something Jessie knew for sure. The problem came when she tried to answer.

"Of course, I missed Swan Harbor."

Sally glanced out the window, and when she turned back, her blue eyes were twinkling. "I bet you missed some things more than others, didn't you?"

She moved on, not really expecting an answer. But when Jessie glanced up, she wasn't surprised to see Cam passing by.

Her heart stuttered for a second before taking off at full speed. He was alone, and there was a purpose in his walk. Was he on his way to see...?

Don't go there, Jess!

She ate another fry and thought back to her walk on the beach. Somehow, she'd known Cam would be on the cliff watching her. He'd been there for three consecutive mornings. A part of her wanted to think it was intentional. In contrast, the other side wouldn't listen.

Her life was what it was because of decisions she'd made—or was it? Could she have made a different choice? But that wasn't an answer she was ready to acknowledge. If she did, then it would mean she'd wasted two years of her life. Two years of *their* lives?

That thought caused the ice cream to settle heavily in her stomach. Jessie pushed it aside, paid for the food, and escaped into the fresh air.

It was summer and the tourist season for Swan Harbor. By July, the sidewalks would be crowded and the beaches full. Shop owners loved it, but most of the residents couldn't wait until September.

She couldn't say if she liked one season more than the other. There were benefits to both. Or at least she'd always thought so growing up. Crowded sidewalks were not her thing.

In an hour, she was expected at the salon, Foxy Lady. There was a wedding tonight, and she needed to be ready. After all, it was the reason she'd returned home.

Was that the only reason?

She side-stepped another visitor and started to cross the road. Suddenly, she was tugged backward just as a bicyclist whizzed past, barely missing her.

It happened in the span of a heartbeat, but she'd known who'd saved her.

Jessie's eyes flared. She quickly pulled her arm free and moved away from the flow of traffic. Her heart raced from the near miss, but that wasn't where her attention lay.

"I, I guess I should say thank you." She met Cam's gaze briefly before looking away.

"Don't say it on my account," Cam's mocking voice intoned. "I would have done it for anyone."

His response left a sting behind, and for a moment, she wasn't sure how to respond. Then, she saw what he was carrying, making it easy to change the subject.

"You must be the one decorating the car. What did you buy?"

Cam smiled, one just big enough to briefly show off his dimples.

"I bought the good stuff."

"Meaning?"

Almost reluctantly, he opened his bag for her to peer inside. He'd bought markers, balloons, and twine."

"Who's bringing the cans?"

Cam shrugged. "That wasn't my job."

"Who's blowing up the balloons?"

"I would assume whoever we can get. Care to blow up a few?"

Jessie's breath hitched. His voice was intimate—a tone she hadn't heard in two years. With it, regret once again rushed through her. She'd missed her chance. Hadn't she?

"Anyway, thanks again. I'm due at the Foxy Lady." Then, as gracefully as possible, Jessie started toward the salon with a different question on her mind. How was she expected to make it through the wedding without falling apart?

The Lighthouse Inn

June 4
4:15 p.m.

Jessie.

Cam ignored the conversation around him and prepared for the next step. The one that involved walking down the aisle—with Jessie on his arm. Something he hadn't considered until the rehearsal, which he hid beneath a facade of happiness.

The few times their eyes clashed, his heart raced. When he'd touched her, it caused his fingers to tingle.

It hadn't affected her, though. Or at least that's what he'd thought the night before. Tugging her back from the crazy bike rider showed him how wrong he'd been.

As soon as their gazes collided, he saw the shadows in her eyes. He'd noticed how she constantly rubbed her fingers over her arm where they'd touched. Those were nothing compared to what happened when she looked in the bag.

Her breath hitched, just as it had in the past. When she glanced up, a rosy hue was spread across her cheeks. Her voice was husky and a touch breathless.

Behaviors that gave him hope. But could he trust them?

He wanted to think he was happy, but he wasn't sure he believed it. Wanted to think he hadn't missed her, but knew he was lying to himself. Wanted to believe Jessie was his past and not his future, but knew that wasn't true.

With one look, he was back under her spell. Just like always, she mesmerized him. Even after she'd crushed him, their hearts were connected and always would be.

That should have made everything easy. Instead, it brought back feelings he'd worked to hide. Feelings that didn't involve love—as he was willing to admit he still loved her. The question was, could he trust her with his heart once again?

Finding the answer was put on hold when the minister pulled the groom away. Seconds later, the bride and bridesmaids joined the groomsmen, and almost unconsciously, his gaze drifted to her.

Jessie was fussing with the bride's dress. She knew where he was standing.

That was evident by the number of times she glanced up. How he felt when it happened didn't help his peace of mind, though.

"It's about time," the coordinator whispered. "Men, find the woman you're escorting down the aisle. Hurry, here comes the music."

Cam started walking toward Jessie, who gave him the once-over. Her silent scrutiny left prickles of warmth dancing along his skin, and his nether regions stirred to life.

A friend. She's only a friend. It was much safer.

Nice words, but did he believe them?

"Ready?"

"I think so."

Cam offered Jessie his arm. When she hooked hers through, he could feel her heat. Could hear the catch in her breath.

He ignored the fact that everyone was watching them. Ignored the heady smell of Jessie's perfume. Ignored how her arm felt in his and focused on putting one foot in front of the other.

What he hadn't considered, though, was that when he stood on the groom's side, she was directly in his line of sight.

"Dearly Beloved," the minister began. "We are gathered here today..."

With every word, the barriers he'd built around his emotions started to crumble. With every line the bride and groom repeated, Cam's dreams of the future reappeared. With every crack in his carefully constructed facade fading away, his heart was no longer safe. Was that something he could accept?

He wanted to say no. Wanted to say he couldn't go through anything like that again. And then...

"I now pronounce you man and wife. You may kiss your bride."

Cam's eyes locked with Jessie's. In them, he saw everything he'd ever wanted looking back at him. Was it still possible to protect his heart? Or better yet, did he even want to?

TWO

The Lighthouse Inn
June 4
7:00 p.m.

Jessie's jaw hurt from gritting her teeth to keep from making a sound. One that would let Cam know he still mattered.

For the past two hours, she'd been sitting next to him on a raised platform. Every time he moved, his leg bumped against hers, and electricity jumped from the point of impact. It brought everything full circle—something she wasn't sure she was ready to face.

"Jessie?" Cam's husky voice broke into her thoughts. "Refill?"

"Sure. Thank you."

"I'll be right back."

Once he was gone, she grabbed the table's edge and fought the need to run screaming from the room. Her head was spinning from Cam's cologne, and her hands were shaking. Behaviors she should have expected but not ones appropriate for a bridesmaid.

"Jessie, "the groom whispered. "Are you okay?"

"I need some fresh air."

"Go." He nodded to the doors behind them. "I'll cover for you."

Jessie stepped off the elevated stage and slipped out an open door. The bouquets of pink, white, yellow, and purple flowers still decorated the ceremony area, but her focus was on the cliff several yards beyond. She dropped her shoes on a chair and, bypassing the arch where Cassie and Ryan were pronounced husband and wife—she could finally breathe.

The wind whipped her long hair around her head and molded the periwinkle dress to her body. With the view below, she could easily imagine living in another time. One where she was the princess looking down upon her charges as they readied for battle.

A fanciful thought, yes. But somehow, the analogy felt right. It hadn't been easy to return home after two years away. However, it had been the *right* thing to do for Cassie, one of her best friends. Then, once committed, there'd been no running, especially when their other friend, Sadie, got involved. Since returning, Jessie had been forced to admit how much she'd missed them—and Swan Harbor.

Laughter spilled from the ballroom, and without even turning, she could feel him watching her. Cameron Hunter was six feet, two inches, with shaggy blond hair, deep dimples, and eyes that undid her. Whether they sparkled with happiness or were dark green with desire, they'd always made her feel as if he could see inside her soul.

Cam had been a part of her life forever, seeing her at her worst and her best. When her life had been torn apart, he'd given her strength and helped chase the darkness away. She loved him, and at one time, he'd loved her. However, upon her arrival in town, seeing him locked in an embrace with another woman left her reeling.

Her brother, Dylan, had shared the woman's identity. Eden Fowler was the only daughter of the Chief of Police and several years her junior. But the sight of another woman in Cameron's arms forced her to be honest with herself. Something she'd been reluctant to do for years.

Cam had always been the one constant in her life, and she hadn't expected that to change. Somehow, the fantasy image of him meeting her at the town line had stuck inside her head. That he'd be waiting for her to return.

However, seeing him with another woman made her realize it was time to *put up or shut up*. Except that meant revealing why she'd stayed away for so long. Could she do that? After all this time, could she explain there'd been a reason why she'd left Swan Harbor?

She'd tried to ignore her feelings when they'd been thrown together as members of the wedding party. A get-together at the arcade, a bonfire on the beach, and other moments meant to celebrate Cassie and Ryan's upcoming nuptials. After every occasion, Jessie sought refuge from her feelings of loss and escaped to Sonny's. Only on the ice had she been able to outrun the demons that never seemed to be far away.

Had it worked?

She thought so until she saw him on the cliff. Until he'd touched her the previous night. Until she'd held his arm as they walked down the aisle. But then, during the ceremony, their gazes had been drawn to each other. That's when her heart stuttered, and some of those empty places began to fill.

Then, he turned away, and the moment was broken. His attention was on Eden, causing an ache deep inside. An ache she'd tried to ignore but one that hadn't completely gone away.

Eden was pretty and kind and devoted to Cameron. Everything he deserved, but...

Since then, the words, '*It should be me,*' were on repeat inside her head. They had her wondering if it was too late for the Princess to win the battle for her own happily ever after.

"Jessie?" Cam placed his tuxedo jacket around her shoulders. "Readying for war?"

She frowned. "Why would you say that?"

Cam shrugged. "I don't know. You just looked so..."

"No war," Jessie replied. Then silently added, *yet.* "Did you need something?"

"It's almost time for the dances. Shall we?"

Jessie retrieved her shoes and returned inside, knowing that Cam and she were being watched. Rather than looking around, though, her entire focus was on the bride and groom. The way they were staring at each other caused her eyes to water.

"You ready?"

Cam pulled her close, and their movements immediately meshed. "There," he murmured. "That's not so bad, is it?"

What she'd both feared and desired happened as the pieces she'd been searching for clicked into place. With him—she was home. Ignoring how she felt hadn't worked. The question was, what now?

That answer didn't come easy. What if she put herself out there, and he rejected her? If that happened, she didn't know how she'd feel. It made her nervous—*he* made her nervous.

Why, though? This was Cam. He'd been a part of her life forever. But the pep talks didn't seem to do any good, and her heart rate wasn't slowing down.

"You're still light on your feet," Jessie quipped. "I won't have to worry about my toes."

"No, Jess," he whispered against her temple. "You don't need to worry about your toes."

His voice was low and dangerous. The unspoken message had her insides waking, wondering what was next. There was much she wanted to say, but the subtle tightening of his palm on her lower back had her resting her head against his shoulder. They would talk … eventually.

"Oh, Princess," Cam sighed, almost as if it was an afterthought.

Jessie held her breath, waiting … hoping he would say more. When he didn't, she couldn't help but wonder if maybe, for the first time in a long time, they were on the same page.

✦

"Jessie, I," he whispered. But then, the dance partners changed, and he was looking into the bride's dark eyes.

"You look beautiful today, Cassie." He attempted to thwart her questions.

"Thank you." Cassie's knowing eyes met his. "But that won't work, you know?"

"No?" he grinned. "I thought women always enjoyed a compliment … or two."

She glanced around his shoulder at where he knew Jessie was dancing with her new husband. "When are you going to tell her how you feel?"

"Eden?" Cam let it hang for several seconds. "She knows how I feel."

"Does she?" Cassie surprised him by asking. "Do you love her?"

"I—" he began but couldn't complete the sentence and settled on, "I care about her … a lot."

"Be careful, Cameron," Cassie warned. "The heart wants what the heart wants."

"And you don't think I know something about heartbreak?" he snapped, not caring if he was being unfair.

"I know Jessie hurt you, but isn't love worth fighting for?"

The question was barely out of her mouth before her new husband whisked her away. It left Cam standing in the middle of the dance floor with much on his mind. That had him heading away from Eden and toward the bar.

"Whiskey, neat," he requested.

While he waited for his drink, his gaze was drawn back to the dance floor. Jessie was laughing, and the words *the heart wants what the heart wants* echoed inside his head. *Damn!* The ache in the center of his chest wasn't what he'd hoped to feel.

Cam reached for his drink and tossed back the entire glass. The liquid burned when it hit the back of his throat. A feeling he relished, though, as he needed something to distract from his inner turmoil.

"You're drinking?" Eden's accusatory tone set his teeth on edge. "You know I don't like the taste of that stuff."

"I didn't ask you." Cam pulled his gaze away from the dance floor to the petite blonde. "I'm sorry. Dance?"

Eden's face lit up, but instead of being pleased, he felt unsettled. The feeling persisted on the dance floor. It had him giving single-word responses until she finally gave up and leaned her head against his chest.

He tried to stay focused on the woman in his arms. But the memory of dancing with Jessie was still too fresh in his mind. He'd been told he had a 'type' by more than one of his friends. Except for height, he could see the similarities between the two women. Both were beautiful, with delicate features, strawberry-blonde hair, and blue eyes. Eden's were like the sky. However, it was Jessie's turquoise ones that lived in his mind. They would twinkle one minute and darken the next, her moods and emotions fully displayed.

The heart wants what the heart wants was on repeat inside his head. Was he ready for the emotional roller coaster? Once the answer was out there, his life would no longer be under his control. Could he trust that this time, what he wanted and what he got were the same things?

❧

The Lighthouse Inn
June 4
10:00 p.m.

Hours later, Jessie followed her friends into the bride's dressing room. As soon as the door closed, Cassie pinned her with a pointed stare. "How are you holding up?"

"Shouldn't I be asking you that?" Jessie pushed Cassie's hands aside to help with the wedding dress laces and sought to change the subject. "Did I tell you how beautiful you looked?"

"Oh, Jessie." Sadie's eyes met hers in the mirror. "Don't you think it's time to talk?"

"Talk about what?" Jessie looked from one to the other and realized her running days were over.

"Well, duh," Sadie arched one dark brow. "Let's see ... Cam?"

"Cam," Jessie sighed. "There's not much to say. He has a new girlfriend, and they appear to be happy."

"Appearances can be deceiving," Cassie intoned.

"Eden seems very ... sweet," Jessie forced out between gritted teeth. "It's just that..."

"You want him for yourself," Sadie finished quietly.

"Well, yeah. But, if he's happy, then aren't I supposed to be happy for him?"

"Cam's being," Cassie waved her hand around as if searching for the right word, "safe. He doesn't love her."

"You asked?"

Cassie tossed her a mischievous grin. "I asked."

"Wait, really?" Jessie fired back.

"Yes, really," Cassie hummed. "He started to lie..."

"But?"

Well," Cassie went on. "He did admit he cared for the girl."

"That's not love," Sadie jumped in. "Which means you still have a chance. Isn't he worth fighting for?"

Was he? Jessie wrapped her arms around her stomach and wandered to the window. Her thoughts returned to how she felt during the ceremony when the vows were read aloud. Of how every time Cam was near, her heart felt whole. More importantly, though, of how when she'd been in his arms on the dance floor, she'd realized he was her home. Was she ready for that battle?

"But Eden's…"

"Not you," Sadie murmured.

"Well, of course, she's not me," Jessie sighed.

"But since he couldn't have you," Cassie pointed out. "He picked someone who resembled you."

"No," Jessie muttered.

"Come on," Sadie argued. "Can't you see it?"

Jessie still wasn't ready to completely give in. "Her hair's blonder."

Cassie rolled her eyes.

"Eden's short," Jessie continued.

"She's also young," Sadie added.

"Eden's safe," Cassie circled back to where she'd started. "He's waiting for you."

"Ha," Jessie scoffed. "I'm not convinced he's pining for me as much as you seem to think."

"Well," Cassie's dark eyes twinkled. "When you catch my bouquet, let's see how long he'll be able to stay away."

"Me?" Jessie laughed. "What about Sadie? She's still single."

"Oh, I know." Cassie exchanged conspiratorial looks with Sadie. "But she's waiting for Gray to come to his senses and figures…"

"If I'm with Cam," Jessie chuckled at their devious minds. "I can put in a good word."

"Exactly," Sadie giggled. "Those Hunter men just need a little push."

Jessie blinked several times to clear her vision. "I missed you guys," she whispered. "Thanks for being my friends."

"Hey," Cassie sniffed. "Don't make me cry and ruin my make-up."

"Sorry," Jessie grinned. "It's been nice to be home."

Sadie and Cassie wrapped her in a group hug. "We're glad you're home too."

"Now, remember," Cassie reminded her. "I'm aiming for you."

"And if someone gets in the way," Sadie giggled, "knock them over."

"Got it."

It was a plan, Jessie thought. Could she go through with it, though? Could she put her heart out there one more time?

Cam had a hard time looking away when Cassie, Jessie, and Sadie returned to the room. Each woman was striking on her own, but there was something about the three together that reminded him of *Charlie's Angels*. One was dark, one brunette, and one light. They were strong, independent women whose bond had been forged years before. He'd learned a time or two in the past, hurt one, you hurt them all.

"Have you spoken to Jessie?" Ben, his friend, and the other groomsman asked as soon as Eden left for the bouquet toss.

"We danced," Cam responded defensively, "and spoke briefly."

"Chicken."

Cam sighed. He knew his friend was right. But....

"I need to," he admitted. "I'm just not sure what to say."

"You tell her she broke your heart." Ben hesitated for a beat. "You tell her you forgive her and want her back."

"I'm dating Eden."

"Dating," Ben repeated quietly. "What if Eden catches the bouquet?"

"What about it? That won't change anything."

"Won't it? You know Eden's going to want more."

"Why do you think so?"

"Eden graduated from college and is ready to start her career," Ben reminded him. "Isn't marriage the next step?"

"So?"

"So, what will you say then?"

Before Cam could answer, a squeal made him look over his shoulder to see Eden push Jessie aside and grab the bouquet.

"Oh, shi..." he barely got out before Eden launched her body into his arms and kissed him.

It took several seconds to regain his wits and create a little distance between them. "Whoa there, Sugar," Cam drawled, his standard nickname tripping off his tongue. "Where's the fire?"

Eden mumbled something, but his attention had drifted across the room to where Jessie stood, watching him. He gave her what he hoped was a '*We need to talk*' look. Before he could move, though, she ran from the room. His gaze sought Sadie's, but when she sent him an accusatory look, all he could think about was it was time to fix things.

"Eden, I," he began, giving Ben a *Help me out* expression.

"Cam's trying to tell you," Ben turned his charm on Eden, "that I'm driving you home tonight."

"What's going on?" Eden frowned.

"Cam needs to take care of something for Ryan," Ben answered smoothly.

"Oh, okay."

Eden's smile dimmed, and for a split second, Cam felt guilty. Then, just as they had all night, the words *'the heart wants what the heart wants'* floated through his head. They reminded him of what was important. With little more than a buzz on her cheek, he went after what he wanted—a second chance.

As expected, he found Jessie on the ice at Sonny's. Illuminated by a single light, she skated to music only she could hear. Her movements weren't as polished as when she'd practiced daily. But as she transitioned from a split jump to an axel and then moved from a salchow to a sit spin, he realized she was lost in her memories.

He watched her for another minute. When he couldn't stay away any longer, he dropped onto an old bench and slipped into his skates. They hadn't been worn since the last time he'd been on the ice with Jessie. It hurt too much, making him think about what could have been. Instead, he'd tried to bury those feelings, living only in the present and choosing safe company.

Until four days ago, he'd been successful. Then, Jessie walked into Randy's Arcade, with Sadie on one side and Cassie on the other. She'd laughed and talked with her friends as if she'd never left.

Every sound had been like a stab to his heart, and every word had caused a sick feeling in his gut. He hadn't confronted her, though. Instead, he'd paid more attention to Eden. While it had temporarily numbed his pain, he'd felt miserable.

He would admit a part of him hoped she'd come home ... to him. Hoped she was ready to give him the chance he'd been waiting for since she was fourteen. However, before they could talk, she'd disappeared. Then, like always, he'd followed, finding her on the ice at Sonny's.

Those times, he stayed on the outside, looking in. Even when he'd placed his beat-up old skates in his trunk, he'd planned nothing specific.

Tonight was different. After watching two of his best friends pledge their lives to each other, he finally admitted safe wasn't working. Cam wasn't sure where things would go. He wasn't sure how he'd be accepted. What he did know was he had to try. As for everything else, there was always hope.

With that in mind, he stepped onto the ice. Wherever Jessie was, he would find her.

When hearts connect ...

THREE
TEN YEARS EARLIER

Jessie's Home
December 27
2:00 p.m.

MOST FIFTEEN-YEAR-OLD GIRLS SPENT THEIR CHRISTMAS BREAK hanging with friends, talking on the phone, and dreaming about boys. But Jessie no longer felt like a typical teenager. Her parents and brother, James, had been killed in a fiery car crash the previous February. Since then, nothing had been the same.

She'd spent the holidays with her brother and the Hunters, their surrogate family. While they'd tried to create a 'normal' Christmas, Jessie had felt out of step. Memories constantly bombarded her, and the dreams she'd thought were behind her had returned. They followed her everywhere, unsettling her in many ways.

Thanks to help from her grief counselor, she didn't dream often. Unless she was lonely or it had been a highly emotional occasion, then they returned. Christmas had been one of those times.

The dreams always began with a mashup of happy memories. Inevitably, though, they morphed into those final moments with her parents.

Jessie stood on the porch, dressed in old sweats, while her mother gave her last-

minute instructions. The longer she stood there, the more the wind blew through her thin clothing, causing a chill to race up her spine.

"Hurry, Ruth," her father honked the car horn. "We'll be late picking up James."

Her mother rolled her eyes. "Men," she retorted. "I'd better go. Remember, we'll be home late."

"Okay, Mom." Jessie shivered, impatient to get inside where it was warm. "Have a good trip."

As her father backed the car out of the driveway, he rolled down his window. "We love you, Princess."

Jessie slowly fought her way up through the grief, the memory of just waving at her parents and running inside weighing heavily on her mind. It was the same as every other time she had the dream. She was angry she hadn't taken the few seconds to return the words.

Whenever the dream appeared, it set the tone for the rest of the day. It brought the darkness that only stayed away when she skated. She tried to fight it. Tried to get involved in listening to the new music she'd gotten for Christmas. While it helped for a short time, eventually ... the darkness returned. Finally, she grabbed her skates and made her way to the frozen pond.

The darkness chased her around the ice longer than she cared to admit. Then, little by little, it faded, becoming lighter and lighter until relinquishing its hold. Once that happened, her skating became less hectic and freer, allowing her to practice different moves.

Stopping wasn't an option. If she did, the darkness might return, and questions would be asked. Ones she'd answered many times before. Ones she was tired of hearing.

Jessie knew Dylan was watching. She didn't have to see him to know that. He'd come outside and stood on the porch ... waiting for her, just in case. While she appreciated he was there, it was easier when she was alone. Then, she didn't have to behave as if things were fine. On the ice, she could follow her heart. Could listen to the feeling inside and just skate. On the ice, she could just be...

Jessie's Home

December 27
4:00 p.m.

Cam climbed into his old pick-up truck and drove toward the Prince's home. Their families had been friends long before he was born. Meaning that, for most of his life, he'd grown up thinking of Jessie, two years younger, as *just Jessie.*

However, the summer she'd turned fourteen, he'd seen her in a bikini top. A female had replaced the tomboy he'd always known. One whose legs seemed to go on forever, and filled out her bikini in all the right places. Suddenly, Jessie was the girl who starred in his dreams. This time, though, in a much different capacity.

The summer and fall before her parents' death, he'd worked to win her heart. But no matter how much he flirted ... she only saw him as a friend. She came to him when she wanted to complain about school, her brothers, her friends, or even other boys. He was stuck in the friend zone, and he didn't know how to get out.

When her parents and brother were killed, Jessie stayed with his family for a few months. He'd gotten close to her, just not in the way he'd wanted ... nor in the way he'd expected. There were nights when he'd been the one to hear her crying. Those were the times he'd offered a shoulder for her to lean on. She trusted him—and he refused to violate her trust.

During one of those nights, he'd decided Jessie needed to be the one to choose what capacity he held in her life. If they were destined only to be friends, he would honor her wishes. Since then, he'd stuck to his plan. He was there if she needed him—whenever she needed him.

In the past, Christmas Day had been a loud and noisy holiday. There had been arguments over sports and pie competitions. Then, once dinner was over, a hockey game on the pond. This year, there'd been none of that. The day had been quiet ... too quiet.

When Jessie and Dylan had gone home, the atmosphere hadn't changed. His parents had gone one way, his brother another, and he'd watched some mindless movie.

It had taken hearing how she spent her days for him to figure out what to do. Especially with the knowledge Dylan was worried about her. They might only be friends, but she was still his princess. She needed to learn that as long as she hurt … so did he.

It hadn't been a tough choice to volunteer to spend time with her. He loved watching her move, both on the ice and off. Jessie was always graceful. But when she was skating, her beauty took his breath away. The way she glided across the ice mesmerized him, reminding him of a swan in motion. She was a joy to watch, and if they didn't talk much … he was okay with that. As long as she was happy, so was he.

When he climbed from his truck, Dylan stood on the porch, but Cam's attention was focused entirely on Jessie. He grabbed his skates and trekked through the snow toward the frozen pond.

Jessie slowed slightly, her eyes never leaving his. The look on her face said she wasn't upset he'd driven over.

"Hey, Princess," Cam called teasingly. "May I join you?"

Jessie tilted her head one way, then another, and he wondered what she was thinking. "Tired of reading?" she finally asked.

"Just couldn't concentrate."

Her look was knowing, but she didn't push the issue. Instead, she inclined her head in that regal way of hers and nodded toward his skates. "Think you can keep up?"

"I guess we'll see, won't we?" He hesitated a beat. "If you'll allow me to skate, that is."

She rolled her eyes. "Put your skates on, Hunter. Then catch me … if you can."

By the time Cam stepped onto the ice, Jessie had zipped past him several times. He waited for her to get close and then tossed a jaunty "Race you!" over his shoulder before upping the pace. If she wanted speed, he'd give it to her.

With longer legs, he thought he had a distinct edge. However, his princess was hot on his heels, seemingly determined to overtake him. Yet, Jessie's attention was on other matters, which never wavered.

Even when his brother arrived to pick up Dylan, she said nothing. She had a mission and wasn't willing to be sidetracked, which was okay with him. It gave him time to observe and be ready for what came next.

The first hour flew by, and he was okay. Halfway through the second hour, he was barely hanging in there. However, when the third hour rolled around, he'd nearly fallen more than once, and it was getting damn cold.

Cam reached a point where only a part of him was focused on her. The other half was working to maintain his dignity on the unfamiliar ice. Jessie was still skating as if the hounds of hell were on her tail, which was why he'd stuck close. If she fell, he planned to catch her.

Their conversation was minimal, with only a word here or there. Finally, her expression softened, and she grinned. Cam's shoulders relaxed, and he let go of the breath he'd been holding. Somehow, it felt like a new beginning.

After another half hour, his legs were turning to jelly, and the lengthening shadows had him searching for a reprieve. The next time around, he pushed in front of her and turned to skate backward. "Want to rest?"

Jessie's eyes twinkled, telling him she was on to him. "What's the matter, Hunter? You a wuss?" She flipped her long hair over her shoulder and took off. "If you can catch me, we can rest."

The laughter in her voice made his heart do several mini-flips. "Not a problem, Princess."

Cam dug into his waning energy and skated past her. He set up and executed a perfect hockey stop, throwing snow around them.

"Not bad."

"Not bad?" Cam huffed. "Did you see how high the snow flew?"

"I said it wasn't bad, but let me show you how it's done." She patted him on the cheek and skated past.

Her hockey stop, as expected, was done perfectly. He winked as he sped past, and the glint in her eye distracted him for a split second.

Unfortunately, it happened in the spot on the ice he'd almost tripped over multiple times. This time, though, he wasn't so lucky. Before he could catch himself, he face-planted and slid several feet before landing at the base of a mound of snow—much of which fell on top of him.

The thought he should bounce to his feet as if nothing was wrong floated through his mind. Then, a handful of seconds later, his muddled brain registered she was near.

"Cam." Jessie brushed the snow off his face. "Cam, are you okay?"

He kept thinking he should roll over, but then her warm hand gently pushed back his hair. The feeling it created had the opposite effect, making him want to stay there forever.

"Please wake up," she whispered. "Cam, please wake up."

Her voice sounded different, more worried than usual. Unwilling to cause

Jessie unnecessary pain, he rolled over and gave her a cheeky smile. "Don't stop touching me, Princess." He wiggled his eyebrows teasingly. "I like it."

Jessie scanned his face for an extra minute. Something told him she was looking for injuries.

"You're okay? Really?"

"I'm fine, but you appear to be a little too ... dry." Cam rolled over, tucking her underneath him.

"Cam?"

"Jessie?"

He tried to keep his eyes on hers, but as if powerless to resist, his gaze landed on her lips. Her mouth dropped open slightly, giving him ideas he probably shouldn't be having. It was only the memory of why they were on the ice that had him changing his mind.

The breath he'd been holding fled. Then, before he could second-guess his actions, Cam grabbed a handful of snow and dropped it in the V of her jacket. "Gotcha," then scrambled several feet away.

"Argh." She jumped up and tossed over her shoulder. "You'd better watch out, Hunter. Paybacks can be a bitch."

❧

Jessie's thoughts were unsettled as she skated away. Whether it was because of something Cam had done ... or something he hadn't, she couldn't say. He'd always been that boy she'd watched from afar, never assuming they were destined to be anything more than what they were. Because of the history between their families, he'd always treated her the same as her brothers, like a sister.

Cam was a flirt. At one time or another, every girl at Swan Harbor High had been affected by his glib tongue, sexy green eyes, or dimpled smile. When the girls disappeared, as they always did, Jessie decided, as his friend, he'd always be there. With that decision made, her crush became easier to manage.

Then she turned fourteen, and Cam looked at her differently. He'd made her feel like a female. From that day on, whenever he was around, her traitorous heart had beaten a rapid pitter-pat.

It had only been the thought he wanted what he couldn't have that had helped her resist. However, it hadn't stopped her heart from flipping when he flirted. Nor had it stopped the little buzz inside when he called her princess. There was something about the way he drawled the word that sent chills racing up her spine.

The accident, however, changed everything in her life. Cam seemed to understand what she needed and always showed up when she least expected him. It was eerie but also made her feel special.

Even more so, since her parents...

With that one thought, the darkness was back. It clawed at her, threatening to pull her into its abyss, only letting her go when it covered her. Jessie's knees started to buckle, and the blackness continued its climb up her legs. She was going down ... and then ... strong arms wrapped around her, bringing her close to a warm male body.

Cam made her feel safe and secure as he held her, preventing the black hole from consuming her. She closed her eyes and burrowed her face into his shoulder while she waited for the darkness to overwhelm her.

When it didn't immediately feel as if she'd been swallowed, she peered through her lashes. All she saw were the changing colors of the ice and snow as the sun began to set.

"I'm sorry." Jessie stepped backward a foot ... and then another.

He cupped her jaw and used his thumb to wipe away her tears. "Never apologize for missing your parents, Jess."

His quiet support took her breath and caused her heart to stutter. She wanted to tell him how much she appreciated his help, but the words 'thank you' seemed too insignificant. If she were braver, she'd kiss his lean cheek to show her gratitude. She just wasn't that brave—yet.

"Think there's an extra pair of gloves in the box in the gazebo?" he whispered.

It was then Jessie noticed his hands were bare. "Where are your gloves? What would your mother say? Come on," she fired off each question in rapid succession. Then, not giving him a chance to answer, she skated off, expecting him to follow.

"Geez, Jess," Cam mumbled. "They're just gloves. I was in a hurry, okay?"

"Males!" Jessie pushed Cam toward the bench seat and rifled through piles of colorful wool. Several minutes later, she found a pair near the bottom and handed them over.

"They were James's."

Cam gave her a crooked grin, then told her about the last time he'd been on the ice with their brothers. While the story was funny and typical, the fact that James would never again be a part of their escapades brought tears to her eyes.

"You alright?" He squeezed her fingers.

Confusion washed over her when, once again, he didn't behave as she expected. "Why are you here?"

"Why are you?"

The reasons she skated hadn't been something she'd discussed with many. Her counselor, Sadie, and Cassie, but with the way Cam had been supporting her, a part of her wanted … needed to explain.

"Sometimes there's a black hole," Jessie began, "that threatens to engulf me, and I disappear." She bit her bottom lip and swallowed the tears that wanted to erupt before continuing, "I keep thinking if I skate fast enough, I can outrun the darkness."

"Oh, Jessie," he murmured. "Does it work?"

"Sometimes … but not always. Now, it's your turn. Why are you here and not with Ben or Ryan? Or," Jessie smirked, "reading Persuasion?"

"You needed me."

The combination of his simple answer and dimples almost had her missing the look in his eyes.

"There's more," she prodded after seeing the slight flare in his green depths. "How would you know if you hadn't talked to Dylan?"

"I didn't talk to Dylan, but Gray made plans for your brother, so…"

"Why didn't Dylan mention his plans?" Then, a light went off, and the date blinked brightly in her head. "Ugh. Today is Dylan's … and would have been James' … twenty-first birthday. I'm such a selfish bff." Cam's hand muffled what she'd been about to say. "Where are they?"

"They're at Swan's Spirits,"

"He'll come home drunk, won't he?"

"Maybe." Cam paused a beat, and his grin grew. "Okay, probably. But I'll be here to help you get him into bed."

"That would be nice." She jumped up and started toward the bench where she'd left her shoes.

"Jess? Where are you going?"

"To make Dylan a cake. Want to help?"

"Are you making a chocolate cake?"

"Of course. Is there any other choice?"

They exchanged skates for shoes, and on the way inside, Cam raised his brows in question. "Can I lick the bowl?"

"Sure, if you help."

"I have to earn my keep?" he muttered. "My mother doesn't make me help."

"Well, I'm not your mother, now, am I?"

She thought he murmured, '*Thank goodness for that,*' but when she glanced in his direction, he was washing his hands and looking down.

Her smile threatened to bloom into a full-fledged grin. It made her realize he'd done it again.

FOUR

Cam's Home
February 17
4:00 p.m.

CAM HAD BEEN REHEARSING HOW HE PLANNED TO BEHAVE WHEN Jessie arrived. He'd play it cool, they'd watch the Olympics, and there would be no pressure—on anyone.

Except, this was Jess, and he wanted to impress her. Since Dylan's birthday, he'd allowed her to set the pace for their friendship. Whether they were skating, watching movies, or just spending time with friends, being together made him happy. He knew she was still in a delicate state, but he wanted to think her smiles were more frequent because of him.

While he allowed her control, it hadn't stopped him from wanting more. There had been moments when he'd almost taken her hand or kissed her. However, one look in her turquoise eyes and he'd backed off.

Today was a new day—one he hoped was different. Their brothers were spending the day at Swan Harbor University, and their friends hadn't been invited. For the first time in a while, they would be alone.

"Are you looking for something in particular?" Mary Hunter came from the laundry room into the kitchen. "You've been staring in the pantry for at least twenty minutes."

Cam gave her a sheepish smile. "Just snacks for watching the Olympics. I didn't realize I'd been standing here for so long."

Mary's eyes narrowed. "Do you need some help?"

"No. I've got this."

"Well, okay." She placed a few folded towels in a drawer and then picked up the basket. "I'd grab the Oreos, Cameron. You know how much Jessie loves those."

"Jessie?" Cam glanced over his shoulder. "Who said anything about Jessie?"

"You didn't have to. Have fun."

He returned to the pantry and reached for the sour cream and onion chips. But, they would give him bad breath, and what if...?

Before he could decide, the doorbell rang. Cam rushed to answer, arriving to find Jessie standing right inside the door.

Their eyes met across the distance, and just looking at her took his breath. He wanted to say something clever, but before he could think of anything, Jessie's attention bounced away.

"Well, hello to you," she greeted his mother's prized possession, a toy poodle called Buttons. "Isn't she adorable?"

The puppy buried her nose in Jessie's neck, making her giggle. Right then, he wanted to be the dog, even if only for a minute or two.

"Cam," Mary brought his attention back to her. "Did you find what you were looking for?"

"Uh, no. I thought I'd let Jess decide."

"That's a good idea. Just don't forget the Oreos."

"You bought Oreos?" Jessie exclaimed.

Her light-hearted tone, followed by a gurgle of laughter at the puppy's antics, had Cam's gaze meeting his mother's.

See? I'm good for her.

A secretive smile crossed Mary's face. It reminded him of those wordless exchanges between his parents.

"Enjoy the Olympics, you two. Let me know if you need anything."

"We will."

She left the room, and for a second, Cam wondered what he'd missed.

"Cam?" Jessie's soft voice penetrated the fog surrounding him. "Is everything okay?"

"It's perfect." Cam thumbed toward the kitchen. "Let's choose some food."

❧

JESSIE GRABBED THE PACKAGE OF OREOS AND A BAG OF CHIPS, then followed Cam to the basement. As soon as she hit the bottom step, she realized the furniture was visible. "You actually cleaned!"

"Hey," Cam gave her a sheepish smile, "it wasn't that bad."

"It was bad," Jessie teased. "Who were you trying to impress?"

He glanced away, and a ruddy hue crawled across his high cheekbones. "My mother thought it was time."

Jessie grinned. "Well, it looks good."

"Thanks."

Cam smiled, and with his sparkling emerald eyes and deep dimples, nervousness had her cramming a chip in her mouth.

"I'd forgotten how good sour cream and onion chips were," Jessie hummed. "Dylan hasn't bought them since he's been dating Catherine. He's worried about his breath."

"Oh?"

"Yeah," Jessie continued. "I..."

What she'd unintentionally alluded to had the words dying. Something new was going on between her and Cam. It was exciting and frightening at the same time.

Jessie reached for an Oreo and, as she nibbled on it, searched for a new topic. That was when she spotted his sketchbook. "Did you finish your project for graphic design?"

A myriad of expressions raced across Cam's face as he spoke about his assignment. So many Jessie had trouble reading them all. He was more animated than normal, using his whole body to explain the project.

"What?" He frowned. "Did I say something wrong? Do I have Oreo on my face?"

"No, it's just obvious you really like that class."

"You know I plan to major in architecture, right?"

"Afterward, do you plan to come back to Swan Harbor and work with your dad and Gray?"

"I think so." He was quiet for a moment. "What about you?"

"College seems too far away. Right now, I need to get through Chemistry."

"I'm here if…"

"You're always there for me."

"And I will always be."

His eyes darkened, and he leaned forward just enough she could touch him.

'Do it! Just do it!'

The longer she sat there, the more Jessie became aware of their connection. One that, while invisible, she could still feel the subtle tightening, pulling her closer to Cam's warmth.

He was so close she could smell the musky scent surrounding him. So close she wanted to smooth her hand along his cheek. Then, just as she reached to touch, music from the TV burst forth, causing her to jump back.

"So, who skates first?"

Cam dropped his head for several seconds before glancing back up. "Looks like the men."

Jessie returned her attention to the skating, but in her mind's eye, she was working to understand Cam's expression. Was it possible he wanted the same thing she did?

He pushed the cookies aside, then settled back against the sofa, kicked his feet up on the table, and stretched an arm across the back. His fingers lay mere inches from her, making her want to scoot closer—just to see if he'd touch her.

When the music from one of the performances captured her interest, it sucked her into the world of figure skating. The athleticism and grace of the Olympic skaters mesmerized her and made her wish she could do those same moves.

"Sorry." Jessie smiled, one that was just a bit shy. "I tend to get lost in what's happening on the ice, wishing…"

"You're good, Jess."

"I'm okay. And working with Catherine has been amazing. It's just…"

"Do you want to do that?" Cam nodded toward the pair skating across the screen.

On the TV, the male skater held his female partner high above his head while they flew across the ice. For some reason, the idea tied her stomach in knots.

"You're joking, right?"

"No, I'm serious."

Jessie side-eyed him. "I'm not sure I could trust someone enough."

"Oh, come on, Princess." Cam hopped up and tossed a few pillows on the ground. "You trust me, don't you?"

"You know I do, but that?" Jessie pointed at the TV screen. "You don't know how to do that."

"Come here, and let's see."

Her heart flipped around several times.

"Trust me, Jess," Cam whispered.

Jessie didn't know what she was thinking when she stood, apparently willing to follow his crazy idea.

"Now, jump into my arms and spread out like a swan."

She studied him for an extra second. "Are you sure?"

"I'll catch you."

Jessie took several steps and then hopped into Cam's arms. His hands closed around her waist, and he lifted her over his head.

"There you go, Princess."

Seconds later, his arms started to shake. She reached to balance on his shoulders, and simultaneously, his legs gave out. They landed heavily on the pillows, in a tangle of body parts.

Jessie pushed straight up, only to get caught in the fire of Cam's gaze. "See, you're not very trustworthy."

One second, she was leaning over him. Then, in the next, he'd flipped them around. "Say that again," he murmured, their faces mere inches apart.

Jessie's eyes flared, and her heart wanted to jump from her chest. "Say what again?"

Cam sighed her name, and for the second time, an invisible string pulled her closer. *Oh my gosh!* Is *this it?*

Right before their mouths touched, Cam grunted, "Buttons! What the...?" was barely out there before his mother yelled that Dylan had arrived to pick her up. The moment was lost, but there would be more.

Sadie's Home
March 15
9:00 p.m.

WHEN THE IDEA OF ATTENDING THE SPRING SLEIGH RIDE AS A group was casually suggested, everyone thought it was a good idea. After all, Cassie was already gaga over Ryan, and Sadie and Ben had been tap dancing around each other for weeks. Secretly, Jessie was thrilled, especially since it meant spending more time with Cam. *Except* the plans had been made before their *'almost kisses.'*

Since *that* night, Jessie found herself caught in an emotional storm. One in which the words, *'Will he? Won't he?'* were on repeat inside her head. It confused her, making it difficult to know what to say ... and how to behave.

"Jessie," Sadie's green eyes sparkled, "they're here! Let's go say hello."

Jessie glanced across the field to where Cassie and Ryan had already paired off. Cam and Ben were nearby, and she couldn't help but notice how good he looked.

"Did something happen between you two?" Sadie put her on the spot.

"No!"

Sadie's expression quickly morphed into a knowing one. "Do you want it to?"

Did she? Jessie dropped her head, and her hair fell around her face. She thought she did. Except, she didn't want to feel pressured.

"I think so."

"You think so?" One of Sadie's brows arched. "Then take back control."

"Take control?" Jessie frowned. "What does that mean?"

"My mama says," Sadie grinned, "boys are just as scared as we are. If you like someone, take control and regain the power."

The scene across the field once again captured her attention. "He is quite fine."

"Agreed," Sadie hummed, "sexy and mussed."

"Ben's nice to look at, too," Jessie felt obligated to note.

"Yeah," Sadie confirmed, "in that boy next door kind of way. But he's not..."

When her voice died before finishing her sentence, Jessie prompted, "He's not...?"

"Never mind," Sadie sighed, "pipe dream."

Jessie had long suspected Sadie had a crush on someone she assumed to be unattainable.

"Take control," she tossed the words right back.

A flirty twinkle sparked in Sadie's eyes. "The Princess learns fast."

"I'm not sure about that."

"Come on, Jess. Quit being a chicken. It's just Cam."

But *just* Cam caused her insides to ping-pong all over the place. *Could* he be as scared as she?

"Come on, Jessie," Sadie pleaded, "you know you want to."

Helpless to resist, Jessie glanced in his direction. Their eyes collided, and '*Run to him,*' was all she heard.

"*Carpe Diem*, right?"

"Exactly!" Sadie giggled.

CAM TRIED NOT TO STARE AT JESSIE, BUT TIME AND AGAIN, HIS gaze was drawn across the field. Since *that* night, he'd felt like he was on a roller coaster. He'd asked himself a dozen times if he'd pressured her. But the answer was always the same—he didn't know, leaving him even more confused.

His goal had always been to take care of Jessie's heart, but no one had warned him about his own. It had been a month, yet he still didn't know what to expect from her. One minute, she seemed normal. The next aloof. Her walls were back up, and he was standing on the outside.

Their stalemate caused an ache in the center of his chest. One he hadn't experienced nor knew how to handle. Knowing his friends were just as clueless when it came to girls left him floundering alone.

After he'd flunked a test, his mom had stepped in with a lecture. On one hand, hearing what she had to say gave him hope. However, on the other, since he'd been told to be patient, and patience wasn't one of his strong suits, the ache in his chest remained. He was left to deal with a one-foot-in-heaven-and-the-other-in-hell situation, frustrating him even more.

He'd needed an outlet for the energy buildup and pulled out his Nintendo

DS®. The game Mario Kart® allowed him to channel the tangle inside. Nothing was more satisfying than being able to race as quickly as he desired, even if it meant crashing a time or two. His only problem seemed to be finding the right balance.

Cam fought off a yawn and wished, not for the first time, the sleigh ride would get underway.

Ben side-eyed him. "Up late?"

"What do you think?"

"I think you stayed up too late playing Mario."

"Maybe," Cam grunted. "It's just..."

"What's going on with you and Jessie?"

"Nothing."

"Right." Ben nudged Cam with his shoulder, forcing him to take a step. "Go talk to her, dickhead."

Cam started toward Jessie, and as the distance between them narrowed, what to say ran over and over in his mind.

"Hi." He used the smile he'd practiced in the mirror. "How are you?" When the question sounded somewhat normal, he relaxed ... at least a little.

"Good." Jessie's eyes met his briefly, then lowered to the center of his chest.

For some reason, the way she was looking at him had him panicking. "Ever played Mario Kart?" he blurted.

"Mario Kart?" she repeated. "No, why?"

"It's a great game."

Cam spent the next few minutes explaining the game. However, when they announced it was time to load the sleighs, he was more than ready.

He, Jessie, and their friends would ride in a smaller sleigh with a seat up front for two and one behind for the other four.

"I'll drive," Cam volunteered, not wanting to be stuck next to or behind his friends.

The look on Ryan and Ben's faces as they climbed up on the back seat and settled next to Sadie and Cassie had him groaning. Once they were seated, he took a fortifying breath and held his hand out to help Jessie into the front.

She climbed up, tucked the blanket around her legs, and lifted the other side. "Coming?"

Cam's lips twitched when he realized Jessie was more affected by his nearness than she wanted him to know. "Am I going to fit?"

"I don't bite, Cam," his princess snapped. "Just climb on the darn seat."

"Yes, ma'am." Her quick inhalation when he slipped beside her confirmed his suspicions. "Comfortable?"

"You seem to be the one having difficulty getting situated. Just go."

Cam set the horses in motion and quickly grew used to the gentle sway of the sleigh. Once they were on the way, though, a decision needed to be made. Did he sit back and let her come to him? Or did he drop the talk of Mario Kart and up his flirt game?

"*Guard Jessie's heart, Cameron,*" he heard his mother say.

"*Remember,*" his mother's voice continued, "*the heart wants what the heart wants.*"

Mario. The decision hadn't been an easy one, but as they rode through the woods, Cam slowly relaxed. He was convinced everything would be fine, even if Jessie's leg slid against his.

That was until there was a quick right bend in the trail, and she slid closer, her thigh aligning tightly against his. Cam bit his tongue, and the sharp pain served its purpose. It took his mind away from how it felt to have a part of her touching a piece of him. His heart raced, his body flamed, and he needed...

Mario ... banana peels ... blue shells ... was on repeat inside until his heart slowed, and his body cooled.

When they arrived at the finish line, where a bonfire was already burning full force, Cam pulled the sleigh into an open spot. The popping of the flames and the creaking of the leather seats served as a backdrop to the various conversations around them.

Initially, he was comfortable with the silence until it became apparent those in the back were communicating nonverbally. Jessie squirmed, the sighs, moans, and slurping noises from their friends making her uneasy.

Cam silently cursed the situation and wished he knew how to relax Jess. While Mario no longer fit the conversation, the time wasn't right for anything more.

He tugged off his glove and pulled his iPod Nano® from his pocket. "Music?"

Jessie studied him for an extra beat. Then, just when he opened his mouth to fill the silence, she whispered, "You have any good songs on that thing?"

"How about this?" Cam handed her one of his earbuds.

A Bon Jovi song soon transitioned to Queen. "You've been in your parent's records again, haven't you?" she teased. "I approve."

With her words, a weight lifted off Cam's chest. "I'm happy to hear that ... Princess." She smiled in such a way his heart raced to keep up with the song's rhythm. *It's a step.*

FIVE

Sonny's Skate & Bowl
April 25
3:00 p.m.

OVER THE NEXT FEW WEEKS, JESSIE'S LIFE SETTLED INTO A routine. While she had less time to spend with her friends, she was doing something she loved. She was still ice skating, but Catherine's approach focused on precision and motor planning. This meant there were times when she'd go over and over a move until it was perfect. Monotonous, yes. However, it also gave her time to think about Cam.

Since the evening of the Spring Sleigh Ride, their friendship had changed. There were times when Cam would look at her a certain way. When it happened, the butterflies in her stomach would take off, her heart would race, her palms would sweat, and every thought would fly from her head. Inevitably, she'd end up staring at his lips. She was fifteen and wanted nothing more than for her first kiss to be with him.

However, there were other times when she overheard him talking about his college choices. Those reminded her of the very real possibility he would leave her behind. Cam had been her constant since her parents' death. If he wasn't around, she'd have to rely on herself, something she wasn't sure she could do.

Jessie had tried to run from the emotions he caused. Tried to pull the walls he'd knocked down back into place. Tried to keep her heart sheltered, locked up tightly. Except, it hadn't worked. Cam had stayed close and, once again, pushed the walls out of the way. The feelings he elicited were scary, though. To offer love, she'd have to allow herself to be vulnerable. Could she do that? Did she want to do that?

Love was a word used by many for a variety of reasons. Sadie loved clothes. Cassie loved babies. Dylan loved Catherine. Except was love something that could be described? Or was it just a feeling? When she looked into Cam's eyes, her heart flipped. Could that be love? Or was there more? Was she overthinking things?

Cam had never given her any indication he 'loved' her. Yet, sometimes when he looked her way, and his green eyes darkened, she had to wonder. Was what he felt for her love?

"Jessie," Catherine called. "Where'd you go?"

"What?" Jessie pulled her focus back to the ice.

Catherine smiled. "I asked where you went."

"I just... Then she realized she didn't want to explain where she'd *gone* and mumbled, "Sorry," and took off around the ice. Once she'd completed the spins and jumps she'd just been taught, Jessie knew she'd made progress.

"There you go." Catherine grinned. "Now, try this." She demonstrated a few complex arm and hand moves that would accompany the spins.

"Okay." Jessie pushed off once again to round the ice. This time, though, all her focus was on what she was supposed to be doing. It allowed her muscle memory to kick in, and she almost unconsciously performed the moves with her body and not her mind.

"Excellent!" Catherine exclaimed. "I think you're ready to compete."

"Compete?" Jessie squeaked, her heart beginning to race. "As in, a competition against others?"

"Sure," Catherine replied. "There's one in July that would be perfect."

"Have you discussed this with Dylan?" Jessie forced out breathlessly.

"Not yet." The banging of the gate signaled Dylan's arrival. "If you're interested, I can talk to him now."

Jessie's thoughts were pinging all over the place. However, the possibility of skating in a competition had always been a dream. She'd discussed it with her mother when they'd watched the Olympics.

"Jessie," Catherine's voice brought her back to the present. "Well?"

"Yes," Jess nodded slowly, then quicker as she got used to the idea. "Yes. If Dylan thinks it's a good idea, I want to do it."

"Perfect," Catherine squeezed her hands in support, "leave Dylan to me."

"Okay."

Catherine skated off the ice and into Dylan's arms. As they started toward the offices, a part of Jessie wanted to follow. She wanted to know what her brother would say. However, she also wanted to grab her phone, call Sadie and Cassie, and squeal with them. Mostly, though, she was waiting for Cam. He arrived every afternoon at about the same time. Some days, he hid in the shadows and watched. Other days, he waited for her, and they talked. Those were the days she liked the best.

Cameron's Home
April 25
5:30 p.m.

CAM GLANCED AT THE CLOCK AND HURRIED THROUGH THE LAST few questions of his assignment. Jessie's practices finished at the same time each day, and he was hoping to get there before Dylan. He wasn't sure why he hadn't asked to take her home. The possibility was there— and it wasn't like she'd never been in his truck. Somehow, it felt like he was pushing her—which he didn't want. Patience was the goal.

Jessie confused him more than any other female he knew. Some days, she looked at him in such a way, Cam felt he could touch the moon. Yet, other times, he felt like he was bouncing his head against a wall. Just why her moods were so mercurial, he didn't understand. Nothing she did, though, changed the fact his heart wanted what his heart wanted.

Once he was done, Cam shut down his computer and grabbed his keys. "Mom, I'll be back in a little while," he called halfway out the door.

"Hold it," Mary halted his escape. "Did you finish—?"

"Yes," Cam interrupted, knowing exactly what she would say.

"Homework's done, the computer's turned off, and I'm dropping this," he held up an envelope, "at the post office."

"Does that mean you signed?"

He'd been lucky to receive two good scholarship offers. Unfortunately, neither were in the state of Maine. One was in New York, and the other in Texas. Either program could fulfill his professional dreams. The personal goals, though, hadn't happened.

"I did." His mother's smile faltered, so he added, "It really was the best offer."

"I know." Mary sniffed. "Your father and I are proud of you. We just wish you were going to be closer."

"Like Gray. I know." Cam gave her a crooked smile. "It's what you get for having your smart son last."

"Oh, you," she laughed, allowing a bit of his guilt to disappear. "When are you going to tell Jessie?"

"How am I going to tell Jessie, is more like it?" he mumbled. "I don't know what she will say."

Mary stepped into the hallway, and a part of Cam wished he would have kept his mouth shut. He needed to hurry if he wanted to get to Sonny's in time to watch any of Jessie's lessons.

"What are you worried about?"

"I don't know." Cam thought about the look on Jessie's face when college came up and shrugged, "I used to be able to read her, but lately…"

"You could read her before," Mary noted, "because you were looking at her with different eyes. Now, you only see what she wants you to see."

"Which isn't much," he confessed.

Mary chuckled. "Nothing worth having is easy. Tell Jessie hello."

Cam just hoped he could come up with the right words to explain to Jessie why he had chosen a college so far away. She wouldn't like it. However, if he were lucky, she would understand.

***

Sonny's Skate & Bowl
April 25
6:00 p.m.

WHEN SHE HEARD THE OUTSIDE DOOR CLOSE, JESSIE TOOK OFF around the ice. Cam had arrived, and with him watching from the wings, she wanted to show off.

She'd been working on her triple axel, and since he hadn't seen it, she circled the ice twice. Her forward takeoff was perfect, followed by three and one-half revolutions. However, her timing was off for the landing. Instead of hitting the ice with just one foot, both hit simultaneously, which sent her sprawling across the ice.

"Damn."

"Need some help?"

Jessie lifted her head to see Cam standing above her. He held out his hand, and when she placed hers in his, the ever-present loneliness dissolved.

"Thank you." He helped her up, and the look on his face scattered her thoughts.

"I wondered if we could talk," he murmured.

"Talk?"

"Yes, please."

Jessie nodded. "Okay, sure, but I'm waiting on Dylan." The mention of her brother reminded her of her news. "Catherine wants me to enter a competition," rushed out.

"A competition? Really?" Cam picked her up and swung her around. "That's great, Jessie. I'm so..."

Jessie's arms circled his neck. Being near him made her dizzy even when he wasn't swinging her around. However, when he stopped moving and she slid down his much larger frame, the feeling of being so close had her tongue adhering to the roof of her mouth.

"Cam," she sighed.

"Jessie." Dylan shattered the moment, causing her to jump backward. "Are you ready to go?"

"Coming." Jessie swallowed the disappointment and gave Cam an apologetic smile. "Sorry."

"Another time?" He walked with her across the ice.

Before she could respond, Dylan shouted, "Have you decided on a college yet?"

Cam's eyes met hers. "UT-Austin," he mumbled, frustration evident on his face.

"Nice. Gray thought that was the one you would choose. Let's go, Jessie. We have a lot to talk about."

"Congratulations, Jess." Cam grinned. "You'll do great."

Philadelphia Skating Competition
July 15
4:00 p.m.

SIGNIFICANT CHANGES WERE MADE TO JESSIE'S TRAINING DURING the months leading up to the competition. Longer practices replaced her flexible ones, forcing her to spend six or seven afternoons a week at Sonny's. Catherine also put her on a healthier eating schedule and added dancing and yoga several times a week. The possibilities excited her, but she couldn't help but miss her friends.

However, since her feelings for Cam hadn't been resolved, Jessie found it easier to be busy. It kept her from dealing with her emotions regarding his going to college in Texas. She understood when he did, things between them would change. Except, that was something she tried not to dwell on. Instead, she told herself their time would come—she just had to be patient.

It hadn't been easy, but she'd decided to stop looking to the future and focus on each day and what it had to offer. Her family and friends were supportive, and the summer flew by. Then suddenly, it was July, and she was on the way to Philadelphia with only Catherine. But standing on the sidelines waiting for her turn on the ice, she wished Cam was watching. His ability to always say the right things would have helped her not feel so alone.

"You okay, Jess?" Catherine whispered.

"I'm okay," Jessie assured her.

Which was true, mostly. It wasn't until they called her group to warm up that she finally relaxed and easily hit her jumps. Her confidence lasted until she skated off the ice. Then, the butterflies inside took off.

"Jessie?" Catherine studied her carefully. "You look a little pale."

"It's not that big a deal," Jessie grumbled. "My butterflies woke up at the same time."

"Oh!" Catherine laughed. "I remember those days. Maybe they will help." She pointed toward the stands.

When Jessie glanced up, tears sprang to her eyes. "You came!" She couldn't believe how much better she felt knowing her brother sat next to Mary, her husband, Clint, and Cam's brother, Gray. But where was…?

Cam's warm hands landed on her shoulders, and what she would say flew away. "Miss me, Princess?"

"But … how?" Jessie glanced from Cam to Catherine and back. "I thought you couldn't come."

"And miss your debut?" He winked, his dimples on full display. "Not a chance. Knock 'em dead, Princess."

"Ready, Jess?" Catherine asked softly.

The butterflies in Jessie's stomach swirled, and her head swam. She handed her blade guards to Catherine, and her eyes locked with Cam's.

"You're ready," he murmured. "Right?"

Her insides settled. "I'm ready."

Cam pressed his cheek against the side of her head, and the smell of his cologne calmed her even more. "Have fun."

Jessie nodded once, and when her name was called, she pushed away from the wall and headed toward the center of the rink.

Once the music started, her body relaxed. She set her arms and feet and let the music flow through her, making her feel like she was one with the ice.

A split jump.

Double axel into a double toe loop.

Sit spin.

A flip jump into a lutz.

A salchow jump into a sit spin.

Double toe loop, single toe loop.

Around the ice, she skated, her excitement growing with every landed jump. She could see the crowd responding, clapping, and cheering, the sounds making her feel more powerful and confident. Someone who had defeated the darkness and didn't worry it would return.

As the music reached its crescendo, Jessie threw herself into her last two jumps and transitioned into a Biellman spin. The crowd's roar caused her heart to race, and she couldn't stop her smile from blooming.

With one last push, she lifted one leg behind her, stretched her arms wide, and slowly undulated them up and down. Then, as the music slowed, she wrapped her arms around herself as if they were a large pair of wings. When the last notes faded, Jessie skated to a stop and bowed her head.

The swan had come to a rest.

With the crowd's roars in her ears, she bowed and skated off the ice into Cam's arms.

On Camerons Boat

August 10

7:00 p.m.

When they returned from Philadelphia, Cam's days became a blur. Jessie had been approached before they'd left the arena and asked if she'd be interested in training in Boston. His feelings regarding her move were all over the place. Somehow, the idea of her waiting for him in Swan Harbor had taken root. The knowledge she wouldn't be caused an ache in his chest. It forced him to face just how much their lives would change.

They had grown close the past few months, but he still caught himself heeding his mother's advice to guard Jessie's heart. She'd known too much loss, and he was determined its fragile state would never shatter because of him. He wanted her to fly free, knowing somehow that even though she reminded him of a beautiful swan, she was still a princess, not yet in full bloom.

On their last night together, Cam decided to take Jessie sailing. He wasn't sure exactly what they would say to each other. It was important to him that she knew he cared. And, he hoped, holding her once more would carry him through the next few months.

Cam sailed his small boat into the middle of the harbor and dropped anchor. There were millions of stars spread out above them. The water was calm, allowing only a gentle back-and-forth motion of the boat. Yet, his insides were racing.

"Lay with me, Princess." He leaned on the deck and clasped her hand in his. "Well, how did I do?"

Jessie rolled toward him and propped her head on her hand. "You expect me to say you did a good job because it's not cloudy tonight, right?"

"Who? Me?"

"Please," Jessie poked him in the side, "you're pretty cocky, aren't you?"

Her choice of vocabulary words created visions in his head. Instead of allowing them to simmer, he sought a safer topic.

"Are you excited about tomorrow?"

"A little," she giggled. "Okay, a lot. I'm worried about Dylan being alone, though. Think he'll be okay?"

"Something tells me he'll be fine." Cam rolled onto his side and imitated her position. "Miss Gold will be there if he needs her."

"True."

Their eyes locked, and the longer he stared, the greater the sinking feeling inside. He was being pulled into their turquoise depths, their connection tightening.

Jessie's hot breath blew across his lips. Her eyes drifted shut, and all he could think about was closing the distance and kissing her.

"Cam?" She cupped his jaw. "Don't you want to kiss me?"

"Come on, Princess," Cam groaned. "Don't do this to me."

"Do what?" Jessie asked innocently.

He rolled onto his back and pinched the bridge of his nose, hoping the pain would help him focus.

"I want to," the words were torn from deep inside, "more than anything, but…"

"Cam," she suddenly filled his vision, "I'm sixteen—"

"And I'm eighteen," he interrupted. "I'm supposed to be the…"

Jessie put her finger over his mouth. "You're supposed to what?" Her lips lightly touched his. "Teach me?" She placed an innocent kiss on his upper lip. "Show me?"

Cam tried to be strong, tried to resist, but she was too close, and she smelled too good. When her sharp teeth nipped at his earlobe, he couldn't hold out any longer. He wrapped his arms around her and pulled her lithe frame flush against his body.

"Open for me, Princess."

His lips played with hers but never stayed long in one place. Her mouth tasted exactly like he'd imagined, and he wanted to go on kissing her forever.

Then, Jessie opened and let him in. Their tongues lazily mated, and Cam's body heat skyrocketed, feeling as if it was on fire.

Just a few more, Cam decided, and dove back in. The kiss went on and on until he felt his self-control waning. It was only then he backed away.

"Don't forget me, Jess."

"Oh, Cam, never." Jessie threw her arms around his neck. "I'll miss you."

"And I'll miss you."

Cam placed one last lingering kiss on her lips before turning away. The trip back to shore was quiet, and way too quickly, he walked her up the steps to her door.

"I hope you find everything you've been looking for, Princess."

"You too, Cam."

Jessie kissed him on the cheek, and he wanted to say he already had. He wanted to tell her she was everything he'd ever need. However, she ran into the house before he could work up the nerve. Once again, he was left on the outside looking in.

Falling in love is easy. It's the next step that's hard.

SIX
PRESENT DAY

Sonny's Skate & Bowl
June 4
11:00 p.m.

'I hope you find everything you've been looking for, Princess.'

That naïve girl hadn't found what she needed in Boston. Nor had she found it in Orono, Charlottesville, or the Philippines. At the time, she'd told herself she was doing what she had to do, but she wasn't that young girl any longer. She was a twenty-five-year-old, pragmatic woman.

At least, that was what she tried to tell herself. Yet it didn't explain why she found it so hard to talk to Cam.

However, with her thigh muscles beginning to protest, the decision to stop might not be by choice, but a necessity. Then what? *Put up or shut up*, floated through her mind as they made another circle around the ice, and what to say continued to evade her.

Since she'd returned to Swan Harbor, Jessie had escaped to Sonny's as a respite from seeing Cam with Eden. After only a few minutes on the ice, the sounds of the rink had settled her, but ... she'd been alone. This time, neither the soft shushing of her blades nor the creaking of the building could calm her insides. Somehow, though, she'd expected that. Their dance had changed everything.

Isn't he worth fighting for?

Sadie's question had Jessie surreptitiously glancing at Cam. She didn't see a twenty-eight-year-old man. In her eyes, he was still the boy she'd been in love with her entire life. Even with his hair hanging in his face and his white shirt no longer crisp, her traitorous heart didn't care. Her heart wanted what her heart wanted. The question was, how did she go about getting it?

An image of Eden catching the bouquet and then kissing Cam floated by. When it felt as if she'd been stabbed in the heart, she knew she couldn't wait.

Jessie flipped around into a T-stop and pinned Cam with a hard stare. "Why are you here?" She hesitated a beat. "Instead of with your new girlfriend?"

A surprised look flitted across Cam's face as he adjusted the direction he was moving. "Why are you?" he tossed back, as he had all those years ago. Except then, they'd been close, and she'd wanted to share with him.

"I asked first," Jessie said childishly, then propped a hand on her hip.

Cam's eyes traveled up her body, and a dimple peeked out. "Well, lookee there," he drawled, "the princess is present."

He exasperated her as he had in the past. "You're not in Kansas anymore, Cam. You can lose the lame accent."

"That's Texas, Princess," he winked. "Now, come sit down. You've busted my balls long enough." Then, not waiting for a response, he skated toward the benches.

Jessie opened and closed her mouth several times, but when she couldn't come up with a good retort, she followed him off the ice. At least, it was his idea to sit first.

CAM GRITTED HIS TEETH TO KEEP FROM GROANING OUT LOUD AS he stepped off the ice and dropped onto a bench. He wanted to take off his skates and free his feet and ankles, but if he knew his princess, she wasn't through running. One little misstep, and she'd take off again. This time, though, he didn't plan on letting her get away.

"Come on, Jess," he encouraged when she hesitated, "it's time."

"What do you expect us to do, Cam?" Jessie sighed. "Should we sit around the campfire and sing Kumbaya?"

"It would be a start." Cam's eyes collided with hers. "Please."

When she muttered, "Okay," then sat next to him, his entire being relaxed. There were so many questions he wanted to ask. However, many of them would make her run. Instead, he decided to start with the simple, and move out from there.

"Tell me about Boston."

"Boston?" Jessie frowned. "You know what happened. I got hurt and came home."

"No, Jess," Cam grumbled. "Tell me something I don't know."

"Let's see," she retorted, in full princess voice. "I woke up at six, had breakfast, then went to ballet..."

"Jessie," he interrupted, "your schedule wasn't what I had in mind."

She sat still for so long, reminding him of when they were younger. Of her high walls and how he'd often felt as if he'd been on the outside looking in. His princess used them like a blanket. Each time she'd pulled them back out, she'd wrap them just a little tighter, and he'd have to chip them away bit by bit.

"When I arrived, I strutted in as if I owned the world," Jessie began.

The tenor of her voice had Cam leaning forward as he strained to hear the soft words.

"I had to learn the pecking order." She gave him a wry smile. "It took getting knocked down a few times before I figured things out."

As Jessie continued her story, for the first time, Cam heard traces of emotions he'd not expected a sixteen-year-old to hide. Loneliness, anger, jealousy, and finally acceptance. The more she talked, the more he wondered if he didn't hold some responsibility for how she'd felt.

Cam tried to remember the feelings of his eighteen-year-old self. Then, he'd not wanted to cause her any pain. What Jessie wanted ... she'd gotten. Was that where *he'd* gone wrong? Was that where *they'd* gone wrong? Had he and Dylan pushed her away too fast? Not just because it was best for Jessie, but because it had been the easiest for them.

He'd been leaving for college, and with Jessie in Boston, he could imagine her happy. Her brother's case was similar, but not really. Had Dylan thought, once she was gone, his job was complete?

Cam couldn't help but wonder if that were true. If so, it explained the distance between them during their first year apart. He'd been in Texas meeting new people, studying, going to football games and parties. However, if he ever felt overwhelmed, he still had his family. For some reason, she'd kept her feelings inside.

Cam watched a tear track from the corner of Jessie's eye. Everything inside wanted to reach out and touch her. Would she allow that? The distance between them still felt too great.

"I finally learned," Jessie murmured, "there would always be someone with cleaner edges. Or someone able to jump higher or spin faster than I could. After all, while I'd been skating since I was four, it wasn't the same as training. If I was lucky, I might win a regional and skate in the sectionals, but it was unlikely. I'd never make the U.S. Championships or the Olympics. For a while, though, I was content."

"Except content isn't good enough for you," Cam claimed, barely holding on to his temper. "Why didn't you say anything? Why didn't you tell Dylan or Catherine?"

"What were they supposed to do?" she cried. "Besides, Catherine knew what training was like. It wasn't as if it had changed much since she'd been in my shoes."

"So, you pretended," he guessed. "Or did you just not talk to them?" Like she'd done with him. He wasn't ready to put that much out there, anyway.

"I did what I had to do."

Cam wanted to take her in his arms and hold her, just like he'd wanted to do when she was fourteen, fifteen, and sixteen. That hadn't changed.

"Why, Jess," he tightened his hand into a fist, "why didn't you tell me?"

Jessie's humorless laugh sent a cold feeling of dread rushing down his spine. "I called you once,"

He searched his memory for a time when she might have called. Yet he came up empty. "When?"

"December, your freshman year," she murmured. "Some girl answered and said you were in the shower. I hung up."

"Oh, Princess," Cam whispered. "It wasn't..."

"Just forget it," Jessie replied. "It's not a big deal."

While Cam couldn't be sure who'd answered his phone that December day, he knew the female hadn't belonged to him. There had been no one for him but Jessie—until he'd gone home the summer after his freshman year.

He'd heard she'd been kissing a boy named Roger, and his heart had shattered. It changed how he'd behaved when he arrived in Austin for his sophomore year.

"Jessie," Cam hesitated until she looked at him. "She was my roommate's girlfriend. Not mine."

"Really?" Jessie arched a brow in disbelief. "You expect me to believe you didn't have girlfriends while in Texas?"

"No one serious," he admitted. "But I didn't go out with anyone until I'd heard about Roger."

"Roger? Who's Roger?"

"You tell me," Cam tossed back. "You were kissing him in the movie theater."

"I was kissing someone?" Jessie frowned. "When?"

The blank look on her face had Cam pushing up on his sore feet and walking several steps away. Was it possible he'd been wrong?

⁂

CAM STOOD FIVE FEET AWAY, YET JESSIE COULD FEEL THE TENSION radiating from him. Based on the question he'd asked, he was beating himself up over something that may or may not have happened. She had no idea what he was talking about, but did it matter?

He turned back around and leaned against the half-wall with his arms crossed. "I'm sorry. I thought…"

"Don't!" Jessie stepped closer to him and put her fingers over his lips. "It's done. Let it go."

"But, I…" Cam looked away, his eyes distressed. "Damn, I'm such an idiot." He captured her fingers in his much larger hand.

The sight of their clasped hands brought tears to her eyes. In the past, even when she thought of him as just her friend, holding his hands was a source of comfort and excitement. But this time, as she stared at them, she felt a keen sense of loss. She wasn't sure how much longer she could continue reliving the past.

"Do we really need to air out everything tonight?"

"Jessie," he tugged her back to their bench, "not just yes, but *hell yes!*"

Her bottom lip was tender from nibbling on it, but that didn't stop her from worrying it between her teeth. What were they doing?

"Why?"

Cam studied her for a heartbeat … then another. But she wasn't willing to back down. This time, she needed him to give her a good reason to lay herself bare, something she'd never been willing to do. His answer would help her decide if she stayed … or left.

He cupped her jaw and angled her face toward his. Jessie's breath stuttered as his lips slowly descended, stopping only when their mouths connected. The kiss was gentle, hesitant, and lasted no more than several heartbeats. But the fine tremor of his hand as their lips separated gave her hope.

"Is that reason enough … for now?"

Jessie nodded when the tears clogging her throat prevented her from explaining her feelings. He'd just given her the answer to what she needed to do to get what her heart wanted. Was she going to be able to handle it?

Seven Years Earlier

Boston
February 20
3:00 p.m.

As time went on, Jessie learned the only way to keep her insecurities inside was to throw herself headfirst into everything she was offered. To the world, it appeared as if her dreams and goals had become a reality. She won ribbons and medals, yet she didn't love her life. Her world grew smaller, and the darkness she'd conquered years before crept back, sneaking around the edges of her consciousness.

Just like before, she was only free when on the ice. For a while, escaping to someplace quiet and skating while lost in her memories worked. However, after spending Christmas in Swan Harbor, the struggle became more difficult. She was torn between her desire to please others and her need to escape. Additionally, what motivated her to work hard at sixteen no longer held the same power at eighteen.

If she hadn't moved to Boston, she would have graduated from Swan Harbor High with her friends. There would have been parties, dances, and laughing between classes. And while her mind had marched right up to the door of dating, she refused to walk through. Somehow, even with all the confusion surrounding her relationship with Cam, it didn't feel right.

But, after two months of soul searching, she realized the problem. She was jealous of the life Sadie and Cassie were leading. They were students at the University of Maine, and while there were some things they complained about, the sparkle in their eyes told another story.

It was the same with her brother and Cam. While she wanted to believe their lives hadn't changed, she couldn't have been more wrong.

Dylan had returned from the police academy and was working for the Swan Harbor Sheriff's Department. Since he'd always wanted to be an attorney, the career change was a bit disconcerting. The same could be said about Cam's behavior at Christmas.

Two years before, when she'd called his phone and another female answered, a little piece of her died. She'd survived by packing her emotions into an imaginary box. When she'd seen Cam over the holidays, though, a hole appeared. It made Jessie realize, if she continued to pursue a life she didn't love, she would never know what might be waiting ahead.

"We leave in ten minutes!" their driver yelled, pushing her to dress faster. First, she needed to get through the large fundraising event Veronica Myers staged every February, and then she'd try to figure out what she wanted for the future.

Several hours later, Jessie waited until her peers were on their way to change before turning in the opposite direction. She'd discovered a smaller women's locker room and planned to hide for a bit. There were days when she didn't mind the constant noise, but today wasn't one of them. Her heavy thoughts of earlier still weighed on her mind, and the constant chatter of her teammates made her want to scream.

When she pushed open the door to her secret place, Jessie was relieved to discover it was empty. She ducked into one of the curtained cubicles, dropped her bag, and sank onto the bench. Her entire body ached, and all she wanted to do was go back to her room and sleep, but the 'older' skaters had to shmooze with the big donors.

Socializing with people she didn't know wasn't high on her list of likable tasks, and fending off drunken advances had grown old. But Veronica had been good to her, meaning she'd do what she had to do.

Jessie pulled off her costume and was digging through her bag when she heard the door open.

"Ugh, Addi," Natalie Harkness's nasally voice intoned. "Did you see that cow out there tonight?"

"Come on, Nat," Addison Simpson, Jessie's primary competition, responded. "She's not that bad. In fact, she's pretty good."

"How can you defend her?" Nat groused. "She took the solo from you."

"I know," Addi sighed.

Jessie realized they were talking about her. While she'd never cared for Natalie, she considered Addi her friend.

"I can't believe you're so calm about it," Nat groaned. "You should be the star, not her."

Jessie's jaw ached from gritting her teeth. She dug her nails into her palms at the hatred she heard in the other girl's voice. Didn't they know how hard she worked? Didn't they care?

"Natalie, let it go," Addi replied tiredly. "I've been watching Jessie skate. I don't think her heart's in it any longer. Maybe she'll quit."

Ah, oh. Experience had taught her that showing weakness could be disastrous. Which meant she hadn't been careful enough to hide her emotions.

"And go back to that quaint little town she calls home?" asked Natalie.

However, the way she posed the question caused a little shiver to zip up Jessie's spine.

"I assume so," Addi replied. "Why does it matter, as long as she's gone?"

"Catherine won't like that," Natalie confided.

"What does Catherine have to do with it?" Addi replied.

"Oh, plenty."

"Stop trying to be so clever," snapped Addi. "It's time to go."

"Well, okay," Natalie popped her gum a few times, "but what if I told you..."

It was several minutes after the door shut before Jessie moved. What she'd overheard was difficult to process. *Was there any truth in it?*

She quickly replaced her costume with leggings and an old sweatshirt. Then she ducked through a hidden doorway and down a long hallway into a rarely used part of the facility.

Catherine won't like that.

The words reverberated inside Jessie's head, and the darkness, never far away, drew closer.

Catherine's why Jessie is here.

Her invitation to train with Veronica Myers had nothing to do with her ability to skate.

A lot of money exchanged hands.

When Jessie stepped into the arena, there was a hush in the air. The room held a small rink surrounded by raised seating. While there wasn't much space to outrun her demons, she was alone.

What Catherine wants, Catherine gets.

The more the words played in her mind, the greater the darkness.

Catherine wanted Dylan, and Jessie was in the way.

Jessie stepped on the ice, and her vision immediately cleared. It allowed her to relax and take in her surroundings. A few cables strung across a corner of the rink led to what appeared to be a sound system. Other than that, it was fine. If she could only skate in circles, she didn't care. What mattered was moving.

She pushed away the thought of the words she'd heard and focused on the one person who had been her champion. Cam. Just his name gave her a sense of peace and brought happiness to her heart.

It didn't take many revolutions before bits and pieces of songs she'd skated to in the past wound their way through her head. A triple loop from this melody, a double axel from another. When the music from her first competition took its turn, she had no choice but to allow the memories to carry her through the routine. She was one with the ice, gliding, jumping, and spinning. With every revolution around the rink, her cares and the darkness that threatened blew farther and farther away.

As she reached the end of the routine, a door opened, pulling her attention away from her location on the ice. It was only for a split second, but long enough for her skate to roll over the electrical cords she'd been avoiding.

Jessie fell, sliding headfirst across the ice toward the sound equipment. That she was going to crash zipped through her brain a second before impact, and her head bounced once ... twice.

"Jessie!" someone screamed as the darkness claimed her.

SEVEN

SEVEN YEARS AGO

King's Castle General Hospital
February 23
5:00 p.m.

Jessie felt like she was floating, and while her eyes refused to open, the sounds around her were familiar. She could hear the steady beep of the heart monitor, the periodic crackle of the intercom, and Dylan.

"Come on, Jessie," Dylan cried in a husky voice. "It's been three days. Come back to me. I can't lose you too."

It wasn't long before someone wearing squeaky shoes entered the room. "Good evening, Dylan," a gentle voice greeted. "Any change?"

"No," Dylan murmured. "Why is it taking so long?"

There was a clicking sound, as if Ms. Squeaky Shoes was checking the beeping equipment beside the bed. Then, a slight tug and cool fingers lifted Jessie's left hand and covered it with the blanket.

"Her body needs time to heal," the nurse answered. "Doctor Watts should be in to speak with you soon."

"Thanks, Sheila," Dylan replied. "I'll be here."

A few minutes later, the nurse's footsteps faded. Shortly after she was gone, Dylan's phone rang, and based on the tenor of his voice, he was talking to Catherine.

Catherine. What was she going to do about Catherine? She didn't want to hurt Dylan, as he had been her hero for as long as she could remember.

"Again!" four-year-old Jessie demanded. Dylan picked her up and tossed her into a huge pile of leaves. As soon as she landed, she rolled off the pile and ran to her brother, James. "Your turn."

"Okay, Princess," James laughed. "Ready?" He tossed her into the leaves.

Jessie giggled and hopped off the pile just as her father drove up in his sheriff's car. "Daddy's home!" she squealed.

Robert stepped out of his car, "How's my Princess?"

"Good, Daddy," Jessie laughed. "Come see me fly!"

"Princesses don't fly," her father teased.

"Oh, Daddy," she giggled. "Watch." Jessie took off running and jumped into the pile of leaves, sending them scattering everywhere. "Did you see?"

One look at her father's face and Jessie knew he was upset, but she didn't know why until he began to scold her brothers. "I thought I told you boys to do this before I got home."

"Sorry, Dad," Dylan jumped in to take the blame. "We got sidetracked. We'll do it now."

In her dream-like state, Jessie watched as her father and James faded, leaving behind her and Dylan. He was the brother who had always taken responsibility for everything, even if it wasn't his fault. And after all these years, she couldn't shatter his world anymore. If he were happy with Catherine, she would figure out how to deal with his girlfriend's betrayal. Even if it meant staying in Boston and pretending she knew nothing.

With the decision made, Jessie allowed the darkness to pull her under once again.

England
March 20

CAM KICKED OFF HIS COWBOY BOOTS, LAY BACK ON HIS BED, AND stared at the new picture of him and Jessie. He'd been looking forward to completing a semester at the University of Sheffield in England. That is until Christmas. After being in Swan Harbor with his princess, the time away hadn't been as exciting as he'd expected. As much as he'd tried to fight it, a part of him was still back in the States with her.

Jessie was eighteen to his twenty. However, his feelings for her hadn't changed since that moment he'd first noticed her as a female. Their time spent together over the holidays had given him new insights into their relationship. As his mother said, the heart wants what the heart wants, and his heart was set on his princess.

He knew the large fundraising event for the Myers Stars had been the previous weekend. Since then, he'd been waiting for news of how she'd skated. However, when no call came, he couldn't shake the feeling he'd missed something.

When the phone rang, Cam pounced. "Hey there, Jessie." He exaggerated his drawl.

"Take off the boots, Cam."

Cam usually relished it when Jessie used her princess voice, but her acerbic tongue had him sitting up. "What's going on, Jess?"

"I..." she hesitated briefly, then tossed out. "How are classes?"

His Jessie radar was firing, and he wanted to push her for answers. Except experience told him if he did, she'd rebuild the wall he'd knocked down in December. With that realization, he spun a tale or two about his professors.

"It sounds nice," Jessie answered.

"So far." He hesitated briefly, then came back with, "How did you skate last weekend?"

"Last weekend?"

"The fundraiser."

"Oh," Jessie took a deep breath, "I skated fine, but..."

When she didn't immediately continue, he grew even more nervous. "Come on, Jess," he sighed. "Tell me what's going on, because I'm imagining the worst."

"I'm okay," she assured him. "I just … I had a silly accident."

"Jessie," Cam pushed a little harder. "What are you not saying?"

"It was nothing." Jessie laughed, but something about her statement didn't ring true. "My skate rolled over a wire, and I fell."

"You fell!" he exclaimed. "Are you okay?"

"I'm okay," she assured him. "My ankle's sprained, and I have a little glue on a head wound. I'm even home from the hospital."

"Home home?" Cam questioned. "Or Boston home?"

"I'm in Swan Harbor."

"How long will you be there?" he asked, knowing he'd be home in early June.

"How long will I be here?" Jessie repeated something she'd always done if trying to avoid answering. What was he missing? "I'm not sure. I guess you'd need to ask my ankle," she tried to joke, but it sounded flat.

"Is that it?"

"What else could there be?"

"I don't know, Princess. You tell me." She was silent for a while, and he thought he heard Dylan say something in the background, but if so, the words were too quiet to understand.

"Cam," Jessie continued in a steady voice. "I'll be fine. You need to worry about getting good grades. You wouldn't want Beau to have a better GPA, now, would you?"

"That was low, Jessie," Cam muttered. "But you're right."

Beauregard Johnson had been his roommate since they were freshmen at UT. Competitive, by nature, they had thrown themselves into seeing who was the best … at everything. Cam realized most were stupid things, like who could burp the loudest or the longest. But there were more serious competitions, like who could eat the most BBQ ribs or jalapeños.

At one time, they'd even competed over women. Except, he tried not to think about those times. He'd finally grown up and decided kissing and telling didn't feel right. Grades were important, though, since high marks meant keeping his scholarship. If Jessie thought that's all he and Beau cared about, well…

"Of course, I'm right," she declared.

"And you're really okay?"

"I'm fine," Jessie replied. "Don't worry about me."

"If you say so." Except there was more going on than she was willing to share. That much was obvious.

"I do," she assured him again. "I'm feeling a little tired, so I'll talk to you later, okay?"

"You take care now ... Princess."

❧

Jessie's Home
March 20

As soon as the line went dead, Jessie's arm dropped. Her hands were shaking so much the phone fell with a clang onto the floor. "Crap." She clasped her hands together, hoping to still them.

"You didn't tell him the entire truth," Dylan accused.

"And?" Jessie knew she sounded petulant. Except she was still in the, '*You do what you have to do mode.*'

The sofa dipped, and Dylan settled next to her. "Why didn't you tell him you were blind?"

"Temporarily blind," she amended.

"Okay," he acknowledged. "Why didn't you tell him you were *temporarily* blind?"

Jessie smirked at the underlying annoyance layered with patience in her brother's voice. She could *see* his sky-blue eyes staring at her solemnly. Could *see* the tic that pulsed on his jaw when he clenched his teeth. That is, *if* she could see.

"You know why. He's almost as protective as you are and would have been on the next plane home."

"But what if he finds out from someone else?" Dylan continued to push.

"You won't tell him." Jessie hesitated a beat, "Will you?"

"No," he assured her. "But there's always Gray or Mary or..."

His brother and mother wouldn't tell him, would they? "Ugh," she leaned against his shoulder, "will you ask them not to? Please?"

Jessie could feel Dylan studying her, even if she couldn't see him. In the beginning, the darkness had been complete. It reminded her of being in a pitch-black room, and no matter how wide she tried to open her eyes; it didn't

63

matter. Her worst nightmare had come to life. The darkness from the fringes swallowing her whole.

Thankfully, that wasn't still the case. In the last few days, the darkness had given way to gray. Like being in a thick fog but unable to see on the other side. Better, but...

"I'll ask," he sighed. "If it lasts much longer, you need to tell him."

What he said made sense, but it didn't mean she enjoyed hearing it. "I know," she conceded. "I just need a little time."

England
March 20

HOURS AFTER THEIR TALK, CAM STILL COULDN'T SHAKE THE feeling Jessie hadn't told him the complete story. He tried studying, doing laundry, and even playing pool. Yet, the tone of her voice lingered. It seemed to be telling him something else. Since jumping on a plane wasn't an option, he pulled out his phone and dialed a familiar number.

"Cameron? Is everything alright?"

Somehow, just hearing her voice settled his nervous feelings. "Hi, Mom. How are things at home?"

"We're all fine," Mary began hesitantly. "How are you liking your classes?"

"Good." Then, because he knew his mother, he told her the same stories he'd shared with Jessie.

"It sounds wonderful," her voice softened. "Why did you call, Honey? Need money?

"I never turn down money," Cam chuckled. "But can't I call ... just because?"

"Sure, you can." Mary paused a beat. "But that's not you. A text here and there. An email now and then. When you call, there's a problem. What's going on, Cam?"

"I'm that predictable?"

"I'm your mother," she murmured. "Moms know these things."

"Is it written in the mom's manual?" he teased.

"You got it," Mary laughed. "But Gray is the same way. And it's much better than a letter once a week, like when your father and I were dating. But," she circled back, "you didn't call to talk about your father's communication abilities or lack thereof, did you?"

"No," Cam sighed. "It's Jessie."

His mother hummed, which could be an entire conversation alone. "I thought as much. Do you want to talk about it?"

The care and concern had him telling his mother everything he'd learned on the phone. He also tried to explain the things Jessie hadn't said. Or he attempted to anyway.

"Have you seen her ... or Dylan lately?"

"Jessie's here?" Mary questioned. "In Swan Harbor?"

"Apparently," Cam replied, "Jessie said she's waiting for her ankle to heal before returning to Boston. Can you check on her ... please?"

"I'll try," Mary promised. "Remember, your father and I are flying out tomorrow night, right?"

"You're going away?"

"Yes, Honey," she reminded him. "We're going down to Florida for a month, just like we have for the last few years. Your father will play golf, and I'll read, relax, and catch up with friends."

For a split second, annoyance flooded Cam's system. Luckily, the rational side of his brain showed up before he said anything too stupid. "Oh, that's right. Well," he hesitated, "if you have a chance, I'd appreciate it."

"I said I would try," Mary answered. "I'll let you know. In the meantime, why not email? You're good at that."

Cam could think of a few choice words, but since it was his mother, he told her to have a good trip and hung up. When he couldn't think of someone else to check on Jessie, he took his mother's advice and emailed. After all, what did he have to lose?

Swan Harbor General
April 20
2:00 p.m.

Two months after her accident, Jessie was willing to admit, silently at least, she was scared. Every other appointment, she'd come away hoping by her next visit, things would be better—until today.

According to the specialist, there was no physical reason she shouldn't be able to see. The swelling in her brain was gone. Diabetes, macular degeneration, cataracts, or any other diseases of the eye didn't cause her problems. She had low vision. Which meant she could see ... a little.

The gray had brightened, leaving behind clouds and tunnels—at least, that's what it felt like. When she looked out at the world around her, it was hazy and indistinct, almost as if she were standing in the middle of fog. The edges of her vision resembled her dreams, and the layers of darkness never went away.

As soon as the car stopped, Jessie's breath caught. "We aren't home, are we?

"No," Dylan released his seatbelt, and the seat creaked as he turned toward her, "but it is where we're going next."

The noise of a siren drew Jessie's attention to the building in front of her. "The hospital?" She could read Swan Harbor General Hospital on a large sign.

"We have an appointment in thirty minutes."

Jessie's stomach clinched with the implications of what he'd said. She didn't want anyone in Swan Harbor to know what was happening. If she went inside, then her secret wouldn't stay a secret. "I can't go in there," she cried, not caring how irrational she sounded. "Dylan, take me home, please."

"Jessie, it's time," Dylan sighed. "The doctor in Portland recommended we see a psychiatrist—"

"I can't," Jessie interrupted. "Please don't make me."

"Jessie," Dylan muttered. "I just..."

She could hear the frustration in his voice, but she couldn't give in. Somehow, she had to convince him to take her to see someone else.

"I'll go see anyone you want me to ... in Portland. Anyone."

Tears were running down her face, and there was a touch of hysteria in her voice. However, if she went into the hospital, that would mean...

"Jessie," Dylan snapped. "Stop it."

"But—"

"I can't!" he all but screamed. "I love you, and I'm trying to do everything in my power for you. But..." Dylan's voice faded, and somehow, she knew he was brushing his hand through his hair. "I can't drive you to Portland several times a week for therapy. I have a job, and my boss isn't happy with all the time I've missed. I just…"

Jessie's heart ached. She was at a loss. Being a burden to the only family she had left wasn't what she wanted. This time, she couldn't even blame Catherine. The fault lay squarely on her shoulders. While her blindness wasn't because of something inside of her, she was the only one holding back.

Why? What could she do about it?

Go inside and see what happens, her inner voice whispered.

Except what if they told her she'd never get her eyesight back? She would be in Swan Harbor, caught between Dylan and Catherine.

There was also the possibility if she went inside, her sight would automatically return. That would mean returning to Boston, so her brother could be happy.

And you would be miserable.

True, but she couldn't continue behaving like a brat. This was for Dylan. Just as with Cam, she'd do what she had to do.

"Okay, you win," she conceded. "I'll go."

"Don't look at it like that, Sis," Dylan pleaded. "I want you to get better … for you. Don't you miss your life in Boston? Friends?"

How did she tell him the truth about Boston? What would he say if she told him she no longer wanted to skate?

"I don't mean to cramp your style, Dylan," Jessie sighed. "I know it's hard having me under your feet. Sometimes, I don't even like myself."

"Jessie, I don't—"

"There I go again," she gave him a self-deprecating smile, "feeling sorry for myself."

"You have every right to be upset," Dylan assured her. "And I love having you home."

"You do?"

"Of course I do," he confirmed. "But is this the life you want to live? That's the question you must ask yourself, isn't it?"

"You sound like a shrink."

Except she'd been asking herself the same question for several months. A part of her knew the answer and what steps she should take, but fear held her back.

"Not hardly," Dylan replied. "But right through those doors, I know a good one, and she's waiting for us. Are you ready?"

"Yeah, let's go." Jessie met Dylan by the rear of the car. If she were lucky, they'd go straight to her appointment and not run into anyone else she knew. If she wasn't...

EIGHT
SEVEN YEARS EARLIER

Swan Harbor General
April 10
3:00 p.m.

WHEN THE AUTOMATIC DOORS OPENED, JESSIE'S SENSES WERE immediately assaulted. The smell of antiseptic, and the sounds from the overhead intercom reminded her of waking up just after her accident. Except that hospital was in Boston, where she didn't care if she saw someone she knew. Entering Swan Harbor General was different. Everyone knew her family, which made hiding her condition more difficult.

At one time, Jessie had been given instructions on how to navigate unfamiliar environments. But stubbornness had kept her from listening. Her steps faltered, feeling like they were mired in mud.

"It's okay, Sis," Dylan murmured. "Just hold on to me."

He hooked her arm around his, which made her feel more secure. It also helped with the strong self-preservation running rampant—as it was fighting to hide the fact she couldn't see well.

They made it through the lobby and down one hall without seeing anyone they knew. However, as soon as they started down a second hallway, the sounds of heels had Jessie holding her breath.

Oh, no! Please not...

"Dylan?"

Her luck had run out.

"And Jessie?"

The muscles in Dylan's arm tightened as they stopped and turned toward the newcomer. "Catherine, what brings you to this side of the hospital?"

Jessie schooled her features and looked the other woman square in her eyes—or at least she hoped so. "Hello, Catherine."

"Why, why are you here?"

"You heard about my little accident," Jessie responded as if it wasn't any big deal. "Right?"

"Well, yeah," Catherine admitted. "I mean, I knew Dylan had gone to Boston to check on you. I just..."

The underlying tone in the other woman's voice had Jessie wondering what Dylan had told her. "My ankle's as good as new. We just have one more appointment today, and then..." she shrugged, aiming for nonchalance.

Dylan squeezed her fingers and stepped far enough away to kiss Catherine's cheek. "I'm sorry I've not touched base lately, but with Jessie and work..."

"It's okay, Dylan," Catherine assured him, the sugar in her voice making Jessie's teeth hurt. "I've been busy with my new job and all."

Don't ask. Don't ask, Jessie chanted internally. Except the manners her mom had encouraged snuck up. "What is it you do?"

"You didn't tell her?" Catherine questioned Dylan in a '*How could you not have told her*?' voice.

"Well, I have been a little busy," he began.

Only to have Catherine interrupt with, "I'm the assistant to the administrator. It's a very important job, you know?"

Jessie had to bite her tongue to keep from asking if that was another description for a secretary or gopher, but in the end, she smiled and offered, "Congratulations."

"Thank you," Catherine responded in her saccharine, sweet voice. When you get back to Boston, Tell everyone hello."

While Catherine said goodbye to her brother, Jessie took a small step to her left and placed her hand on the wall. The strain of pretending was wearing thin, and she might scream if they couldn't continue on their way in a minute.

"You didn't tell Catherine about your vision." The censor in Dylan's voice had her blinking back tears of frustration when they resumed walking.

"Sorry, I just..." The words died, as what could she say that hadn't been said before?

"We're here."

Dylan opened the door, and the moment Jessie stepped over the threshold, her heart rate skyrocketed. She closed her hands into fists so tightly her nails dug into her palms. But it was the only way to keep them from shaking.

She'd spent more days than she cared to remember in these offices, waiting to speak with her grief counselor. To the left was Merlene's office. And to the right...

"Jessie," her name whispered in that soothing voice settled her. "I've been waiting for you."

Even though she'd promised herself she wouldn't cry, tears instantly sprang to Jessie's eyes. "Hi, Mary." She brushed the wetness away. "Thank you for seeing me."

Doctor Mary Hunter, Psychiatrist, had been Ruth Prince's best friend. With her blonde hair, sparkling brown eyes, and infectious laugh, people were drawn to her. She'd been a lifeboat to Jessie and Dylan when their world had fallen apart.

"Hey, Sweet Girl," Mary murmured. "Come sit so we can talk."

As Jessie walked into Mary's office, she tried to make sense of the multitude of feelings inside. There was relief because she was talking to someone she knew and trusted. That was mixed with worry about what came next. Wrapped around them was panic her secret was out.

Once she settled, Mary explained the continued vision problems were psychosomatic, which didn't surprise Jessie. It only reiterated what she'd kind of figured out herself. That for some reason, *she* was causing the problem, and she was the one who needed to fix it.

But how did she go about doing that? Was working with the woman she thought of as her second mother the answer? Could Mary help her understand the internal stress she felt?

A bright pattern on the carpet caught her attention, and an image of a small girl sitting on the floor flitted through her mind. It made her smile, something she hadn't done much of lately.

"What are you thinking about?"

Mary's voice sounded far away, and it took Jessie several minutes to float up from the memory. "Did I ever play here when I was young?"

"You remember that?" Mary asked, sounding surprised.

"I think so." Jessie wrinkled her nose as the images began to play in her head. "I had my Polly Pocket dolls with me."

"And Cameron kept stealing them," Mary replied with a laugh.

"Cam was there?" Jessie dove back into the picture, searching until she located the scene. She was sitting on the floor playing with her dolls, and he had a pile of blocks in front of him. "He was building ... I think."

"Legos," Mary confirmed. "I should have known Cameron would grow up to be an architect. He was always carrying around a backpack full of those blocks. Even when you two were young, he always had a soft spot for you."

Jessie ducked her head, fighting not to let her smile fly free. "Speaking of Cam..."

"You don't want him to know, do you?

"No," Jessie admitted. "Cam would be on the first plane home."

"I hate keeping secrets from my family." Mary lightly touched the small scar on Jessie's forehead. "In here, though, I'm your doctor. What we talk about stays between us."

It wasn't a matter of not trusting Cam's mother. Nor was it a matter of not trusting her doctor. It had more to do with the fact that once something had been said aloud, it had to be handled.

"Is that anything I say?"

"Anything," Mary confirmed.

"I, I think they may be right," Jessie admitted.

"Right about what?"

While Jessie couldn't see the tiny nuances of Mary's expression, she knew she was being studied. "I'm feeling internal stress." She took a deep breath and put the rest of it out there. "I don't want to be in Boston any longer."

Mary's quick inhalation said that hadn't been what she'd expected. "Do you want to stay here?"

"Oh, no," Jessie quickly pushed that idea away. "I want to go to the University of Maine with Sadie and Cassie."

"Oh, that's wonderful," Mary exclaimed. "But," she paused, and Jessie knew precisely where the conversation would go. "SAT scores, applications, etcetera. It's long past admission dates for the fall."

"I know it's late," Jessie acknowledged. "And I understand it's a long shot. However, they have rolling admission, so maybe…"

"You really want this, don't you?" There was a hint of something in Mary's voice that had Jessie relaxing.

"Yes, I do."

"Then I'm with you." Mary's happiness lightened Jessie's heart even more. "I think your mother would approve."

The statement caused feelings Jessie hadn't expected. She understood passing the exam might not be easy. However, she also understood each problem needed to be taken a step at a time—first school, then Catherine.

Six Weeks Later…

Jessie's Home
June 10
7:00 a.m.

Jessie pulled one of Cam's old Swan Harbor High sweatshirts from a drawer and slipped it over her head. It was too big, and even though she'd not worn it for years, she could still smell him. Wearing it was comforting. The butterflies, however, were still busy in her stomach, and she couldn't stay still.

Her mind spun in multiple directions with everything the last six weeks had brought. It had been a time full of growth and eye-opening situations. Some of them were just okay. Most of them were positive, giving her new insights into who she'd been, who she was, and who she wanted to be.

It hadn't happened overnight. Somehow, Jessie had gotten it in her head that her eyesight would magically appear once the secret was out. When it hadn't happened, it left her discouraged. It was only when she started studying for the SAT, Jessie knew she was on the right path.

However, even with a positive attitude, pockets of fear still existed. What if her scores on the SAT were low? Or if the University of Maine refused to admit her at such a late date? What should she tell Dylan about Catherine, or Cam, if he found out about her accident.

Some days, the list of problems felt insurmountable. On those days, the darkness grew closer. At other times, though, she was able to follow Mary's advice and take the problems one at a time.

Her biggest obstacle to date had been taking the college admittance exam. Because of her low vision, Jessie had asked for several concessions. Special lighting, larger font, thicker paper, and a computer, which allowed her to complete the test alone. Once that was over, she'd felt an enormous sense of accomplishment, and the possibility of independence had seemed real.

That had been the day Mary had taken her to lunch, and she'd met Hayden, Sally's eleven-year-old nephew. With his parents gone, he'd moved across the country to live with people he barely knew. One look at him, and Jessie had known what he was feeling. She'd decided she would be there for him if he needed to talk.

Somehow, though, helping him began to help *her*. She started to see how much she'd always depended on others—her parents, Cam, Dylan, and even the coaches in Boston. Sharing her story with Hayden had been liberating in many ways. It showed her that helping others made her feel good.

Except the longer her life was in limbo, the more she worried about who knew her secrets ... and who didn't. While Cam still didn't know, his family did, as did Sally, Hayden, Dylan, and others. The longer her vision was distorted, the more the wagons circled around.

They'd done a good job of protecting her and Cam. Now, though, it was all on her. When he arrived, she had to have the right words to explain everything. Maybe then, they could go forward ... together.

Jessie's Home
June 10
7:30 a.m.

CAM HAD FALLEN INTO BED AFTER TRAVELING THE BETTER PART of twenty-four hours. He wanted to blame his inability to sleep on the fact that his internal clock was still on U.K. time. Instead, he'd finally acknowledged it all revolved around Jessie.

For two months, he'd known something was off. Yet, every time he'd said something—asked someone, he'd gotten the same answer. It's Jessie's story. She has to be the one to tell you. What the hell did that mean, though?

Cam grunted with frustration and rolled over. His eyes drifted shut, and then—just like the other times, his mind clicked back on. Finally, he gave up. His heart was trying to tell him something, and it was time he listened. Especially since his princess was in Swan Harbor, and he had no idea for how long.

He jumped from the bed and into an invigorating shower. With the cobwebs temporarily dispersed, Cam grabbed a bagel and headed toward the Prince's home. He had questions, and he wanted answers.

The streets were quiet, and before he formulated what to say, he turned onto the Prince family drive. The moment he did, he knew things were off. During the holidays, Jessie had hounded Dylan until he'd brought out all the decorations and strung lights from one side to the other. Any other year, those would have been removed not long after the first, but yet, six months later, the lights still hung from the eaves.

"Oh, Princess." Cam climbed from the truck and jogged up the steps, his stomach tied in knots. "It's going to be bad, isn't it?" He knocked, and while he waited for the door to be opened, his palms started to sweat.

"Yeah?!" Dylan bellowed. Then, as if he'd just registered who it was, relaxed slightly, "Oh, Cam. It's you."

The gruff voice of the man who opened the door was a shock, but not as surprising as his appearance. His clothes looked like he'd been wearing them for days. Dark blond stubble covered his face, and his hair was sticking up at odd angles. What was most telling about his state of mind, though, were his eyes. Dylan's eyes usually sparkled with life and light, but the ones looking back at him were bloodshot, as if he'd been drinking too much.

"Dylan," Cam asked hesitantly, "what's going on?"

Was he prepared for what was going on inside the walls of the house? The same feelings of neglect and disarray from the outside continued inside. The air was stale, and piles of clutter and chaos were everywhere. This wasn't the cozy Prince home he was used to seeing.

Cam stared at Jessie's brother, slouched half-asleep on the sofa. "What's going on, Dylan? You look horrible."

A yawn so large Cam heard Dylan's jaw pop kept him from answering immediately.

"Watch it, Kid," the other man slurred. "I'm tired. Been working extra shifts."

It was summer, so maybe his answer made sense, but Cam still sensed more was happening. "Where's Jessie? I heard she's been home for months."

Dylan stared at him for so long, Cam wasn't sure he would get a response. Finally, he offered, "There was an accident."

"Well, hell, Dylan," Cam barked impatiently, "I know about the accident. But why is Jessie still here? She led me to believe she was fine."

"Jessie lied," Dylan's words had Cam stepping back in shock. "She's blind."

His blunt response had Cam clearing off a place to sit. "Why is this the first I've heard about it? What's being done?"

"It's Jessie's—"

"Don't give me the '*It's Jessie's story*' line," Cam snapped. "I need to know what's going on."

"Look," Dylan took a deep breath, and his voice came out stronger than when Cam had arrived. "Jessie is an adult. I might not have agreed with her decision not to share her disability, but it was *her* decision. Talk to her."

Which was all true, Cam decided. However, he still needed to know what to expect before he talked to her. "Jessie sees nothing?"

"Sorry," Dylan muttered. "I shouldn't have blurted out she's blind. I should have said she has low vision."

"Which means what exactly?" Cam scoffed, working to maintain his temper.

"She sees," Dylan sighed, "but not clearly. I'm sure she can explain it better."

Cam took a deep breath and relaxed back in his chair. "How's Jessie handling all this?"

Dylan ran a hand through his already mussed hair. "Initially, while it kept her off the ice, Jessie treated it like she expected to wake up one day and she could see again. Then, days turned into weeks, which turned into months. One minute, she was anxious, and the next introspective. She did a lot of thinking and not much sharing."

"Thinking," Cam grumbled, "about what?"

"No idea," Dylan admitted. "Jessie spent time on the computer and with your mom. Since she didn't seem unhappy, I didn't push."

The knowledge she'd been with his mom and on the computer was a bit disconcerting. He'd sent Jessie several emails, but her brief responses made him feel like the internet hadn't been a priority. What could she have been doing?

"My mom said nothing."

"Doctor-patient thing," Dylan pointed out.

"Maybe," Cam mumbled. "It still doesn't explain why she didn't tell me. We're friends. I could have helped."

"Jessie knows that Cam," Dylan assured him. "She was worried you would drop everything and run home."

Which was true, Cam thought. Something Jessie had known, as well. It didn't make it any easier, though. He'd helped her after her parents' death, and a piece of him was pissed she hadn't told him the entire truth ... no matter what. The thought of her having to go through something like this alone was tearing him up inside, and he wasn't sure how to handle the feeling.

Except she wasn't alone. She had your mother.

Another part of the entire situation that annoyed him. Cam hated being left out of the loop.

"Will she see me?"

"I don't know," Dylan sighed. "Jessie's upstairs if you want to try. I'm tired and heading to bed for a few hours before returning to work. Good luck!" He smirked just before he disappeared down the hallway. "You'll need it."

Of that, Cam had no doubt. Jessie was stubborn and fiercely independent, but for her to hold something this serious back from him felt unnatural and a little unsettling.

But why shouldn't she?

Where that thought came from, he wouldn't explore. As far as he was concerned, they were a team. He just had to convince Jessie of that.

NINE
SEVEN YEARS EARLIER

Jessie's Home
June 10
7:45 a.m.

CAM TOOK THE STAIRS TWO AT A TIME, FIGHTING NOT TO FOCUS on his own emotions. Anger, hurt, and what felt like betrayal were at war inside his head. But this wasn't about him. This was about Jessie.

When he reached the landing, the same feeling of neglect he'd noticed downstairs remained. There was a burned-out bulb on one end of the hall, and the only door opened was the one belonging to the bath. The rest were closed, blocking out any light from the outside.

As if being pulled by a string, Cam headed toward her door and couldn't help but think it was quiet ... almost too quiet. There was no music or voices from the television—which at any other time would have meant no one was home. In fact, it was so quiet he wondered if Jessie had run—her walls once again back in place.

Her bedroom door was ajar, and with a soft push, it swung open. Jessie was lying in the middle of her bed, wrapped in one of his old sweatshirts. Headphones covered her ears, and her fingers tapped the beat of the music on her flat stomach.

Seeing her lightened the worry he'd been carrying since talking with Dylan. But frustration at the situation had him holding tight to the door-facing to keep from rushing to her side.

He tore his gaze from her delicate frame and quickly scanned her room. The walls were purple and covered with the same old posters. And, in one corner, the same stuffed animals were piled high.

The same, yet not the same, Cam thought, as a prickle of awareness had him turning his attention back to the bed. He could have sworn her eyes lit up when they connected with his.

"Cam?"

Hearing her soft voice propelled him across the room. "Hey there, Sugar." He picked her up and settled her on his lap.

"Sugar?" Jessie rolled her eyes. "I don't think so."

She curled against him, and he couldn't help but tighten his arms around her. Nor could he stop from burying his face in her sweet-smelling hair.

"You win ... Princess." But that wasn't anything new. Jessie always won. Cam sat still for a few more minutes before his impatience had the question, "Why didn't you tell me?" bursting forth.

"Why?" The tone of her voice had him wondering if he would get the runaround. "You can't tell me you've never made decisions for my own good."

"Well, hell, Princess, that's—"

"Don't tell me that's different," she snapped, her old fire rearing its head. "I wanted to ensure you didn't ignore what you were supposed to be doing." Jessie scrambled from his lap to pace around the room, "Besides, it's over, and a moot point. You finished your semester, and I did what I needed to do."

"And what was that?" Cam fired back, already angry to be put on the defensive.

"Things," she replied, absently stacking the books on her desk. "Just things." Jessie turned back toward the bed, her body language defiant.

"Things?" He sauntered closer. "Dylan didn't mention taking you to Sonny's to skate. He only said you spent time with my mom. Why?"

"Who are you to question what I do?"

A part of him knew she was pushing his buttons. However, it didn't stop him from closing the distance between them. "I'm the man who..." His green eyes clashed with her turquoise ones. They weren't vacant as he'd thought they'd be. Nor had they lost any of their power to tear him apart.

Cam took one more step, cupped her elbows, and pulled her against his chest. There was a moment of satisfaction when her eyes widened, but then her gaze dropped to his mouth.

"This." He placed a feather-light kiss on her lips. "This." Cam repeated the movement, this time a little harder. "This right here gives me the right to worry."

His lips covered hers in a kiss he tried to control, but couldn't. He was feeling too much, and everything inside came pouring out.

Her hands tangled in his hair, tugging him closer to her fire. It was a contest of wills as their lips, teeth, and tongues fought for superiority. Their breathing echoed in the room, chasing the anger away, leaving only want and need behind.

Cam wrenched his mouth from hers. "Wait."

"WAIT?" JESSIE'S FOG-FILLED BRAIN WASN'T SURE SHE'D HEARD correctly. "But, I like." And she did. She loved kissing Cam. Besides, as long as his mouth was busy, she wouldn't have to worry about those questions she might not be ready to answer.

"I like it too, Princess." Cam kissed her again. "But we need to ta—"

Jessie cut off his words, locking their mouths together. It had been so long since he'd held her, she needed to be in his arms a little longer. His kisses had always been like a drug, enticing her to take a little more, to stay a little longer. He tasted like flavored coffee, smelled like his cologne, and felt like home.

Cam wrapped his hand around her hair, holding her head still. "Jessie, not that I don't ... love ... what we're doing, but I will not allow you to distract me."

She dropped her head against his chest. "What do you want to know?"

Talking about everything wasn't high on her list—but she might as well get it over with. She knew Cam, and he wouldn't let it go. In the meantime, there were things she'd share, and other things that, well...

Jessie fought to maintain eye contact as Cam studied her, making her feel like he was trying to read her mind. The longer he stared, the more she wanted to see him. Then, she'd be able to read his expressions, hoping to find out what types of questions to expect.

"Come sit." Cam settled her on the bed next to him. "Tell me what happened."

"I told you," Jessie huffed. "I skated over a wire and fell."

"Come on, Princess," Cam taunted. "You can do better than that. Where were you? Why was the wire there?"

Question after question came pouring out. Ones she'd expected him to ask but had done everything she could to ignore. Jessie leaned into him, worrying her bottom lip, a habit that had worsened since her accident.

"It was," she began, "just before the party, and I was stalling..."

"You didn't want to go?"

"Hardly," she admitted with a humorless laugh. "I learned to hate those parties."

"Why?"

What could she say that wouldn't make him want to take someone on to defend her honor? "It all felt pretentious," she shrugged. "Besides, I was tired."

There were things she held back, such as Catherine's part in everything, but she shared the rest. Even the fact she'd decided she didn't want to skate any longer came pouring out.

"What can you see?"

"It's hazy." Jessie tilted her face toward his. "Kind of like looking through a window covered with condensation. Except..."

"Except?" Cam pushed.

"You know how when you look through a tube?"

"And can only see straight ahead?"

"Yes," Jessie hummed. "Now, that's how I see."

"It's changed?"

"Yes, I can see a little better." Jessie cupped his jaw. "I can see this."

Cam's hand covered hers, rubbing back and forth over his scruff. "It's fairly new," he murmured. "I thought it made me look sexy."

"Hmm, I like it." She wouldn't tell him he looked sexy with it, as his ego was big enough without her help.

"You didn't think it was too rough?" he asked, the tenor of his voice low and sexy.

Jessie felt her cheeks heat because when he'd kissed her, she'd been so lost in the moment she hadn't even noticed. "No." She rubbed her cheek against his beard. "It makes you look very mature."

"Really?" Cam yawned, quickly covering his mouth. "Sorry. I couldn't sleep until I saw you."

"Well," Jessie replied. "You've seen me, so go home and sleep."

"Oh, Princess," he breathed. "Are you trying to get rid of me?"

His nearness had Jessie's heart racing, and she wanted nothing more than to spend a few hours in his arms. However, there were still things she'd yet to share, such as her plans. Which, thankfully, his tired brain had yet to process.

"Come on," she tugged on his hand, "you can come back later."

Cam followed almost docilely down the stairs. "Now, Jessie," he looped his arm around her and pulled her close. "If I do, what did you have in mind?"

The sexy timbre of his voice sent a thrill through her system, but he was making her head spin. "I thought you could take me skating."

"Did I miss something?"

"It depends…"

Except Cam forged ahead, not giving her any chance to argue. "You fell and hit your head, right?"

"Yes."

Cam stepped closer, then held his arms up on each side of her, two fingers on one hand and three on the other. "You can't see how many fingers I'm holding up, right?"

"Well, no," she snapped. "I told you that."

"So, how do you expect to see where you are on the ice?"

Jessie stared at him for a handful of heartbeats, hoping her vision would clear and she could see the subtle expressions on his face. His voice sounded curious, but she wondered his intent. Without those cues, she couldn't be sure.

"You'll be my eyes, silly," she tossed at him playfully. "Now, go sleep."

Cam took her hand and lightly nuzzled her temple. "But, Jessie," he whispered in a tone meant to coax information from her. "Are you sure skating is a good idea?"

The longer she was with him, the more her resolve weakened. It would be so easy to step into his arms. He'd only been back a day, and already so much had changed. Plus, he was confusing her.

"Trust me." Jessie pushed up on her toes, kissed his cheek, and somehow manipulated him out the door before he could offer any more arguments.

Once he was gone, she couldn't keep the silly grin off her face. The box she'd closed her feelings for Cam in had just crumbled, and she had no clue what to do.

Good thing Sadie and Cassie were coming home because she needed some pointers ... sooner rather than later.

***

Cam's Home
June 10
10:00 a.m.

CAM WAS STILL IN A DAZE WHEN HE ARRIVED HOME. HE'D GONE TO Jessie's expecting a kitten and found a fox. But the memory of how she'd defended her decision when compared to the woman who'd curled against him, had him backtracking. She was a fox with a smattering of kitten and a slice of lioness.

Somewhere, though, he was missing a piece of information. He just wasn't sure what it was. However, his Jessie radar told him she'd run off and leave him if he didn't catch up soon. Something he wasn't willing to risk.

He tossed his keys on the table and followed his nose to the kitchen. "Mom?" Cam called over the noise of the mixer.

"Cameron!" Mary stopped what she was doing to hug him. "Welcome home."

"You're not at work."

"Still as observant as ever," she teased. "I thought I would make you breakfast, and we'd catch up."

"But ... you don't cook," Cam frowned. "Is something wrong?"

Mary laughed. "Can't a mother cook for her wayward son if she wants?"

"Well, sure." Cam thought longingly of his comfortable mattress upstairs. "I was just going up to bed."

His mother's brown eyes met his. "Sit down and have a few pancakes." She continued stirring for several minutes before adding quietly, "Please."

"Can I help?"

"Sit."

Mary told him what had happened in town while she poured pancake batter on the griddle and checked on the bacon in the microwave. Except, every time he thought she might 'fill him in' on Jessie, she'd skip to another topic.

Finally, she set a plate on the table before him and gave him the opening he'd been waiting on.

"Did you just come back from seeing Jessie?"

"Yes," Cam sighed. "Why didn't you tell me?"

"Well, it wasn't—"

"Don't say it was Jessie's story," Cam retorted. "That's what you said when I was in England. Hell, even Dylan told me the same thing, but..." He bit off the rest of what he was going to say and offered, "It would have been nice to be warned."

"What would you have done differently?"

"I could have..." His mother was only speaking the truth, though. Even if he'd come back early, there wasn't anything he could have done. "You're right," he admitted. "I just..."

"I understand," Mary conceded. "But this is Jessie's fight, and she's come a long way."

"Jessie said her vision problems are caused by internal stress," Cam murmured. "Do you know what that is?"

"She's shared," Mary replied. "However, I don't think I know all of it."

"Walls," he sighed. "Jessie is good at building walls."

The possibility of having to scale those walls once again frustrated him. But the woman he'd held ... kissed ... those walls were different than the Jessie of the past. Would it be easier for him to get around them this time?

"You know, Cam," Mary carried their breakfast dishes to the sink, "I don't think you need to worry about Jessie. She's going to be just fine."

"Then what should I do?"

"What do you think you should do?" she turned the question back at him.

Kiss her some more was the first thing that popped into his head, but he didn't think that was appropriate.

"Be her friend," Cam finally responded, knowing it was what his mother expected him to say.

"That's a start."

The look on her face made him think his mom knew more about his feelings than she'd let on. But with lethargy suddenly weighing him down, he opted not to follow up.

"I think I'll head to bed now. I've lost count of the hours I've been awake."

"Do you think you have enough energy to unpack first?" Mary closed the dishwasher and followed him from the room. "I'll do your laundry while you're sleeping ... that is if you brought home dirty clothes."

"Oh, just a few," he quipped.

"That's what I thought. Just drop them in the bathroom."

"Sweet. Oh, and Mom, Jessie wants me to take her skating. Do you think it's a good idea?"

A huge smile crossed Mary's face. "I think Jessie is getting to know Jessie," she responded cryptically. "Let her spread her wings."

Cam nodded absently, but as he unpacked, he had the feeling there was more to that message than he understood.

Jessie's Home
June 10
6:30 p.m.

AFTER RECEIVING GOOD NEWS IN THE MAIL, JESSIE SPENT SEVERAL hours on the phone planning her future. With that done, though, she wanted to shout it to the world. However, there was one hurdle ... explaining everything to Dylan.

That she hadn't told him she was studying for the SAT and wanted to attend college gave her slight pause. She'd convinced herself it was because she'd not wanted to hear the disappointment in his voice if she failed. With the results in, she couldn't delay any longer.

"Jessie?" Dylan stepped into the room. "Is everything okay?"

"Yeah, why?" She wiped her palms on her pants and took two glasses from the cabinet.

"Well, you said you needed to talk to me." Dylan moved in sync with her, anticipating what had to be done and placing food on their plates. "Here, let me." He reached for the glass she was filling with ice.

"I can do it." Jessie jerked the glass away, and the quick movement almost had it slipping from her hand. "Damn!" But she didn't like how irrational she sounded and relented, "Sorry."

Dylan was quiet while he helped her get dinner. Then he asked in his calm way, "Why don't you tell me what's got you so riled up? Was it seeing Cameron?"

"No. I need to tell you something, and I'm afraid you'll be mad."

"You're my sister, Jessie. You know you can tell me anything."

His comment had tears rushing to her eyes. "Can we eat and then talk?"

"Sure, Sis."

Thirty minutes later, Jessie picked up the letters and sat on a sofa across from Dylan. "I need to know something before I go any farther." She kept twisting her fingers together, trying to keep her hands steady.

"What is it, Jess?" Dylan sounded tired, but again, without seeing the little nuances of his expression, she was left to guess ... or be quiet.

"Why didn't you tell Catherine about my injuries?"

That question had been swimming around inside her head since April. If it was because they had broken up, that could change what she would say, but if not...

While Jessie couldn't see clearly, she could tell Dylan was running his hand through his hair. Finally, he leaned forward and clasped his hands together. "Honestly, I thought I had."

"What? How could you *think* you told her?"

He didn't immediately answer, and her mind's eye filled in the blanks from memory. While he worked through what he wanted to say, he would shift. First, he'd lean forward and then back in the chair. Then, he'd nibble on his left thumb cuticle.

"Dylan?"

He hesitated briefly before offering, "Catherine was out of town on hospital business when I got the call. You were the only thing I was focusing on."

Which was part of the problem. Especially since Catherine wanted her out of the way so she could have Dylan to herself.

"Then, for three days," he continued in a husky voice. "You were in a coma, and all I thought about was I couldn't lose you too. It was a horrible time."

Jessie blinked, remembering him talking to her while in the hospital. But the only thing that stuck out in her memory was the emotion in his voice and not the words.

"What about when I woke up?"

"You were still my primary focus."

A part of her felt like she could take everything Dylan said at face value. Except it didn't fit with the hospital visit. At that time, he'd been waiting for her to tell Catherine about her vision issues, making her think both were guilty of holding back.

Was Dylan aware Catherine was jealous and felt the need to protect his sister?

"Are you still dating?" Jessie blurted. "She hasn't been around."

"You didn't want anyone to know about your vision issues," he reminded her. "No one has visited until Cameron. Even your sessions with Mary were away from the house."

When Dylan didn't pursue that conversation any further, she let out the breath she was holding, "Is Catherine the one?"

He let go of a laugh. "You don't ask the easy ones, do you, Jess?"

"Well?"

Dylan fidgeted for a handful of seconds, "I want what mom and dad had … or what Mary and Clint have, and … I'm not sure if—"

"If Catherine is the one," Jessie filled in the blanks.

"Maybe," he replied absently. "Anyway, was Catherine what you wanted to talk to me about?"

Jessie pulled the letters out from under her legs. "Kind of. Here."

She shoved them toward him, fighting to sit still. While he was reading, her bottom lip found its way between her teeth, and she kept playing with her fingers, trying to steady her nerves. Dylan looked up a few times, and she was sure his expression was a mixture of delight and surprise.

"Well?" Jessie pushed once he was done reading. "Are you okay with my decision?"

"Am I okay?" he repeated quietly. "Oh, Jess."

Jessie squeaked when he jumped up and pulled her into his arms.

"I'm *very* okay with it! And Jess," Dylan stepped back far enough so she had to tilt her head up slightly, "I'm very proud of you."

"Thanks. I'm kind of proud of me too."

"You should be," Dylan congratulated her again. "I have a few questions, though."

"Okay. Have time for some ice cream?"

A layer of guilt for keeping things from him slid away when he chuckled. It lightened her load, and somehow, she knew everything would be okay.

TEN
SEVEN YEARS EARLIER

Jessie's Home
June 11
11:00 a.m.

THE NEXT DAY, CAM WAS STILL TRYING TO PROCESS EVERYTHING he'd learned. It wasn't a big deal if Jessie didn't want to skate any longer. If he were honest with himself, he liked the idea because it meant they could spend more time together. But why hadn't she said something if she no longer wanted to skate?

"Let her spread her wings," his mother said. But what did that mean? Jessie had given him bits of information and then intentionally distracted him. That made him curious. He had a question or two for her before he took her to Sonny's.

"My vision issues are psychosomatic."

"She's shared a little," his mother answered.

"Sometimes there's a black hole that threatens to engulf me, and I disappear," Jessie had told him right after her parents' death.

Was that why she wanted to go to Sonny's? Would skating blow the darkness away and clear her vision?

"I think Jessie will be just fine."

Of that, he knew—as he planned to do everything in his power to assure it.

Cam climbed from his truck, ready with his list of questions. But Jessie wasn't waiting for him in the manner he'd expected. He found her pacing from one end of the porch to the other.

"Jess," he called several times before she acknowledged his presence.

"Oh, hi," Jessie responded nervously.

Her top teeth, holding her full bottom lip captive, caught his attention. "Is that all?"

"What?" she frowned. "Should I have said, 'Oh, hello, Cam?' Or were you expecting me to ask where you've been?"

The comments spouted in such a waspish manner shouldn't have turned him on, but they did. "No, Sugar." He grinned, knowing she'd have something to say about his word use. "I was thinking you forgot something." He tapped his bottom lip and waited with bated breath.

Jessie's gaze traveled to where his finger rested, and he saw indecision come and go. Suddenly, she tugged his mouth down to meet hers.

The kiss was everything he remembered. This time, he took advantage of what she offered.

"I'm sorry I didn't make it back last night." After every word, Cam dove back in, taking whatever she was willing to give.

"I spoke to your mom."

That might have surprised him in the past. However, considering their recent relationship, he should have expected it.

"Do you still want to go, or...?" He wanted to kick his behind the minute he opened his mouth. Some questions needed answers, and there was no time like the present.

"In a minute," she stepped back, "sit with me?"

Cam stared into her blue eyes, which were cloudy but not from her vision issues. Something was going on, and she wanted to talk.

"Of course."

Jessie wasn't sure why she was so nervous. Cam would be happy for her, she was sure. However, once he knew, everything became real.

That meant everything they'd been tap-dancing around for years would need to be addressed.

"Here." She handed him her acceptance letter. "I know after our talk yesterday, you have questions. This should answer them."

Cam took the envelope and removed the single page. While he was reading, it was impossible to look away. She was hoping for a sign—happiness, anger, excitement—something to give her an idea of what he was thinking.

"Well?"

"Congratulations, Jess." Cam appeared happy. He also sounded confused, which had her preparing for his questions. "Why didn't you tell me?"

"Do you need to know everything?" Jessie pushed up from the swing and put a little distance between them.

"I..." he tilted his head, studying her, and she swore she wouldn't be the first to break. "No, not everything ... but this is big."

Stop it, Jess, her internal voice scolded. *Listen!*

"I'm sorry," Jessie sat back down and angled toward him. "No one knew, not even Dylan. This was for me. And you know what? It feels amazing."

Cam cupped her jaw, and his thumb settled in the center of her chin. "I'm proud of you, Princess." He kissed her, one so tender, her senses came alive. Her breath stuck in her throat, her heart raced, and goosebumps rushed from the point of impact. "So..." he murmured against her mouth, "we have the summer together?"

His voice's huskiness made her want to crawl into his lap and wrap herself around him. However, the way he was making her head swim had her tightening her butt muscles to stay firmly planted.

"Yes," barely escaped before he kissed her again, this one just as electric.

"Good," he whispered. "I'm sure we can find some things to do."

He angled her head just enough to deepen the kiss and dissolve her control. It didn't take long before Cam scooped her up and onto his lap.

After years of imagining what being in his arms felt like, she realized her dreams were nothing like reality. The way he brushed his hand up and down her back, the heat from his chest, and the way his body hardened against her hip made her skin come alive. She wanted closer ... but was unsure how to get there.

Time lost all meaning until a car door slammed, penetrating the fog surrounding her.

"Dylan!" Jessie jumped off Cam's lap, ready to face her brother. Until she realized her mouth probably looked well-kissed.

"I'll get my skates," she suddenly blurted before running into the house, leaving Cam to fend on his own.

CAM'S THOUGHTS WERE SLUGGISH, BUT HE HAD THE wherewithal to fold one leg over the other just as Jessie's brother ran up the steps.

"Isn't that great about Jessie? I bet you're happy she'll be close. I must admit I was a little taken aback when she told me, but..." When he saw the '*What the hell's got into you*' look on the other man's face, Cam bit off the rest of what he wanted to say. After all, he'd been rambling.

"What's going on?" Dylan asked instead of answering the multiple questions he'd been tossed.

Hell would need to do the proverbial freeze before he would share exactly what had been going on.

"I came to take Jessie skating. My mom thought it would be a good idea."

"Mary thought it would be safe?" Dylan asked softly.

"Mom suggested I let Jessie spread her wings." Cam thought that was an interesting analogy, considering what his princess reminded him of every time she skated.

"Seems our Jessie is spreading her wings," Dylan hesitated a beat, "in more ways than one. Take care of her," he quipped on his way inside.

Cam had to work to keep his mouth closed as he processed the double meaning behind the words. However, before he could consider them any further, Jessie returned with her skate bag slung over her shoulder and her eyes shining.

"Ready?" She headed toward his car, her eagerness evident in every step.

"Are you in a hurry, Princess?"

Jessie tossed a sexy smile over her shoulder and climbed into his truck. It made him think about being alone and helping himself to more kisses. A thought that had him turning right out of her driveway instead of left.

"Where are we going?"

"To Sonny's."

"Okay," Jessie stretched out the word. "Why are we going the long way?"

Cam snatched her hand and interlocked their fingers. "What if I say I'd like a little more time alone with you?"

Her quick inhalation and the tightening of her fingers around his told him the idea wasn't all bad. However, since he couldn't take her where he wanted … yet … he opted for a drive-by instead.

"I thought I'd show you something."

"Oh?"

"Yes."

With Lover's Cove just ahead, Cam slowed down and wondered what Jessie would say if he pulled into the parking lot. No, they weren't ready for the commitment the Cove promised. Someday, though, he'd take her there.

"The ship looks lonely," Jessie murmured, referring to the seventeenth-century Spanish galleon, a staple in Swan Harbor forever.

"Lonely?" Cam questioned. "She has Jonesy."

Jessie giggled. "True."

"Can you see him?"

"Jonesy?"

"Yes."

"His shape," Jessie whispered.

Jonesy was a white, mute swan that appeared sometime in the 1960s or 70s. He arrived every spring, never straying far from the ship, recently turned into a restaurant. Jack, the owner of Captain Jack's Fine Dining, proclaimed Swan Harbor's hope revolved around the duo. However, everyone knew Jack was eccentric and mostly paid him no mind. But it didn't stop Cam from thinking if the whole hope story was true—it would explain some of the oddities in his hometown.

"Soon," he promised. "Soon, you'll see Jonesy's white feathers."

She gave him an impish grin. "I hope you're right."

"I know I'm right." Cam winked. "I'm always right."

He climbed from the truck and hoped his nerves would settle. While his mother might think Jessie needed to '*spread her wings,*' he was on the verge of hyperventilating.

"Are you ready?"

"I'm ready. Come on."

He took her hand, grabbed their skates, and led her into the building.

Memories immediately bombarded him, and he couldn't help but wonder if the same had happened to Jessie.

"Are you sure?" Cam asked once more.

Jessie squeezed his hand. "Let's go."

She took off toward their usual bench, which gave him a few minutes to admire the fit of the leggings and tight tank she was wearing. By the time he sat down, she'd already slipped into one of her skates.

"Let me help." Cam reached for the laces on her skates.

"I've got this."

"Well, okay." He went to work on his laces, understanding her need but not liking it. Jessie was finished with the first skate and had moved on to the second before she glanced up.

"It never changes, does it?"

"What?" The abrupt topic shift had him running to catch up. "Your skates? Sonny's?"

"Sonny's." Jessie smiled. "The smells, the sounds. I'm hoping the feel of the ice, too. Ready?"

"Lead, and I'll follow."

Cam took her hand, and they stepped onto the ice. Her smile lit up the room, and heaven help him. He thought her kisses were potent, but what he'd felt as an eighteen-year-old was nothing compared to what he felt now.

Sonny's Skate & Bowl
June 11
2:00 p.m.

AFTER BEING OFF THE ICE SINCE FEBRUARY, IT TOOK A FEW STEPS before her natural affinity returned and Jessie could relax.

"How's it feel?" Cam murmured.

"Good," she hummed, "but different too."

Holding Cam's hand and hearing his voice calmed her and settled those last-minute nerves. She'd worried when she stepped on the ice for the first time after the fall, that's all she'd think about. When that wasn't the case, it felt like she'd been given a gift.

"How's your vision?

"My vision is…" Until he'd asked, she hadn't noticed her tunnel was wider. "Better," Jessie replied, excited the edges seemed lighter. "How close to the side are we?"

Cam hesitated, making her wonder if he planned to ignore the question. "About five feet." His reluctant response had her lips threatening to lift. It didn't, however, deter the direction her thoughts were traveling.

As long as she kept looking from side to side, Jessie could figure out where she was on the ice. Once they reached their bench, she started counting her steps, working to get a handle on the timing. Things felt familiar, and the more they skated, the greater her confidence.

"Let me go, Cam."

"Let you go? Why?" He tightened his hold on her.

"Let me skate. I can do it. Please, let me try."

"Well, hell, Princess," Cam sputtered. "You're going to give me a heart attack."

Jessie ignored him and focused only on what she wanted to do—a sit spin. Once she set up, she threw her leg in the air and landed on one foot, intending to spin around.

She could feel the ice beneath her skate, and just as the thought, *I've got this,* floated through her mind, her concentration broke … causing her to fall. *Nice move, Prince.*

"Jessie!" Cam shouted.

"I'm okay!" Jessie brushed off her hands.

"Are you sure?"

"Positive." She grinned. "I fell when my vision was perfect."

"Don't scare me, Princess." Cam skated around her, "You're going to try it again, aren't you?"

"I'm going to try a jump."

Jessie skated off, her entire focus on the steps. She set up and executed a single axel and landed it perfectly.

"Whoop, Jessie!" Cam swung her around. "That was amazing!"

"Thanks. Except it was only a single." But she couldn't deny it helped her confidence—almost as much as he did.

"All right, Miss Prince, what's next?"

"Watch." Jessie skated away to set up another jump. When she landed a double axel, triple lutz, she couldn't keep the squeal of excitement from escaping.

Cam was there and pulled her into his arms. "You take my breath away, Jessie," he whispered against the side of her head.

"Isn't that a good thing?"

He tightened his arms around her, pressing her flush against his hard body. "A very good thing." Their lips met in a kiss so hot she was sure the ice was melting around them.

"Jessie!" Her name being squealed broke through the fog Cam's lips caused. "Jessie!"

She pushed out of Cam's arms. "It's Sadie and Cassie! They're home."

"That they are," Cam nodded toward where they were standing, "and brought Ryan and Ben with them."

"Race you!"

Jessie took off with Cam's "Hey, no fair!" ringing in her ears.

She won but knew it was because he'd let her. He made her feel so much more than she'd ever allowed. How was she going to keep her heart safe? Better yet, did she even want to?

༄

Randy's Arcade
July 15
7:00 p.m.

OVER THE NEXT FEW WEEKS, CAM SPENT AS MUCH TIME WITH Jessie as possible. It had been three years since they'd been in the same place for longer than a few days, and the only word he could find to describe how he felt was liberated. He'd harbored feelings for her for years, but being able to act on them was more than he'd ever imagined.

For the first time, he felt free to think of her as more than *'just a friend.'* She was his girlfriend, and he was determined to experience all the *'date-like'* activities with her possible. He wanted the movies, long walks, dinners, and bonfires—all ending with the traditional date night activity ... kissing—lots and lots of kissing.

Cam loved kissing her and helped himself to those kisses whenever possible. Unfortunately, his wayward body and the way it hardened when she was near had caused a few uncomfortable situations. Being caught sporting a hard-on in front of the entire town was not his idea of a good time. Nor did he enjoy holding objects in front of his lap, hiding behind tables and chairs, or wearing a long jacket. Plus, tighty-whities should be outlawed.

At one time, Mario Kart had worked to prevent embarrassment, but bigger problems needed bigger distractions. He came up with three ideas, two of which had been successful. The first was used when he should have been working on something at the office. Instead, he'd gotten lost in a memory of the evening before, and his body had immediately stood up to salute.

He'd recited building codes—effectively deflating the problem. It had been a close call, too, as his dad and Gray walked into the room, and he had to think fast.

The second time had been at home, when he was lounging on the patio talking on the phone. Jessie's voice turned him on, and the memory of how she looked in her bikini had his flag flying high within seconds. Then he heard his mother coming and silently repeated the rules to be a successful architect. He'd been saved from embarrassment when his flag had fallen.

Several days later, Cam met Ben and Ryan at Randy's to play pool. He was easily distracted and more than once, thought about going home. Except, he knew Jessie was—

"Wow!" Ben interrupted his thoughts. "What did you do to make Jessie so happy? She's practically glowing."

Cam frowned. "What?"

"Jessie." Ben nodded toward the door.

Cam heard her laugh before he saw her, and when he did, he was struck dumb. Jessie sparkled with more light and life than he'd seen from her since her parents' death. She was wearing a short skirt that showcased her long legs. Her tank top was the same color as her eyes, and her strawberry gold hair hung down her back. His blood rushed south, and he had to grab the edges of the seat to keep from running to her.

"Did you finally give her the old vavoom?"

Ben's crude comment made Cam want to punch him. "Cut it out, Matthews," he snapped. "It's not like that with Jessie."

"Oh?" Ben leaned across the table. "How is it exactly?"

It was something—that much Cam knew. But how did you give words to a feeling you'd never experienced? One that consumed your entire being and filled you up, making you think it might explode out of you any moment?

"Jessie's different," Cam replied, hoping he'd appeased his friend.

"She's hot," Ben kept pushing. "Look at those legs."

"Did you see Cassie?" Ryan jumped in.

"Of course." Ben took a sip of his beer. "She's looking quite fine, too. Why don't you go talk to her, Romeo?"

"Alone?" Ryan squeaked. "What if she ignores me?"

"Just go talk to her," Cam sighed. "You never know until you try."

"I remember saying those same words to you some time ago." Ben laughed. "I've got an idea. Let's all go."

Cam hesitated. Jessie had been excited to reconnect with her friends. Did he want to get in the middle of that?

"Come on." Ryan took one more drink. "Let's go."

"I think the girls wanted to be alone," Cam warned them. "This might not be the best time to try to make up with Cassie."

"Come on." Ryan nudged Cam forward. "It will be okay."

"Well, I guess," Cam capitulated. "But don't say I didn't warn you."

The girls met them halfway, and when Jessie kissed him, the Pythagorean Theorem popped into his mind. It was the only thing that might save him, as all his blood was hanging out down south.

⁂

"Cam." Jessie wiped her lipstick off his mouth and took a step back. "Hi."

"Hi yourself." Cam grinned, and his dimples popped. "Coral isn't my color?"

"No," she playfully touched a place on his shirt, "maybe a nice pink to match those little dots."

"I'll remember that." His eyes twinkled, and he looked like he wanted to say something more, but their attention was pulled toward their friends.

"I told you," Cassie's dark eyes sparked. "I'm not ready to talk to you yet. Maybe never."

"But, Cassie," Ryan cajoled. "I'm sorry. Can't we talk … outside?"

When Jessie's eyes met Cassie's, she saw satisfaction at winning whatever battle she had with Ryan.

"Fine," Cassie fired back, her voice clipped. "I'll give you ten minutes."

"Any idea what that's about?" Cam whispered, and his hot breath sent tingles racing down her spine.

"No clue." Jessie glanced at her other friend. "But I'd better go, or someone will drag Sadie onto the dance floor."

Cam hugged her. "Just remember you're spoken for," he reminded her before kissing her quite thoroughly in front of everyone.

He'd not done that before, which threw her off a little. "Wow." Jessie watched him until he was out of sight, all the while admiring his fine ass.

"I believe you've been holding out on me." Sadie linked their arms and guided her toward a table. "Now, I know why you suggested Randy's."

"That wasn't," Jessie began.

"Sure, it wasn't," Sadie disregarded her comment. "Now, sit down and spill."

Jessie worked her lip over several seconds while what to say and how much to say sorted itself out. "Okay," she admitted. "Something is bothering me."

"Do tell." Sadie's green eyes sparkled. "What's Cam done?"

"Well," Jessie sighed, feeling a little like an idiot. "It's not so much what he's done, per se, it's more what he's not done."

Sadie frowned, and then, as if a light went off in her head, her brows rose sky high. "He's not done anything?"

"Well, we've kissed," Jessie murmured. "A lot. Just anything else ... nope."

"Hasn't even tried, huh?" Sadie toyed with the straw in her glass for a heartbeat or two. "Who made the first move?"

"I kissed him first." Jessie glanced around to make sure they weren't being heard, "But that was three years ago. This summer? Him. I *have* attempted to push his buttons a few times, though," she admitted with a wicked smile. "It just hasn't gotten me very far."

"Well," Sadie stated matter-of-factly. "It appears you need to do more button pushing."

Her face heated as several possible ideas raced by. "Oh, I don't know. Like what?"

A devilish smile settled on Sadie's face as she leaned in. "First, I would..."

ELEVEN
SEVEN YEARS EARLIER

Jessie's Home
August 12
8:30 a.m.

Jessie was in that space halfway between asleep and awake. Since she wouldn't see Cam again until Thanksgiving break, he'd promised to make the day memorable. What he didn't know was she had a few ideas of her own.

Her phone buzzed, and her heart began to race. "'Lo."

"Good morning, Princess," Cam whispered in his sexy voice. "You're awake, right?"

"Maybe. Why? Did we have plans?"

"Be ready in fifteen minutes," he replied. "Wear jeans, and bring your swimsuit."

"Fifteen minutes?" Jessie squeaked. "That's not long enough!"

"You'd better hurry then," Cam warned. "Don't make me drag you from your bed."

"You wouldn't."

"Try me."

She could hear the challenge in his voice and had to admit a part of her wanted to do just that. "You're not very nice. You could have warned me you'd be here so early."

"Now, Princess," Cam's husky voice caused a shiver to race up her spine. "Don't be testy. I'll see you in thirteen minutes."

Since she was secretly happy he'd shown up so early, she jumped from bed. It was okay to let him win sometimes, especially when she had a few things planned on her own.

❧

Cam chuckled at how fast the shower started after he'd hung up. "And you didn't think I could get her out of bed."

Dylan grinned. "My sister's stubborn."

"Agreed."

"But," Dylan continued, "you've been good for her this summer. When I saw her lying in the hospital bed, I thought…"

"Jessie wouldn't want you dwelling on that image."

"I know." Dylan folded his arms over his chest. "What's on the agenda today?"

Just as it had a few times over the summer, Dylan's protective dad mode appeared. For some reason, it made Cam want to push the older man's buttons.

"A little of this, a little of that," he quipped, earning the expected frown.

"Hey," Dylan snapped. "That's my sister."

"You've reminded me of that several times this summer," Cam pointed out. "I'm not likely to forget it."

"See that you don't."

"How can I when you remind me quite often?" Cam hesitated a beat, then, to decrease some of the tension, offered quietly, "You don't need to worry," and gave Dylan the answers he wanted.

Jessie ran into the room, reducing the tension even more.

"You made it." Cam grinned.

"Did you doubt me?" She kissed him, then glanced from him to Dylan. "Is everything okay?"

"Everything's fine," Cam murmured. "I was just promising Dylan I'd take care of you today."

Jessie slipped her hand into his back pocket and dug her fingers into his ass. The look in her turquoise eyes dared him to say something.

Her challenge caused Cam's balls to tingle. His blood heated, and he wondered if he was going to have to resort to reciting the Pythagorean Theorem. Getting a hard-on in front of Dylan wouldn't endear him to the other man.

Jessie took several steps away and picked up her bag. "Dylan knows that, don't you?"

"I do. Have fun. I'll see you later."

"Sorry about that. I pushed a few of his buttons, and things got a little out of hand."

"About what?"

"You," his lips hovered over hers briefly, before settling in for a taste. "But you're worth whatever he wants to throw at me."

"Maybe I should tell you I'm sorry," she gave him a wry smile. "I didn't realize my big brother was being so ... well ... fatherly."

"Dylan doesn't want to see you hurt," Cam offered on the way to his truck. "Don't worry about it."

He opened the door, but rather than sliding inside, Jessie stood still, waiting for what, he wasn't sure.

"What's going on, Cam?"

"Nothing. Why?"

She took a step closer and slid her arms around his neck. "I trust you."

Cam nuzzled her temple. "You have no idea what you do to me."

"Oh, I think I have some idea."

"Jessie," Cam groaned. "Are you sure we aren't being watched?"

"Spoilsport." Jessie tossed a sexy grin over her shoulder and settled in the center of the bench seat.

"Behave." Cam kissed her, one that was hard and much too brief. "Otherwise, you won't get your present."

"Present? What is it?"

Cam closed his fingers around hers to stop them from wandering up the inside of his thigh. "Patience, Princess. We'll get there."

Jessie groaned inaudibly. She'd tried several of Sadie's suggestions, but each time, he maneuvered out of the situation. His skittishness reminded her of wanting her first kiss. It had taken weeks until persistence had finally paid off.

It wasn't long until Cam pulled into Buck's Flying Steeds.

"Horseback riding?" Jessie grinned. "Hence the jeans."

"You're quick, Princess. Ready?"

Jessie slid into Cam's arms. His heat reached out to wrap around her, and just as she anticipated the feel of his lips on hers, he stepped back.

"Are you okay with this?"

"Why?" She gave him a flirty smile. "Did you think I wanted more?"

Cam's eyes twinkled, but he didn't say anything. It reminded her of her secret that would make his upper hand fall by the wayside. Of that, she had no doubt.

Buck arrived with Buttercup—a pretty sorrel mare for Jessie, and Atari, a black gelding for Cam.

"Atari will want to lead," he warned them. "Have fun."

Cam was much more comfortable on a horse than she. His blond hair fell over his forehead, his t-shirt fit snugly, and suddenly, she wanted nothing more than to be held.

'*We'll get there*,' he'd promised, which, if she had anything to do with it, they would, and soon.

Thick trees lined the trail as they climbed toward a plateau. Swan Harbor was spread out below with the church where his parents were married in one direction. In another, a covered bridge connected town roads to county ones, and not far from the base of the mountain, they were building a new park.

Atari had no intention of enjoying the view, though, and pranced from one observation area to the other.

"Damn horse," Cam muttered.

"You don't care for Atari's plans?"

"Not hardly."

"Oh?" Jessie hummed. "Should I be nervous?"

"What do you think?"

"I can't wait," she tossed over her shoulder before riding off without him

Atari pranced around until Cam gave the horse free rein, and he took off after Buttercup.

As he passed Jessie, Cam made the mistake of looking at her. His thoughts scattered, and his blood rushed south.

"Cat got your tongue, Cam?" Jessie kicked her horse into a trot.

She didn't get far before Cam went after her. With his horse's longer stride, he quickly caught up and stopped several feet away.

It was a struggle not to jump down and rush toward her. She had on jeans that molded her thighs, and her strawberry-gold hair blew wildly around her shoulders. If that wasn't enough to distract a man, she'd added a minuscule bikini top, and the sight set his blood on fire.

"Jessie…"

Her name was pulled from deep inside, where he'd tried to bury his wants. Seconds later, Buttercup stopped nearby, and his gaze collided with hers.

He stalked across the sand, tugged her down, and into his arms. "Can you feel that? Can you feel what you do to me?"

A slight tremor raced through her, and she pressed a little closer. "Surely, you aren't complaining, are you?

"Oh, hell, honey," Cam nuzzled her temple, "you're going to be the death of me."

"And that's bad?"

"No, it's very, very good. But something is going on. What?"

"I'm … I'm giving you," she paused briefly before continuing, "memories so you won't forget me."

Cam bit his lip, thinking the pain would clear the lust from his brain for a few seconds. He trailed his finger from the top of her bikini up underneath her chin, forcing her to look at him. "Princess, everything we do is memorable. But this," he kissed one corner of her mouth, "this is playing with fire."

His lips settled on hers, and when she grabbed hold of his hair and opened for him, Cam nearly exploded. He lost track of how long they stood there communicating only with their mouths and hands. It didn't take much for his body temperature to skyrocket, and those impure thoughts to rush back around. If they were alone, Jessie's legs would be wrapped around him, and her much softer parts aligned with his hardness.

"Wait!" Cam wrenched his mouth away. "We can't."

"You don't like?"

"You know damn good and well I like." He turned them back toward the corral and looped his arm around her. "However, our time's about up, and besides, there's more."

"More kisses…" Jessie waggled her eyebrows suggestively, "or more activities?"

"Both."

On the way back to the truck, he had to wonder if the next part of his plan was a good idea.

Swan Harbor Docks
August 12
4:30 p.m.

When they drove into the dock parking area, Jessie's heart took off at the possibilities. "We're going sailing?"

"I want you to myself," Cam admitted, "but after that display on the beach, I'm wondering if it's a good idea."

"Oh?"

"Are you okay with this?"

Jessie soothed the little frown line between his brows. "I trust you."

"But maybe you shouldn't, Princess. I'm…" Cam's eyes flared, and he reached for her hands. "Wait! You saw the Catalina! Can you see me … clearly?"

Jessie's eyes filled with tears. Only then did it register, she could see him. "I can. It happened when you rode past me. Finally, the darkness is gone."

"Oh, Jessie." He pulled her across his lap and kissed her. One full of fire, and so hot she wasn't sure she could handle it.

"Princess," he groaned. "You're killing me here."

"Sorry." Jessie jumped from the truck, grabbed her bag, and started toward the boat. "Race you!"

He caught her quickly and carried her onto the boat. "I've got you, Princess."

"No," Jessie hugged him, "I've got you."

"Are you ready?" He kissed her again. "The quicker we leave..."

"The quicker we're alone."

"Yes, please."

Cam gave concise instructions, and within minutes, they were headed out to sea.

"I can handle this," he called above the sound of the wind. "Why don't you go put on your suit?"

Jessie grabbed her bag and slipped below deck and into the head. It was small, barely big enough for her to turn around. When she pulled off her jeans and dropped her shirt, she studied her barely-there bikini.

It was royal blue and made of two sets of twin triangles. One set covered her breasts and the other below, with both sets fastening with matching ties. When wet, she was pretty sure the material hid nothing. She'd never wear it on the local beach, but with Cam ... sometimes a girl had to do what she had to do.

Since the boat was still moving, she wanted to wait until Cam could focus on just her. She pushed open one side of the mirrored cabinet. It held typical items: toothpaste, several wrapped toothbrushes, mouthwash, dental floss, and a box of...

Her hand shook when she picked it up, and a part of her wanted to rip open a packet. Wanted to *see* and *feel* what was inside.

She didn't know why she was nervous. That hadn't been there earlier. Why, though?

Was it seeing the box? Where had it come from? Had Cam put it there? Or did it belong to Gray? Should she take a couple up onto the deck, or should she...?

What would Sadie do?

Take a pocketful.

But *what* did she want?

❧

Since Jessie disappeared below deck, he both feared and anticipated her return. If just seeing her in jeans and a tiny blue top had drained all of the blood from his head, he wasn't sure he could handle the entire suit.

Cam dropped anchor, put away the mainsail, and turned his attention to the ladder. He'd just dropped it into the water when the air vibrated, charged with the connection between him and his princess.

"Cam?"

The hesitancy in Jessie's voice had him whirling around, unwilling to make her wait any longer.

She stood a few feet away, with the sun painting a halo around her slender frame. Her bare feet sported blue polish. With one knee bent, her long legs were on display, and the mere thought of them wrapped around him made him grip the railing.

Blood rushed to his balls, stealing his breath, and anticipation zipped along his skin.

In less than three strides, he'd invaded her space and tugged her against his chest. "This wasn't what I was expecting."

"You don't mind, do you?" She had on one of his flannel shirts. It hung mid-thigh, and the sleeves were folded over several times.

"Well," he fingered the points of the collar, "the blue plaid matches that little top you were wearing earlier. Were you cold?"

"A little."

Cam tightened his arms around her and brushed a kiss on the side of her head. There was more going on with his princess than being cold, but he'd let her set the pace. He always did.

"My shirt looks better on you than it ever did on me."

"That's good. I might steal it."

"No stealing necessary. I'll gladly give it to you."

"Really?"

"Anything, Jess," he whispered. "Anything."

Cam put a little distance between them and tried to ignore his disappointment that Jessie, the siren, had been tucked away. "My mom packed us a picnic. Are you hungry?"

"Mary knew what you'd planned for today?"

"Well, she knew *some* of what I'd planned," he admitted.

"I could eat."

He spread out a blanket and let Jessie dig through the basket. Once they started eating, whatever pressure they'd put on themselves seemed to disappear. She laughed more, and her natural gestures became smoother and less erratic.

For the next few hours, he kept his eyes where they belonged, but just barely—until one of the shirt's buttons slid apart.

When it did, he could see a little more of Jessie's silky skin. Not long after her thighs were exposed, the top buttons opened, expanding his view. His heart raced, and he quickly reached a point where it was jump in the cold Maine water or find a distraction.

Cam handed Jessie the small box he'd intended to be her birthday gift in July. At the last minute, he'd chickened out, worried it was too much. But with them going in separate directions, he needed her to know how he felt.

"I hope you like it."

"You're nervous..." Jessie murmured. "Why?"

"What if you don't like it?" He shrugged. "What if it's too much?"

"Don't you know it doesn't matter?"

"Are you sure?"

"Very. What matters, Cam, is that it's from you."

Something inside him settled. "Open it."

Jessie tossed the wrapping paper in the basket and lifted the lid. "It's beautiful." Her voice was breathless as she looked at the heart-shaped diamond pendant. "I can't believe you gave me a diamond heart."

Cam's breath caught. He cupped her hand and pressed it against his chest. "It's not the first heart I've given you."

"No?"

"No." He kissed their entwined hands. "You've held mine far longer than I can remember." Then he paused a heartbeat and added, "I love you, Jessie," words he'd never spoken to anyone but family.

"Oh, Cam," she whispered. "I love you too."

"That's very good. May I put it on you?"

"Please."

Cam fastened it around her neck, and the sight of it lying against her breastbone took his breath. "It's beautiful." He glanced up, and their eyes met. "You're beautiful."

"What now?"

The suggestive look in her eyes belied the hesitancy in her voice. He didn't think it was possible, but his dick hardened even more, and he wanted nothing more than to touch.

"Come here." Cam hooked a finger in the one remaining button and tugged her closer. "Let me show you."

Jessie popped the last button, dropped her shoulder, and allowed the shirt to fall away.

At the sight of the tiny scraps that barely covered her nipples, he forgot to breathe. One tug, just one tug, and the suit would be a memory. He wanted to bury himself in her softness.

"Cam?"

"Let me show you." He pulled her close, lowered her to the deck, and captured her lips.

THE TINGLE JESSIE ALWAYS FELT WHEN IN CAM'S ARMS HAD RUN earlier, but it was back and threatened to become a storm. His mouth teased, caressed, and slid against hers until she barely knew who she was. Her focus centered on the feelings he was pulling from deep within.

His touches were everything she'd dreamed about. One minute, hard, and the next soft. He caressed her breasts and then, before she could catch her breath, cupped her butt cheeks. A multitude of sensations and emotions raced through her, telling her one thing—to get closer.

Cam rolled them over, and her top fell away. His thumb glided over her raised nipple, causing her breath to hitch. Pressure grew, and the words '*More! More!*' were on replay.

One rough palm captured a firm peak, and sparks zipped straight to her core. Goosebumps spread from wherever they touched. She couldn't get enough, wanting more, hoping the feelings would last forever.

"Jessie." Cam cupped her breast and slid his thumb back and forth over her nipple. "You have no idea how long I've dreamed of this."

Me too!

The words wouldn't form, though, as all her focus was on how it felt to have Cam touching her. One second, she was floating, and tension built inside, growing with every new touch. Then, in the next heartbeat, the slow, tender caresses were replaced by quick, rapid movements.

Stop, she wanted to say, but felt too awkward, too embarrassed.

He squeezed her breast, a touch that should have had her body softening, and the excitement inside growing. Instead, an image of what he was doing made her want to giggle, and acted like a bucket of water, snuffing the flame.

Slow down! Yet Cam's caresses moved faster, and his breathing became more erratic.

"So good." He kissed her again, and the slow mating of their lips stoked the fire back to life once again. "So soft."

He trailed feather-like touches over her flat stomach, and her bottoms fell open.

*W*hen he stroked between her thighs, the gentle touch caused sparks to return. Jessie stilled, waiting for the heart-racing, blood-pumping experience she'd read about.

But then he moved too fast, and she tensed, wrapping her fingers around his wrist. She didn't know *what* she needed, besides regaining some control.

"My turn."

"But..."

"My turn."

Jessie pushed Cam onto his back, loosened the ties of his board shorts, and slipped her fingers beneath. He was hard yet velvety smooth, and she couldn't wait to explore his body closely.

She wrapped her fingers around him, causing him to jerk against her. "Can't wait. Need..."

Jessie plucked a foil packet from the pocket of the plaid shirt and pushed Cam's hands away. Surprisingly, he lay back, seemingly to allow her to touch, but the second she did, he took over.

"Kiss me," she begged, hoping to bring the fire back.

His kiss was soft, and once again, the buzz inside took hold. Cam rolled over on top of her and hiked her left leg over his hip.

Oh my! Oh my! Oh my!

Their gazes were locked together, and slowly he began to move. What she saw in his eyes was too much, too intense, and so overwhelming, she couldn't breathe.

Her eyes slid shut, and she opened her senses. While it might not feel exactly as she'd expected, she wanted to remember everything. Wanted to remember the sound of the waves as they bounced softly against the hull. To remember the smell of saltwater lingering in the air, and the gentle sway of the boat, rocking her world. Right then everything changed between her and Cam, and she never wanted to forget the moment.

He hovered above her, and she kept waiting until finally, she chanced a peek through her lashes. The tendons in his neck stuck out as he struggled for control. That didn't last long before he shouted his completion, leaving her waiting for the fireworks described in her romance books.

It took her an extra second to understand he was waiting for her. Not knowing what else to do, Jessie shuddered, and the way he rolled them onto their sides said she'd done the right thing.

Except she couldn't help but think there should be more.

Focus on what you have, not on what you think you should have.

"I'm not ready to let you go," she murmured against his neck.

He kissed her tenderly. "Don't Princess. Don't ever let me go."

Without hope, there would be no happy endings.

TWELVE
PRESENT DAY

Sonny's Skate & Bowl
June 4
11:30 p.m.

THE MEMORY WASN'T ONE OF HIS FINEST MOMENTS. MORE THAN once, he'd wanted a do-over. Except, do-overs weren't always an option.

"Did you regret what we did?"

"What did you say?"

"Did you regret giving yourself to me that night?"

"What do you think?" Jessie snapped right before skating away.

Cam sighed as every glide of her skates showcased her inner turmoil. He'd expected her to run but hadn't thought that question to be the catalyst. At least she'd waited until he was rested.

He called her name a few times, but either she ignored him or couldn't hear. If he had to guess, he'd say the former, which had him skating in front of her and performing a messy hockey stop.

"Jessie," he laughed at the exasperated look on her face, "answer my question."

"Oh, please, Cam," Jessie retorted. "I didn't give myself to you like some maiden from the 1800s. I was there because I wanted to be."

Some of the tension he'd been carrying dissipated. "I owe you an apology," he muttered. "I'm sorry I was a selfish jerk that night."

"Yes, you were." She lifted a brow and tilted her head in that regal manner of hers. "Feel better now?"

He didn't, which annoyed him as she wasn't making it easy. "Is that why we never did it again?"

"Did it?" Jessie barked out a laugh. "What? Are we still in high school?"

"Well," Cam huffed, "was it?"

"There are other ways to be intimate," she quipped. "Don't worry so much. Over the next few years, you more than made up for being," Jessie made air quotes, "'a selfish jerk.' I always wondered who taught you so much."

Her voice had gone from flirty to flinty in thirty seconds, again making Cam's lips threaten to curve. "No, she," he admitted with a sheepish grin. "I read article after article on the internet."

"For some reason, that makes me feel better." Jessie patted him on the chest and took off again.

She kept him off balance and was back to busting his balls on the ice. Would he always need to chase her?

"Jessie."

"What?"

She'd stopped under a light resembling a beacon, drawing him closer. Her features still captivated him, but there was a maturity there that hadn't been present the last time he'd seen her. Was that because it had been two years, or was there more going on in her life he didn't know?

His gaze drifted around her face, cataloging the differences. Her hair was more red than gold and shorter, her curls resting on her shoulders instead of halfway down her back. She was still thin, but her curves were more rounded, making him cram his hands into his pockets to avoid reaching for her.

"More questions, Cam?"

Jessie tossed a curl over her shoulder, and the light captured the sheen of gold circling her neck.

He didn't ask and wasn't sure he could have stopped, but he lifted the chain with his heart out from under her dress. "You still wear it."

The smile that crossed her face was a little shy and a little sad. "It's still my favorite piece of jewelry."

Why he'd never been able to give his heart to anyone else suddenly made sense. His heart still belonged to Jessie and always would.

"I'm glad."

His answer was simple, but inside, he couldn't stop thinking about when he'd planned on giving her another piece of jewelry. Was there more to the story he didn't know? Plausible, yes, especially after everything he'd just learned about Catherine. Was it possible, though?

"There's more, isn't there?" Her gaze skittered away, confirming his suspicions. "Finish it?"

This time, just like he had so many times before, he held out his hand and waited for her to decide. He needed her to show him she was ready to meet him in the middle.

"You're right." Jessie placed her hand in his, and his heart rate took off.

They skated halfway around the rink, and while her hand remained in his, she didn't continue speaking.

"Can we sit?" he asked quietly, wanting to be able to look at her while she spoke.

⁂

A PART OF JESSIE HAD KNOWN SHE WOULDN'T GET AWAY WITH half the story. The other part, though, hoped it wouldn't matter. She'd wished they could start over, even if it were unrealistic.

Cam was lagging, using her to carry him along. "You're tired, aren't you?" she accused when she noticed he was breathing hard.

"What makes you say that?" Cam muttered while massaging his quads.

"You weren't keeping up out there."

"Since when have I ever kept up with you, Princess?"

His response took her aback for a second, causing her to study him a little closer. Same shaggy hair, tall, lean frame, and sexy dimples. His eyes, though. They were different.

"If it was such a chore," Jessie grumbled. "Why continue?"

"Now, Princess," Cam grinned, dimples popping in his lean cheeks. "You know the answer to that as well as you know your name. His gaze lighted on her heart pendant, causing hers to flip a few times. "Now, the story...?"

Jessie rolled her eyes, unwilling to allow the little flips her heart was engaging in to cause her to do … or say … anything irrational.

"You know the story."

Over the next six years, their romance and her life had grown into everything she wanted. He'd graduated with his architecture degree when he was twenty-three and received a full ride to the three-year Master's program at Yale. He was closer to her yet still so far away.

She'd started college a year behind her friends but, determined to graduate with them, she'd worked extra hard. There had been heavier schedules in the fall and spring and classes over the summer. However, when she'd graduated at twenty-two, Cam had driven from Connecticut to Maine for the ceremony. Everything in her life had been falling into place.

"I was so proud of you that day." He squeezed her fingers, lost in the memory. "While it disappointed me you hadn't chosen a graduate school closer to Yale, I understood. People don't turn down a full scholarship to the University of Virginia."

"True," Jessie agreed.

"Then what happened?"

If he was trying to hide the pain he felt, he wasn't doing a very good job. Except, right then, Jessie struggled to hide anymore. After all, she also knew a thing or two about pain, much of which had yet to be shared. "Then came grad school. We both had two more years, and life was busy."

"Just stop it," Cam snapped. "You're trying to make me think we fell apart because of the distance between us. That's a damn lie."

Jessie dropped her head, hoping he couldn't read her expression. "What does it matter, Cam? You apparently made peace with it. I have to say, after two years away, I wasn't expecting to see you and some girl engaging in PDA as soon as I drove across the town line."

The minute the words were out, she wished she could call them back. She sounded like a jealous shrew and not a woman who'd moved on.

⁂

CAM WINCED, WISHING HE COULD CHANGE MUCH OF HIS behavior from the past four days, but he liked knowing his princess still had claws.

"Jealous?"

"No," she spit too quickly for him to believe her.

"What do you want to know, Jess?" He studied her, wondering why she diverged from the timeline and what she was after.

"Did you wait until I was gone before you started seeing her?" Jessie reached for the heart necklace and slid it back and forth on its chain. "Eden seems quite young."

Cam refused to tell her about his lowest point because it no longer mattered. "If you really want to know, just ask."

It had been about a year after Jessie disappeared from his life, and his mother caught him at one of his lowest points. Mary told him if it were meant to be, it would be, but if Jessie drove back into town the next day, how would he feel? Would he like the man he'd become?

"I cleaned up my act, and a few days later was in Sally's waiting on Hayden—"

"You stayed connected to Hayden even after I left?" she asked.

"Of course. Hayden was hoping you'd make it back for his graduation."

"I tried." Jessie sighed, and if he hadn't been watching her so closely, he would have missed it. "I couldn't get a flight."

"Hayden's a whiz on computers. I heard he broke into the school's mainframe and changed a few grades." Cam chuckled. "Except no one could prove it was true."

"Sounds like him."

Her arched brow and flashing blue eyes pushed him to answer, "I thought she was you. I was at Sally's and saw…"

He'd seen a flash of strawberry blonde hair walking by the windows and ran after her, thinking it was Jessie. When she'd turned around, his heart had fallen, landing at his feet.

Eden was sweet, but at the time, she was still in college, studying to be a teacher. He'd considered her safe.

"And the kiss?" Jessie prompted. "You looked quite involved, and she caught Cassie's bouquet, so … should I expect an announcement sometime soon?"

"It means nothing that she caught the bouquet."

"Have you taken her to Lover's Cove?"

"Would it matter?" he shot back without answering the question.

"Well, you know the legend," she continued.

That was when he finally understood what she was after. The legend had couples getting engaged if they made love in Lover's Cove.

"No," Cam replied. "I've never been to the Cove with Eden."

"Oh."

Jessie's response was small and hesitant, something he didn't need to dissect. Just as she had the answer she wanted, so too did he. In her roundabout way, she'd told him a second chance was still there.

"You're stalling, Jess." Cam took her hand and held it between his. Hers was ice cold, which worried him. "Let's finish this."

FOR A SPLIT SECOND, JESSIE THOUGHT HIS WORDS HELD ANOTHER meaning—that he wanted to be done with her. However, one look in his eyes and she knew she'd misunderstood.

The memory of his kiss and the rightness of her hand in his gave her the courage to continue. "After spending a few weeks visiting Cassie in Washington, D.C., and Sadie in Augusta, I was excited to get home."

"To me?" Cam squeezed her hands a little tighter.

Jessie smiled, took a deep breath, and plunged forward...

Two Years Earlier

Jessie's Home
June 10
3:00 p.m.

Jessie stepped from her car just as Catherine stormed out, leaving the door to slam behind her.

"This is your fault," Catherine snapped. "You're like that bunny that keeps coming back."

"What are you talking about?" Jessie retorted. "I just got back into town. Whatever problems you're having, they're yours."

"Dylan was mine ... until you," Catherine made air quotes, "hurt yourself. After that, everything changed."

"Did Dylan finally get wise to your ways?" Jessie sneered. "Because if so, it's about freaking time. I didn't tell him you paid to have me sent away. If I had, he would have kicked your ass out of his life long ago."

Catherine reared back as if she'd been slapped. "You knew about that?"

"That you paid to get me out of town?" Jessie couldn't believe how controlled she sounded. "Hell, yes, I knew. You managed to lose him all on your own. How'd that happen, anyway?"

"It wasn't my fault," Catherine grumbled. "I just found him in bed with someone he called Molly. He said, '*His heart wanted what his heart wanted*' or some other trivial statement."

"Way to go, Bro," Jessie quipped. "I knew he was smart."

"Oh, I'm not giving up." Catherine moved closer, forcing Jessie to take a step back. "I always get what I want. This isn't the last your family has heard from me."

She stormed to her car and, with a squeal of the tires, roared off. When the dust settled, Jessie noticed the unfamiliar car parked beside Dylan's.

"The infamous Molly must still be present." She slammed the trunk and climbed back into her car.

⚶

THE NEWS JESSIE WAS IN THE BUILDING REACHED CAM BEFORE SHE did. It allowed him to be there when she stepped off the elevator.

"Princess!" His lips covered hers in a short but very thorough kiss.

"Well, that was nice." Jessie slid her arms around his neck. "Will you greet me like that every time I come to visit?"

"Just as often as you'll let me." Cam manipulated them into his office. "Are we still on for dinner tonight?" he asked, punctuating each word with a kiss.

"We are," she confirmed. "I understand Dylan has some news to share with me first."

Cam chuckled. "Would that be about Molly?"

Jessie playfully punched his arm. "Why didn't you tell me?"

"Not my news."

Jessie stuck her tongue out. "That's not very nice."

"Oh, I can be nice." Cam kissed her again, one of those soul-wrenching kisses that ratcheted up his need and made him wonder if he could leave work early.

Several loud raps on the door had them jumping apart. "Cameron," Gray smirked, "the meeting starts in five."

Cam's head dropped onto Jessie's shoulder while he tried to control his breathing and body. "I'm sorry," he sighed. "I'll see you about seven."

"Okay," she kissed him again. "I'll be waiting."

He watched her walk down the hall and look at her phone as she entered the elevator. The evening couldn't come fast enough to please him. His plans involved a special piece of jewelry for his princess.

Present Day

Sonny's Skate & Bowl
June 4
11:45 p.m.

EVEN AFTER TWO YEARS, THE MEMORY OF THE TEXT MESSAGE she'd received stood out sharply in Jessie's mind. But she hadn't been willing to risk harm to anyone she loved, and she'd left town with barely a word to Dylan.

Except that was then, and now ... Dylan and Molly were married...

"How could you have just left, Jess?"

The pain in Cam's voice killed her, and she wanted nothing more than to fall into his arms. If that happened, it had to be with only part of the truth.

"You left me!" Jessie took several steps away.

This time, he didn't give her any space but stalked toward her. "Your memory seems to be faulty, Princess," Cam taunted. "I've been right here for the past two years. You're the one who left."

Her heart pounded so loudly, she imagined the entire town could hear it. "But you didn't come after me," she cried. "For the first time, you didn't come after me."

Before the last word faded, Cam cupped her elbows and tugged her against his hard body.

"I'm here now, Princess." He kissed her lightly. "This time, I'm not going anywhere."

Jessie couldn't breathe, couldn't think, could only feel. He held her as if she were precious and had no desire to let her go again. How had she thought she could live without him?

Their lips reluctantly parted when the door opened.

"I'm not ready to let you go," Cam murmured when she tried to see who had come in.

"But..."

"Jessie."

Cam tucked her against his side, and together, they faced Dylan.

"You've been crying." Dylan gave Cam a disgruntled look. "Are you okay?"

Cam's fingers dug into her waist, and without thinking, Jessie dropped her head against his shoulder.

"I will be." She smiled at Cam. "I think so, anyway."

"You will be." Cam kissed her nose. "I'll call you tomorrow?"

Jessie nodded, and with another brief kiss, Cam tugged off his ice skates and left her alone with Dylan. Suddenly, the burden she'd been carrying weakened her knees, and she dropped back onto the bench.

"How'd you know where I was?"

"Let's see," Dylan hummed. "It started when Sadie sent a text to Molly..."

"Who sent you searching?"

"Wasn't hard." His blue eyes took on that fatherly look. "Don't you think it's time to fill me in?"

Her phone rang, saving her from having to respond immediately. *Cam!*

Jessie swiped her finger across the screen, and the message sucked her back in time.

"No!"

"Jessie?" Dylan's eyes grew wide when he got a look at the message. "Damn, Sis. We're going home and calling Cameron. You shouldn't have to carry this alone.

Maybe, she thought, *just maybe, her heart would win.*

Isn't love worth fighting for?

THIRTEEN
PRESENT DAY

Cam's Home
June 5
12:45 a.m.

Cam glanced back at Sonny's once more before climbing into his car. Now that he'd found Jessie again, he was afraid to leave. Worried once he drove out of the parking lot, the events of the evening would turn out to be a dream. One like so many he'd had since she'd left.

He stuck the key into the ignition but couldn't make himself turn it. Instead, he checked his messages.

One from Ben, letting him know Eden was asking questions.

Another from Eden, wondering if he was home.

And, a last one from his mother asking about him and Jessie. Somehow, she'd known he and Eden weren't a lifetime couple. That spot was reserved for a certain strawberry-blonde, turquoise-eyed siren who had captured his attention when they were kids. Now that she was back, he would do everything possible to ensure she stayed.

Slow down and guard your heart, he could hear his inner voice say.

It was too late, though. The heart wants what the heart wants, and his heart wanted Jessie. But first, he had to break things off with Eden.

On the drive home, Cam thought about the conversation he hoped Jessie was having with Dylan. She needed to come clean with him. After all, she'd been trying to protect her brother. Whatever she decided, he would support her, something he should have done two years ago.

Cam found Gray in the den, holding a highball glass and staring into the night. He poured a splash of whiskey and slid into the chair opposite him.

"I didn't expect you home until tomorrow. Did you and Tia fight?"

"We decided we're better off as friends." Gray swirled the ice in his glass for several seconds before taking a drink. "What about you? How was the wedding?"

"Eye-opening," Cam surprised himself by admitting. "I've been with Jessie the last few hours."

"It's about damn time," Gray barked out a laugh. "You've been stalking her since she returned."

"Whuh—what do you mean?"

His brother gave him an '*I'm not stupid*' look. "Come on, little brother," Gray chided. "It's been years since you've stepped on the ice, yet the second Jessie was back in town, out came your skates. What happened?"

Cam tossed back the rest of his whiskey and tried to decide how to answer. Finally, he offered, "You're right. I did pull them out."

"Why?"

"I knew she was returning to Swan Harbor for the wedding, but wasn't sure when," Cam began. "Then she strolled into Randy's with Sadie on one side and Cassie on the other. It only took a look for all those feelings to come rushing back. I panicked," he continued, not proud of what happened next. "I flaunted my relationship with Eden, wanting to hurt Jessie as much as she hurt me."

"But sometime that night," Gray guessed, "Jessie ended up at Sonny's, and you followed."

"Yeah," Cam sighed. He'd been talking to Ben, and suddenly, it felt like he couldn't breathe any longer. Felt as if all the air had been sucked out of the room. It wasn't long after he'd made excuses, dropped Eden at home, and gone searching for Jess.

"She was at Sonny's, as I'd expected. Except I couldn't force myself to open the door, and like so many other times, I watched her skate. I was once again the man on the outside, looking in."

A corner of Gray's mouth lifted. "So your heart tried to tell you something long before you listened."

"Seems so." His quiet response had Gray arching a brow, pushing him to continue. "After the bonfire, I followed Jess to Sonny's again. I took out my skates and reached for the door, yet I couldn't force myself to walk through. I was still lying to myself about my real feelings."

"Something happened at the wedding," Gray guessed. "Am I right?"

"There were several epiphanies tonight," Cam admitted. "Did you know Catherine has a vindictive streak and comes from money ... big money?"

"Catherine from money?" Gray hummed. "I guess that makes sense, but she's never flaunted it. How'd it come up?"

The retelling of what Catherine had done to keep Dylan seemed almost surreal. "It's like a movie, but in the end, Jessie won."

"Does Dylan know?"

"He showed up at Sonny's." While it was good that the secrets were exposed, Dylan needed to work on his timing.

"Take it slowly, Cam," Gray cautioned. "I don't want to see you hurt like last time."

"I know." Cam's phone buzzed, and a message from Dylan appeared. "We've been asked to come to the Prince's home tomorrow morning."

"Why?"

"I've no idea." Cam frowned. "That's all the message says."

"I guess we'll find out tomorrow," Gray mumbled around a yawn. "I'm going to bed. I'll see you in the morning."

"Night." Cam's thoughts were spinning. What could Dylan want? Was this about Catherine, Jessie ... or Molly?

He set the alarm and climbed the stairs to his old room. Perhaps it was time for him to think about a home of his own. A place where he and Jess could live ... together.

❧

Jessie's Home
June 5
8:00 a.m.

Jessie's eyes drifted to the photo of her and Cam. Looking at it reminded her of all their hopes and dreams for the future. Ones that had sustained her through those lonely nights while in the Philippines. She'd brought the picture home, hoping things would be different. Hoping that maybe there was still a chance those dreams could become reality. But when she'd seen Cam with Eden, she'd shoved it in the drawer. After last night, she'd removed it and set it on the top of her dresser. Hope had returned. First, though, she needed to tell Dylan about Catherine.

Her brother met Molly not long before that infamous situation. A visit to The Beachside Inn, a chance encounter, and true love was born. Dylan's heart wanted, and the rest was history. They were a sign that happily-ever-afters were possible.

"Jessie," Dylan stuck his head in her room, "Cameron and Gray will be here in a couple of hours."

"Okay. I'll shower and be right down."

"Molly's making pancakes. She wants to know how many you want." His face lit up as always when he mentioned his wife's name.

"It depends," Jessie muttered tongue-in-cheek. "Are they better than yours?"

"Hey, take that back," Dylan grumbled. "But yes, my wife can cook."

"Then I'll have a couple, thanks."

As soon as the door shut, Jessie rolled over, and her gaze again drifted to the picture. If things were different, she'd text Cam to tell him good morning. However, until he knew the entire story, she couldn't help but feel like she was walking on eggshells.

What to say and how to explain remained at the front of her mind as she showered and dressed. Dylan was printing copies for everyone, so all she had to do was fill in the blanks. That shouldn't be too hard ... right? Except, why was she so nervous?

'Because love is worth fighting for.' Something she'd always known but had been too scared to do just that.

Now that she was back in town, was the happy ending she wanted with Cam still waiting for her?

There's only one way to find out. Fight for what you want.

For years, she thought that was what she'd been doing. Fighting to protect those she loved. But just as Dylan wanted the same kind of relationship their parents had, so did she. He'd found his happy ending with Molly. *She* wanted that with Cam.

Jessie grabbed a file from her suitcase and stepped into the hall, her mouth watering at the thought of homemade pancakes.

Except there was no buttery goodness wafting up the stairs like her brother had promised. Just a scorched, *'someone burned something'* odor that had her running to the kitchen.

"What's that—?" Jessie immediately whirled around. "Oh!"

"Jessie!"

"Sis!" Molly and Dylan shouted simultaneously.

"We are so sorry!" Molly apologized, and Jessie could hear scrambling behind her as they worked to put their clothes right.

"No, I'm sorry," Jessie replied, her back still turned. "You're used to having the house to yourselves, so..." She was glad they still had their clothes on ... or at least mostly. "I should have made more noise."

"Coast is clear." Dylan breezed by her. "I'll just go make those copies."

"*Chicken,*" Molly muttered.

"I'm sorry you're embarrassed," Jessie laughed. "It's so nice to walk in on him after all those times he did the same to me."

"You and Cameron?" Molly glanced up, then right down, her cheeks sporting bright pink patches.

"Yes." Jessie laughed, as the memory was funny now. "One time, Dylan came home, and Cam and I were..."

While they mixed up some fresh pancake batter, Jessie entertained Molly with silly stories. Thirty minutes later, Dylan returned just as they'd placed the plates on the table.

"Sorry about that, Sis." He kissed the top of her head before sliding into an adjacent seat. "Now I know how you felt."

"It feels good being on this side for once," Jessie snickered. "Paybacks are so fun."

Dylan glanced up, and his blue eyes locked with hers. "We will get to the bottom of this."

His serious, determined, and worried expression should have made her feel better. Instead, it reiterated the heaviness she'd been carrying around for years. "You think?"

"I know."

She couldn't help but hope he was right. Working with the orphanage in the Philippines was rewarding, but she wanted to be in Swan Harbor. With her family … and with Cam.

Thankfully, Molly jumped in, and they spent several minutes discussing the town and summer crowds. From there, they moved to the news that her brother was running for Sheriff, the same position her father and grandfather had held.

"Dad would have approved," Jessie smiled. "He used to grumble and say he didn't understand why you wanted to be a lawyer. Thought you'd make a damn fine deputy."

Dylan laughed. "That sounds like dad."

The conversation continued for another few minutes. Only when Molly mentioned picking something up did she tune back in.

"Wait," Jessie exclaimed. "Are you getting a dog?"

"Yes."

"When? What kind? Why?"

There had always been a dog or cat in their home before her parents' accident. Afterward, though, Dylan thought it was too much work. Apparently, her brother had changed his mind.

"Molly wanted one." Dylan gave her a sheepish smile. "He's an English Shepard, six-weeks-old, and we haven't decided on a name."

"Show her his picture, honey," Molly encouraged. Then, to Jessie's surprise, Dylan pulled out his phone to show off the puppy's photo.

"He's adorable." Jessie exchanged conspiratorial grins with Molly. "Is he with a breeder?"

"No," Molly hurried to explain. "Maggie … one of the teachers I know, adopted the mother and"

"You couldn't resist." Jessie … grinned.

"Something like that." Molly exchanged a look with Dylan, making her feel like she'd stepped into a private moment.

When she glanced down and realized the syrup on her plate was congealing, Jessie knew it was time. "We need to talk about Boston."

"Boston?" Dylan's eyes narrowed. "What about Boston?"

"About why you were never asked for money."

"I never thought about it," he shrugged. "Until one day, someone at Sally's asked how I could afford it.”

"What did you say?”

"I told them you were on a scholarship,” Dylan replied. “Why?”

"A scholarship?”She frowned. “Who told you that?”

"Catherine. Why are you bringing this up now?”

She’d expected his answer and question, making it even more difficult to dig into the past.

Jessie glanced from her brother to Molly, then to the clock. “Because I need to tell you something before Cam and Gray arrive.”

Cam’s Home
June 5
9:00 a.m.

AFTER A NIGHT OF DREAMS INTERWOVEN WITH MEMORIES OF what might have been and what was, Cam woke feeling logey. Something that made it difficult not to dwell on the negative.

When Jessie walked out of his life without a word, she’d taken his hopes and dreams for the future. Now that she was back, and they had talked, his perfectly constructed walls around his emotions were gone. His head was telling him to take things slowly. Telling him not to rush forward too quickly, but to take everything one step at a time.

Except the heart wants what the heart wants, and with it speaking, he wanted to jump in with both feet.

He showered, dressed, and then dug through his drawer, looking for the diamond ring he’d bought so long ago. It still sparkled, and the idea of sliding it onto Jessie’s finger caused his heart to race.

Someday, he promised himself. Someday.

Cam left the ring in the box on his nightstand and jogged downstairs to find Gray perusing the contents of a pastries. “When did you go to Paula’s?”

"While you were in the shower,” Gray mumbled. “There’s no food in the house.”

"Sorry,” Cam answered around the bite he’d just taken. “With the wedding and all, I’ve not been home much.”

Gray's grunt had him making a mental note to go shopping. He liked the idea of taking Jessie but needed to break things off with Eden first—not a task he relished.

"Let's go." Cam tossed his napkin in the trash. "The quicker we find out what's up, the faster I can work on my future."

"Aren't you impatient?" Gray helped himself to a third doughnut before heading toward the door. "Remember what I said about being careful?"

"Careful-smareful."

Cam reached for his keys and noticed his hand was shaking. He was excited, but a part of him was also nervous. Until everything was out in the open, he worried something would stand in the way of the happily-ever-after he wanted with Jessie.

"You're acting more nervous than when you were a teenager," Gray snickered.

"Matters more now," Cam fired back.

Which couldn't be more true. Somehow, he understood whatever happened once they walked through the door was important—very important.

"Well, let's go, Romeo," Gray quipped. "Your future's waiting."

On the drive over, they talked about the pier project Hunter Construction had recently undertaken. The entire dock area had been remodeled, and shops, restaurants, and arcades were being built. One end would be anchored by the Spanish galleon, and the other by Siren's Song, a nightclub he was working to design.

"We need an office manager," Cam grunted, thinking about the pile of files stacked on the conference room table.

"I know," Gray sighed. "But you know how Dad feels about that."

"That was a long time ago," Cam pointed out. "We should ask him again."

"Go right ahead," Gray laughed. "The last time I did, Dad ignored me."

A situation with an office manager years ago had soured their father on giving someone that much control. However, since it was Cam and Gray running the office, perhaps it was time.

"Maybe when they come back from Florida," Cam offered.

He pulled into the Prince family home driveway, and the first thing he noticed was how different the house looked from that long ago summer.

Molly had been good for Dylan ... and for the old house. It no longer felt neglected but was full of hope and happiness.

They knocked, and when the door opened, Cam froze.

"Cameron?" Molly murmured. "Are you okay?"

"I, I'm fine." He smiled, one big enough to showcase his dimples. "You're looking well."

"Grayson, come in. Dylan and Jessie are—"

"—Leaving you to do all the work." Cam grinned, unable to take his eyes off Jessie's face, when she entered from the kitchen.

"Exactly," Molly's green eyes twinkled. "You know, I did hear some interesting stories about you and Jessie this morning. I'm surprised Dylan didn't shoot you."

"Oh, shmmph," the word was cut off when suddenly his lips were occupied in a much more enjoyable activity.

"Sugar," Jess laughingly finished when she stepped back.

"Definitely, sugar." Cam kissed her again. "Morning, Princess. Did you talk with Dylan?"

"I did." Jessie nodded. "But there's more."

Their eyes met, and while he wasn't sure what he was seeing, his heart sank.

"More? What does that mean?"

Jessie leaned a little more of her weight against him and took a deep breath. "That's why you're here. Come sit, and I'll explain everything."

Cam settled next to Gray on one of the sofas. When Jessie exchanged serious looks with Dylan, his heart rate spiked, and the knots in his stomach tightened.

"What's going on, Prince?" Gray groused. "Cam filled me in on Catherine's behavior, but I'm unsure how that affects me."

"There's more to the story, Gray."

Dylan's response was clipped, and his blue eyes were shooting fire. It was obvious he was hanging onto his temper by a thread. But why?

"Just spit it out," he finally snapped. "Catherine's out of the picture..."

"We don't know that for sure," Jessie's quiet voice had his heart triple-timing. "But it's not just our family being targeted."

"Come on, Princess," he reached for Jessie's hand, "spill."

"It's you too, Cam," Jessie cried. "The threats involve your whole family."

"Our whole family?" Gray barked. "How?"

"Healthcare fraud," Jessie whispered.

Cam's thoughts spun off in multiple directions, and feeling sucker-punched, he fell back against the sofa.

FOURTEEN

Jessie's Home
June 5
11:00 a.m.

THERE WAS SILENCE FOR ABOUT THIRTY SECONDS, THEN ALL HELL broke loose, and everyone started talking at once. Jessie's heart raced, and as the noise grew louder, the sick feeling in the pit of her stomach churned faster. Her breath caught in her throat, and the darkness she'd kept at bay for years peeked out.

No! She slammed it back down, and her eyes sought Cam's. *Isn't love worth fighting for?*

There was no longer any doubt about that answer. Yes, of course it was! This time, though, she would fight ... *with* him ... *beside* him. This time, she wouldn't allow anyone to have power over their happiness.

To gain control, Jessie whistled. The shrill pitch broke through the white noise the voices had become until, once again, silence reigned.

"I know you have questions." She looked slowly from person to person before settling on Cam. "Let me get the story out, and then you can ask, okay?"

"Sorry about that, Princess," he murmured. "But fraud? Come on."

Jessie picked up the folder she'd been carrying for two years. "Everyone knows about my confrontation with Catherine, right?"

At the acknowledgment of the four others in the room, she continued, "When Catherine told me she wasn't giving up, I thought nothing about it and drove to HCI."

"That was the night we were to meet later," Cam replied. "It was the night you never showed."

The look on his face and the tenor of his voice told her how much she'd hurt him. However, this wasn't the time to get into that. Jessie sent him an apologetic smile and said, "As I was leaving HCI, a text message arrived. It was from an unknown sender and said:

> You have two hours to leave town, or this will be
> on the Swan Harbor News front page tomorrow.
> Imagine how many lives you'll ruin then.

"The person behind the text sent two attachments."

"Jess," Dylan's '*I can't believe you didn't tell me*' voice interrupted.

"I'm sorry," she cut him off. "All I can say is, I thought I was doing what was right."

"Show me," Cam commanded.

Instead of giving him the folder, Jessie removed two pieces of paper and read,

"Local Doctor Investigated for Fraud

An anonymous source has reported that Doctor Mary Hunter is being investigated for several healthcare fraud cases. She has been a practicing psychiatrist at Swan Harbor General for many years, and the implications could devastate her career and her husband's business, Hunter Construction. We will keep you apprised of this case as we learn more."

When Jessie finished reading the short article, she handed it to Cam so he could see the attached picture. It showed Mary sitting at her desk, surrounded by files. Her expression said she was upset about something.

"There was also a handwritten note."

Jessica,

An audit of hospital records can turn up so many skeletons.
**False Billing*
**Improper Diagnosis*
**Mishandling of Medications*
And many other 'secrets,' leading to Malpractice.
There goes her license. There goes her career.
Do you know what happens next when they're finished auditing
her records? They'll go after Hunter Construction, Inc. (HCI)
books. That means your precious Cameron and his pain-in-the-ass
father and brother will be out of a job.

Gray growled, "Hey, what did I do?" earning a laugh from Cam when she read the last line. For some reason, the fact they'd been able to laugh in the middle of such a serious situation filled her with hope. Was it possible love really could conquer evil?

"The note ended with,

You'll enjoy where you're going. A one-way ticket is waiting for
you at Logan International. Once you arrive in San Francisco,
someone will meet you and prepare you for the rest of your journey.
You're not needed in Swan Harbor, but the children in the
Philippines do need you. See, I'm not so bad.

"Was it from Catherine?" Cam snapped. "If so, I have a few things I'd like to say to her."

"It's unsigned," Jessie explained.

Still," Cam's brow furrowed, "there's no way any of what you read is true. Plus, it happened two years ago. Surely, it's no longer relevant."

Dylan handed Jessie another folder. "I wish that were true. But another message arrived after you left Sonny's the other night."

"Not..." Cam began.

"I'm afraid so," Jessie admitted.

"What this time?" Cam asked.

Jessie dropped into the chair adjacent to where he was sitting and linked their fingers. "It's bad."

Cam's green eyes darkened. "How bad?"

She pulled several photos from the folder and handed them to him. "These were attached."

He looked down at the pictures, and his stare grew hard. One photo showed Mary Hunter behind bars, wearing an orange jumpsuit. A second showed her being removed from her office in handcuffs, and a third was of her mugshot.

"Damn!" Cam snapped. "But these aren't real." He passed the photos to Gray. "My mother has never been arrested."

Before Jessie could think of anything to say, Dylan jumped in, "We know that. However, no one from either family will be safe unless we figure out what's happening."

"Is that it?" Cam asked when it had been quiet for a handful of seconds.

"Almost." Jessie took another piece of paper from the folder. "There's another 'article.'"

"Read it," Cam barked impatiently.

Jessie tried not to take offense at Cam's vocal tone, especially since his anger was completely normal. It was just that somehow, she couldn't stop feeling responsible — even knowing how irrational that sounded.

Local Doctor Indicted

Doctor Mary Hunter was indicted and charged with multiple counts of healthcare fraud, including falsifying claims, writing phony prescriptions, and ordering medical tests not needed. She is facing fraud allegations of over one million dollars.

This reporter has also learned several counts of pending embezzlement involving her husband's business. (HCI).

Doctor Hunter has been a practicing psychiatrist for over thirty-five years and has medical privileges at Swan Harbor General. If found guilty, she could face up to ten years in prison.

Jessie passed the article and a few pages with columns of numbers on them to Cam and turned to the short letter.

Jessica,

You can remain in Swan Harbor, but there's no happy ending for you and Cameron. Stay away from him or else.

When she finished reading, Jessie angrily tossed the note on the table and jumped up to pace.

"Great choices, huh?"

Her choices sucked. She could leave Swan Harbor and be miserable away from her family ... and Cam. Or she could stay in Swan Harbor and be miserable without them. Had she been born under a black cloud? Every time happiness was close, something beyond her control seemed to take it away.

Cam pulled her into the safety of his arms. "Jessie, we're going to fix this."

"How?" Jessie could feel the darkness rising. "It all seems so..."

The word hopeless almost tripped off her tongue, but wasn't that how she should have felt after her fall? Yet, somehow, with Cam's help, she conquered it.

The gentle murmur of Dylan and Molly comforting each other had Jessie stepping back and tangling her fingers in Cam's shirt. His green eyes mesmerized her, their message of love promising her the world. *He's worth fighting for!* With those thoughts, anger took hold and pushed the darkness away.

"We can't let whoever is doing this win."

Cam cupped her face. "We want the same things, right? A life ... together."

"Of course." Jessie kissed him, and the anger and love inside merged. They gave her strength for what came next. "It will be a fight."

"One we're going to win," Cam promised. "But how?"

"Hell," Dylan's smile turned dark. "We investigate, which I do very well."

"No!" Molly and Jessie both shouted.

Dylan crossed his arms over his chest defensively. "But, it's what I do. Why no?"

Jessie moved to her brother's side. "You're running for sheriff. You're the law. I kept secrets so you could have your happy ending, and now that you have it, I won't let you throw it away."

"But I'm the investigator," Dylan all but shouted.

Jessie took his hand, hoping he understood why she was so adamant he stayed out of it.

"I remember Dad saying you could solve any crime if you have all the pieces. We just need to find them."

Dylan looked like he was going to argue. Except, she could tell he knew she was right. He just didn't want to admit it.

"Face it, Prince," Gray joined the argument. "You've been bested. While you might have the badge, sometimes we're all investigators."

"He's right, Dylan," Jessie took over. "I'm a therapist, and every time I get a new case, I investigate while trying to help the person find a solution."

Cam slipped his arm around Jessie in a gesture of solidarity. "And Gray and I search for weaknesses in everything we build or design."

"You need to let us do this," Jessie replied softly. "You know I'm right."

"Fine," Dylan barked, "but on several conditions."

"Whatever," Gray sighed. "Say your piece, then take your pretty wife for a Sunday stroll."

"Number 1," Dylan looked at Jessie before turning his gaze to Cam, "you two can't be seen together."

"What!?" they shouted.

"Think about it," Dylan went on. "The letter states Jessie needs to stay away from you or else. Aren't you worried about what that means?"

"But..." Cam's arm tightened around her back.

"He's right." Jessie forced herself to step away from Cam's heat. "I was in town for a few days before the wedding, and there were no texts."

"Then I followed you to Sonny's," Cam whispered.

"And as soon as you left," Jessie answered, "a new message arrived."

"Damn!" Cam stalked across the room, anger radiating off of him in waves.

❧

CAM MEASURED THE DISTANCE BETWEEN WHERE HE WAS standing and Jessie. He was tempted to carry her away and let their brothers fight this battle. Except she deserved more. *They* deserved more—meaning if they wanted a life together, they needed to fight—something they should have done two years ago.

"Okay," he sighed. "What else?"

"You won't like this either," Dylan warned. "But, to Swan Harbor, nothing must appear different."

"You're not saying?" Cam sputtered. "Are you sure this is necessary?"

"I am," Dylan nodded. "Until we know more…"

Cam cut a glance in Jessie's direction and prepared for her to put up a fight. Instead, she surprised him.

"Eden did catch the bouquet," Jessie pointed out. "How would it look if you suddenly dumped her?"

"I don't care how it would look," Cam blurted. "Eden's not the one I want to marry."

One of Jessie's red gold brows flew up. "I should hope not."

"I'm sorry," Dylan sighed. "But you need to continue dating Eden. For the time being, anyway."

"Except this time," Jessie sauntered toward him, "there *will* be a few conditions."

The touch of jealousy added a layer Cam hadn't anticipated.

"Oh?"

"Yes!" Jessie tilted her chin up a notch. "Got a problem with that?"

Problem? Certainly not!

"We'll talk about it later." Cam tucked her against his side, then looked to Dylan. "What else?"

Dylan separated the pieces of paper into several piles. "Like Jessie said, you need to solve the puzzle. These," he pointed to the pictures, "are either real or ones that have been cropped or photo-shopped. You need to determine a time frame and see if you can differentiate them from the originals."

"Can we ask Mom when they were taken?" Cam was pretty sure he knew the answer, but…

"Not just yet," Dylan replied. "There's no need to upset her." He separated two sheets from the rest. "These look like ledger sheets of some kind. Find an accountant you trust and see if they can make sense of them."

"An accountant?" Jessie grinned. "I know just the person."

"Sadie?" Cam teased.

"Long legs and ponytails," Gray recalled with a smile.

Jessie snickered, causing Cam to send her a questioning glance.

"Later." Her eyes twinkled with devilish merriment, making him wonder what he was missing.

"And last," Dylan hesitated an extra beat. "I can't believe I'm saying this, but you need someone who's computer savvy."

That was an easy one—even if it might not be viewed favorably.

"Just be careful," Dylan warned them. "If this…"

"It will be fine." Cam pulled his princess a little closer to his side. "I'll take care of Jessie."

"We'll take care of each other," Jessie clarified, her sign to him he wouldn't be going rogue on this mission.

"Together," Cam echoed.

"Be careful." Dylan slowly looked around the room before his gaze landed on Jessie. "Don't make me worry about you."

When she walked away to talk to Dylan, Cam once again pulled out the photos. There was something familiar about bits and pieces of a couple. Overall, though, he couldn't explain why he thought that to be true.

Gray pointed to the one of Mary in a prison cell. "Why do I feel as if I've seen this before?"

"I had the same thought," Cam admitted. He took out the one of Mary sitting at her desk. "This one seems familiar, as well."

Jessie appeared, looking over his shoulder at the photo. "I … I've seen that before. Or at least a picture that looked similar to this one. I'm just not sure where."

"Mom was at the hospital when it was taken," Gray noted a framed photo in the background. "That's been there for years."

"That picture was taken when my mother was pregnant with me." Jessie smiled. "They were celebrating."

Gray noted, "Hot fudge and ice cream at Sally's. That's my kind of celebration."

"Once we get the dirt on Catherine, you can buy," Cam quipped.

Gray took the folder. "Gladly. I'll dig around Mom's pictures. Jess, you'll ask Legs about the accounting, right?"

Jessie nodded, and her turquoise eyes sparkled once again. "Won't be a problem."

"And I'll check with Hayden regarding computer hacking," Cam added.

"Alright," Gray glanced around, "Dylan left?"

"Took his pretty wife for a stroll," laughed Jessie.

"Good for him," Gray murmured. "I think we've got a good plan. We'll reconvene in a few days ... covertly and make Dylan proud. Now, it's time to go eat."

Cam nodded. "Okay. Give us a few, will you?"

"Make it quick," Gray advised. "Your car's been here long enough."

As soon as the door shut, Cam tugged Jessie into his arms. "I hate this."

⁂

JESSIE RELAXED AGAINST HIM, AND THE FEELING OF HOME IN Cam's arms was as strong as ever. This time, though, there was another kernel of something inside. Hope, maybe.

Cam buried his face in her neck. She could feel a slight tremor in his body and wished she could make everything disappear.

"Are you okay?"

"I hate this," he repeated. "The last few days, I've been a jerk to you ... *and to Eden.*"

"To both of us?" Jessie stepped back and forced him to look at her. "Why do you think to both of us?" He dropped his arms, and his expression scared her. "Come on, Cam," she goaded, "spit it out. Did you sleep with her and pretend it was me? Is she pregnant?"

When all the color drained from his face, her knees almost buckled. *Where had that question come from?* He'd pretty much said he hadn't slept with Eden. Besides, this was Cam, and she trusted him.

"No!" he shouted, the anger on his face making her wince. "You know I never..."

"I know!" Jessie brazenly grabbed his waistband and pulled him close. "I'm sorry. I shouldn't have... Just your behavior around her was..."

"I wanted to..." Cam loosely wrapped his arms around her waist. His voice dropped an octave, and his expression caused her heart to flutter. "I know it wasn't easy seeing me with her."

"Why do you say that?"

He kissed her once, twice, never holding it long enough for her to get comfortable. "Because if our roles were reversed, and I saw you in the same situation, I'd want to kill him." When he kissed her again, it was longer, threatening to suck the very breath from her lungs.

His choice of words was so anti-Cam, Jessie almost laughed, but then she saw his expression.

"I know you don't mean that literally." She kissed him like he'd kissed her. Smaller kisses, leading toward a deep, dark, dangerous one that stole her breath and had her holding on.

Jessie thought she'd remembered how his kisses made her feel, but the swooping, swirling way her insides were moving was new. She wanted to drag him upstairs and get reacquainted with other parts of him, too. The knowledge she couldn't, though, at least yet, had her stepping back.

"I love you," she said, the words that had only been insinuated. "I just want you to know … in case … you know."

"I know." He smiled, one so big and … so sexy it took her breath.

"You know?" Jessie huffed. "It's customary when someone says they love you, for you to say it back."

"Oh, it is?" Cam's green eyes glittered, causing her heart to flip flop. "Okay, Princess," he drawled, "you win, as usual."

Jessie held her breath, waiting to hear the words she'd dreamed of for years. He hesitated—one, two, she counted, but when he still hadn't said anything at ten, she nipped the bottom of his chin. "Well?"

"There's that frosty princess voice. I…" Cam's whispered words sent chills zipping down her spine. "I love you, Jessica Marie Prince. I always have, and I always will."

Tears filled her eyes, so much so she was once again looking at Cam through a foggy lens.

"Don't cry, princess." He gently swept the wetness away. "It kills me when you do."

"These are good tears," Jessie sighed. "Very, very good tears."

"Really?" His lips lingered on hers. "I'm glad because I do … I love you."

"Show me," Jessie begged, unwilling to let him go. "Give me something to tide me over."

"You're killing me, Princess," Cam groaned. "But I've never been able to resist you."

He kissed her, one of those soul-stealing kisses, turning her thoughts into mush and weakening her knees. Jessie tangled her hands in Cam's shirt and held on. If she were lucky, she'd survive to see another day ... and get another kiss.

FIFTEEN

Hunter Construction, Inc.
June 10
5:00 p.m.

OVER THE NEXT WEEK, MORE OFTEN THAN NOT, CAM FOUND HIS focus drifting in directions it shouldn't. He needed to attend to the building he was designing for the pier, but the plans weren't coming together. Instead, he spent his days waiting for Hayden to find something to help them with their case. His evenings were reserved for long phone calls with Jessie.

His princess was the bright spot in his life. While he couldn't be with her physically, it hadn't stopped them from reconnecting. After spending long hours with her on the phone, he felt his heart was whole again. He met the Jessie she'd become and was realizing how, in some ways, she'd changed. What he'd learned only gave him more reasons to love her, which made being apart even more difficult.

When she asked what the last two years had looked like, he willingly shared with her—just not all. There were feelings and emotions he'd bottled up that hurt too much to revisit. He didn't readily offer loneliness, sadness, anger, jealousy, and emptiness. Since the questions had gone unasked, he kept them buried—so far, anyway.

In many ways, the woman she'd become surprised him. This one spoke her mind and seemed much more comfortable fighting for what she wanted. She challenged him one second, then the next said something that made him love her more. The pull between them was stronger than ever and seemed to strengthen each day.

Jessie had spent time asking subtle questions about his relationship with Eden. That she was jealous was obvious. Her emotions, though, caused him to feel like he was on a roller coaster.

One minute, he was on top of the world because she cared enough not to want to share. Then, the next, he would crash because she wouldn't have to if they weren't in this predicament. Although, in his eyes, no real 'sharing' was being done. His heart was Jessie's—always had been—always would be.

She'd taken the comment regarding her conditions to his '*pretend*' dating to heart. For the past four days, she'd sent a morning and an afternoon text, listing them.

From her first one,

> Jessie: Condition #1. No tongue when kissing.

To her tenth,

> Jessie: Condition #10. No whispering sweet words in Eden's ears.

Cam relished them, as they were a tangible reminder she was back in his life. It had been five days, and he'd received ten comments.

However, after she learned he was taking Eden to Randy's, her texts came faster and more often. Some of them made him chuckle. Others, though, made him happy their roles weren't reversed. The never-knowing kept him on his toes and hyper-aware of his phone, to the point that as soon as it buzzed, he gave up the pretense he was working.

> Jessie: Condition #25. No loving nicknames. You may call her Sugar. After all, you use it when you can't remember a female's name.

"News from Hayden?"

Cam glanced up to see his brother standing in the doorway. "What?"

"News from Hayden?" Gray nodded toward the phone.

"No, it's from Jessie." Cam tossed his phone on his desk and leaned back. "I'm shocked she could read me so well … and," he blew out a breath, "a little embarrassed at my behavior."

"Is that a good thing or a bad thing?" Gray shut the door and slid into a chair on the other side of the desk.

"I can't decide." Cam frowned. "It's just one more item to deal with when this is over." He shoved the thought away for later and turned to business. "If you're here about the building, I'm not done."

"I'm not," Gray retorted. "But why the hell not?"

"Can't get it right," Cam confessed. "Now, why are you here?"

"I found one of the pictures." Gray flipped open a magazine and laid it on the desk. Then, he separated the pages so the pictures were side by side.

Cam studied his brother for an extra second before glancing down. As soon as he saw what Gray had discovered, a sharp whistle escaped before he could stop it. "Damn, Bro. You hit the jackpot."

Doctor Mary Hunter had been featured in a two-page glossy layout in a prominent Psychiatry magazine. She was seated behind her desk, and files were stacked high around her. In the original, she was leaning forward with her arms resting on the folders, and her expression was one of pride and excitement. This was a stark contrast to the one Jessie had received.

"Photoshop," Cam spit out in disgust. "Why would someone go to all this trouble?"

"Your guess is as good as mine," Gray retorted. "It's a good thing Sadie spotted a copy of the magazine in the picture, or—"

"Wait, what?" Cam interrupted. "Sadie was with you last night?"

"Uhh," Gray stood so fast he knocked over the chair. "So, what if she was?" His petulant voice reminded Cam of when they'd gotten in trouble as boys. "Is there a problem with it?"

"Now, I'm going to give you a warning," Cam tossed his brother's words back. "Take it slow. Sadie is a lovely person, but she's a ball buster with men."

His brother's eyes hardened so much, Cam had to blink several times to make sure he was seeing what he thought.

"Speaking from experience?" Gray snapped, jealousy dripping from every word.

"Not hardly!" Cam laughed. "My heart has always belonged to Jessie. But hurt one—"

"—Hurt them all," Gray acknowledged. "Already got the lecture."

"Jessie?" Cam guessed.

"Yes," Gray's sigh was long-suffering. "She was texting threats."

Cam gave his brother a break and returned to studying the pictures. "So, if the expression was changed to convey mom was upset about something, where did the person find the picture?"

"No idea. But this isn't the end."

"Good luck." Cam folded the plans on his desk and shoved them in a drawer. "I'm taking off. I've got a date."

"Sounds like you need the luck," Gray teased. "All those conditions and all."

Cam couldn't help but think the statement had some measure of truth. His *date* wasn't going to be just a simple evening out. Feelings—not only Eden's but Jessie's—had to be considered.

Once again, he was guarding hearts, leaving him to wonder if he also needed to worry about his own.

Jessie's Home
June 10
6:00 p.m.

JESSIE HAD BEEN STARING AT THE PICTURES OF MARY HUNTER FOR hours, trying to decide if they'd been photoshopped and where. Primarily, though, she needed to keep busy. If she didn't, she had to deal with Cam going on a date ... and it wasn't with her.

"Find anything?" Molly peered over her shoulder. "You've been sitting there for hours."

"We found out where this came from." Jessie pointed to the picture of Mary sitting at her desk. "But there's nothing new on the rest." She lined up the other three images in order of arrest, mugshot, and behind bars. "I just can't shake the feeling I'm missing something."

Molly separated the photo of Mary behind bars from the others. "You know, there's something familiar about this one. Let me think about it a little more. Maybe the pieces floating around in my head will eventually come together."

Jessie closed her eyes and tried to push away the pity party tears. "Unlike some people, I've nowhere else to be."

"Oh, Jessie," Molly sympathized. "I can't imagine how difficult it is to know he's close, yet you can't claim him as yours."

"It's harder than I thought it would be," Jessie admitted. "Cam's going out with Eden tonight, and I just want to scratch her eyes out."

Molly laughed. "I'm afraid I'd want to do more than that. But is there any reason...?"

Jessie glanced in her sister-in-law's direction to see her eyes alight with mischievousness.

"Are you thinking I should...?"

"I am," Molly chuckled. "Randy's has so many nooks and crannies you never know whom you might run into."

Several possibilities ran through Jessie's mind. She had to admit that Molly was right. Randy's had multiple floors and hidden closets. There was even a storage room that, when they were younger, she used to sneak into with Cam.

"Thanks, Molly." Jessie hugged the other woman. "You've been a big help."

"Knock him dead, Jess. I'll let you know if I have any further thoughts on the picture."

"Thanks." Jessie grabbed her phone and punched a button. "I'll talk to you later."

Randy's Arcade
June 10
6:30 p.m.

CAM PARKED HIS CAR IN A LOT NOT TOO FAR FROM RANDY'S Arcade. When Eden had suggested it, he'd thought it a good idea. Especially when he heard they were meeting her friends. The music and someone for her to talk with would keep her occupied, taking some of the pressure off him.

Except then he'd found out '*why*' they were meeting her friends.

"I was so surprised when Abby showed me her ring," Eden prattled on. "Luke pulled out all the stops. Isn't that nice?" She linked her arm with his and pressed her breast against his as they walked.

"Very nice." Cam made a mental note to kick his ass several times when all this was over. Yes, Eden was pretty. Except had she always gone on ad nauseam without saying much?

"You've been quiet." Eden pressed even closer. "Is there something going on?"

Cam tried to put a little distance between his bicep and her anatomy. Had she behaved this way before, and he hadn't minded? Or had he just not noticed?

"It's just a work thing." He tucked his hands in his pockets, hoping to create more space between their bodies.

Eden said the appropriate things, but then her voice faltered, and her steps slowed at the same time. "Oh, Cameron!" Her sugary voice warned him not to turn around. "Isn't that the most beautiful ring?"

He could feel the blood drain from his face. *What had he been thinking?* Since Randy's had no parking spaces, Cam pulled into a city lot nearby. That it was right next to Joanne's Gems hadn't been considered.

The possibility it wasn't what he thought raced through his mind. Then he looked at the store's display. A part of him wanted to laugh. Eden had chosen a ring similar to the one he'd purchased for Jessie. Except for explaining his laughter, well...

"Wouldn't it look wonderful on my finger?" she gushed.

It would look wonderful on a finger, all right. It just doesn't belong on yours.

"Eden," Cam took a deep breath.

"Yes, honey?" When he met her gaze, a dreamy look crossed her face. It had him searching for a delicate way to escape the situation.

"We've only been dating a few months..."

"I know." Eden batted her eyes. "Sometimes, though, that's all it takes."

Which Cam understood. Once he'd started seeing Jessie as a female, that was all it took. After that, no one else stood a chance.

"You're so young," he tried a different tactic. "You have your whole life ahead." Then, he forcibly directed her away from the window and toward Randy's.

"And I want to spend it all with you." Eden slipped one arm around his waist and her hand into his back pocket.

It had him thinking about Ben's words from the wedding. Since Eden had caught the bouquet, she'd become more territorial. Or had her behavior changed when Jessie returned to Swan Harbor?

He couldn't deny multiple questions were piling up, many of which wouldn't be answered until everything was over. It left a bitter taste in his mouth and reminded him of his delicate situation.

When Cam opened Randy's door, he was immediately bombarded by memories. The arcade had been a fixture in Swan Harbor long before he was born. It had three floors and multiple spaces that seemed to evolve as often as the town.

The first floor housed video games, everything from old-fashioned pinball machines to the latest combat ones. In the center of the room was a large staircase, and as they moved toward the second floor, the bells from the electronic games gave way to the quieter clacking of balls from the pool tables.

Eden stopped and caught him unawares. When he ran into her, she tossed a sultry smile over her shoulder.

"What?"

"Oh, nothing." She wiggled her ass against his stomach. Then, with a wink, she proceeded up the stairs, adding a pronounced sway to her hips.

Cam was sure one, if not two, of Jessie's conditions had been broken. Determined not to break another, he looked away quickly. Especially since condition number thirteen was '*No staring at Eden's butt.*'

On the third floor, they were greeted by a large group of Eden's friends, who had come to celebrate Abby and Luke's engagement. Several tables had been crammed together, and when they were seated, Cam found his chair on the edge.

Everyone was paired off—and young, making him feel old, older than the six years separating him from most. Something that was even more glaring when the waitress arrived with their drinks. A glass of whiskey for him, glasses of champagne for Eden and a few others, and lemonade for the rest. It had him wondering if the nondrinkers were even legal.

Which was another '*What were you thinking?*' moment, like so many he'd had over the past week.

He wanted to put aside the last two years and move on with the future. And even though Hayden kept saying he was '*Working on it,*' those words weren't much of a consolation prize.

Cam stretched his long legs under the table and placed his arm along the back of Eden's chair. Her hair flirted with his wrist, and he might have fingered the strands before. Except Jessie's condition number four, '*No playing with her hair,*' kept running around in his head.

The thought had a corner of his mouth lifting as he picked up his glass and swirled the amber liquid. When he tossed back a drink of the alcohol, he could feel Eden's displeasure.

"Must you drink that stuff?" she muttered. "The smell and the taste is just so..."

"Well then, Sugar," Cam quipped. "It's a good thing I didn't offer you a drink now, isn't it?" Eden humphed, and his eyes met the laughing ones of the guy sitting across the table.

"Are you two engaged?"

"No!" he exclaimed.

At the same time, Eden responded, "Not yet, Bart."

"I'll give you six months," Bart grinned, rubbing his thumb over the small diamond on his fiancée's finger.

Cam thought he heard Eden say something about it not taking that long, but their meals were delivered before he could say anything. However, with the devil inside of him cackling with glee over the expected comments he'd get over his meal, he let it go.

He didn't expect the smell of spicy hot wings and beer to be much to her liking. This proved true as he ate, pointedly ignoring the dirty looks Eden tossed his way.

Once finished, he wadded up his napkin and dropped it on his plate. Then, just like every other time he'd eaten the wings, he felt a large burp welling inside. In deference to his company, he bit back the need to '*let it rip.*' Instead, he turned his head away and met the mischievous eyes of his princess.

When Jessie sashayed by wearing a straight, black miniskirt, a tiny green top, and strapped sandals, showcasing her long legs, he fought the need to run after her. Especially when he realized she was on her way to dance, followed by Ben, Sadie, and an overly muscled blond.

Cam told himself he was looking out for his brother's best interests and asked Eden to dance. However, once they were on the floor, it wasn't Sadie and her partner who captured his attention. Jessie was laughing at something Ben said, and even though he knew how she felt, he couldn't stop the tiny kernel of jealousy that sparked to life.

As they danced, Eden lightly rested her cheek against his chest. However, after only a dozen steps, her head popped back up.

"Eww," she wrinkled her nose delicately, "you smell like beer and hot wings.

His devil peeked back out, and he knew his mama would disapprove, but a guy had to do what he had to do. Cam swallowed a little air, produced a burp, and blew it into Eden's ear. "It was delicious, too."

When he looked over her shoulder, it was into Jessie's twinkling eyes. He was trying to decide how to switch dancing partners when, surprisingly, Eden took the initiative.

One second, he was dancing with Eden, and the next, Jessie was in his arms. It had occurred in such a smooth manner, he had to wonder if perhaps the manipulations hadn't been all one-sided.

"This is where you're meant to be."

"And don't you forget it," Jessie tossed back.

Cam took advantage of the dark dance floor and, with some subtle movements, manipulated them away from the others and into a corner. He pressed her hips into the cradle of his, and when her breasts flattened against his chest, a shiver of pleasure zipped straight up his spine.

"Oh, Jess," he breathed into her ear. "I must be breaking a few conditions."

"Not nearly enough," she whispered against his throat.

"Are you trying to kill me?"

Their eyes met, and everything she was feeling was there. He wanted to tell her he was sorry. Wanted to tell her, she was always on his mind. Except before any of that could happen, the song began to fade.

Cam nuzzled her temple, then brushed his lips across her cheek. "I love you."

Her hand slowly slipped from his as he walked away, leaving a little piece of his heart behind.

※

Jessie wasn't sure how long she floated inside a fog, reliving how it felt to be in Cam's arms. Minutes later, she imagined she could still feel the touch of his hand and his hot breath as he whispered love words in her ear.

She'd come to Randy's hoping to see him, but she hadn't expected anything else. Dancing with him was wonderful, and she wanted more.

When she returned to the table, and Sadie didn't immediately jump in with questions, Jessie knew something was happening.

"Did you get a love note from Gray?

"What?" Sadie glanced up, and for a second, her expression was blank.

"Your phone," Jessie nodded toward the device, "did you get a love note from Gray?"

"Oh," a sly smile crawled across Sadie's face. "I wish, but no." She leaned closer and lowered her voice, "They're from Hayden."

"Oh? Anything interesting?"

"They're ledger sheets." Sadie turned her phone so both could see the screen. "Here's the person's name, and over here," she slid the form so it moved to the left, "there are amounts. But these letter and number combinations, I don't know what they mean."

"I63.9, F33.1," Jessie read and understood immediately. "Those are diagnosis codes."

Sadie frowned. "How do you know that?"

"I'm a social worker," Jessie reminded her. "I had to do clinicals, and we used those for billing."

She took the phone and slid her thumb around to see all the columns. "When a patient comes in, you give them a diagnosis or reason for your service. Then," Jessie pointed to another code, "depending on what the person needs, there are one or more codes billed to the insurance company."

"Okay, that makes sense." Sadie sent a quick text, then grabbed her wrap and purse. "Hayden is printing these out for me to study. Wish me luck."

"Hey, this involves me. I'm coming too."

When they started down the stairs, Jessie glanced over her shoulder but couldn't see Cam.

"Why don't you go on ahead?" Jessie decided. "I'm going to stop at the ladies' room and tell Cam what's up."

"I'll see you in a bit," Sadie replied absently, her attention still on her phone.

Jessie ducked into the ladies' room and sent Cam a quick text. When she walked out, someone clamped one hand over her mouth and dragged her through an open door, slamming it closed behind her.

SIXTEEN

Randy's Arcade
June 10
9:30 p.m.

HER PULSE IMMEDIATELY SPIKED, ONLY TO RACE FASTER WHEN her body recognized her captor.

"Cam." Jessie wrapped her arms around his neck and attached her mouth to his.

The kiss was one of those toe-curling ones where you can't get close enough. Her heart raced, her mind went blank, and all she could do was feel.

Cam tangled one hand in her hair and slid the other under her skirt. He cupped her butt and pressed her closer to his heat. His tongue swept across hers, and their lips fought for dominance, neither willing to let go of the other.

"Wait!" Jessie tore her mouth away. "Where's ... you know?"

"Forget about her." Cam backed her against a shelf. "*This* is more important."

He palmed her ass and pushed her skirt up enough to tug her leg up over his hip. "Doesn't this feel good?" Cam established a steady back-and-forth motion, each forward move causing his hardness to press against her much softer body.

Damn, Jessie thought. After two years apart, he still had the power to send her need skyrocketing. Except was this what she wanted?

Yes, her body answered when he sucked on a sensitive spot just below her ear. His hand skimmed up her side, and he whispered a kiss across her cheek.

"Are you aiming to break all those conditions?" Jessie tongued the notch at the base of his throat.

"Is that a problem, Princess?" He swooped back in for another taste.

If he hadn't been holding her between the shelf and his hard body, she would have melted into the floor. "Oh, Cam." Jessie's eyes suddenly filled with tears. "Do you know how often I've dreamed of this over the past two years?"

"Every single damn day." Each word was punctuated with a kiss. One that was just a little harder lasted just a little longer than the one before.

"Me too," she confessed, pushing closer, needing more.

"Princess." Cam cupped her face, and his thumbs swept over her cheekbones. "Tears?"

Jessie wanted to tuck herself against him and let the world go on without them for a few hours. "We should leave," she lowered her leg, not answering the question. "At least we had one dance, right?"

"I want a lifetime of dances, though," he murmured against her mouth.

His kisses were like a drug, sending her flying one second and begging for more the next. Whenever he spoke of wanting a future with her, the feeling was so enormous, her insides threatened to burst.

The door to their private space was suddenly yanked open, causing her heart to sink.

"What the hell is going on in here?"

Cam pushed her behind him. "Ben, what the hell?"

Jessie peered around Cam's shoulder into Ben's curious eyes. "Nothing. Nothing's going on."

"Uh, yeah," he smirked. "Lover boy here is wearing your lipstick and probably sporting a rather painful hard—"

"Shut up," Cam snapped. "It's not what you're thinking."

"Oh?" Ben lifted a brow. "Then what is it?"

"It's..." Jessie's panicked look met Cam's annoyed one. They needed to tell him something. The question was, what?

"You'd better hurry and come up with what to say," Ben pushed. "Young Eden is already looking for you," he nodded toward Cam.

"We can't tell you," Jessie sighed. "You're an attorney, and we don't want you to get in trouble."

"Give me a dollar." Ben held out his hand.

"A dollar?" Jessie frowned. "Why?"

"Because if I'm your attorney, then whatever you say is attorney-client privileged."

"It's not just us," Cam admitted. "It's bigger—much bigger."

"I'm on your side," Ben crossed his arms over his chest, "both of your sides."

Cam's groan was barely audible as he pulled Jessie close and nuzzled her temple. "Take him to meet the others. I'll get there as fast as possible."

Jessie smiled, knowing it didn't quite reach her eyes. "I suggest you look in the mirror before you find your girlfriend." She tried to lighten the mood by rubbing at the lipstick on his mouth.

Cam sent her an understanding look. "Go on," he whispered.

She squeezed his hand and stepped out of the closet.

"We'll see you in a few," Ben murmured.

"Take care of her," Cam called as they walked away.

"Sure thing." Ben placed his arm around Jessie's waist and purposefully planted his hand on her butt cheek.

"He won't like that," Jessie muttered.

"True," Ben agreed. "But now, he has other problems. Eden at one o'clock."

"Crap," Jessie groaned. "I was hoping I'd get out of here without having to talk to her."

"Oh, don't worry," Ben replied. "She's too busy looking for her date."

They'd almost reached the staircase when Eden called, "Did you find him, Benji? I've looked everywhere."

"Oh, I found him." Ben snickered so softly, Jessie thought she'd imagined it. "He's in the men's room. I think those wings gave him the runs."

Jessie couldn't stop the giggle that snuck out. "That was mean," she laughed. "But I loved it."

As soon as they were out of sight, Cam ducked into the men's room. Ben's familiarity with Jessie had stoked a jealousy he hadn't expected. It made him realize just how difficult seeing him with Eden had to be for his princess—something he'd known but hadn't understood.

He swiped at the lipstick stains several times, then studied his face in the mirror. To his untrained eye, his lips looked a little puffier than usual, and the scruff hairs around his mouth were tinted. Other than that, all traces of his make-out session with Jessie were gone. And since he didn't plan on allowing Eden close enough to study him carefully, he thought he'd be fine.

"There you are." Eden pounced as soon as he stepped into the hallway. "I've been looking all over for you."

"Why?" His brief reply earned him a frown.

"Are you okay?" She studied him more carefully than he was comfortable with, causing him to press his lips together. "Ben said you were sick."

"Oh, he did?" Cam took her elbow, intending to get her to leave.

"He did," Eden nodded. "Ben blamed it on your dinner."

"Well, you know how it is, sometimes," he replied in an elusive way.

"I know," Eden whined. "The gang is going to Sonny's, and I was hoping..."

"Sonny's, with you?" Cam bit off what he wanted to say, as there was no way in hell he'd go to Sonny's with her. Instead, he hummed, "I probably should just go home."

She frowned. "It's not even 10:00 p.m. And it's Friday."

"Go with your friends," Cam encouraged. "I don't mind."

"But..." Eden frowned. "I'd be alone."

No, he wanted to say, you'll be with your friends. Except before he could hustle her out, she smiled, making him worry about what she was cooking up.

"I'll come take care of you."

"You'll what?"

"Take care of you," Eden repeated.

"No," Cam barked. "I don't think so."

"But why?" she continued to push. "Don't you like to be taken care of?"

"I'm a grown man," he retorted. "I'll probably just sleep. So, would you like me to take you home?"

Eden sighed, one of those long-suffering ones that made him worry about what was next. "Fine, I'll just go home. We should go say goodbye."

Cam glanced up the staircase, and the thought of returning to the third floor and Jessie not being there made him a little nauseous.

"If you don't mind," he rubbed his stomach for good measure, "I'll get the car and meet you out front."

Eden glanced up, and the innocence in her blue eyes should have made him feel guilty. Instead, it just made him anxious.

"You do look a little pale," she murmured.

"I'm feeling a little weak, as well," Cam added another symptom.

"Go get the car. I'll be right out."

She reached to lay her hand on his chest. Unconsciously, Cam stepped back. The look on her face woke him up enough to realize what he'd done. He squeezed her fingers, then nudged her up the stairs.

"I'll see you out front."

Cam retrieved the car and, as soon as Eden was seated, headed toward her home. He could feel her watching him on the drive, almost as if she knew something was different but wasn't sure what. Thankfully, she didn't push, and it wasn't long before he pulled up in front of the house she shared with three others.

"Now that you've graduated, are you going to move?"

Eden smiled, and suddenly, warning signs began flashing in his head.

"It depends."

"On?"

"You, Silly. Us."

"Us?" His brows flew north. "What do *we* have to do with it?"

"Well..." The warning signs in his head stopped flashing. Instead, they glowed bright red, telling him he shouldn't have pushed. "On when I move in with you."

Her answer caused him to rear back. "With me? I didn't—"

"We'll talk about it when you're feeling better," she cut him off.

"Let me walk you to your door," he offered, in a hurry to get her out of the car.

"That's okay. You should go rest." Instead of climbing from the car, a strange look crossed Eden's face. "You smell like perfume, and it's not mine."

"Get over it," Cam snapped. "You've forgotten you're the one who switched dance partners."

"Whatever. Go home. You're mean when you don't feel well." Eden scrambled from the car and slammed the door.

When he drove off, he glanced in the rear-view mirror and noticed she hadn't moved. A game was going on in her head, and he didn't know the rules. It just added one more reason to kick his butt.

⚜

Above Sally's Diner
June 10
10:30 p.m.

JESSIE PACED IN FRONT OF THE DOOR, WAITING FOR CAM TO arrive. She'd done her job—bringing Ben to the diner. However, waiting for her *boyfriend* to take his *girlfriend* home was making her antsy, especially after spending time in his arms. While it had been wonderful, it reminded her of what she was missing.

She'd already annoyed Sadie and Hayden one too many times. And since she couldn't answer Ben's questions, she'd left him to wait alone. Something that had her hanging out by the door, watching the clock.

Their meeting place—an abandoned apartment above Sally's—gave them the perfect opportunity to 'hide in plain sight.'

Jessie checked the time once again. It was five minutes later, and her anxiety had risen another notch. She should have given Cam more conditions. Or put a tracking device on him.

Suddenly, the door flew open. Jessie's muscles tightened as she prepared to jump into Cam's arms. Then she realized it wasn't the Hunter man she was waiting on.

"Oh, it's you."

"Well, it's nice to see you too, little sis," Gray drawled, sounding both sincere and mocking.

Jessie thumbed over her shoulder. "Sadie's in the back with Hayden. So, behave."

"Thanks." Gray winked on his way by.

Grayson Hunter was a good-looking man and had never been shy about using those looks, especially if he wanted something. He was slightly shorter than Cam, with light brown hair, blue eyes, and a lean frame that had drawn female attention for as long as she could remember. Something that worried her about his relationship with her best friend.

Less than a week ago, Sadie hoped for an 'in' with Gray. However, since the first night the 'group' met, they'd been inseparable. It made Jessie feel like she was the one who needed the 'in.' At least they could be seen together in public, and no one would care.

"What's put that pucker right here?" Cam rubbed his thumb between her brows, causing her to jump. "You were so focused, you didn't even hear the door open."

His pout made Jessie want to laugh because if anyone should pout, it wasn't him. "I'm worried about Sadie," she admitted. "I don't want her to get hurt."

Cam hummed. "I've had the same thoughts about not wanting my brother to get hurt."

"Really?" Jessie frowned. "I can't see that. Sadie has wanted Gray for years."

"They're adults, Princess. Now greet me appropriately." He tugged her closer and puckered his lips expectantly.

Jessie leaned forward just enough so her lips hovered close to his. She could smell the spices from his earlier meal and feel the heat from his breath. Sinking against him would be so easy.

"First," she placed her finger in the center of his chin, "how many of those conditions did you break tonight?"

Cam grinned, causing his dimples to pop. "Do you really want to know?"

"I asked, didn't I?"

"There's that princess voice I love so much."

"Cam," Jessie warned.

"I broke several," he whispered, "with you."

"Are you sure—?"

Cam cut off her question with his mouth, but she wouldn't complain. Instead, she tangled her fingers in his shirt and enjoyed the kiss. It was wonderful, but they were both holding back. That much was obvious.

"Where's Ben?"

"He's waiting across the hall," Jessie murmured. "But we need to explain to the others first."

They found Gray and Hayden looking over Sadie's shoulder, all three sporting somber expressions.

"What?" Jessie tightened her hold on Cam's hand.

"In a minute," Gray grunted. "Why the hell is Ben here? He's a lawyer—"

"Just hold on," Cam interrupted before his brother's mad grew too far out of control. "He caught Jess and I—"

"What!" Gray snapped. "You know what could happen if you're seen together."

Sadie grabbed his hand. "Gray, look at me."

When he looked down, and Jessie saw the tenderness for her friend on his face, her fear over their relationship dissolved.

"Let them talk," Sadie murmured.

"Ben's on our side," Jessie explained as soon as possible. "More importantly, though, if there's trouble for Hayden ... or Mary, we might need him."

"But," Gray tried again.

"We hire him," Cam replied, anticipating the next question. "Shall we?"

⚜

Cam found Ben scrolling through his Twitter feed, looking bored. "Are you sure you want to hear this?"

"I'm here, aren't I?" his friend sighed. "Now what's going on?"

"We want to hire you." Cam handed three one-dollar bills to Ben. "Are we good?"

"Just so you know," Ben quipped, "that might buy you a minute."

"Let's hope we don't need it," Cam muttered.

"What's this about, Hunter?"

"Come with us." Cam led Ben into the other room and nodded toward the work area. "Someone is threatening my mother if Jessie and I are together."

"We're trying to find out who," Jessie continued. "It's why I stayed away for so long."

Ben propped his hands on his hips, his blue-eyed stare almost making Cam uncomfortable.

"I don't want to know all the 'how,'" he replied, "but what do you have so far?"

"Not much," Cam answered.

Sadie spread several sheets of paper on the table and pointed to the first one. "Hayden sent me these earlier. They're ledger sheets from an accounting program that 'appears' to be from Mary Hunter's private practice."

Cam frowned down at the pages. "You're saying those are payments for patient visits, right?"

"We think so," Sadie answered.

"And how do you know they're moms?" Cam followed up.

"I used the passwords you gave me," Hayden explained. "They opened her office's billing program."

"Mom works for the hospital," Gray muttered. "Why would she have her own billing program?"

"That's not something I can explain," Sadie sighed. "I can just tell you what these papers say. And, if they're true, quite a few dollars were billed over the last ten years or so."

"Can you tell where the money came from?" Jessie asked. "Or where it was deposited?"

"Hayden?" Sadie tossed it back to the younger man. "He was working on that when Gray showed up."

They turned their attention to Hayden's monitors. One of them showed the ledgers. The other one had Cam questioning his decision to bring in the younger man.

"Wait, Hayden," he commanded. "Don't tell me you're breaking into the bank computers."

"Okay," a cheeky smile crossed Hayden's face, "I won't, but look..."

Hayden explained that while the accounting program didn't have a person's name, it did have a routing and account number. He'd tracked the routing number to Swan Harbor Trust, one of the town's oldest and most respected banks.

When Cam saw how easily the younger man had broken into the bank's computer system, he had second and third thoughts about the process. He tugged Jessie closer, thinking he should have listened to his inner voice and taken her and run.

"It'll be okay." Jessie squeezed his hand.

He wanted to look away from what was happening before him—except he couldn't. Every time he tried, something pulled him back to the numbers flashing on the screen.

"I found the account." Hayden traced his finger along the line to an amount. "Holy mackerel, there's almost a million dollars in there."

"Whose account is it?" Cam asked, even though he wasn't sure he wanted to know.

"Oh..." Hayden's voice faded. "Maybe I'm wrong." He started to erase the entire program.

"Stop!" Cam placed his hand on Hayden's shoulder. "Pull it up."

Jessie's nails dug into his arm as they watched the account information appear on the screen.

"Oh, my." She buried her face against his chest.

"Account holder: Mary Evans," Cam read. "It was opened in 1986."

"Why would Mom open a savings account in her maiden name after marriage?" Gray mused.

"Hiding something," Ben intoned.

"Ben!" Jessie shouted. "That's awful."

"Sorry," he shrugged. "Just joking. Who opened the account?"

Hayden tapped a few more keys, "Looks like someone named Colleen Richards. Do you know her?"

"Richards?" Cam searched his memories for the name.

"Could Colleen be Belle Richards' mom?" asked Sadie. "Wasn't she in your class?"

"Miss Richards?" Hayden muttered. "The librarian?"

"That's her." Ben dropped onto a nearby chair. "Belle's grandmother raised her. Her mom disappeared when she was young. Five or six, I think."

"How do you know this?" Cam frowned. "I don't remember you ever dating her."

"We went out a few times the summer before I left for law school," Ben replied. "It was nothing."

"So now what?" Jessie mumbled.

"Let me dig around a little more," Hayden responded. "Maybe I can find something else that will help."

"Okay." Cam tightened his arms around Jessie. "Call me if you find something."

"Will do. Night," Hayden waved them off but never looked back up.

Cam let Gray, Sadie, and Ben leave first, as he wanted a few minutes alone with Jessie.

"I want to be the one to take you home."

"I want that too." She kissed him, but it wasn't nearly enough. "Since Sadie drove to Randy's, Ben offered to take me home. Will you be okay?"

"Do I have a choice?" Cam kissed her again, not giving her a chance to answer. "I'll be fine. However, tell Ben to keep his hands off your butt." He palmed her ass cheeks and pressed her against him. "That's my condition number one."

"Ha!" Jessie laughed. "I told him you wouldn't like that."

"Not one bit."

It took several more kisses before his insides settled, and he could let her go. As soon as he was sure she was gone, he took the stairs down.

His evening hadn't gone the way he wanted. From the discussion about a ring—with the wrong woman—to the bank account. The discoveries unsettled him, even more so when he realized they probably weren't over.

He gunned his car, and the powerful engine roared to life. The need to spend the night wrapped in Jessie's warmth burned deep in his gut. Except something told him Dylan wouldn't allow him inside their home.

When he drove away from Sally's, Dylan was climbing out of his car, parked in front of the Sheriff's Department. Cam glanced in his rear-view mirror to find Dylan watching him. Somehow, he knew he'd see the Deputy later. But in what capacity—as a sparring partner or writing him a ticket?

SEVENTEEN

Jessie's Home
June 14
3:00 p.m.

Jessie spent her weekend at Sonny's, mulling over the puzzle they were trying to piece together. With the most recent finding pointing to Mary, she wasn't willing to sit back and allow Sadie and Hayden to do all the work.

She was also unsettled after a weekend of terse conversations with Cam. He was hurting, but so was she. That didn't mean she didn't understand his need to be alone. It didn't mean that when he'd asked her to go with him, it hadn't taken all her willpower to say no. Once she had, though, he'd taken off on his own, and after two days, she was still waiting.

"Jessie!" Molly burst through the door. "Remember the picture I said looked familiar?"

"Yeah."

"Look what I found while volunteering at the hospital."

Jessie stared at the picture on Molly's phone, and a spark of hope rekindled. "Oh wow, where did you find this?"

"At the hospital. I finally remembered seeing a similar photo, and voilà."

Molly grinned. "I give you Doctor Arthur Dean, the psychologist whose office isn't far from Mary's."

Jessie tried not to get her hopes up, but Molly was right. The pictures looked very much alike. She dumped the photos on the table and sorted through them, searching for the one with Mary behind bars.

When she found it, she noted that Mary and Author wore orange jumpsuits. However, in Arthur's photo, he held a sign that said, *'Bail me out and help us meet our goal for the new hospital wing.'*

"Molly," Jessie blinked several times to keep her eyes from filling with tears, "this is amazing. It's the same, except Mary's sign has been erased."

Molly grinned. "I did good, didn't I?"

"Yes, my dear sister, you did very well. Now, if we can find the picture of Mary..."

"Sorry, Jess," Molly sighed. "I ran out of time, or I would have looked more."

"You found one of the photos." Jessie waved away Molly's concerns. "We only need one more. Besides, this gives me something to do. I've been feeling rather helpless."

"You still haven't heard from Cameron?"

"Not yet."

"He'll call," Molly assured her. "You know that, right?"

"Oh, I know. It's just..."

"Jessie," Molly giggled. "If you tell Dylan I said this, I'll deny it."

"Tell him what?"

"Males pretend to be tough, but deep down, they're just as scared as females."

"So, what you're saying is, I need to *'Take back the power?'*" The same thing she'd heard from Sadie when they were teens.

"You got this."

"Thanks, Molly."

Jessie shoved the photos back into the envelope and grabbed her purse. "I think I'll poke around the hospital a little more. Maybe I'll get lucky."

"Just be careful, Jess," Molly warned. "You know who works there."

"I'm not likely to forget."

Jessie forced herself to take the shortest route possible to Swan Harbor General. When she stepped over the threshold, memories washed over her.

The all-consuming grief after her parents and brother's death. Plus, her fear over the possibility of her vision issues being discovered before she told Cam. Those were juxtaposed with her sense of accomplishment when telling Mary about her high SAT scores.

She started in the mental healthcare wing, where the psychiatrists, psychologists, social workers, counselors, and therapists' offices were located. Photos lined the walls, some of which she had seen before and others new. The hospital staff photos behind bars were found near the end. However, Mary's picture wasn't included.

"Jessie? What brings you to the hospital?"

Oh, crap! Oh, crap! Oh, crap!

Jessie slowly turned around and attempted a smile. "Catherine, I just noticed these pictures on my way to say hi to Merlene."

"Aren't they great?" Catherine indicated the photos. "I found stacks of these left behind in my office and thought they'd look nice on the wall."

"How old are they?"

It was a miracle the conversation sounded normal. If she could find the answers, it would be worth the creepiness she felt while in the other woman's company.

"Hmm," Catherine shrugged, "nine or ten years, I think? It was for a fund drive held around Halloween."

"Where are Mary's photos?" Jessie blurted before she'd thought through the question.

"Mary?" Catherine frowned. "I'm not sure. Maybe they're in her office."

If Catherine is the one after us, why would she send me to Mary's office?

"Thanks. I'll ask."

"Good luck." Catherine took several steps before turning back. "How's Dylan ... and Molly?"

"They're fine," Jessie answered, wondering where Catherine was leading. "Just fine."

What might have been a sheepish expression flitted across Catherine's face. "I know this is awkward, but everything worked out. He's going to be the next sheriff. You're back in Swan Harbor, and with Cam, and I'm—"

"No, I'm not," Jessie interrupted, worried Catherine was fishing. "I'm not with Cam. He's with Eden." A statement that twisted her stomach every time she uttered it.

"Oh? I just thought ... anyway, good luck with your search."

Catherine hadn't gotten far when she answered her phone with a giggly voice and wearing a flirtatious smile.

What was that all about? Was there more going on than they knew?

Out at Sea
June 15
5:00 a.m.

CAM TOOK A FEW STEPS ONTO THE DECK, A CUP OF COFFEE IN ONE hand and his phone in the other. The sun had just peeked over the horizon, reminding him it was early and another day had passed. Yet, he still hadn't spoken to Jessie.

He could admit he was wrong. Could even admit he was behaving like a dick. His issue was how to make it better—especially when he couldn't look into Jessie's beautiful turquoise eyes and tell her what was in his heart.

Logically, he knew he'd behaved like a child. That by going off on his own, he'd tossed up walls just like she'd done so many times.

His excuses were numerous. They had started when Ben touched Jessie and ended when the bank account was discovered. When multiple emotions raced through him, and he had no one to talk to, he'd run instead of fighting for what he wanted.

Three days alone at sea had given him a new perspective. The cobwebs in his head were blown away, giving his creative juices room to flow. He'd mostly finished the plans for the music club, and then his thoughts turned to Jessie. After many years of living in his head, his dream for them was on paper. If he were lucky, it would show her where she stood in his life and what kind of future he wanted with her.

Were pictures really worth a thousand words?

Cam turned on his phone, and when message after message appeared, he considered tossing it in the ocean. He glossed over most and ignored others. Right then, only Jessie mattered.

He snapped a picture of his drawing and attached it to a text,

Cameron: I'm sorry, Princess. I do want a future
with you, and promise to fight for it ... and for you.
Never forget that I love you

Once it was winging its way through cyberspace, Cam listened to Hayden's message. The excitement in the boy's voice propelled him into action.

After a quick shower, Cam sailed back to shore. He docked the boat and, without stopping by the house first, started toward Sally's. Sadie and Gray's togetherness made him envious and eager for everything to be over.

He found Hayden in the workroom, bent over his computer. "It's about time you showed up," the younger man snapped. "You've missed a lot."

Cam frowned. "What has you so bent out of shape?"

"You," Hayden's curt reply took him aback.

"Me? Why?"

"Jessie."

The word felt like a slap, something he probably deserved.

"I hurt her," Cam sighed. "I was a jerk and promise to make it up to her. But shouldn't she be the one yelling at me?"

"Oh, don't worry. She will."

"And I deserve it."

"Agreed," Hayden retorted. "You deserve whatever Jessie throws at you."

That should have been you, Cam's inner voice whispered. *You should be the one championing Jessie.*

"I *will* talk to Jessie," Cam murmured. "But tell me, why are you so excited?"

Hayden upended an envelope and spread the photos on the table. "Jessie found these pictures with a little help from Molly ... and Catherine."

There were multiple photos of his mother, all dressed in an orange jumpsuit. The first three showed her being arrested by the Chief of Police, her mugshot, and in a jail cell holding a sign that said, '**Bail me out and help us meet our goal for the new hospital wing.'**

"So, it was something for the hospital?" Cam sifted through the rest, most showing behind-the-scenes activities. "And she was 'arrested' by Eden's father. But why didn't he say he knew my mother?"

"Maybe he doesn't," Hayden replied absently, already back on his computer. "Maybe the police just arrested the docs or something."

"Could be," Cam agreed. "When did Jessie bring these by?"

"Yesterday."

"I'm sorry. I screwed up," Cam repeated. "I know it's no excuse. It's just been a lot…"

Hayden glanced up and pinned Cam with the most serious expression he'd seen on the boy's face in years. "We all have difficulties. But you're behaving like a douche. I was a kid when we first met, yet Jessie let you help her when she was hurt. Trust her. Don't blow it."

Cam's head dropped at the enormity of those words. "I'll do my best."

Hayden's eyes locked with his for another second, making Cam fight to maintain the connection. Finally, as if he'd decided something, he turned away and pointed to his computer. "Now, let me show you what else I found."

Swan Harbor Beach
June 15
10:00 a.m.

UNABLE TO SLEEP, JESSIE DROVE TO THE BEACH EARLY TO WATCH the sunrise. However, she knew that wasn't the whole truth. Mostly, it had to do with making sense of Cam's behavior the last few days.

She didn't know how to handle the man who had run. The Cam Hunter she remembered was kind, caring, and patient. Someone who was always there when she needed him. Someone ready to take her skating one minute and dance with her at Randy's the next. He was a man who turned her inside out with his kisses and made her feel special. Yet, she couldn't say if he'd ever *needed* her.

Emotionally, she didn't think so. Certainly, not in the same way she'd needed him after her parents' death and her accident. Was the dynamic in their relationship so unbalanced he didn't think he could rely on her? If that were the case, had he always felt that way, and she'd been too young or … too selfish to notice? Or was it a new behavior—one that started after she left?

She glanced at the photo again. It caused her heart to race and a subtle tremor in her hand. Was he saying what she thought?

Cam had drawn a picture of a house with a snow-covered yard. He and Jessie stood on the porch watching a young girl with red-gold hair skate around a small pond. Her eyes filled, and warmth rushed through her. She wanted the future the photo promised.

"Whatcha looking at?" Sadie settled next to her. "A house?"

"It's something Cam drew. Do you think it says what I think?"

Sadie grinned. "If you think it says he wants a life with you, then yes. Cam wants that life with you."

"He has a funny way of showing it," Jessie grumbled.

"Cam's a man."

"True. I just wish they weren't so confusing."

"Remember what my mama always says," Sadie intoned.

"I know, I know," Jessie laughed. "Take back the power. Molly already gave me that lecture."

One of Sadie's brows arched. "Then why are you down here?"

Jessie waved toward the sea. "Because the man I have a beef with is out there somewhere."

"No, he's not."

"He's not?"

"Cam's at HCI."

"Are you sure?"

"Cam was at Sally's when I arrived," Sadie replied. "He said he was on the way to work."

"At work?" Jessie frowned. "Really?"

That he hadn't tried to find her bothered her more than she wanted to admit.

Remember, you can't be seen together!

Didn't make it any easier.

"Jess," Sadie whispered. "It will work out."

Jessie side-eyed her friend. Her green eyes were twinkling, and her skin was glowing. She was happy—because of Gray. How long had she pined for Cam's older brother?

"I'm sorry. Did you need something? Is that why you're down here?"

"My eyes were crossing from staring at numbers," Sadie sighed.

"Have you learned anything new?"

"The names listed on the ledgers aren't real people."

"They aren't real people?" Jessie hesitated a beat. "What does that mean?"

"I think it means the money in the bank didn't come from insurance companies," Sadie murmured. "Where it came from, though, I'm not sure."

"Is Hayden working on it?"

"He is."

"Now what?"

Sadie looked at her nails. "Interested in a manicure and pedicure at the Foxy Lady? I could use some pampering."

"Only if we can get ice cream afterward," Jessie answered. "I need a treat."

Sadie linked their arms as they started up the pier. "Well, duh. We can get ice cream and then check on Hayden. Maybe we'll get lucky, and he's found something new."

Hunter Corporation, Inc.
June 15
3:00 p.m.

HOURS AFTER TALKING TO HAYDEN, CAM WAS STILL TRYING TO understand everything he'd been told. To say it was mind-boggling was an understatement.

Hayden discovered that when he entered Mary's password, the system kicked him into another server. One that did not belong to the hospital. Once inside, he found ledgers, and those led him to the bank account.

With the discovery, though, came more questions. If the names listed didn't belong to real people, where had they come from? There was also the money. The million dollars in the bank account with his mother's name was real.

Was everything because of Catherine? If so, why? However, if not, who could hate his and Jessie's families so much they wanted to destroy them?

Cam put aside his questions and studied the plans for the club. He couldn't go any further until he met with the owner. Theoretically, he could work on the ice cream store plans until he had answers, though his concentration wasn't worth much.

He jogged back to Sally's and found Hayden in the same position as earlier.

"Find anything new?"

"Another accounting program for your mom's office," Hayden mumbled. "But this time, I know they're real."

"How?"

"I traced some names to other departments within the hospital system," Hayden responded. "I even got into the hospital banking records. Need a few bucks?"

"Don't even tease about that," Cam growled.

Hayden laughed. "Man, you need to relax."

"Sorry," Cam sighed. "I just want this all to be over."

"I get that." Hayden hesitated a beat. "Have you talked to Jessie?"

"No." He hadn't heard from her, making him wonder if she even liked his picture. "I said I would talk to her."

"You did. For now, though, go away and let me work. I'll send you a text when I find something new."

"Fine, fine," Cam sighed. However, as soon as he stepped outside, his heart sank. He grabbed the door to run inside—but it was too late.

"Cameron." Eden shoved her phone back into her pocket. "I was just leaving you a message … again. We need to talk."

There were quite a few people he needed to talk to, and Eden wasn't at the top of his list.

"What is it, Eden?" he offered tiredly.

"Where have you been all week?"

Her voice had him clenching his jaw to keep from saying something he shouldn't. "Working. Why?"

"Working?" Eden's brow rose in disbelief. "Really?"

"Really," Cam answered impatiently. "I'm on my way to eat. If you want to talk, you can join me." He took Eden's elbow and started toward the front of Sally's.

"But I've already eaten."

"I thought you wanted to talk."

"Fine." Eden pulled her arm free and chose a table in the center of the room.

After Cam ordered, he followed her at a much slower pace. Hindsight told him he should have given her more information, as it might have satisfied her. Since he hadn't, though...

"You wanted to talk, so talk."

"One of my friends saw you at the gym on Friday," she retorted. "I thought you were sick."

Cam shrugged. "I took something for my stomach and hit the gym."

"Why didn't you call me? I wanted to go to Sonny's. I've told you how much I love it there, yet we've never gone."

"And we never will," he snapped without thinking.

"What?"

The hurt sound of her voice penetrated his annoyance enough for him to realize what he'd said. "I just mean, Sonny's holds a lot of memories I'd rather—"

"—Not relive."

The word was far from what he'd been thinking, but instead of going there, he went with it.

"That works."

"Still," Eden whined. "You could have called."

"I didn't. Get over it."

When he looked away, he caught sight of Jessie. She was standing just outside the front door, talking to Sadie. His heart kicked up a few beats, and he had to fight to stay seated.

"What are you looking at?" Eden glanced over her shoulder just as Jessie jumped out of sight.

What the hell?

"Cameron?" Eden laid her hand on his arm. "What's going on?"

"It doesn't matter."

Thankfully, Eden didn't push, and he was allowed to continue to stare. It wasn't long before Jessie stepped back into sight. This time, though, she wasn't alone. As soon as he saw who she was with, his head swam, and he had to hold on to the table to remain in his chair.

"No!"

"Cameron?" Eden tightened her fingers around his wrist. "Who is it?"

"Roger." His heart raced at full speed for a handful of seconds, then it shattered and fell at his feet.

EIGHTEEN

Sally's Diner
June 15
4:30 p.m.

By the time Cam gathered his thoughts, Jessie, Sadie ... and Roger were gone. Were they out front?

"I just remembered a meeting." He tossed some bills on the table and rushed out the door before Eden could slow him down. But Jessie was nowhere to be seen.

"Damn!" Cam raced to the sidewalk and perused up and down the street. When he didn't see them, he ran across the road and headed up Main Street.

The image of her greeting Roger was burned in his brain, almost to the point it made him nauseous. Had she not liked his picture? Or did she not understand it? The possibility of his screw-up having permanent damage caused him to run a little faster. He skirted several buildings before he caught sight of Jessie's shiny hair. Seeing the trio—had become a duo, had him grabbing the side of the building for support.

"What the hell?!"

They stopped in front of Swan Harbor's Spirits and Wine, which had him jumping into a doorway when Jessie glanced over her shoulder. That's all he needed—for her to see him skulking around in her wake.

Once they'd disappeared inside, Cam sprinted across the street. The honking horns should have caused concern. Except he couldn't be bothered and pressed his face against the window, trying to see where they were sitting.

With the tinting too dark for him to see much, Cam ran back to the office and slammed the door so hard it bounced against the hinges.

Jessie's comments about Roger floated through his head.

"…I didn't go out with anyone until I heard about Roger."

"Roger?" she frowned. "Who's Roger?"

"You tell me," Cam shrugged, "you were kissing him in the movie theater."

"I was kissing someone?"

Had he been wrong? Was the man's name not Roger? If that was so, who was it?

Cam glanced wildly around the room, searching for what—he wasn't sure. Air. He needed air.

"Cam?" Gray stepped out of his office. "What's going on?"

"Plenty!" Cam pushed the door open so hard it bounced off the wall.

"Hold on!" his brother yelled.

"You want to talk," Cam barked. "You'd better keep up."

Swan's Spirits
June 15
5:30 p.m.

Jessie and Tyler had been sitting in Swan's Spirits for less than an hour when Sadie rushed in. She had several shopping bags hanging from her arm and a Cheshire Cat grin on her face.

"Oh, these are my favorites." She helped herself to a shrimp puff. "I'm sorry I took so long. There were just so many things I liked."

"Oh?" Jessie hummed. "Did you buy out the store?"

"Not hardly," Sadie giggled. "But I think Gray will approve."

"You could show me," Tyler teased, "just in case you need a guy's opinion."

"Nice try," Sadie laughed. "Now, finish filling us in."

Jessie was pleasantly surprised when they ran into an old friend from college in front of Sally's. Tyler James was tall, dark, and handsome, with a Tennessee drawl few females could resist. When he sang, every female swooned and wanted to get closer.

Except her. To Jessie, Tyler wasn't Cam. Which had made it easy to be his friend. Then, they'd graduated and gone their separate ways. She'd heard he'd gotten married and nothing else until...

Jessie fought not to get lost in the memories. Fought to step back to see how running into Tyler on the fateful day two years previous had changed her thinking.

After she received the threatening text, she raced to Logan International. There, she ran into Tyler and his three-month-old daughter, Bethany. That was when she learned his wife had died during childbirth. Hearing about someone else's problems allowed her to shove aside her grief. That had become the catalyst for her to let go of her anger and give her future up to fate and hope. If the heart truly wanted what the heart wanted, then somehow—if she were meant to be with Cam—they would be.

"You're too quiet, Jessie." Tyler tapped the back of her hand. "Did I put you to sleep?"

"Sorry." Jessie grinned. "I think my early morning is catching up with me."

Before he could respond, a stranger slid into the empty chair next to him. "Are you Tyler James? I saw you in concert in..."

Jessie exchanged looks with Sadie. "I'm gonna go." She hurried from the table and stopped by the bar to cash out.

"Here you go, Sugar," Krystal, the bar's owner, handed her a receipt. "It's nice to put a face with someone I've heard so much about."

"You've heard about me?" Jessie frowned.

"Definitely." Krystal popped her gum several times. "There was one night when Cameron was in here. He had quite a few things to say."

"Cam," Jessie swallowed hard, "talked about me? When was that?"

"Hmm," Krystal worked over her gum for a few more seconds. "I'd say it was a couple of years ago."

"What did he say?"

"Oh, honey..." Krystal leaned closer. "That boy was..."

Cam's Home
June 15
9:30 p.m.

CAM HAD TO HAND IT TO HIS BROTHER. GRAY HAD GONE WITH him to the gym and run a few miles along the beach. After they'd come home, a shot of whiskey and his brother were waiting when he returned downstairs.

He tossed back the drink and weighed the heaviness of the glass in his hand.

"I wouldn't," Gray warned. "Especially not with Mom's crystal."

"The satisfaction might be worth her ire," Cam's toneless reply had Gray lifting a brow. "Okay. Let me get something."

He ran to the basement, dug through a desk drawer, and unearthed a wrinkled envelope. More than once, he'd thought about tossing it, especially since keeping it around almost as some sort of punishment.

"Here," Cam tossed the envelope onto Gray's lap. "This might explain a few things."

Gray opened the flap and pulled out the two photos. "Where did you get these pictures of Tyler and Jessie?"

"Who the hell's Tyler?" Cam snapped. "That's Roger. Look on the back."

Gray flipped over one picture, an 8x10 photo of Jessie hugging the man she'd been with outside of Sally's. On the back was a short note.

Jessie quickly replaced you, didn't she? His name is Roger. Remember him?

Where did this come from?"

"Read the other one." Cam indicated the second image, which showed Jessie and the same man looking down at a baby girl.

Jessie has moved on, so should you. Some memories only bring us pain.

Gray returned the photos to the envelope and tossed them on the table. "Who gave you these?"

"I don't know," Cam shrugged. "I'm wondering if they're from Catherine. After all, she wanted Jess out of town."

"She succeeded, though." Gray tossed the envelope on the table. "What would she have gained by using those photos?

"To keep me from going after Jessie?" Cam offered, not really buying the possibility.

"Maybe," Gray conceded. "What would she have gained by using those photos?

"No," Cam sighed. "I found the first one waiting for me in my car the night Jessie left."

The pain that rippled through his body with the admission surprised him. He thought he'd dealt with those ghosts, if not before Jessie returned, then when they talked at Sonny's.

"And the second?"

"The next summer," Cam replied. "I was with Ben and had decided to fly to the Philippines and bring Jessie home. When I got in my car—"

"—The second picture was waiting."

"Yeah."

"Where were you when you said you were flying to the Philippines?"

"Sally's, why?"

"Someone had to have heard you were leaving."

"Which means they put the picture in to stop me," Cam muttered. "And it worked!" He stomped to the window and stared into the darkness, calling himself several colorful names.

If he started making a list of all the 'should haves' since things had gone south, he'd fill up a page.

"How do you know his name's not Roger?"

"Sadie," Gray's simple answer made sense. "They went to college together. In fact..."

The pregnant pause had Cam turning back toward his brother. "What are you not telling me?"

"Tyler, as in Tyler *James*," Gray emphasized, "is our client."

"Ahh, damn!" Cam had spent weeks thinking about Tyler's club, and now...

"Have you talked to Jessie?"

"Not yet. I just…"

"Sit!" Gray pushed Cam into a chair. "I'm only saying what Mom and Dad would say if they were here."

"I don't want—"

"Tough," Gray snapped. "You've been acting like an ass, and I'm tired of it."

An ass, a dick, neither words very flattering and not something he enjoyed. Cam wanted a way out. It was just…

"Look, Cam," Gray went on. "Your whole life, you've been the golden child. You made the grades, got the girls, excelled at sports, etc. We have parents who've been married for many years."

"And?"

"Your whole life, there's only been one thing you haven't had control over." Gray paused for emphasis. "Jessie. I suggest you talk to her. Don't throw away the best thing that's happened to you."

"But…"

"No buts," Gray snarled. "Just do it."

Except that was easier said than done when you couldn't be seen together. That meant he needed to be creative to find a way to tell his princess he was sorry.

Jessie's Home
June 15
11.45 p.m.

WHAT SOUNDED LIKE THE BUZZING OF A FLY KEPT JESSIE FROM sinking deeper into sleep. When it buzzed again, she swung out and knocked it on the floor. It was then she realized the noise had come from her phone.

"Crap!" She wrenched her eyes open and peered over the side of the bed in time to see the screen light up. When Cam's picture flashed, it kicked her heart rate into high gear.

> Cameron: Can we talk?

They needed to talk. Was she ready?

Jessie: It's kind of late.

Cameron: Look out your window.

His quick response gave her pause.

Cameron: Please, Princess. I need you.

Words that, for some reason, she'd wanted to hear.
The same text buzzed once more. This time, she couldn't resist.
Jessie tossed the blankets aside and padded to the window. Cam stood just below, using a flashlight to highlight the large pieces of paper he held.

Princess,
I was an ass.
Let's talk, please.

Should she go down?

Jessie: What if we're seen?

Cameron: We won't be. Trust me.

Did she trust him?
When she looked inside her head and heart, there was no question.

Jessie: Give me a few minutes.

She slipped on her shoes and pulled a sweatshirt over her pajamas. Then, she quietly made her way downstairs.
Cam wrapped her in his arms as soon as she opened the door. Their kisses were slow and languorous, interspersed with loving words. It would be so easy to allow the heat between them to spin out of control. Except both

seemed to be aware of just that and were fighting not to let their passion burn too hot.

"Jess," Cam whispered against her lips. "We need to…" He dove in for another hard kiss.

"We do." Jessie took a half-step back and noticed she'd inadvertently crushed the flowers Cam had brought. "Oops, sorry about that."

Cam chuckled, and the sound was so sexy it caused a zip of electricity to race up her spine. "I'm sorry, Princess." He gave her a yellow rose. "I love you." Then he handed her a red rose. "I behaved like an ass."

"You did." Jessie laughed at the look of dismay her agreement caused to flash across Cam's face. "However, the flowers are a nice touch."

"It pays to know people."

"You got Charley out of bed?"

"Oh, no," Cam snickered. "I got Ben out of bed. He's the one who woke up his father."

"What are you going to owe him?"

"Who knows? You're worth whatever the cost."

"Oh, Cam."

He tucked her against his side, "Are you ready to talk?"

"If you are."

Jessie knew Cam was nervous. There was a slight tremor in the arm around her, and he kept glancing in her direction, making her wonder if he thought she might disappear.

"Oh," she exclaimed when they reached the gazebo. "You've been busy."

He'd covered the bench with a blanket, and a camping light cast shadows around them. In the center was a large envelope.

"It's not much," Cam nodded toward the bench seat. "Warm enough?"

"I'm fine." Jessie patted the spot next to her. "Will you sit by me?"

Cam hesitated for a moment before settling beside her and lacing their fingers. He ran his hand through his hair, then suddenly jumped up and moved to the far side of the gazebo.

When he started talking, and his gaze bounced all over the place, never meeting hers for long, Jessie melted. He was adorable in his shy, awkward way, a side of him she'd not seen often.

"I'll admit my life has been easy," Cam veered in a direction she hadn't expected. "I did well in school, had plenty of friends, and was okay in sports."

"Plus, all the girls swooned over you," Jessie quipped.

Cam ducked his head as if he was embarrassed. It was several minutes before he continued.

"My parents were always there for me, and I was fortunate when it was time for college. With all that said, there was always one thing I couldn't completely make mine."

"What?"

"You."

His quiet reply caused her heart to flip. "People aren't possessions."

"Oh, I know," he sighed. "I just meant there were times when I needed you to choose me."

"I did," Jessie jumped in to respond. "Every time I came home from school, I chose you."

"Did you, Jess?" his eyes bore into hers. "Or did I choose you?

"But Cam," Jessie whispered. "Didn't we choose each other?

<hr>

"I thought so," Cam answered. "Until I heard you'd been kissing Roger."

"But I told you, I didn't," Jessie jumped in.

"I know that now," he sighed. My only excuse is I was a nineteen-year-old idiot, and when I went back to school in the fall..."

"Oh? Are you going to tell me the story about competing with your roommate? What was his name?"

"Beau."

"Yeah, that's it," she grinned. "Is that when you and Beau competed for girls?"

Cam had to fight to keep the shocked expression off his face. How had she known? "I'm so—"

"Don't apologize," Jessie cut him off. "Go on."

The relief he felt she didn't want to relive his sophomore year was only minimal, as there was more he needed to confess. "That wasn't the last time I'd heard about you and Roger."

"I don't know a Roger," she repeated.

"You accused me of not coming after you when you left," Cam powered on as if she hadn't said anything. "This was why I didn't." He handed her a photo.

Jessie glanced down at the picture and then back up. "Because I was hugging Tyler?"

"Flip it over." His heart pounded as she did so.

"Oh, Cam," Jessie cried. "You thought I'd run off with another man?"

"I…"

"But you knew I loved you. Didn't you?"

"I was a mess that night, Jess."

"I know"

"You know?" Cam frowned. "How?"

"Krystal from Swan's Spirits told me," Jessie explained. "She said your mom and Gray had to take you home.

"Yeah, it wasn't pretty." His days during that time were dark. So dark, even knowing they were behind him, they still caused a bad taste in his mouth. "Once I was sober, my mom sat me down and told me in a good relationship, both parties have equal power."

"Your mom is a wise woman."

"She is," Cam sighed. "However, it was a while before I listened enough to clean up my act. That's when I told Ben I was going after you."

"But you didn't."

He gave her the second picture, and Jessie quickly flipped it over to read the inscription. "I still feel like I'm missing something. When did you know this picture wasn't the truth?"

"I overheard Dylan and Molly talking," Cam admitted. "They'd just returned from their honeymoon, and I heard them mention your name."

"But they didn't say anything about a child?"

"No," Cam sighed. "That's when I decided it was all an elaborate hoax. I'd hoped when you came home for Christmas…"

"Except I didn't, which was when you 'mistook,'" Jessie put the word in air quotes, "Eden for me."

"I was a fool, Jessie," he whispered. "There's only one you, Princess."

"I'm glad you know that." Her haughty voice had returned, and even though they had to hash out the rest, his lips twitched. "Now sit down," Jessie continued in her bossy way, "and let me tell you about Tyler.

"Your princess voice turns me on." Cam scooped her up and settled her on his lap. "But you know that, don't you?"

"Everything turns you on."

"When it comes to you." He gave her a hard kiss but very thorough kiss, then waited until she was ready.

Jessie brushed her fingers down his cheek. "Shall I start?"

Just tell me, Jess," Cam instructed. "Secrets don't work."

"Well, okay." She skipped over the part of the story he knew and went straight to when she'd run into Tyler at Logan International.

"I don't think he noticed I was crying," she murmured. "Because when he hugged me, Bethany was squished between us."

Suddenly, Jessie jumped up and reached for the pictures. "Bethany..."

"What about her?" Cam glanced at the picture, but there was no sign of a baby.

"Tyler was holding her." Jessie's eyes met his. "Bethany was removed."

"Damn," Cam snapped. "Someone was at the airport and sent the pictures to Swan Harbor."

"To Catherine?"

"Who else?" he asserted. "It has to be. Hopefully, Hayden can help us prove it."

Jessie leaned her forehead against his. "I can't believe someone would go to this much trouble to keep us apart."

"I can't either," Cam hummed. "Now, tell me about Tyler."

The story of Tyler's wife giving birth to a healthy baby girl and then hemorrhaging to death had Cam holding Jessie a little closer. He wasn't sure how the other man had gone on with his life but guessed it had been for his daughter.

"My heart was broken," Jessie continued. "I had to leave to save your mother and was feeling pretty miserable. Then, I heard Tyler's story. It was one of love, loss, and life, and I realized something."

"What?"

"I realized that twice in my life, I'd suffered," she murmured. "Each time, you were there for me. That was when I decided if we were meant to be, somehow, it would happen."

"Oh, Jess." Cam brushed away her tears. "I'm so sorry I never came."

"We both have regrets," Jessie whispered.

"We do," he agreed. "It doesn't make it any easier, though."

"No. But you know what?" she continued, as if not expecting a response. "When Cassie asked me to attend her wedding, I thought maybe it was a sign. I was scared to get on the plane."

"Why?"

"I don't know. Maybe I was worried my dreams wouldn't come true."

"And which dream is that, Princess?

"The one where I can do this," Jessie kissed him, "whenever I want."

"Feel free to do just that."

"Yeah, right," Jessie retorted. "Most of the time, I must stand in line behind your girlfriend."

Cam was back to kicking his ass for behaving like a dick. For the time being, he ignored her comment and moved on.

"Why didn't you come to see me?"

"You know why," her princess voice was back. "As soon as I drove into town, you were getting hot and heavy with another woman."

"I'm sorry about that," he sighed. "Eden had just passed her exams and..." Secretly, though, he loved that Jessie was jealous.

"Hmm, well," she grumbled. "It looks like I need to add that to my conditions."

"Don't worry, Princess." Cam kissed her hand. "I have no plans to get hot and heavy with Eden."

"I feel like I'm living in some bad fairytale."

"This is no fairytale, Jess. It's real life, and we will get our happy ever after. I promise you that."

Jessie's silky hair slid through his fingers as she twisted around and straddled his lap. "Isn't this where we seal the promise with a kiss?"

Cam's body jumped from half-mast to full throttle, and a million ideas rushed through his head. "You're killing me here, Jess."

She pushed against his hardness and ratcheted up his need—which he hadn't thought possible. "But what a way to go ... right?"

For that, he had no argument.

NINETEEN

Jessie's Home
June 16
1:00 a.m.

Jessie was lost in a sensual haze when her lone functioning brain cell began yelling mayday. She tried to ignore it, but when she did, it yelled louder.

"Cam." She pushed back slightly.

"Hmm..." He latched onto a sensitive place on her neck, causing goosebumps to dance along her skin.

"We can't." Jessie hopped off his lap and moved several feet away. Then her eyes met his, and the look in them had her grabbing hold of the railing. If she hadn't, she would have jumped back into his arms.

With his blond hair in disarray, puffy lips, and his shirt unbuttoned, he looked like a model. Her eyes lazily drifted over his smooth chest and flat stomach, but when she reached his unbuttoned jeans, she slammed on the brakes.

Oh, man! Jessie stepped out of the gazebo and away from temptation. What had they been thinking?

You weren't.

Which was the truth. They weren't thinking but only feeling. She had to believe their time would come. After all, they'd sealed it with a kiss.

Cam came up behind her and linked their hands. "Wait for it."

"Wait for what?" was barely out of her mouth before she saw one ... and another ... and then another. "Lightning bugs!" Her heart fluttered as memories of catching them with her dad and brothers floated by.

"How did I do?" He swept their linked hands in front of them.

"You want me to think you created this, right?" Jessie side-eyed him, and the cheeky smile on his face reminded her of the night of their first kiss. "Okay, you win." However, instead of growing bigger, his grin faded, and it was once again time to talk. This time, the confession would be hers.

"Come, sit." Jessie took a deep breath and began, "Cam ... my time in the Philippines taught me a lot ... about life ... about myself."

"Really?" He hesitated. "Like what?"

"I finally admitted to myself I was a spoiled brat," she murmured. "Sometimes, I look back and wonder why people put up with me."

"You weren't—"

"Stop," she cut off his denial. "I had my parents, your parents, my brothers, Gray, and you, allowing me to do whatever I wanted. Come on ... don't tell me it didn't annoy you. I always got my way."

The guilty look that crossed his face had her pushing on. "Mary told you partners should be equal, right?" At his nod, she continued, "That means both must give and take. You always gave, and I always took. Our balance was way out of whack."

"I didn't mind."

"Bull," she called his bluff. "The fact you believed the stories about Roger tells me something was going on."

"That was a long time ago."

"Then why did you run away and not talk to me for three days?" Jessie whispered. "Why weren't you sure I'd chosen you?"

CAM'S EYES MET HERS BRIEFLY BEFORE SKITTERING AWAY TO watch the fireflies. "You've changed," he hesitated a beat, finally meeting her gaze head-on. "I'm only realizing how much."

"I grew up," Jessie replied. "It's about time, don't you think?"

"I thought you were perfect."

"Ha!" she laughed. "A perfect brat, maybe."

"But I loved that brat." He smiled, showing off his dimples. "However, the woman you've become," Cam's voice dropped an octave, "she takes my breath away."

"Is that a good thing? Or is it why you ran?"

Cam adjusted on the bench, tired of his nuts feeling like they were in a vise. "Jessie, I ran because, for the first time, I needed you ... and while you were there, I couldn't have you."

"What?"

"You were right about the power between us being out of whack," he sighed. "When we were young, you needed, and I was there. I liked being needed. Then, as we grew older and our relationship changed, you were the first thing on my mind when we came home."

"I..."

Cam shook his head, needing to finish what he was trying to say.

"Fast forward to 'that night...'" He leaned on his knees and dropped his head.

"Tell me." Jessie forced him to look at her.

"I had a ring that night." Her quick intake of air told him she hadn't expected that answer. "Hours after my mom and Gray put me to bed, I sobered up enough to find the ring and took it out onto the patio. I almost threw it into the ocean."

"Oh, Cam. You didn't?"

"No." He kissed the top of her head. "My mother stopped me and said she'd hold it for me until it was time for me to give it to you."

"Sounds about right."

"The last time they were in Swan Harbor, she left it on my dresser," he admitted. "I want to marry you, Jessica Marie Prince. But between the news about the bank account and you not letting me spirit you away, I needed some time to think. I'm sorry."

"I get that," she murmured. "Except I wasn't rejecting you. You just need to rely on me like I rely on you."

"I love you." Cam leaned in for a kiss.

However, before he reached his destination, Jessie placed her finger on his chin to stop him. "Changes and all?"

"Of course." He kissed her. "The drawing I sent you was my promise to you."

"The house?"

"Our house," Cam reiterated. "My dad gave Gray and me some land, and someday ... I want to live there with you."

"I want that too," Jessie murmured. "You didn't just choose me, and I didn't just choose you." She kissed one cheek and then the other. "We chose each other."

Her last kiss melted the rest of his insecurities, and Cam took full advantage of her offering.

Jessie's House
June 16
7:00 a.m.

JESSIE WANDERED INTO THE KITCHEN IN SEARCH OF CAFFEINE. It had been late—or very early—when Cam had kissed her goodnight. Then, her dreams were disturbed by an early morning phone call to meet at Sally's.

"Rough night?" Dylan hummed.

The hours spent in Cam's arms had morphed into graphic dreams. When she woke up and realized they were only dreams, frustration had taken root. A cold shower had helped ... but it hadn't completely dispelled the images.

"Not particularly, why?"

"Late night?" Dylan came back with. However, his 'dad-look' said he knew exactly how late she'd come in.

"We had a lot of things to talk through."

"And did you?"

"I think so," she sighed. "I'm just ready for everything to be over."

"Has there been any progress made?"

Jessie refilled her coffee cup and wished she could talk to Dylan, but...

"Some. It's just—"

"—Better if I don't know what it is," Dylan guessed.

"Something like that."

"Just be careful," he warned. "You are, aren't you?"

"We're being careful," she assured him. "And as soon as possible, I'll fill you in."

Dylan studied her for a few more minutes before washing his cup and sticking it in the dishwasher. "Do you need a ride?"

"No, I'm going to drive. Thanks."

She watched him go and, with a few minutes to spare, let the memory of Cam's words float through her head.

"Jessie, I ran because, for the first time, I needed you ... and while you were there, I couldn't have you."

Goosebumps raced up her spine at the thought. In a way, he'd shown her. His desire had been evident in every kiss, every touch, and every look. She'd wanted to see how far she could push him. Unfortunately, pushing his buttons triggered her own as well.

Her phone buzzed, and without looking, she knew it was him.

Cameron: Are you on your way?

Jessie: Thinking about it.

Cameron: Thinking about it? What else are you thinking about?

Jessie: Wouldn't you like to know?

Cameron: I bet I can guess.

Jessie: You think?

Cameron: I know.

Jessie: I wouldn't be too sure if I were you.

Cameron: You can show me when you get here.

"Oh!" She giggled, and heat climbed up her neck.

Jessie: I'm on my way.

Cameron: I expect a kiss when I see you.

Jessie: Oh? Are you sure that's not playing with fire?

When a text didn't immediately arrive, Jessie put her cup away. She grabbed her bag and had just climbed into the car when her phone buzzed again.

Cameron: Honey, there are ways to keep my balls from turning blue. You know, we could…

Jessie's face heated at where that text had taken her active imagination. They could. Just not as long as she lived with Dylan and Molly.

Jessie: Cam!

Cameron: Is that a maybe?

A little zip of excitement slid along her skin, and more memories of their heavy petting session threatened to distract her even more.

Jessie: I call uncle. I'm on my way.

The traffic moved easily until she was closer to the center of town. There, the streets were more crowded and slower, a testament to the beach crowds' arrival. Jessie drove into Sally's parking lot, surprised to find Ben and Cam in a serious conversation.

When she climbed out of her car, Ben was strolling toward her.

"Right on time. I like that in a woman."

Jessie frowned. "What's going on?"

Ben grabbed her shoulders as if he planned to kiss her on the cheek. Instead, he whispered, "We're being watched."

"What?" Her gaze flew from Ben's to Cam's, then back. "Where?"

"Across the street." Ben placed his hand at the center of her back and guided her toward his car. "The diner's packed. Would pastries from Paula's be alright?"

"Do we *really* need to drive?"

Ben grinned, almost as if he were enjoying the cloak-and-dagger behavior. "I'm banking on the person following you so Cam can slip into Sally's without being seen."

"That makes sense," Jessie replied. "What about Sadie and Gray?"

"They should arrive in the next few minutes." Ben parked not far from Paula's. "We're just taking a tiny detour."

Jessie followed him into Paula's, where they bought a dozen donuts. From there, they ducked into Ben's father's flower store and into a back room.

"Now what?"

"Just wait."

Ten minutes later, Ben murmured, "The coast is clear." Then led the way out a back door.

On the way to Sally's, Ben made a point of staying out of sight. Several times, she wanted to giggle but didn't think he'd appreciate her laughter.

"Here we are." Ben ushered her into Sally's and up the stairs.

"It's about time," Cam grumbled when they reached the second floor. "What took so long?"

"We brought donuts," Ben quipped. "That should make up for the delay."

Cam's possessiveness gave Jessie a little thrill. However, it didn't stop her from wishing things were different.

As soon as they were alone, Cam pulled her into his arms. "What did I tell you I wanted first thing?"

"What did you tell me you wanted?" Jessie tossed the question back.

"Sugar."

"You've forgotten my name already?" she teased.

"Haha."

"I'm just making sure."

"Never, Princess. But just so you know." Cam nuzzled her temple. "No one whispers sweet nothings except me. That's my condition number two."

"You didn't like that?"

"Hell no." He kissed her, stealing other thoughts from her mind.

❧

Above Sally's Diner

June 16

8:30 a.m.

CAM WAS RELUCTANT TO LET JESSIE GET TOO FAR AWAY WHEN they walked into the workroom. Yes, he was feeling possessive. However, for the time being, it was only when they were 'working' he could touch her the way he wanted. It was a sad state to be in. He just hoped it wouldn't be much longer. The idea someone was watching her ... watching them—made him nervous.

"Okay, we're all here," Cam grumbled. "What did you find?"

"You go first," Hayden mumbled around the bite of donut he'd just taken.

"Ben was right." Cam glanced from Jessie to Gray. "Someone was across the street watching Sally's."

"And you couldn't see who it was?" asked Gray.

"Not before they disappeared into the City Hall."

"Were they watching me, or were they watching Sally's?" questioned Jessie.

"Just be careful," Ben reminded everyone. "We don't know who we're dealing with."

"And I really don't want any blowback on Dylan," Jessie murmured.

"Or our parents," added Gray.

"There's more." Cam pulled the pictures and quickly explained when and where he'd gotten them. "We figured out the photos were taken at the same time, at Logan International."

"But the baby was removed," explained Jessie.

"Which means someone followed or was waiting for you at the airport," Ben surmised.

"And either sent or brought the picture back to Swan Harbor," finished Gray.

"It had to be sent electronically," Hayden noted. "Especially if it was photoshopped and put into your car that night."

Ben was quiet for several moments while he moved around the room. Cam felt like his friend was about to give a summation, hoping to convince a jury.

"Jessie," he began. "You think Catherine's father paid for your time in Boston?"

"I think so," Jessie hummed. "I don't know where else she would have gotten that much money. I just heard, '*What Catherine wants, Catherine gets,*' and then something about money exchanging hands. No names, though."

"What do you know about Catherine's father?" Ben prodded.

"Nothing much. Catherine only talked about her mother. She gave me the impression her father wasn't in the picture."

"Let's see." Hayden's fingers flew across the keyboard. "Richard Gold has been divorced once, and Catherine is his only child."

"What does Daddy Gold do?" Cam still wanted to know why his family ... and Jessie's, had been targeted.

"Looks like he manages hedge funds and dabbles in commercial real estate," Hayden continued reading.

"Are there any noticeable ties to Swan Harbor?" Ben suggested another possibility.

"He donated a million dollars several years ago to Swan Harbor General," Hayden answered.

"I'd bet that's the same time those pictures of Mary were taken," mused Jessie.

"Dates match," Hayden confirmed. "And it looks like he's donated to several local elections, including Dylan's opponent."

"So, it involves daddy somehow," Gray offered. "But why? I still don't see why she'd target my family."

Cam didn't either and fought with himself daily to avoid driving by Catherine's office and forcing her to talk.

"My turn." Sadie nodded to Hayden, who opened a file on his computer. "These are the fake ledgers we first found, and to the best of my knowledge, these people: Sandy Swan, Polly Dee, Frieda Driver, Sunny Iceland, Liberty Freeze, and all the other names in this program are not real."

"None of them?" Jessie frowned. "Going how far back?"

"Ten years or so," Sadie shrugged. "It's the same names repeated, just different amounts."

"No pattern?" asked Ben.

"No," Sadie confirmed. "And before you ask, we don't know where the money came from."

"I'm working on it," Hayden offered. "But…"

"Hayden did find his way into the real books for Mary's department," Sadie quickly said in defense of the boy.

"And?" Cam pushed. "Is there *any* good news?"

Jessie rubbed her hand back and forth over the tight muscles in his back. It made him think about what she'd said the night before—about relying on each other. He had to admit he kind of liked it.

"We know these are real people," Sadie explained, "because Hayden could track them through other hospital departments. I hate feeling like I'm invading someone's private life. Mary saw a lot of people she knew."

"But nothing tells us who is doing this?" Cam spit out, and only Jessie's hand in his kept him from saying more.

"Not yet." Hayden's smile grew into a *'child who found the cookie jar'* one. "But I discovered someone snuck an event-program into the hospital's computer system."

"Meaning?"

Something in Hayden's expression lit a little spark of hope inside Cam.

"Event programming means that when something happens, it triggers another, which triggers another, etc," Hayden explained.

"Like a Rube Goldberg machine?" Cam questioned.

"Similar," Hayden agreed. "It's like a domino effect … but let me show you."

He grabbed a couple of whiteboard markers and drew a large rectangle in the center of the board. Inside, he drew several small squares. Then, on the outside of the large rectangle, he drew four sets, each containing a square, a circle, and a triangle.

"Okay." Hayden pointed to the larger rectangle in the center and, in full academic mode, continued, "This is the hospital. Its computer system is a large mainframe capable of running many programs simultaneously."

Hayden then drew a set of arrows that formed a circle around all the squares within the big rectangle. "The event-program was circling inside the network, waiting."

"Waiting for what?" Cam studied the drawing, and then, as if a light clicked on, he answered, "The passwords."

"Seems so," Hayden replied.

"So, you broke into the mainframe, added those passwords we gave you, and," Cam made quotation marks with his fingers, "an event was triggered?"

"That's what I'm saying." Hayden drew a quick stick figure above the large rectangle. "I broke into the mainframe and hit the program, asking for passwords. Entered those, expecting to be sent deeper into the mainframe—"

"However, those passwords kicked you somewhere else." Sadie indicated one of the smaller squares outside of the large rectangle.

"Yeah." Hayden pointed to the same square as Sadie. "The ledgers were here. We traced them," he noted a circle, "to the bank. The question is, what's next?"

"Does the money stay in the bank," Sadie indicated the circle, "or go somewhere else?" Her finger landed on the triangle. "You've only found one set of books, right?" When Hayden nodded, she continued, "Then why do you have these other three options?"

"Mr. Fowler used to say, *'Why program only one event when you can take on the whole party?'*"

"What did you just say?" Cam's attention was pulled from the diagram.

"Mr. Fowler," Hayden repeated. "My AP Computer teacher."

Cam's eyes darted to Jessie's. "Damn. That's Eden's older brother. You don't think...?"

"That Eden's involved in this?" Jessie questioned.

"Is there any way to determine how long the program has been waiting?" Cam wondered. He didn't like what he was thinking, but if Eden was involved...

"That doesn't explain the bank records," Sadie noted. "Those go back ten years or more."

"True." Cam paced across the floor and replayed the last few months with Eden. Her father was quite a bit older than her mother and had been married before. His conversations with Aaron Fowler had been brief. "Makes about as much sense as Catherine doing all this."

"When solving a mystery," Jessie added softly, "it's often right in front of your face."

"Now what?" Cam sighed.

"It's a tedious process," Hayden explained. "But I'm looking into several things. First, I'm trying to find where the money came from. Second, I'm trying to find out who set up the programming. I'm also trolling Catherine's computer."

"We're running out of time," Jessie murmured. "I have to leave in a month or so."

She'd told him about flying back to the Philippines the previous night. But she'd only be gone for six weeks. Cam tugged her into his arms and hugged her.

"If we can't be together, though…" she whispered.

"I'm not going to lose you, Princess." Cam couldn't entirely hide his fear. "We won't stop fighting."

"Promise?"

"I promise." He only hoped that was one promise he'd never have to break.

TWENTY

Calliope's Dress Shoppe
July 9
3:00 p.m.

Jessie ran her hand along the rack of colorful clothes. Since finding out about her 'surprise party,' she'd pinched herself several times. She'd spent twenty-three of her twenty-five birthdays with Cam, and he always made them special.

Which was why she convinced Molly to go shopping with her. She was hunting for an outfit to remind him that no matter what, he was always in her heart and on her mind.

When she was young, she loved her birthday. There was always a princess cake, with streamers and balloons scattered everywhere. Her favorite part, though, was the pink princess birthday crown she wore year after year.

As she grew older, the theme varied, but the sentiment remained. Everyone treated her like a princess—something that explained why she'd been so spoiled.

Her memories, though, always returned to her fourteenth birthday. It was the final birthday she'd spent with her parents and James. Additionally, it was also the first time Cam saw her as a girl.

That year, her birthday was mid-week. She knew they were up to something when her mom rushed her out of the house early in the day to go shopping with Cassie and Sadie. It was more suspicious when her dad hadn't gone to work, and her brothers were up before noon.

Then, as her mother backed out of their driveway, she heard a familiar but unexpected sound. She didn't have to look over her shoulder to know the Hunter family was heading to her house in their beat-up old truck. They were planning a surprise, and it had to be big.

While shopping, she thought about asking questions. She hadn't, though. Instead, she waited until her friends were dropped at home to ask.

"What's my birthday surprise, Mom?"

Ruth jerked the car wheel just a little too hard. "Birthday surprise? We went shopping, had lunch, and you and your friends spent a few hours at the beach. And," she glanced down at Jessie's bare stomach, "you got a new bikini."

"I did." Jessie lightly touched the emerald green bandeau top, still a little shocked her mother bought it for her. "I certainly don't look like a nerd in this."

Ruth laughed. "No, my darling daughter, you do not."

"But that doesn't answer my question. What could the Hunters, Dad, Dylan, and James be doing without us?"

"Picked up on that, did you?" Ruth laughed. "I'm surprised you haven't figured it out long before now."

Jessie thought back over the last few weeks, but nothing seemed out of place, "So, it's something you've been planning for a while?"

"Maybe," Ruth teased. "After all, you're not a little girl any longer."

"My room!" Jessie shrieked.

"Shh." Ruth placed her finger on her lips and winked. "You didn't hear anything from me."

As soon as the car rolled to a stop, Jessie yanked her seatbelt off and ran inside, her mother's "Wait for me so I can take pictures" trailing in her wake.

She raced up the stairs, the smell of paint growing stronger the closer she got to her room.

"Happy Birthday, sweet girl." Mary greeted her when she reached the top of the stairs. "I hope you like it."

"Thanks, Mary!" Not waiting for an invitation, Jessie raced into her bedroom.

The room was just like she told her mother she wanted. On the purple walls, posters of Michelle Kwan, Sasha Cohen, and Kelly Clarkson hung. Her stuffed animals were organized in one corner, and her new bedding made her feel grown up and not like a child.

"Oh, Cam! You helped, too?"

She twirled around twice, fighting the need to giggle with happiness. When, after a few minutes, Cam hadn't said anything, she glanced over her shoulder. He was standing in front of the window, staring at her, but his expression was unlike any other time.

His eyes grew wide and raked down her body, causing. Jessie's thoughts to scatter and goosebumps to dance along her skin. Cam's stare made her feel pretty, sexy, powerful, and very female.

⚯

CAM'S GAZE SLID DOWN JESSIE'S BODY, FROM HER EMERALD GREEN bikini top to her bare midriff and low-riding denim shorts, only to return to her top.

'She has ... boobs' bounced around in his head at the same time his adolescent body stood up and took notice.

"Did you help paint?" Jessie brushed her hand across his cheek. "Purple looks good on you."

His face tingled from where she'd touched him, but he couldn't get his brain and mouth to connect.

'This is Jessie,' he kept trying to tell his body, but then 'She has boobs!' would roll around again.

"How do you like it, Jessie?" His mother's knowing eyes took everything in before he could turn away. "Ruth is on her way with her camera."

Cam glanced at his mother and then at the packaging he held. "I, I," he swallowed and tried again. "I'll just go throw this away." Then he rushed out the door.

The memory of feeling like he'd been punched in the gut when he saw her that day was just as fresh as if it had happened yesterday.

Then again, Jessie took his breath away whenever he looked at her. He was counting the days until he could tell the whole world.

A door slammed somewhere in the house, reminding him he'd been lost in the past for too long. He closed the ring box he was holding and set it on his nightstand, along with his proposal plans. Then, with a last look in the mirror, he headed to Sally's.

When he arrived, the diner looked the same as any other Friday night, except for the **Closed for a Private Event** sign on the door. The tables were removed for dancing, and the counter was lined with food. Multicolored spotlights, balloons, and streamers floated everywhere. It no longer resembled just a diner but a party place fit for his princess.

The party was small with only a few select people invited. Also, Eden was in Rhode Island helping her friend Abby with wedding plans, meaning he was a free man.

That realization added an extra bounce to his step. It also earned him more than his share of gripes whenever he got in the way.

"You need to relax," Ben scolded him when Sadie repeatedly growled.

"I know," Cam sighed. "I'm just looking forward to spending an evening with friends."

"And not having to walk that fine line," Ben added.

"You said it."

The week had been tough. He'd taken Eden on a few 'dates,' making him more aware than ever of Jessie's conditions. He knew how his princess felt about the entire ordeal. Had even experienced those same feelings when he'd learned she spent time with Tyler. Their condition lists were growing, and until everything was over, he couldn't see that changing anytime soon.

"You're okay with Tyler being here?" Ben gave a subtle nod toward the door.

Cam glanced over in time to see Sadie hug Tyler, not surprised when Gray was hovering close by. "Yeah. As long as he stays away from my girl, I'm okay with him."

"Which one?" Ben laughed.

Cam swallowed his response when someone shouted, "Everyone, be quiet! Jessie's here."

The door opened, Jessie stepped in, and Cam's eyes immediately locked with hers. He knew he should probably look away, but he couldn't. That connection between them wouldn't allow it.

Her long-sleeved, emerald green top was the same color as her bikini all those years ago. Instead of denim shorts, she wore a tiny black skirt showcasing her legs. How was he expected to stay away from her?

When the song, *I Knew I Loved You* began, Cam took her into his arms, encountering nothing but skin. "You're trying to kill me, right?"

"Moi?" Jessie's turquoise eyes glittered under the colored lights. "But look at you," she ran her hand across his shoulder, "purple looks good on you."

"You always look beautiful, Princess." His voice dropped an octave, "However, there's just something about you in this color of green..."

"I bought it for you."

"And I thank you for it." Cam pressed her hips closer, making it a struggle for his body to behave. Engaging in a bit of frottage with Jessie wasn't something new. With her, he was used to having one foot in heaven and the other in hell.

Sally's Diner
July 9
7:30 p.m.

JESSIE BURROWED HER NOSE AGAINST CAM'S THROAT, AND A shiver raced up her spine. Every time he rubbed against her, and she could feel his body's reaction, her insides jumped up and screamed, *Here I am! Here I am!*

"The party wasn't a surprise, was it?" His gentle question broke the bubble threatening to surround them.

"How did you know?"

"Come on, Princess." Cam glanced down and then right back up. "I know this isn't your usual Sally's wear."

"True," she laughed. "And you're right. I tricked Molly into spilling."

"Poor Molly. I'm surprised she didn't catch on. I mean, she does teach first grade."

His teasing tone had Jessie automatically sticking her tongue out. Desire flashed in Cam's eyes, making her realize what she'd done. Later, they promised. Thankfully, the song ended before she could embarrass herself, and Cam left her with Sadie.

"Happy Birthday, Jess!" Sadie hugged her. "You're shaking. Are you okay?"

"I will be." Jessie took several deep breaths. "I think my outfit backfired, that's all."

Sadie stepped back. "Well, if it's any consolation, Cam's wrecked too. I wouldn't be surprised if he isn't looking for a way to climb into Sally's freezer."

"Thanks." Jessie laughed. "That image helped."

"Hey, what are best friends for?" Sadie grinned. "Let's mingle."

It was a struggle for Jessie to keep her focus on Sadie or the person she was talking to. If she didn't, she unconsciously searched for Cam. Then, just like when they were kids, the words *'Run to him'* played loudly in her head.

"Come." Dylan drew her onto the dance floor.

"Afraid I might get myself in trouble?"

"Not you," Dylan chuckled. "Cam."

"Cam?" Jessie glanced around until she found him dancing with Molly. "What did he do?"

"His feelings for you are written all over his face," Dylan whispered. "I just want you two to be careful."

"I'm sorry." Jessie's head dropped against Dylan's chest. "I probably should have put a stop to the party. It's just..."

"The heart wants what the heart wants," Dylan murmured.

"And you know something about that, don't you?"

Dylan's face turned red. "Why do you think I stepped in?"

"So, I should thank you for saving us?"

Before Dylan could respond, the diner door opened, and several people entered. "It's Tia," Jessie grinned. "And... Her voice faded, and an uncomfortable feeling worked its way through her system.

"Do you want me to get rid of her?" Dylan growled.

Jessie wanted to say yes. However, if she did, it might cause more issues than keeping quiet.

"Not unless there's a problem. Just keep Cam away from her."

"Okay. Be careful."

"Yes, Dad," Jessie giggled. "I'm always careful."

As she walked away, she heard him mutter, *"Except when it comes to Cam,"* but continued toward her high school friend with determined steps.

"Jessie!" Tia Patterson hugged her. "I'm so sorry about Catherine. She showed up with Belle, and I didn't know how to get rid of her."

"That's okay." Jessie watched Catherine and Belle take drinks, then melt into a corner. "Dylan is married to Molly, so it doesn't matter."

"If you say so," Tia hummed.

"I'm fine," Jessie assured her. "What are you doing these days?"

"Just managing The Beachside Inn." Tia shrugged as if to say, nothing much.

"Nana Patterson retired?"

As soon as she said the words, Tia's expression said the news wasn't good.

"I wish," Tia's lower lip trembled. "It's only been a few months, but I still miss her."

"I remember her brownies," Jessie smiled. "Remember when we..." Her voice faded when she realized she'd lost her audience, and not wanting to be rude, she introduced Tyler.

"Do you mind if I steal Tia for a dance, Jess?"

"That's not up to me." Jessie glanced at Tia and realized it was a moot point. "Have fun, you two."

She went looking for Sadie but was waylaid by Hayden. "I think I found something."

"Really? What?"

"I've been watching for abnormal activity, and something pinged today. If there's more, I'll get a signal and disappear."

"If I don't see you," Jessie murmured. "That's a good thing?"

"That's a good thing," he nodded.

"Is it with—?"

"Catherine," Hayden interrupted. "Miss Richards, what do you think of the party?"

Jessie's knees almost gave out before she could make an excuse and leave. There was no way she could make small talk with that group.

Sally's Diner
July 9
9:30 p.m.

Cam watched Hayden come back into the main room with Catherine and Belle.

"What the hell?" he muttered when he realized Jessie wasn't with them.

"You can't," Gray hissed. "Let Sadie check on her. We have other problems right now."

"What?" Cam couldn't imagine anything more pressing than Jessie, and then Gray nodded toward the door. "Did you...?"

"Invite them?" Gray shook his head. "No. But here they come."

"Can tonight get any worse?" Cam caught sight of another new arrival. "Well, damn!"

"Cameron," Mary hugged him. "It's so good to see you. Where's Jessie?"

"Mom, Dad," Cam gave his brother a look he hoped screamed, *'Help!'* "I thought you were staying in Florida."

"We were," Clint gave Mary an indulgent smile. "But your mother..."

"I just had to see my girl," Mary exclaimed. "Where are you hiding her?"

"I..."

"Cameron!" Eden, the other uninvited guest, threw her arms around his neck. "I missed you."

Every coherent thought fled as he disentangled Eden's arms. "You're supposed to be in Rhode Island," he retorted.

"Oh, we finished everything early," she leaned in as if expecting a kiss, "and I just had to be here to wish Jessie happy birthday."

"That's uh, well, nice," Cam stammered, thankful when Tyler happened by. "Could you please entertain the lovely Eden while Gray and I get our parents settled?"

"Mary? Clint?" Jessie's excited tone was the only thing that could have calmed him right then. "You're here!"

"Happy Birthday, sweet girl." Mary grabbed onto Jessie as if she was a lifeline. "Oh, how I've missed you."

When Jessie broke down in his mother's arms, Cam exchanged concerned looks with Gray. His mother would not let things go.

"Have you been keeping my boy in line?" Mary hugged Jessie with one arm and slipped the other around Cam. "He's missed you so much. Do you know, I've prayed daily for you to come home ... where you belong?"

The look on Jessie's face screamed, *'Help.'* He just wasn't sure what to do.

"I've loved being home," she sighed. "I didn't realize how much I'd missed it until I arrived."

Jessie glanced in his direction, and Cam fought not to get lost in her turquoise eyes. It was as if his heart was reaching for hers, and it took every ounce of his strength not to tug her into his arms.

"Dad, why don't you dance with," Cam caught himself before he gave away too much, "Jess?"

"Come on, Princess." Clint's expression said he had questions. "Dance with this old man."

"Do you have something to say, Cameron Clint Hunter?" Mary addressed the elephant.

When you're twenty-eight, and the evoking of your middle name makes your knees quake, it isn't good.

Cam led his mom onto the dance floor. "Welcome home. We've missed you."

"Nice try," Mary glanced toward where Clint had Jessie laughing. "You might as well say it. I'll find out, eventually."

Not if I have anything to do with it. "Mom," he whispered. "Things are complicated with Jess."

Mary's brown eyes dove into his. "Do you love her?"

"I," unerringly, his gaze found Jessie, and the thought he could lie flew away. "More than life itself. But ... I'm with Eden tonight. You have to trust me."

"Oh, Cam," she sighed. "What have you gotten involved in?"

"What makes you think...?" Her lifted eyebrow had his words fading

"Switch partners?" Clint smoothly traded Jessie for his mother.

Jessie's hand settled on his shoulder, and her thumb brushed the side of his neck. "Are you okay?"

"Better with you in my arms." Cam pulled her a little closer. "What about you? Tell me about earlier."

"It was nothing much," she replied. However, something told him she only gave him part of the story. "Hayden was just telling me something."

"About the case?" Cam looked around the room but couldn't see the boy anywhere. "Where'd he go?"

❦

"He's gone?" Jessie's heart sped up, and that little kernel of hope sparked to life.

"I don't see him, why?"

"Hayden thinks he found something. He said if he left, it was a good thing." Jessie slowly scanned the room until the sight of an uninvited guest stopped her. "Why is your girlfriend here?"

Cam dropped his head against hers. "Eden said she came back to wish you a happy birthday."

"Ha!" Jessie snorted. "Eden's trying to protect her property ... you."

"People are not possessions, Princess." He tossed her words back.

"You don't belong to me?" she asked innocently.

His eyes twinkled, his dimples peeked out, and his lips whispered across the rim of her ear. "I belong to you, just as you belong to me," he promised in a husky voice.

"Just so you remember that." Jessie wanted to say more, but the song ended, and Eden appeared.

"Happy Birthday, Jessie." Eden linked her arm through Cam's. "This is a great party."

While there was a territorial glint in Eden's eyes, Jessie couldn't see anything vindictive.

"Thank you."

Except she couldn't stay and make small talk. If she did, the temptation to claim Cam as her own wouldn't be easy to ignore. That had her excusing herself and starting across the room. As she did, she could feel the heat from Cam's stare. It woke her nerve endings and caused them to tingle.

Jessie tried to return her attention to the party. But the wild feeling inside refused to settle. Especially when she felt her every move was being watched. She ducked into the ladies' room and locked the door, hoping for a small respite.

Even that didn't last long, though, when Sadie knocked. "Are you okay?"

Jessie pushed open the door and stepped out. "I'm fine."

"Cam said Hayden found something," Sadie whispered. "What?"

"I don't know," Jessie shrugged. "He said if there were signs of movement, he'd leave."

When they thought they heard someone coming, Jessie waved her friend toward the main room. "Go on. I'll follow in a bit."

As soon as Sadie walked away, Jessie spotted the alley door. If only she could escape to Sonny's. Except she couldn't do that to her family. They'd done something special for her, and while she appreciated it, she only wanted one thing.

"However, a little cool air won't hurt." Jessie stepped outside, and a gust of wind whipped her hair around her head.

TWENTY-ONE

Sally's Diner
July 9
10:30 p.m.

When Sadie returned from the back alone, Cam's worry meter jumped up a notch. "You didn't find her?"

"I found her," Sadie replied. "But we thought someone was coming, so—"

"—She sent you out first?"

"She did," Sadie hummed. "Don't worry. Jessie said she'd be right out.

A shard of fear zipped through Cam. "Then where is she?" His eyes clashed with Gray's, the fact they'd been spied on still on their minds. "Shouldn't she be here by now?"

"I'm sure she's fine, Cam," Gray murmured. "There are extenuating circumstances as to why you can't keep watch on her all the time."

"Don't you think I'm aware of that?" Cam snapped.

"Calm down." Sadie placed a hand on his arm. "I'm sure Jessie just needed a little downtime. She probably went back into the bathroom."

Cam looked from Sadie to Gray and then back to Sadie, "You thought you heard someone coming?"

"Right." Sadie drew out the syllable longer than needed. "We were talking about Hayden."

"What's that boy done now?" Mary stepped off the dance floor into their circle.

"Hayden's getting excited about going away to college," Sadie jumped in

The look on his mother's face said she wasn't buying their attempts to side-track her. Which meant he'd do what he could do.

"I'm a little worried about Jessie," Cam admitted.

Mary studied him with dark eyes that saw way too much. "Is she okay?"

"I'm sure she's fine." Sadie waved her hand toward the room. "Jessie's probably hiding out for a little peace and quiet."

"And miss Y.M.C.A.?" Mary answered, tongue-in-cheek.

The response caused Cam to let go of the breath he was holding. His mother told them she'd forgo the questions ... at least temporarily.

"We're going to dance." Clint sent him, then Gray, a pointed look. "We won't be long."

"Get the feeling we're screwed?" Cam watched his parents for a few minutes. "Any second now, the questions are going to start."

"I feel like I got caught sneaking out of the house," Gray grumbled.

"Or helped yourself to dad's bourbon."

"That wasn't me," Gray chuckled. "It was Dylan."

"Watch it," Dylan warned. "You wouldn't want to spread rumors about the future Sheriff."

"Rumors?" Gray hummed. "Let's see. What about the time we...?"

Cam ignored Dylan's and Gray's attempts to one-up each other and went back to searching for Jessie. He was tempted to go looking for her. Except there was still the little complication of Eden and Catherine....

"Why is Catherine still here?" He nodded toward the back of the diner. "And what's going on between her and Belle?"

"Who cares," Dylan snapped. "Why Catherine thought it was okay to just barge into the party, I don't know."

"Catherine and Belle are arguing about something," Molly answered.

Dylan side-eyed his wife. "Why do you say that?"

She sent Dylan a look, causing Cam to bite his lip to keep from laughing.

"It's perfectly obvious. Look at how they're standing. Look at how their hands are positioned. Look at their angry expressions."

Cam had to admit there was something to what Molly had just explained. Especially when, a few seconds later, Catherine flounced across the floor and said something to Tia. Shortly afterward, she ran from the diner, with Belle not far behind.

"Well, that was interesting," Dylan quipped.

"Cameron," Eden materialized by his side. "I'm going to leave."

"Everything okay?" he felt obligated to ask.

"I'm just tired." Eden sighed. "I'll see you later." Then, she ran out the door.

For half a second, Cam wondered what had happened. However, his anxiousness over Jessie pushed everything else away and sent him on a search.

She wasn't in the back hallway, nor did he find her in the bathroom. When he pushed the stall doors open, and there was still no sign of her, his heart beat a little harder … a little faster.

He searched the kitchen and looked in Sally's office. Then he took the stairs to their work area. However, as soon as he hit the top step, he knew she wasn't up there. That was something he could feel.

"Hayden," Cam stuck his head in their office area, "have you seen Jessie?"

"I saw her earlier this evening. Why?"

"I can't find her and…"

Hayden frowned. "Do you want me to help look?"

Cam thought about it but then decided if Hayden was on the trail of something that could help them, it was more important.

"You keep working."

"Okay, let me know."

"Will do." Cam ran back downstairs and slid into the front room. "Jessie's missing!"

"We'll look at Sonny's." Dylan and Molly ran out the front door. Then Gray and Sadie left to check the parking lot.

"I'm sure she's fine." Mary squeezed his arm in a show of support. "Let me double-check in the bathroom. It's possible you just missed her."

Cam followed her into the hallway, and the way the wind whistled through a crack caused the hairs on the back of his neck to stand up. He glanced around and finally noticed the alley door wasn't completely closed. When he reached to shut it, something had him pushing instead, opening it wider. What he saw on the other side caused his heart to stop and a chill to race up his spine.

"I found her!"

Jessie was lying at the base of the stairs in a tangle of arms and legs. There was blood on one side of her face. Her stillness, though, scared him the most.

"Princess," he whispered. "Open your eyes for me."

"Cam!" Mary exclaimed. "What happened?"

"I don't know," Cam snapped. "But I'm not leaving her." He removed his polo shirt and applied the cotton to Jessie's wound.

"Cam..."

"Shush, Princess." He smoothed his other hand over her cheek. "You've got a nasty cut. We're taking you to the hospital."

"I'll go have your father bring the car around," Mary replied. "You'll be okay?"

"I'm fine, Mom. Just go." He readjusted the cloth and gave Jessie his full attention. "Can you hold this in place so I can carry you?"

Jessie laid her hand on his, then lifted the cloth slightly. "Your purple shirt is ruined."

"I can get another shirt. You, though," Cam picked her up, "there's only one of you."

"Cam."

"Just hold on," he whispered. "Just hold on to me."

Swan Harbor General
July 9
11:00 p.m.

Jessie dropped her head against Cam's shoulder. She wanted to focus on his bare chest and musky scent. However, her pounding head and spinning stomach kept pulling her attention to them.

"We'll be there shortly." Cam kissed the side of her head. "You scared me to death.

"Sorry." She swallowed the bile that threatened to rise. "It wasn't on purpose."

He chuckled, but he never stopped what he was doing. One minute, he was slowly smoothing his hand across her back. The next, he was massaging her muscles. His touch, though, was what mattered. Cam comforted her in a way no other person could.

"I'm okay," Jessie assured him. "But did someone call my brother? He might flip."

"Already taken care of," Mary tossed over the back seat. "Dylan will meet us at the hospital."

It wasn't long after that they arrived. When the car jerked to a stop, Jessie had to clamp her molars together to keep from throwing up.

"Let me get your door." Mary jumped from the car to help.

Cam kept his arms around her and turned toward the opened door. However, the touch of the cool breeze on her behind had her yelling, "Wait!"

Her panicked cry stopped Cam's movements, so he was half in, half out of the car. "What?"

"My skirt."

"What about it?"

"I don't think she wants to flash the entire hospital, Cam," Mary explained, coming to her rescue.

"Oh."

Jessie wanted to laugh at his sheepish reply but didn't have the energy. Thankfully, Cam got her inside with her dignity intact. Then, all she had to worry about was her spinning stomach.

While Jessie waited for the nurse, Mary disappeared, leaving her alone with Cam. He couldn't settle and paced around the room like a caged lion. The combination of his frenetic movements and the bright lights caused her head to pound harder. Finally, she gave in and let her eyes drift shut.

"Here, Cam," Mary returned and tossed him a scrub shirt, "put this on."

A few minutes later, the door opened again, and a nurse rushed in. "Hi, I'm Audrey. How are you feeling?"

"Like I was hit by a truck."

Jessie was poked and prodded for the next several hours, as they moved her from one department to another. With each new person she met, she complained about her head. However, they all said the same, *'You have a concussion and need to be watched. We can't give you anything because you have alcohol in your system.'*

That didn't help her head. Nor did it put her in a good frame of mind. Especially when she ended up being tucked into a hospital bed and not sent home as she wanted.

Cam hovered nearby and asked the same question repeatedly, "Are you comfortable?"

"Stop it," Jessie growled, irritated by the entire situation. "My head hurts, otherwise, I'm fine."

He brushed her hair back, then kissed her softly. "I wish I could crawl in next to you and hold you."

"Me too."

The door banged against the wall, and Dylan rushed in. "Are you okay?"

"It's just a little cut," Jessie explained. "I didn't even need stitches."

Dylan propped his hands on his hips, and his 'dad look' flashed across his face. "That's it?"

"That's it," Jessie began.

Then Cam jumped in to help. "She's telling you the truth, Dylan."

"Good." Dylan's smile relaxed. "Feel like answering a few questions?"

"Questions?"

"Yeah, like, what happened?"

"I cut my head," Jessie grumbled. "What else do you need to know?"

Dylan's look and vocal tone caused Jessie's heart to skip a few beats, increasing the intensity of her headache.

"Jessie," Cam's soft voice settled her, "why were you in the alley?"

She thought back to the last thing she remembered at Sally's. "It's no big deal. Between Catherine and Eden showing up, I needed some air."

"And that's when you opened the alley door?" asked Cam.

"Yeah. It was windy when I pushed the door open. Then, I stepped outside..." Jessie's voice faded as the rest of what she remembered made no sense.

"What happened then, Princess?" Cam prompted. "Did you fall? Hear or see anything ... anyone?

His question had her breath coming faster. She closed her eyes and tried to put herself back in the alley. "I heard something. It sounded like a shoe scraping. Then, somehow, I lost my balance and fell."

"Anything else?" Dylan pushed a little more. Except all that did was cause her head to pound again.

"No," Jessie rubbed her temple, "I need to stop thinking right now, though. My head hurts."

"Okay, Sis." Dylan kissed her on the forehead. "Mary's going to stay with you tonight."

"But..." Jessie looked to Cam for help.

"It's not a good idea, and you know it," Dylan reminded her. "In fact, he needs to leave ... now. Let's talk." He looked pointedly at Cam, then walked out, she was sure, expecting to be obeyed.

"I'll talk to him, Princess." Cam kissed her softly. "Maybe I can stay instead of my mom."

"You know that won't happen." Mary returned to the room from wherever she'd gone.

Cam winked, kissed her again, and whispered, "We'll see," before going to talk to Dylan.

❧

As soon as Cam walked out of Jessie's room, Dylan hauled him into an empty one. "Just what in the hell have you gotten my sister involved with?"

"What are you *talking* about?" Cam yanked his arm out of Dylan's hands. "You know exactly what we're working on."

Dylan stared at him for several seconds before stalking across the room. "Right. Jessie said there have been some developments, but she wouldn't tell me what."

"There have," Cam offered minimal information.

"Is there something I should know?" Dylan subtly changed the question.

"Just say it," Cam finally barked. "You're obviously tiptoeing around *something.*"

"Yeah, okay." Dylan ran his hand through his hair. "There was a piece of plastic pipe not far from where Jess was found. Rusty, my partner, is looking into it."

Cam's breath caught, and he had to grab hold of the closest thing to keep from running back into Jessie's room.

"Do you think someone was out there and hit her?"

"It can't be ruled out," Dylan admitted. "Now, *has* anything happened?"

"Someone was watching Jessie last week and then followed her away from Sally's," Cam explained. "We thought, maybe…"

"What?!" Dylan yelled. "Why are you just now saying something about this?"

"You know why," Cam sighed. "Jessie doesn't want you involved. We're still hopeful we can do this on our own."

"What have you found?" Dylan came back with.

There were a few ways Cam could answer that might get him in trouble. However, if the roles were reversed…

"Are you sure you want to know?"

"No," Dylan immediately answered. "But this is my sister."

"We've found a web of things that make no sense," Cam explained. "Unfortunately, none allow us to pin everything on Catherine."

"Well, damn."

"My thoughts exactly," Cam agreed. "Hayden was working on something earlier tonight, so I'm hopeful. In fact, I could use a ride back there. I want to give Jess her birthday gift."

"How long is this going to take?" Dylan asked. "I want my sister safe."

"And you don't think I want the same thing?" Cam blew out a frustrated breath. "You don't think it's killing me not to be with her every day? I love her, Dylan, and want — hell, have wanted to marry her for years. Having her here and not being with her is worse than when she was gone."

"The heart wants what the heart wants."

"It seems so." Cam hesitated a beat. "Now, about that ride."

"Fine, you can give her your gift." Dylan led the way out of the room. "But just so that you know, you're still not staying with her tonight."

Swan Harbor General
July 9
11:30 p.m.

JESSIE WOKE FROM A SHORT NAP AND FOUND MARY SITTING NEXT to her with questions in her eyes. "What do you want to know?"

"You can read me that well?"

"Maybe." Jessie shrugged. "Or maybe I've just been waiting for them."

The look on Mary's face grew melancholy. However, she didn't start talking right away. Instead, she moved to the window and stared out for several minutes.

"Tell me about the last two years," Mary surprised Jessie by asking. "When you left, Cameron was devastated."

Jessie ducked her head to hide her tears. She wasn't hearing anything new. However, that didn't lessen the pain.

"There were reasons," she paused, not knowing what else to say. "I'm sorry."

"Jess," Mary crossed the room and sat directly on the bed. I know some of your secrets. When you're ready, I'd like to hear the rest. For now, though, tell me about your work while you were away."

"I grew up." Jessie's laugh felt uncomfortable. "While there, I worked with children displaced by the Typhoon."

"That must have been tough."

"It was," Jessie murmured. "But those children needed me. They'd lost everything. Yet, a kind word, a gentle touch, or a smile brightened their day."

"Children are very resilient," Mary replied. "Just like you were. Am I right?"

"I see what you did there."

"You do?"

"You pulled the conversation back to my well-being." Jessie raised a brow. "Didn't you?"

"Guilty," Mary admitted. "Am I wrong, though?"

"No, you're not wrong." Jessie smiled. "You always told me behind every cloud, there was a little sun. It took a while, but you were right."

"I'm a mother." Mary grinned as if that was the answer to everything.

"When my parents and James were killed," Jessie went on. "I was fortunate. I had Dylan and your family–"

"We're your family, too," Mary interrupted. "Always have been... always will be."

"I told you I was lucky." Jessie blinked several times. "During my time in the Philippines, I learned the world didn't revolve around me. That to be truly happy, I needed to be strong enough to take an active part in my happiness."

"Is that what you're doing now?" Mary's expression said, *'I'll know if you lie.'*

"I'm trying."

"And Eden?" Mary tossed the other girl into the mix like a professional.

"You're quite good at that, aren't you?"

"What?" Mary's smile was innocent.

"Getting the information you're after," Jessie replied.

"I'm a mother of two boys," a corner of Mary's mouth lifted, and her eyes twinkled, "and a psychiatrist, so … yes. I usually get what I'm after."

Jessie was tempted to share the burden she'd carried for years. However, they were no longer just hers.

"Why aren't you mad at how I treated Cam?"

"I see what you did there."

"I learned from the best. You didn't answer the question, though."

"The heart wants what the heart wants," Mary murmured. "And your heart and Cam's have always wanted each other's. When it's time, you'll find your way."

"Because things happen in Swan Harbor when they're meant to happen?"

"Because love has its own timetable. Also," Mary's eyes twinkled, "because things happen when they're meant to happen."

"I hope you're right," Jessie whispered. "I love…"

The man of her dreams walked into the room, stealing her words and making her want so much.

⚜

"You love?" Cam prompted.

"I love ice cream." Jessie's eyes sparkled.

"And if I brought you some?" Cam strolled toward her. "What will you give me?"

He knew what he wanted, but with his mother in the room, would he get it? Or could he get his mom to give them a few?

"How about…?" Jessie glanced around the room, and finally, their eyes locked. "What do you want?"

Cam's heart picked up speed, his balls tingled, and he wanted. "Mom, will you give us fifteen minutes … please? I'd like to give Jessie her gift."

"Sure, honey," Mary whispered something in Jessie's ear, causing her cheeks to blush. "I'll be back in fifteen."

He waited until his mother had closed the door before sauntering close enough to touch. "What did she say to make you turn so red?"

"She told me to give you what you want. So ... Cam," Jessie's voice lowered, "what is it you want?"

"You, Princess." Cam cupped her jaw. "I just want you."

"That's it? There's nothing else?"

"What else is there?"

Jessie tapped her bottom lip like he'd been wont to do a time or two. "Come here."

Cam leaned close enough, and his mouth hovered over hers. He could feel her breath every time she exhaled. It took all of his willpower not to dive in. "Here?"

"Closer."

He hesitated a beat and then another. However, he couldn't resist and locked their lips together.

She moaned in approval, giving him the opening he needed. Their tongues danced, lighting the fire that was never completely dormant when it came to her. The hotter the kiss grew, the faster his head spun, the more his heart raced, and the harder his... All he wanted was to climb into the bed and never let her go.

"Sorry about that." Cam backed up several steps. "There are some things that shouldn't happen in a hospital."

The shell-shocked expression she wore probably mirrored his own.

"Rain check?"

"Oh, Princess," Cam sighed.

Instead of taking that line of conversation where he wanted, he held the ice cream he'd brought up with one hand and her birthday gift with the other. "Your choice."

"How about I open the gift," she smiled, "and we share the ice cream?"

"A woman after my heart," he quipped.

"I thought I already had your heart."

"Always." Cam handed her the flat box and waited for her to unwrap her gift. She wasn't any quicker opening gifts at twenty-six than she'd been at nineteen. "Just rip it open."

Her grin was mischievous, as she knew exactly what she was doing to him. His heart sank to the pit of his stomach, and his hands closed into fists until ... finally.

"Oh, Cam." Jessie's turquoise eyes met his. "How could you?"

Cam took the box and gently removed the silver bracelet. "How could I not? It's us." He pointed to the three hearts, a larger silver one, rimming a gold one, and inside of those, a diamond-encrusted, solid one. "Three hearts, representing our love yesterday, today and tomorrow."

"It's beautiful." She held her arm aloft, and he fastened it for her. "Thank you. Now, come here."

He kissed her, but as much as he wanted to sink into her, he tempered his response. *Soon. Very soon.*

"Ice cream?"

Jessie's sigh was just as long-suffering as he felt. She took a bite and swirled her tongue around the spoon, giving him ideas he should not be having with his mother on the way back.

"You're not behaving, Princess."

"No?"

"No." Cam lowered his voice. "I told you there were —"

Jessie shoved a spoonful of ice cream in his mouth, effectively shutting him up. However, he hadn't given up hope that someday...

TWENTY-TWO

Sally's Diner
July 12
12:30 p.m.

ONCE JESSIE RETURNED HOME FROM THE HOSPITAL WEARING HER new bracelet, she thought she'd be riding a high. Instead, just the opposite seemed to occur. Her focus was gone, and her insides refused to settle. Since she couldn't be with Cam, she grabbed her skates and drove to Sonny's.

The ice, the sounds, her movements — those were familiar. Yet, no matter how many times she circled the rink, her thoughts refused to settle. It reminded her of when she'd first arrived in Swan Harbor.

She finally ended up at Sally's, ordered a plate of fries, a strawberry milkshake, and mulled. That was when she finally admitted what was going on. There was too much uncertainty surrounding her. Much of which she had no control over.

"Jessie?"

"Hi, Mary."

"Am I late?" Mary slid into the booth and nodded toward the half-eaten plate of fries. "I thought I was going to be early."

"No, you're fine." Jessie pushed the plate away. "It's just been one of those—"

"Abby, where were you?"

Jessie glanced up in time to see several girls converge on a booth behind Mary. When she recognized them as the friends Eden and Cam had been with at Randy's, her stomach churned.

"Did you hear?" one of the girls asked. "Cameron will be so surprised!"

"My Cam?" Jessie mouthed.

Mary shrugged as the girls continued.

"What did Eden do?" asked Abby.

"Oh my gosh," another girl cried. "It's so..." she drew out the vowel, "*romantic*. We're picking up something for her."

As one, they moved to the counter, retrieved a large basket of food, and, in a giggling group, disappeared out the door.

Mary laid a motherly hand on Jessie's. "What's going on, sweet girl?"

"What do you mean?"

"Okay," Mary backed away. "What's got you so down?"

"I'm not ready to leave."

"Are you worried about Eden?"

"Out of sight, out of mind," Jessie quipped.

"Oh, Jessie," Mary sighed. "Remember what I've always said."

"The heart wants what the heart wants."

"And my son's heart recognized your heart as its mate long ago," Mary replied in a husky voice.

"What?"

"It was your fourteenth birthday," Mary began. "Your mother planned that day for weeks."

"I wondered how she kept it a secret," Jessie laughed. "I didn't think she'd paid attention."

"Oh, she paid attention. Ruth worried everything wouldn't go as planned."

"How did you convince the boys to help?"

"Bribery. What else?" Mary chuckled. "Except Cameron. He willingly volunteered."

"Cam was still there when I returned from the shopping trip. The way he looked at me that day was..."

"Like a man whose heart had just found its mate," Mary circled back to her earlier comment.

"He had purple paint on his cheek," Jessie whispered. "Just like the shirt he wore at my party."

"I'm sure that was on purpose."

"You think?"

"I know." Mary tapped her new bracelet. "Try not to worry about Eden and Cameron. You hold his heart."

"I'll try. It's just…" Her phone rang, throwing off her thoughts. The possibility Cam had called had her listening to her voicemail.

"Jessie, what is it?"

"They canceled my flight."

"Does that mean you don't have to go?"

"No," Jessie glanced at the text she'd just received. "They put me on tonight's red-eye."

"Cameron will want to see you before you leave."

Jessie had to bite her tongue to keep from saying, *'If he's not out with Eden.'* "I want to see him too. I'll try to call him after I finish packing."

"He was meeting with a friend of yours today." Mary frowned. "I think he said his name was Tyler."

"Cam's designing Tyler's club," Jessie explained. "It's going to be opposite the Spanish galleon on the pier."

"Oh," Mary smiled. "I wondered what would go there."

"Cam and Gray have big plans for the pier, don't they?"

"They got that from their father," Mary laughed. "Don't get them started on it, especially if you're in a hurry."

"Speaking of…"

"Cam won't be happy if he misses you."

"Hopefully, he won't. I guess I'll have to skip lunch. I'll see you when I get back."

"Just remember, Jessie. Cam's heart has chosen.

"Thanks, Mary. I'll see you later.

Where was Cam, though? And would she see *him* later?

Lover's Cove
July 12
6:30 p.m.

As soon as Cam was parked, he read the note one more time,

> Cameron,
> Meet me at Lover's Cave tonight at 6:30. It's time we make all our dreams come true.
> Your True Love

He couldn't help but think there was something off about the note. Jessie was the only person he'd ever invited to Lover's Cave, and that was the night she'd left. But if she'd written the note, why hadn't she signed it, princess?

Lover's Cave's legend stated if a couple made love there, they'd be betrothed before the year's end. He'd always planned on proposing to Jessie in this little romantic spot. Why, he wasn't sure. Somehow, he felt if he did, their union would be blessed. And since the road to their happily ever after hadn't been smooth, they needed all the help they could get.

Cam hurried around the large boulders guarding the entrance and was greeted by a faint glow.

"Jessie."

When he stepped into the cave, several things registered at once.

Candles had been strategically placed, just like he'd written on his list.

There was a basket from Sally's, with a bottle of champagne chilling nearby, just like he'd written on his list.

The cave was also alive with music. If he had to guess, the music playing was also on his list.

Except, while the decorations didn't trigger an alert. The person waiting for him in the center of the cave certainly did. A huge warning sign in his head started flashing '*mayday, mayday.*'

She was wearing nothing but a bright green bow.

She was holding a diamond ring.

Except, she wasn't Jessie!

"Eden!" he snapped. "Put some clothes on!"

Cam tossed a blanket in her direction, then quickly turned away and waited for her to dress.

"I'm covered," Eden replied sullenly.

He turned back to face her, pleased to see she was covered. "What's going on here?"

"Gee, Cameron," she retorted, her little spark of temper surprising him. "Can't you tell?"

"But..." It took a few minutes to gather his thoughts enough to know where to start.

"When have I ever given you any indication I would propose? *And,* how did you find the ring and my list?"

"I thought you loved me," Eden snapped. "I'll admit, I was slightly concerned when I heard Jessie was returning to town. Except, when you saw her—*you* kissed *me. You* invited *me* to the festivities *and* the wedding. Then, when I caught the bouquet, I *thought* you wanted *me.*"

"I told you at Randy's the other night we weren't there yet," Cam reminded her. "Didn't you hear what I said?"

"Yeah," she shrugged, "but I thought you wanted to surprise me. After all, this ring is like the ones I showed you at Joanne's."

Cam's phone buzzed, but he decided everything needed to be out in the open. "Eden, I take full responsibility for behaving like a jerk." He hesitated for a heartbeat, trying to decide how much to say.

"What's the matter, Cameron? Cat got your tongue?"

"I shouldn't have acted like I did after Jessie came home," he admitted. "I was running from the truth."

"Jessie?"

"Yeah."

"And this ring?"

"I bought it for Jessie two years ago."

Eden's breath hitched. "Two years ago?"

"Yeah."

"Jessie still loves you."

"What?"

"Jessie still loves you."

"I know that, but how do you?"

"I overheard it at the party the other night."

"Who?" Cam fired back. "When?"

"Catherine," Eden replied, "and her friend that works at the library."

"Belle?"

"I guess." She glanced away, and an embarrassed look crossed her face. "I was getting a drink, and they were in the hallway. I didn't know who was talking until they returned to the front room."

"What did they say?"

"One said, '*Wait, I thought they were broken up.*' Then the other said, '*I don't think so. Have you seen how they look at each other?*'"

Catherine was watching them all evening, he realized. Was she also responsible for Jessie being hurt?

"I'm sorry, I wasn't honest," he opted for partial truth. "I've tried to stay away from her."

"I thought Jessie was coming to meet you the other morning at Sally's," Eden told him. "But then I saw her get into Ben's car."

"You were spying on us?"

"No," she quickly denied. "I'd just finished having breakfast with my father, and there you were."

Cam wanted to ask if she'd followed Ben and Jessie but didn't want to sound too paranoid.

"And the ring and list, Eden?" he prodded. "How did you get those?"

"I dropped by your house to give you back your sweater. Gray let me in, and there they were."

"On my nightstand," he cried. "Why'd you go up to my bedroom, anyway?"

"I don't know. I just..."

"Where's the list?"

"I'll get it."

While Eden got the list, Cam checked to see who'd called. Knowing it was Jessie had him wanting to grab his things and run. However, his mama had raised him better than that.

"Here." She shoved the paper toward him. Except when he took it, he couldn't help but feel like it was tainted.

"Thank you. Do you need help cleaning this stuff?"

"No. I can do it." Eden's lower lip trembled, making him feel like a bigger heel.

"I really am sorry."

"Yeah, me too."

He had his finger ready to replay Jessie's message before he'd even reached his car.

"Cam, it's me. Uh, Jessie. I know I'm supposed to leave tomorrow, but my flight was canceled, and they put me on one tonight."

Tonight? No!

"I'm on the red-eye to San Francisco out of Logan International, so I'm leaving now. I'll, I guess I'll see you in August."

Cam checked the time and, without thinking, jumped in his car and revved the engine. There was no way he was waiting six weeks to see her.

Swan Harbor
July 12
6:45 p.m.

JESSIE LOADED HER SUITCASE AND SLAMMED THE TRUNK. SHE'D spent the last few hours watching the new parents play with their puppy, Wilby. Except, she couldn't wait any longer. It was too hard ... too lonely.

"I'd better go."

"It's not even 7:00 p.m.," Dylan pointed out. "You still have several hours before you need to be at the airport."

"I know," Jessie sighed. "It's just..."

"You didn't get to talk to Cameron?"

"He had a date," she replied, not trying to hide the bitterness in her voice.

"I'm sorry, sis. I know this has been hard on you."

"Stop," Jessie interrupted, not wanting her brother to shoulder the blame. "You just suggested what you thought was right. It still didn't make it any easier. How would you like watching Molly go out with some other guy?"

"Not going to happen," he growled.

"Maybe not," Jessie conceded. "It just sucks to be kept apart from the person you love. Especially if it isn't by your choice."

"I get that."

"Of course," Jessie went on with a smile. "When Catherine caught you and Molly, you just used the heart wants excuse. I bet that sounded quite sincere with you in the buff."

Dylan blushed, making her laugh. "I'm sorry, I shouldn't tease you."

"It's not very nice," he agreed. Then swiftly changed the subject. "You'll be back in six weeks?"

"That's the plan."

With one last hug, Jessie climbed into the car and backed out. She thought about driving past Cam's house. Thought about driving past the pier. Even thought about driving through town, thinking maybe she'd be able to find where Eden had planned his surprise, which was so … romantic.

Instead, she turned in the direction of the Cove Highway loop. It would take her the long way around town and not through it, decreasing the chances she'd spot Cam and Eden in a lip lock.

Her heart felt heavy when she reached where the Cove loop joined with Cove Highway. Even more so when she drove past the sign **Leaving Swan Harbor**. Jessie's vision grew blurry, and she gripped the steering wheel tightly, determined not to fall apart.

She rounded the bend where the forked roads met, and a flash in her rearview mirror caught her eye. A car from the sheriff's department, with its lights flashing and horn blaring, was closing in fast.

Jessie pulled to the side of the road and climbed from her car just as the cruiser slid to a stop behind her. "What happened?" she yelled, its headlights blinding her.

A car door opened, slammed, and a tall frame appeared. "Going somewhere, Princess?" Cam strolled closer. "You didn't even say goodbye."

Hearing his voice caused Jessie's heart to race, and the look on his face made her knees weak. However, she didn't plan on making things easy for him after what he'd put her through—whether intentionally or not.

"I wasn't the one who was busy," she exclaimed. "Did you have a good time with your girlfriend?"

❧

Cove Highway
July 12
7:30 p.m.

Cam's lips twitched. "Heard about that, did you?"

"I think the entire town heard about it. 'It's sooo," Jessie mimicked the girl's exaggerated speech, "'romantic. So was it?"

He took several more steps toward her but stopped a foot away. "If that's true, then I wonder what they're saying now?"

"Why? What happened?"

Cam pulled the ring out of his pocket. When Jessie's eyes widened, and the pulse at the base of her throat sped up, a little zip of electricity raced through him. "Eden found this and assumed it was for her."

"Oh."

"Yes, oh. She set up a proposal, using my list—"

"Wait," Jessie interrupted, "you have a list?"

"Princess." Cam took the last step, wrapped his hand around her waist, and tugged her hips against his. "I've been making a list for years."

"Oh." Her eyes kept darting to the ring and back to his.

"Don't worry," he assured her. "I didn't say yes."

"I should hope not." That princess voice of hers caused his balls to tingle, and before he could stop himself, he swooped in for a hard but very thorough kiss.

"Proposing to you on the side of the road wasn't on my list. Once all this mess is over, though, watch out."

"Are you sending a warning?" Jessie's hand slid up his chest to curl around his neck. "Or a promise?"

Her hot breath whispered across his lips, practically short-circuiting his brain. "Both."

The word was barely out of his mouth before his lips were on hers. Again and again, he dove back in, each kiss growing a little hotter, lasting a little longer.

Cam dug his fingers into her back muscles and tugged her hips into the cradle of his, showing her exactly what she did to him. She was his heart—always had been—always would be.

"It's killing me to let you go."

"It's killing me to go."

"We'll Skype?"

"I'd like that."

"Maybe we can…" Cam wiggled his brows suggestively.

"Cam!"

"Hey, you said not as long as you're living with Dylan and Molly," he reminded her. "You won't be living with them."

"No, but I do have a roommate," she pointed out.

"But do you have your own room," Cam nuzzled her temple, "and a door with a lock?"

Jessie ducked her head, and a slight blush crawled across her cheekbones. "Maybe."

"What would it take for me to raise that maybe to a definite?"

He kissed her again, but this time, their kiss was different. It was a kiss full of promises. A kiss to show her there was no need to worry.

"Can I come visit you in a few weeks?" Until he voiced it, he had no idea how much he wanted it to happen.

"Maybe," she teased. "We'll talk about it once I'm there."

"Can I drive you?" Cam offered just as his car was parked behind Dylan's cruiser.

"I wish," Jessie sighed. "However, I think you have some explaining to do."

Cam glanced over his shoulder to see Dylan strolling toward them. "You think?"

Jessie giggled. "Dylan looks like he has a few questions."

"Yes," Dylan retorted. "I do. Like why you had to steal my car to track down my sister?"

Cam considered and discarded several choice words. However, he chose the easiest: "It's all perfectly innocent."

Dylan side-eyed him, then kissed Jessie on the cheek. "Drive safely, Jess. Let me know when you arrive."

"Yes, Dad. Can you give us a few?"

When Dylan was gone, Cam hugged Jessie a little tighter. "I love you, Princess. Come back to me."

"I love you too." She smoothed her fingers over his cheek. "Don't forget me."

"Impossible."

Cam kissed her once more, then settled her in her rental car. When she drove off, she took a little piece of him with her. Slowly, he made his way back to where Dylan was leaning against his cruiser.

"What do you want to make this go away?"

Dylan's brows flew up. "You're trying to bribe an officer of the law?"

"Oh, no, no," Cam clarified. "I'm trying to bribe my future brother-in-law."

"Get in the car," Dylan thumbed over his shoulder, "*your* car. And give me my keys."

"They're in *your* car," Cam replied. "Thanks, Dylan. I'll talk to you later."

On the drive home, he rehearsed what he planned to say to Gray for allowing Eden into his room. If he hadn't, maybe that whole debacle could have been avoided.

Except you'd still be with Eden, his subconscious whispered. So, perhaps it had been one of those blessings in disguise.

Cam skipped into the house and tossed his keys on the table. He was happy, probably happier than he'd been for years. And even though Jessie wouldn't be back in Swan Harbor until the middle of August, they would communicate, and maybe...

"Is that you, Cameron?" his mother called from the living room.

He was tempted to make a wise-ass response, instead yelled, "I was just going to get a snack. Can I get you something?"

"Could you come in here for a minute first?" Mary pushed.

When he walked into the front room, and Gray was sitting across from his parents, several colorful words flew through his head. "What's up?"

"Your father and I have a few questions," she began.

"And we're expecting answers," Clint added.

"Sure, if I can," he prefaced, hoping that allowed him to hold back certain information.

"You can start by explaining these." Mary laid out the damning pictures.

"Then move on to this." Clint laid out the bank account printout.

"I'm sure Gray can explain these much better than I," Cam tossed his brother under the bus.

"Don't look at me." Gray held both hands up in surrender. "It was his girlfriend's secret."

"Jessie?" Mary murmured.

"Yeah, Mom," Cam admitted. "We recently found out Jessie left—and stayed away—to protect you ... and dad. We've been trying to find out who's doing this. We think perhaps, Catherine, but what does she have against you?"

His parents exchanged a look that seemed to be an entire conversation. "I can tell you why," Mary surprised him by saying. First, though, I need you to start at the beginning."

TWENTY-THREE

Hunter Construction, Inc.
August 20
10:00 a.m.

Cam propped his feet on the conference room table and thought about an earlier conversation with his mother. She had something on her mind. He hadn't figured out what when his father rushed into the room.

"You shouldn't be daydreaming at work," Clint teased.

"Sorry."

"Jessie?"

"No, mom."

"What's your mother done now?"

"I was hoping you could tell me," Cam grumbled.

Clint shrugged. "I didn't notice anything different." However, something about his father's tone had Cam paying closer attention. "You'll have to give me more information."

"I don't know how to explain it, except to say she's seemed different lately. Almost as if she has something on her mind ... or up her sleeve. You're saying you've not noticed anything?"

Clint's eyes twinkled. "What I've noticed is she wants her boys to be happy. Since Jessie left and Sadie returned to Augusta, you've both been quiet."

"I know that. But you're not planning to get in the middle of things, right?"

"Why would you think that?" Clint came back with, just a little too quickly.

"You said you would let Gray, Jessie, and me see things through," Cam reminded his father.

"Am I stopping you? Have I asked you how things are going?"

"Well, no," Cam hedged. "So, you're saying what exactly?"

"Just like I promised," Clint replied. "I'm not interfering with what *you* started. Nor am I asking you to stop."

He was up to something. However, getting his father to spill wasn't an easy task.

"Now, here's what I need." Clint circled back. "I'm looking for the Fisher proposal."

Cam pushed the file across the table. "Anything else?"

"How are the plans for the new French bakery coming?"

"They're done. Is that it?"

"You know…" Clint glanced around the room. "You boys should hire an office manager."

Cam's brows shot up, surprised his father had even brought up the subject. "Isn't that a dirty word, as far as you're concerned?

"This isn't about me," Clint replied. "It's about you and Gray and what you need. With all the work the pier project will bring, you need someone to keep you organized."

"It would make things easier."

"As much as I hate to admit this," Clint added. "It would make things easier for me, as well. Since I'm only in the office for certain projects, it would be nice if I didn't have to spend so much time looking for them."

"You're just used to someone picking up behind you," Cam teased. "It's a shame you couldn't talk Nancy into staying."

"That's what I get for retiring before I was ready. Nancy is now living the high life at Sunset Cliff Retirement Village."

"Would you and mom ever consider moving into a retirement facility like that?"

"Cameron!" Clint brushed his hand through his salt-and-pepper hair. "Just because there's snow on the roof doesn't mean there's not fire inside." He winked, then strolled from the room whistling.

Cam sat there for a few seconds, thinking there were some things children shouldn't have to hear.

❧

Above Sally's Diner

August 20
12:30 p.m.

JESSIE PARKED IN AN OUT-OF-THE-WAY SPOT NEXT TO SALLY'S AND bounded up the stairs two at a time. As far as everyone knew, she wasn't due back for three days. However, while she was away, she'd made a decision. She was done running. *This* time, she was going to confront the problems head-on. Her happily-ever-after with Cam awaited her, and she planned to fight for it.

When she reached the second floor, she took a deep breath and marched into the work area.

"Mary?" Jessie exclaimed. "What's, uh, what's going on?

Hayden smiled sympathetically. "She knows Jess." He angrily hit his knuckle against the board. "It's too late, though."

"Too late?" Jessie frowned. "What do you mean it's too late?"

"The money's gone," Hayden sighed.

"The money's gone? Are you sure?"

"Positive. And, all traces of the event-driven program have been wiped."

"How? When?"

"Before you left, I told you something was happening," Hayden began. "Remember?"

"Yes. What was it?"

He handed her a list. "Suddenly, several things happened at once. Money started disappearing from the bank account in Mary's name, only to appear in another. There were various amounts, and they occurred at random times. Sometimes, I could follow the money—other times, I couldn't."

"Do, do you think *whoever* opened those accounts is on to us?" Jessie waved toward the ledgers.

"I don't know," Hayden sighed. "Maybe the transfers are part of the event."

"Was there a pattern?"

"Pattern?" Hayden frowned. "I didn't see one."

"Why don't you show her what you found?" Mary prompted. "It helped me understand everything better."

Understand better? How had Mary found out, anyway?

"Remember these?" He pointed to the four sets of a square, a circle, and a triangle around the large rectangle.

"Those are the fake ledgers and the bank account in Mary's name," Jessie replied.

"Like I said," he continued, "the money from *'Mary's account'* started moving. Sometimes, it ended up in another account in the same bank." Hayden indicated the triangle in the first set. "Other times, it left that bank only to end up somewhere else."

"Somewhere else?" Jessie hummed. "I'm assuming that's what those other sets represent."

"That's right." Hayden indicated the three sets outside the large rectangle. "Money traveled into these four accounts and," he pointed to a square inside the rectangle, "into this one—"

"Wait!" Mary exclaimed. "That's inside the hospital. What kind of hospital account allows transfers from just anyone?"

"I think," Hayden hesitated, "it's the account used during the hospital wing fundraiser."

"But that was ten years ago! Why wasn't the account closed?" Mary frowned. "Has this been going on for all that time?"

"It fits the time frame," Jessie replied. "For both, when the pictures were taken, and the fake ledgers were created. As to why now? I guess because I came back."

"Did all of this happen at once?" Mary asked.

"It started ten years ago or so," he supplied. "Money would go into the account for a few months, stop, and then start again."

"Besides the fundraiser, what changed ten years ago that caused someone to come after me?" Mary questioned. "It doesn't fit."

Jessie knew there was a history between Mary, Clint, and Catherine's mother. Except, that hadn't happened ten years ago, more like twenty-five or more.

"It was when I moved to Boston," Jessie whispered. "If Catherine is behind it, maybe she thought it would help her get Dylan."

"It still doesn't make any sense, but go on," Mary continued. "What happened to the money once it was moved?"

Hayden drew a diamond on the edge of the board. "Money from those five accounts ended up here."

"Wouldn't it have been easier to worry about only one or two extra accounts?" Jessie murmured. "Or even send it directly from the account in Mary's name to the offsite one?"

"Easier, yes," Mary nodded. "But not as simple to hide."

"And even with five," Hayden went on, "they saw quite a bit of action."

"Saw?" Jessie repeated. "That's what you meant by the money being gone, right?"

"Yeah. If the money were local, I would have been able to track it."

"But because it's offsite," Jessie snapped, "it's 'gone.'"

"Yeah."

"Gone, where?" Mary asked.

"It's in the Cayman Islands," Hayden grumbled. "If you know someone who could break into those banks, well…"

For a second, Jessie thought she might throw up. "We were so close."

"I said the money is gone." Hayden's smile turned wicked. "I didn't say all hope was lost."

"No?" Jessie's breath caught. "Tell me."

"These accounts," Hayden indicated the four 'accounts' the money had flowed in and out of, "are in Catherine's name."

"Really? Are they really in Catherine's name?"

"Yeah." Hayden reached for a piece of paper. "In 1987, Brenda Smith opened the oldest account at Swan Harbor Trust. Then, eight years ago, Sharon Gold opened one at The People's Credit Union."

"Catherine's mother," Mary sighed.

"The other accounts were opened two and three years ago, respectively," Hayden continued. "One was opened at SHB by Ellen Weiss and the other at First Bank by Jan Atkins."

"Nothing like hiding in plain sight," Jessie muttered.

"You were the one who said the answer is often the easiest." Hayden grabbed two more files. "Also, I found Photoshop on Catherine's computer."

"Any chance there were copies of the photos on her computer?"

"No."

"But couldn't she have Photoshop on another computer?" Jessie pushed. "One at home, you couldn't get into."

"She could."

Jessie refused to give up. If she wanted to win, she needed proof Catherine was behind everything.

"So, let me see if I have this straight." Jessie used the board's visuals. "The money was transferred from Mary's account into four accounts, each in different banks. Those were in Catherine's name. As well as to an account inside the hospital?"

"Yes."

"And then to the account in the Cayman Islands, right?"

"Yes."

"So why can't we show all this to the police?"

"The easy reason," Hayden pointed out, "is because the accounts in Catherine's name are empty, and the event-driven program has been removed. There's no evidence."

"Are there other reasons?" Jessie wondered aloud.

"Because if you turned all this in, you'd have to tell where it came from," Mary stated. "Which would—"

"Get us in a lot of trouble," Jessie sighed, meaning it circled back to Dylan and why she hadn't wanted him involved.

"Some have more to lose than others," Mary murmured.

"I need to take back the power." With the words out in the open, a sense of peace washed over her. She had to confront the enemy head-on. If she did, she could save Dylan, Hayden, and the others, but her happy ending would be that much closer.

"Jessie, wait!" Mary called. "There are some things you need to know before confronting Catherine."

❧

Hunter Construction, Inc.

August 20

1:30 p.m.

CAM LEFT THE STACK OF FOLDERS ON HIS DESK AND WENT looking for Gray. With Jessie moving back home, he was anxious to start the search for an office manager. It would make life easier and decrease the hours he needed to spend in the office.

He hadn't been completely surprised when he learned why Catherine hated his family so much. Especially when he heard it involved her mother, Sharon Michaels-Gold.

Sharon married Richard Gold, an older man, when she was barely eighteen. They moved to Boston and quickly had Catherine. However, Sharon never enjoyed the limelight and soon returned to Swan Harbor.

In 1987, Clint hired Sharon as his office manager. She ran the office, leaving his father free to grow the business. Three years later, she made the mistake of thinking there was more between them, and all hell broke loose.

Sharon started leaving Clint notes, calling his house late at night, and dressing provocatively. That soon escalated into erasing phone messages, stuffing hotel receipts in his pockets, and making comments suggesting Mary was seeing other men.

When Mary found '*nude*' photos in Clint's briefcase, they confronted Sharon as a team. She was hospitalized, and Catherine was sent to her father in Boston. Catherine didn't see her mother again until she was eighteen and attending Swan Harbor University. He wasn't sure how it would end—just knew it was time.

Cam found Gray in his office, staring out the window. "Gray?"

"What?"

"Are you okay? You look tired."

"I am," Gray sighed. "I was just thinking about something."

"What?"

"After Jessie left, and you fell apart," Gray began. "I used to wonder how you could have allowed her to have so much control over your happiness."

"I'm sorry, Gray. I told you Sadie could—"

"Don't say it," Gray snapped.

The intensity in his brother's voice had Cam taking a step back. "Okay, then tell me what Sadie did."

"Besides, go back to Augusta?" Gray let go of a dry laugh. "Isn't that enough?"

After Jessie left Swan Harbor, Sadie returned to her job in Augusta. For the past six weeks, Gray drove to her apartment every Friday, returning home on Monday morning.

"It's Friday," Cam noted. "Aren't you usually on the road by this time?"

"Usually, yes."

"But not this week?"

"Sadie had to leave with her boss to do an audit."

"Away?" Cam's brows arched. "Overnight?"

"Apparently."

"When are you going to ask her to move home?"

"For what?" Gray barked. "She works for the top accounting firm in Augusta, lives in a fancy apartment, wears nice clothes, and drives an expensive sports car. What is there in Swan Harbor?"

"You." Gray's blue eyes clashed with his green. "Do you love her?"

"How can I love her?" Gray sighed. "We dated for three weeks before she left and six weeks long-distance."

"The heart wants what the heart wants."

"So I've been told," Gray murmured. "Do you need something?"

Cam thought about shooting off at the mouth but decided his brother was dealing with powerful emotions and got to the point. "We need to advertise for an office manager."

"Did dad—?"

"Yes. Let's make a list."

Swan Harbor General
August 20
2:30 p.m.

With the knowledge of why Catherine hated the Hunters,

JESSIE RUSHED INTO THE HOSPITAL. SHE WAS HALFWAY ACROSS the lobby when Mary caught up with her.

"You don't have to do this alone. Your family is right there with you."

"I know," Jessie replied. "And while Catherine's initial hate was toward you and Clint, I'm the one who made this mess. If I had trusted in Cam ... trusted in what we had—we wouldn't be in this situation."

"Okay, sweet girl," Mary whispered. "I'll wait right here."

"Thank you."

Jessie breezed into Catherine's office, locked the door behind her, and turned to face her '*dragon*.'

"Jessie?" Catherine's brows rose in question. "I didn't know you were back."

"Stop with the Miss Innocent act," Jessie snapped. "I know."

"Just what do you think you know?" Catherine asked curiously.

"I know what you've done to keep me away from Swan Harbor. What you've done to keep me from my happy ending."

"Jessie," Catherine began. "I—"

"Oh, stop it!" Jessie barked. "You know damn well what I'm talking about. The pictures, the fraud, the threats."

"Threats?" Catherine frowned. "What threats?"

"Yes, threats. Even after everything you've done to make my life miserable, I still have a hard time believing you could be so selfish."

"Selfish?" Catherine exclaimed. "How was I selfish? You wanted to train, and I gave you the opportunity. You should thank me."

"I worked hard and earned everything I was given. You, on the other hand, were way too manipulative just because you wanted Dylan. I find that rather pathetic."

Catherine let loose a dry laugh. "Whatever. It's over, and you look no worse for wear. I think we're done."

She turned her back, leaving Jessie feeling slightly unsettled. What was she missing? How could she get Catherine to stop denying her actions?

"You need proof?" She dropped the folders on Catherine's desk. "Well, here you go. Look at those and then try to deny you weren't responsible for everything.

Catherine glanced through each page, taking more time on some than others. Jessie kept waiting for her to boast, gloat, or something.

"Is that enough proof?"

"You think I sent these?" Catherine tapped the folders. "Is this it?"

While the question might have been odd, it fit Catherine's need to deny until she no longer could.

"I know you sent them. But that's not all."

"By all means." Catherine waved her hand over the pile of folders. "It's obvious you're not leaving until you've laid it all out. So, give it to me."

Jessie systematically retold the story, from the articles to the pictures, using the folders she'd brought as visuals.

"So, this was why you were looking for Mary's pictures? Did you find them?"

"Of course." Jessie hesitated. "You made copies and spent time on Photoshop."

"I didn't," Catherine denied.

"Then you must have found someone gullible enough to help." Jessie frowned. "Was it Belle? Eden? Or did daddy dearest find a flunky for you?"

"If I'd done this, I wouldn't need help," Catherine smirked.

Jessie filed that information away for later and dropped the pictures of her with Tyler.

"Looks like you weren't too lonely." Catherine grinned. "He's quite the catch."

"He's a friend," Jessie retorted. "I told you, I know it's you."

"Well, you need to do better than this." Catherine rested her interlocked fingers on the desk. "So far, you've got nothing."

"This isn't nothing." Jessie laid the printouts for the five accounts on the desk, each showing two hundred thousand dollars going in and out. "Looks like a nice bit of change. "

"What the hell?" Catherine tensed and immediately started flipping through the checking account printouts. "I don't see any money."

"True," Jessie hummed. "You know that, though, don't you? It's off in the Cayman Islands waiting."

"I guess it's vacation time."

"Why pretend ignorance?" Jessie frowned. "That's not like you to give someone else credit for your misdeeds."

"And what would my ultimate goal be?"

"To make the Hunters pay for how they treated your mom. To make me miserable because you think it's my fault you lost Dylan." Jessie shrugged. "Take your pick."

"What exactly do you want?" Catherine's voice had grown soft. "What will make you go away?"

"Just admit your part in this misery."

"That's all you want?" Catherine asked. "For me to admit my part in ensuring you were miserable?"

"Yes. Tell me why you would treat someone like this?"

Catherine's face morphed from confusion to vindictiveness, reminding Jessie of that afternoon she caught Dylan with Molly.

"Oh, come on," Catherine snapped. "Why wouldn't I? Look at you, perfect little Jessie, with her handsome brother. She loses her mommy, daddy, and duplicate brother, yet she still comes out on top."

"Don't say that!" Jessie screamed. "I was fourteen!"

"Well, la ti da," Catherine retorted. "I was five when your precious Mary and Clint attacked my mother. What do you have to say about that?"

"They confronted her. Her mind wasn't right, and she got sick. That's not my fault."

"Oh, right," Catherine hissed. "Nothing is Little Jessie the Princess's fault. You were supposed to fail in Boston. Yet you did fine. Then, your successes continued in college. But me? Did I get what I wanted?"

"The heart wants what the heart wants," Jessie murmured.

"And did yours get what it wants?" asked Catherine. "From where I'm sitting, you're still waiting to be rescued."

"Excuse me?" Jessie cried. "Where did that come from?"

"The whole town knows you've been mooning after Cameron for years," Catherine taunted. "But I don't see a ring on your finger. If you wanted to be together, nothing would keep you apart. Not even this mess you dropped on my desk."

"You're right," Jessie murmured. "I should have fought harder. But that's on me! That's my sin. Why did you find it necessary to go after Cam's family? Was hurting someone that important to you?"

"Yes! I wanted you and every bleeping member of the Hunter family to be miserable."

"How could you have been so vindictive?"

"You made it easy," Catherine snapped. "I just had to follow you to

Boston, then click, click, and was back in Swan Harbor before I was missed. Like I said, in a small town, if you listen, you learn things."

Jessie wanted to kick herself for letting down her guard because, sadly, what Catherine said rang true.

"You're a selfish, pathetic woman. As long as you hate yourself, you'll always be alone. The woman you are now is unlovable."

"Oh, I have plenty who love me."

"That's sex. You wouldn't know love if it hit you over the head. Leave my family alone, or we'll go to the police. That million dollars would be a bear to explain."

She rushed from Catherine's office, leaving a huge weight behind, and found Mary waiting, just as she'd promised.

"Are you okay?"

"I'm," Jessie paused. "I'm free—a little sad, mad, and every emotion in between."

"Why would you say that?" However, Mary's dark eyes said she understood—perhaps more than she did herself.

"Catherine admitted her part but also said I helped her."

"Because you didn't tell Cameron everything?" Mary guessed.

"Yeah. Stupid, huh?"

"Oh, sweet girl." Mary put a comforting arm around her shoulder as they walked toward the car. "I was young and in love once."

"Except you talked to Clint."

"Not at first," Mary admitted. "Then your mother had a few choice words for me, and well..."

"Really?" Jessie laughed. "I never knew that."

"There are many stories you've not heard," Mary grinned. "Now that you've slain the dragon, we have all the time in the world."

TWENTY-FOUR

Hunter Construction, Inc.
August 20
6:40 p.m.

CAM UPLOADED THE AD FOR THE OFFICE MANAGER AND NOTED A few things he wanted to deal with the following week. Then he shut down his computer and fought not to feel sorry for himself.

Sadie's plans had changed, and Gray raced to be with her. Then, his father left earlier than expected, leaving him alone ... with no reason to rush anywhere, especially home.

His cell buzzed, and Cam's heart ticked up a few beats when the screen flashed his princess's face.

"Is everything okay?"

"Fine, why?"

"You called on my cell," he murmured.

"I did." Jessie paused. "That's okay, though, right?

"You know it is. But what's going on, Jessie?"

"I have a surprise for you."

This time, it wasn't her princess voice that turned him on. That was the husky tenor, making him feel she had just promised him the world.

"Oh?" Cam hummed. "Does this mean we can finally—?"

"Cam!" she cut him off with a giggle. "Stop."

"Spoilsport."

"Well, if you don't want your surprise," she teased.

"I want it. I want it," Cam assured her. "I love surprises."

"You do?"

"I do," he whispered. "I especially love the kind that involves just you and me."

"Then I think you'll like this one," Jessie purred.

His blood rushed south. "Is clothing optional?"

"Maybe."

"Princess," he pleaded. "It's not nice getting a man all worked up when his girl is over eight thousand miles away. Especially if we can't—"

"Who said I'm eight thousand miles away?" she interrupted.

Cam's heart raced. Could she mean...?

"Jessie?"

"I'll send you a picture. You have twenty minutes."

By the time the text arrived, his hands were shaking so much he almost dropped his phone. Minutes later, he was on his way to his destination.

The parking lot closest to Lover's Cove was empty, much like the last time he'd taken the same journey. This time, he had zero doubts. Jessie's note was the same one he sent her years ago. They got it wrong then. Now, though, their happy ending was waiting.

Princess,

The legend guides a heart so true to find its mate before the year is through. At 7:00 tonight, my heart will wait for you. Come to me if yours waits too.

Cam was filled with so many emotions he was hard-pressed to name just one. He tossed his phone onto the console and hurried toward the giant boulders guarding the entrance.

The glow from several candles led his way into the small cavern. "Jessie?"

When she stepped out of the shadows, his heart stopped. Why though? Why was this time any different?

Was it the way the candlelight highlighted the gold strands in her hair? Was it the way the dress outlined her figure? Or was it because the moment was so huge?

"You look beautiful."

"Thank you."

Cam's heart raced, and he wanted to run to her. But he held back, needing to savor the moment.

"You were right about not being eight-thousand miles away."

"One should never assume."

"It seems so. You're home early."

"That's a very astute observation, Mr. Hunter."

Her voice and stance were relaxed in a way he hadn't seen in years. Something had happened.

"Why didn't you let me know?"

"I told you," she reminded him. "I have a surprise for you."

"You did say that." Cam grinned. "Although, you know, when I arrived for my last surprise, she was naked."

Jessie's turquoise eyes flashed. "Should I call her?"

"Why?" Cam gave her a cheeky smile, knowing it showed off his dimples. "When it's a princess I want." He took several steps closer, never looking away. "I missed you."

"You're sure you missed me?" she retorted. "And not ... the naked one?"

"Come over here." Cam crooked a finger. "And I'll show you just how much."

Jessie hesitated as several expressions crossed her face. Then, she smiled, and in the next heartbeat, she was in his arms, where she belonged.

His mouth crashed onto hers, and the kiss zipped from tepid to steamy within seconds. He had never been able to describe what she did to him   how she made him feel. With just a look, she undid him and put him back together.

His balls tingled, his dick hardened, and his need skyrocketed. In no time, their passion spun out of control, and he wanted only one thing—Jessie.

"When?" Cam barely managed before their lips connected once again.

"Ten." He thought he heard, but realized it didn't matter. She offered her mouth freely, and talking wasn't high on his list of priorities.

Jessie nipped his earlobe, and his knees almost buckled.

Cam skimmed his hands down her side, and a shiver raced through her. "You're killing me. Why don't we—?"

Jessie's hand landed in the middle of his chest. "We need to talk."

"Don't you think talking is highly overrated?" He nuzzled her temple, hoping to tempt her to see things his way.

"I need to say something."

The seriousness in her voice had him taking a step away. "What is it, Jess?"

"I'm sorry," she offered hesitantly.

"What are you sorry for?"

"I'm sorry I shut you out two years ago. Sorry I didn't come to you when the first message arrived."

"You're sorry?" he replied. "The mess we made isn't only your fault. A relationship runs two ways."

"I get that," she sighed. "Do you think we've learned from our mistakes?"

"Of course, we've learned. Life is messy, though."

"And we aren't perfect," Jessie murmured. "So, we'll make mistakes."

"Probably."

"This won't happen again. I don't think I could—"

He kissed her, swallowing the rest of her words. "We've learned the power of communication, Princess. That will carry us forward."

"Do you think so?"

"I know so."

Her ring was on his nightstand instead of in his pocket. If only he'd known she was on her way home.

"Jessie, I..."

❧

"I'm not done yet." Jessie placed a finger on his lips. "I want you to walk with me."

She led him further into the cave, where she had left a few items from their past.

"I don't know what I expected when I returned. However, I know it wasn't a walk through our past."

"The past makes us who we are," Cam murmured.

"I'm only realizing how true that is," Jessie grinned. "It can also show us where we went wrong ... or rather, where *I* went wrong."

"Jess, you're not the only one who made mistakes in the past." Cam brushed his finger across her bracelet chain. "It didn't stop me from falling in love with you. Like I said, I loved you then. I love you now. And I'll love you tomorrow."

"The past, the present—"

"—And the future."

"Let's finish our walk in the past, shall we?"

"What did you have in mind?"

She pointed to a dried flower and a ticket stub beside their skates. "Those are from our first date."

"Mission Impossible III?" Cam smiled, causing his dimples to pop. "Why did you consider that our first date?"

"There were differences that night." Jessie hesitated. "You gave me a flower. You held my hand. And I spent the entire evening anticipating our first kiss."

A sheepish smile crossed his face. "I chickened out. I was afraid you'd feel rushed."

"It's a good thing I took the initiative," she quipped. "Or I might still be waiting."

"Now, Jess." He tugged her close for a hard, hot kiss.

"You think not?" Jessie looked pointedly at the blue-plaid shirt she'd appropriated after the night they'd first made love. "There was another step I had to encourage, as well."

"Yeah, and it was so bad we never did it again," he mumbled.

She bit her tongue to keep from saying, '*We talked about this.*' Then she noticed his expression and realized after all these years, he still fretted about it. For some reason, that touched her deep inside—an outward sign he truly cared.

Jessie cupped his face. "Cam, it's why there are do-overs. You get to fix what you didn't like."

"There's quite a bit to fix."

"It wasn't perfect," she conceded. "But that didn't change how I felt about that night."

Cam's green eyes darkened, and he closed her hands in his. "It doesn't?"

"No. I gave a piece of myself to you that night. The feelings were very, very powerful."

"I felt the same way." A wry smile crossed his face. "Well, when I wasn't beating myself up for my performance."

Jessie grinned at how fragile the male ego was—especially about some things. "I think it's time to leave that in the past. After that night, you showed me a few things that curled my toes and made my insides scream for mercy."

His grin started small. "You enjoyed those things?"

"And I look forward to reminding you just how much."

"How about now?" Cam sidled a little closer and kissed her neck. "After all, we're both available."

"Not just yet." Jessie handed Cam her diary. "It all started on my fourteenth birthday."

"My heart chose you that day." His smile turned devilish. "It was the day I realized you had boobs."

"You're such a romantic."

"What can I say?" Cam dimpled, and his green eyes twinkled. "I'm a guy."

"Read what I wrote that day." Jessie handed him her diary and pointed to where she wanted him to pay attention."

Dear Diary,
Today, I turned 14.

"Skip to there." Jessie pointed to the bottom of the page.

Cam looked at me differently today. He made me feel like a female. My heart raced, my mouth dried, and I wanted to ask him what he was thinking. Then Mary came into the room, and the moment passed. Someday, he's the man I will marry. Jessica Prince Hunter sounds perfect.

"I couldn't agree more."

The huskiness in his voice caused her insides to tingle, and goosebumps skated across her skin. Her nipples pebbled, and she wanted to push him down and climb on.

"I love you, Cameron Clint Hunter."

"And I love you."

"Good." Jessie swallowed the lump lodged in her throat. "We've overcome everything life has thrown at us, and for the most part, we've done it together."

"And we always will," he murmured.

She thought about telling him about Catherine but decided against it. This moment was theirs—and only theirs.

"Cam..."

"Princess."

"Will you marry me?"

"Aren't I supposed to ask you that question?"

"I want you to know that I'm choosing you." Jessie picked up the ring box from where she'd left it. "Your mom gave this to me."

"Seems I need to have a talk with my mom."

Her breath caught. "Are you really upset?"

Cam smiled, one of those lazy ones that melted her inside and made her want to promise him everything.

"How can I be upset?" he whispered. "When everything I've ever wanted is standing before me."

"Oh, Cam."

"Will *you* marry me, Jess?"

From his too-long blond hair, to his dimples like craters in his face, he was adorable.

"I love you."

"So, will you ... marry me?"

"In a heartbeat."

Cam slid the diamond solitaire onto her finger and kissed her hand. Then, in one smooth motion, he tugged her against his chest and meshed their mouths.

Her thoughts scattered, and all she wanted to do was feel. She had waited far too long to love him ... not only with her heart but also with her body.

"Oh, Jessie," Cam sighed. "Do you know what you do to me?"

He latched onto a sensitive spot on her neck, and her senses went haywire. Her knees buckled, and she would have ended up on the ground if she hadn't grabbed hold.

"Probably, the same thing you do to me." Jessie pulled his shirt from his pants and spread her hands across the smooth skin of his back.

Want.

Need.

Mine.

"More."

He palmed her butt and pressed her softness against that hard ridge behind his zipper. "More?"

"Yes, please."

⚜

CAM SWUNG JESSIE INTO HIS ARMS AND, IN THREE LONG STEPS, stopped next to the pallet she'd prepared. "Are you sure about this? Are you sure you wouldn't rather make love in a bed?"

"What's the problem?" she teased, and her hot breath sent a shiver up his spine. "Are you getting too old for a pallet?"

"I'll show you old," he murmured against her mouth.

There was an impatience in their kiss. An impatience to get closer and make up for all the time they were apart. And while a part of Cam wanted to slow down and enjoy each moment, his body was saying, *'There's no way in hell you're going any slower.'*

He tugged off her dress and tossed it aside. She pulled his shirt over his head, and everywhere she touched, the embers burned to life.

Jessie skimmed her hand up his hardness. His body jerked with need, and when she moved away, he burned even more.

"Let me." Cam ripped open the button, but before Jessie touched him again, he captured her hand.

"Spoilsport."

"Oh, Princess, you have it all wrong," Cam warned. "If you touch me, my dick will take control, and the fun might be spoiled for both of us. We wouldn't want that to happen now, would we?"

"We definitely wouldn't want that."

Jessie slid her hand down the back of his pants, sidetracking him enough he forgot to remove his shoes.

"Do you need some help?" Jess arched a red-gold brow, and her turquoise eyes sparkled.

"Are you worried I might fall on my ass?"

Jessie's hot gaze landed on his crotch, then lazily drifted up his bare torso. The embers grew a little hotter, each nerve ending begging for attention.

Her hands slid up his chest, and she lightly flicked his nipple. Cam's breath caught, and he started to shake. Yet, it was nothing compared to what it felt when she squeezed him and trailed a finger up his length.

"Uh, Princess." He covered her hand with his. "You are making this very hard."

"That's the point, Cam." She chuckled. "I thought you knew that."

Cam tossed his shoes one way, and his pants another, and then just looked at Jessie. She was stretched out on the palette, offering him everything, and was so beautiful, tears rushed to his eyes. He had spent so many years dreaming of this moment he wanted to make it perfect.

"I love you," she whispered, almost as if she could read his thoughts.

"I love you too."

"Then what are you waiting for?"

"I don't know."

"Shall I show you what I want?"

"No, Jess." Cam crawled over her, hovering just above her mouth. "I've got this."

"Are you sure?"

He lowered just enough to brush a kiss across her lips. "Remember, Princess. It's not a race ... it's an excursion."

Cam captured one arm, kissed the inside of her wrist, and placed it beside her head. When Jessie reached with the other to pull him closer, he kissed her again.

"Remember, it's an excursion."

"What's an excursion?"

"Making love."

He latched on to her mouth and settled in for a nice, slow taste. It wasn't long before she hummed with pleasure, allowing him to sweep his tongue inside and turn up the heat.

"Sometimes, you encounter obstacles." Cam dropped kisses along her shoulder until he reached her bra strap. "Then you have to remove them." With nimble fingers, he slid the straps off and popped the front clasp. "No matter how difficult ... or how simple."

"You're quite good at that," Jessie sighed. "Have you been practicing?"

"I *am* an artist," Cam reminded her gently.

"So noted."

"Now, where was I?"

He kissed her again, striving to rein in the heat. But it was a struggle. While his mind screamed for him to slow down and enjoy, his body wanted to hurry to that final goal. This time, it was all about her.

"Watch it, Princess."

Cam brushed feather-light touches across her breasts, over her flat stomach, and pushed her panties out of the way. She was so soft that, for a moment, he worried his hands were too rough. But then she shivered delicately, and goosebumps broke out across her skin, telling him he was doing exactly what needed to be done.

"When on an excursion," he sucked one tight peak into his mouth, "you can travel in a horizontal line." Cam whispered kisses across her chest to latch onto the other peak. "Then other times, a vertical path is needed."

He lazily made his way from her sternum to her navel, tasting, testing, tempting. "Sometimes, you might need to take a round-a-bout road." A kiss was dropped on one hip bone. Another on her stomach. He nipped her breast. Then, worshipped her lips.

"No rules?" Jessie muttered when he lifted his head slightly.

"No rules," he confirmed, continuing his assault on her senses. "There's a time for soft and slow ... and a time for hard and fast."

With each description, he showed her what he meant. Her moans and sighs were the music, guiding him from one place to another, bringing her higher and higher.

He brought her up, then backed away, only to repeat until her movements grew frenetic, and she came apart in his arms. Cam wanted to savor the moment, but his control was almost gone.

"Are you ready, princess?"

Jessie dug her fingertips into his ass cheeks and wrapped her legs around his. "Don't make me wait any longer."

"No, Jess," he breathed against her mouth. "I think we've waited long enough.

Cam slipped on protection, and with the words from long ago reverberating in his head, '*It's not just inserting Tab A into Slot B, but it's all about hitting the right spot,*' connected their bodies for the first time in forever.

"Cam."

Jessie's body tightened around his, and with very little time to savor, they soared over the top together.

SHE FLOATED, HER SKIN SO SENSITIVE IT FELT LIKE EVERY NERVE ending across her skin was firing at once.

"That was…" Cam's breath caught, and knowing he was worried, the imp inside had her stretching out her response. "Well put together."

"That's it?" His brows arched. "That it was well put together."

"What should I have said?" She hesitated. "Should I have said it was amazing? Or would you have preferred terrific?"

"That would be a start." Cam propped his head up so he could look down at her. "Well put together … what does that even mean?"

"It means," Jessie tugged him down and kissed his cheek, "from your kisses," she dropped one on his mouth, "to your touches," her fingers danced down his side, "to the ending, was … perfect."

His eyes sparked, and he smiled, showing off his dimples.

"Really?"

"From the way I reacted," she whispered, "did you have any doubt?" The answer was in his eyes. Pleasing her had been a priority. "Oh, Cam," Jessie wrapped her arms around him. "Maybe we can do it again, and I'll show you just how much…"

A noise just beyond the mouth of the cave caused Jessie to panic. Before she could move, Cam grabbed a blanket and tossed it over them. It had barely fluttered down when the beam of a flashlight hit them directly in the eyes.

TWENTY-FIVE

Lover's Cave
August 20
9:30 p.m.

"Move the damn light," Cam snapped. "You're blinding us."

It took several seconds for her eyes to adjust, which gave the little spark of fear inside time to grow. Who was behind the flashlight? Was it Catherine coming to exact her revenge? Was it Eden trying to get Cam back? Was it...?

Jessie glanced over Cam's shoulder, relieved but not completely surprised to see their visitor was Dylan. The look on his face reminded her of the times he'd caught them in embarrassing situations. Except, this time, there was something different.

"Sorry," he replied sheepishly when their eyes met.

"Sorry? That's all you have to say?"

"I, uh, I hope I didn't come at a bad time."

Jessie buried her head in Cam's chest and hoped Dylan would disappear. "Think he'll leave if we ignore him?"

"I have my instructions," Dylan grumbled. "Otherwise, there's no way in hell I would have come down here."

"Instructions?" Jessie peered back around Cam's shoulder. "Who sent you?"

"Molly."

"Molly?" Jessie frowned. "How does Molly know where we are? I haven't seen her since I've been back."

"I'd bet it was the Swan Harbor gossip line, Princess," Cam murmured. "Have you forgotten how busy it can be?"

"It's nice to know some things never change," she giggled. "Think they're up to date?"

"If they're not, I'd be happy to shout it from the rooftops," Cam offered.

"Just get dressed first, Hunter," Dylan retorted. "I'd hate to have to arrest you for indecent exposure."

"Dylan, why are you here?" Jessie grumbled.

"You're late."

"Late? What are we late for?"

"The family is waiting to congratulate you," he finally revealed. "And I want to hear what went on at the hospital."

"Hospital?" Cam murmured. "When were you at the hospital?"

"According to the gossip line earlier today," Dylan responded before she could. "Jessie was with Mary."

"You were with my mother?" Cam frowned. "Is that when she gave you the ring?"

"Yes and no." Jessie glanced from Cam to Dylan, then back. "I'll explain everything later. I promise."

"I'm going to hold you to that, Sis." Dylan suddenly chuckled. "You know, one good thing came out of this."

"Agreed." Jessie grinned. "We're engaged … finally."

"Well, that too. But I was referring to the fact that now, when you bug me about Catherine catching me—"

"Go away, Dylan. We'll see you in a little bit."

"Just remember," Dylan reminded them, "a bit isn't long."

"Jessie, what...?" Cam began as soon as they were alone.

"I know you have questions," Jessie cut him off. "I was going to tell you, but..."

"There were more important things to talk about?"

"Partly, I think."

"Just not completely?"

"Not completely, no." She soothed her hand down his lean cheek, and the diamond on her finger caught her eye. "I didn't want to share. For a few hours, anyway, I just wanted it to be about us. Does that make sense?"

"I get that, Princess." Cam slid his hand up her side and palmed her breast. "I, for one, am very grateful." His thumb glided over her nipple, and a little charge rushed along her skin. "You know, I think I have an idea."

"You do?" Except it was a rhetorical question, as his body told her what he wanted. "What did you have in mind?"

"Well, it goes a little like this." Cam pushed her over onto her back, but his artist's fingers were never still. They feathered, stroked, and glided across her torso, each move a little bolder than the one before. "You don't think Dylan would come back after us, do you?" he whispered against her mouth.

Jessie couldn't pull her thoughts together. He touched her, and her skin came alive.

"I, I, I'm not sure."

Cam sucked one of her earlobes into his mouth. "Well, then, we'd better get busy. I need a few more memories to tide me over."

"Show me."

"My pleasure."

His lips met hers, and for that moment in time, everything else ceased to matter.

Cam's Home
August 20
10:30 p.m.

CAM STEPPED OUT ONTO THE PATIO, AND THE SOUND OF THE waves immediately lowered his frustration. He'd wanted to hear about Jessie's conversation with Catherine. However, now he had a war going on inside of him. One side was proud of her for being strong, the other half was floundering.

"Here, Son." Clint handed him a high-ball glass. "I thought you could use this."

"How'd you know?"

"I've been in your shoes."

"With mom?"

"Who else?" Clint chuckled. "Take the situation with Catherine's mother, for instance."

"Mom said you confronted her together," Cam replied.

"Except, I don't quite remember it that way," Clint laughed. "It was my morning to take Gray to school, and, in my rush, I forgot my briefcase."

"And you asked Mom to bring it to you," Cam surmised.

"That's what happened," Clint nodded. "In the meantime, your mother discovered the photos. When she arrived at the office, she was spitting mad and spoiling for a fight."

"Just not with you?"

"No, thank goodness. Mary trusted me."

"So, what happened?"

"I heard her yelling at Sharon from down the hall." Clint let go of a light laugh. "When I walked in, I wasn't sure who needed to be rescued."

"That's where Jessie and I went wrong," Cam sighed. "Or at least partly. We didn't trust each other enough."

"Trust and communication are the foundations of a good relationship," Clint murmured. "It's also the first thing that can break down."

Which was something he and Jessie had learned the hard way.

Cam leaned back on the railing and watched his fiancée show off her ring to Sadie and Molly. His body still buzzed from their time together. He wanted more. The question was, where?

With his parents back in town, the house was just a little too crowded for what he had in mind. Could he convince Jessie to move into an apartment with him? Was that what they needed to do to be together? They had been apart for too long. Now that she was his—he needed her close.

"Cameron," Clint pulled his attention back. "We all spoiled Jessie when she was young. She was the only girl between our two families. That being said, she's blossomed into a fine young woman. I'm happy you've found your way back to each other. I don't believe I've ever seen her so happy."

That his father had called Jessie spoiled wasn't anything Cam hadn't heard before ... most recently from Jessie herself. His father's assessment of the woman he loved was spot on. Her smile was bigger, and he had never seen her look more beautiful.

"To be honest," Cam circled back. "I can't decide if I'm more annoyed about Jessie confronting Catherine alone. Or if it's the fact there won't be any repercussions for messing with our lives."

"Who said Catherine wouldn't suffer?" Clint retorted, and there was something dark and dangerous in his voice Cam hadn't heard before.

"Dad," Cam warned. "You said—"

Clint held up his hand. "I know what I told you. And I didn't interfere with what *you* were doing."

"You just did something on your own?"

"Well," Clint paused a beat. "*I* didn't do anything."

"But someone did?"

"Yes."

"And?" Cam prodded. "What was it?"

"It wasn't much," Clint hedged.

"Dad."

"I asked Blake, in IT, to ensure nothing was left behind that could blow back on you all ... especially Hayden. While I understand why you thought you needed to take care of it on your own—"

"We did it to protect you, Mom, and Dylan," Cam said.

"I'm aware of that," Clint nodded. "And I don't mean to sound like I'm belittling your abilities, but sometimes experience does pay off."

"Meaning, you think if we would have talked to you and Mom earlier, things wouldn't have gotten this far?"

Clint shrugged, which was essentially a non-response. It had Cam wondering if there was more to his father's cryptic comments.

"And repercussions?" he questioned. "Without where the information came from, how can any of this lead back to Catherine?"

Clint's blue eyes twinkled. "Unfortunately, Blake can't just offer up the financial records—even if he were to discover something. That doesn't mean he won't '*do what he can do*' and keep the information safe."

"You mean *if* it's needed," Cam corrected.

"No, I mean *when* it's needed," Clint reiterated. "There's too much money flowing in and out of those accounts for it not to be missing from '*somewhere.*' And someday, when Swan Harbor deems it's time, we'll find out."

"Because things happen in Swan Harbor when they're meant to happen."

"Exactly. As for Catherine," Clint chuckled. "Her personal life is about to get a little sticky."

"What did you do?"

"Oh, not much. Your mother's devious mind helped with this one."

"Dad."

"Oh, okay. Blake..."

JESSIE GLANCED OUT THE WINDOW TO SEE CAM THROW HIS HEAD back and laugh at something his father said. Since she'd shared her story, he'd not said much. That had her wondering, was he upset or just happy it was all over?

"I told you everything would work out," Sadie grinned. "Eden never stood a chance."

"You did say that. I just wish..."

"Don't go there, Jess," Sadie scolded. "Be happy. You and Cam have waited a long time for this."

"Speaking of waiting," Jessie sent Sadie a mischievous smile, "what's going on with you and Gray?"

Sadie's eyes twinkled. "Do you really want to know?"

"Not that," Jessie sputtered. "You know what I'm talking about."

"I love him," Sadie whispered. "I want to be with him. But..."

"What's keeping you apart?"

"Besides distance, you mean?"

"Well, yeah."

"A commitment," Sadie admitted. Words Jessie had never heard her friend say.

"Wow!"

"You're telling me," Sadie sighed. "Gray and his college girlfriend dated for years, but that went nowhere. What if he's not the type to commit to one woman forever?"

"She didn't hold his heart," Jessie replied. "I think his heart was just waiting for you."

"Don't I wish. I've wanted…"

"The heart wants what the heart wants. Remember that."

"I know," Sadie sighed. "And my heart wants Gray. But does he want me?"

"Cam told Gray to ask you to move back to Swan Harbor."

"Really? When?"

"I think it was earlier today."

"And what did Gray say?"

"Gray's not sure he's enough of a reason," Jessie hummed. "He used the whole '*She has a good job, nice apartment*' excuse."

"So, I just need to convince him he's enough." Sadie glanced over her shoulder to where Gray was talking to Dylan. "I love his parents, but when they returned to town, it put a damper on certain activities."

Jessie snickered. "I was just thinking the same thing on the way over here. Maybe it's time for the Hunter boys to give the house back to their parents and—"

"—Take up residence somewhere else," Sadie agreed. "I should suggest that."

"You know," Jessie glanced back out the window, and her eyes locked with Cam's, "maybe I should suggest the same thing. I'm going to go talk to my fiancé."

Sadie squeezed her hand. "Good luck."

"Good luck to you too, Sadie. Maybe someday, instead of just best friends, we can be sisters."

"That would be … amazing," Sadie replied. "It's a long-time dream of mine."

"Look at this!" Jessie flashed her ring. "Dreams do come true."

"Fingers crossed," Sadie giggled, "and toes too."

Jessie watched her friend walk toward Gray, and something told her she didn't need to worry. The way he looked at Sadie told a story all of its own. However, the question of how it played out was still up in the air.

In the meantime, she had an agenda to discuss with Cam. One she thought would be advantageous to both.

She found him on the patio, laughing at something Clint had said. They turned toward her with identical expressions, pushing her to ask. "Who are you plotting against?"

"Who, us?" Clint shrugged. "No one special."

"Uh huh," Jessie hummed.

"Really. It's no one special," he reiterated. "Ask Cam, he'll back me up."

Jessie laughed. "Now, I see where Cam and Gray get their '*ability to dance around tough answers*' behavior."

Clint gave her a look that said, '*Who, me?*' But the smile on his face told a different story. "I'm going to go see what Mary is up to." On the way inside, he kissed Jessie on the side of the head. "You two behave."

"Do I want to know?"

Cam tugged her into his arms and buzzed a kiss across her forehead. "It depends on the question."

"Do I want to know what you and Clint were discussing?"

"You know how you found my mother with Hayden when you got to town?"

"Yeah," Jessie nodded. "I was surprised, but with everything going on, I never asked how it happened. I thought your parents promised to stay out of it."

"They didn't stay out of it," Cam laughed. "They stayed out of what *we* were doing."

"Ah, they used semantics to get around their promise," she realized. "So, what did they do?"

Cam explained what the IT guy was doing, which mostly went over Jessie's head. What she found interesting was what was going to happen with Catherine."

"You're saying Blake will leave some crumbs, so the hospital has to audit their departments?"

"Supposedly."

"And that Catherine used her work computer—and work funds—to buy sexy lingerie?

"She did," Cam hummed. "You know that's a no-no."

"And that's it?"

"Oh, no. There were other expenses the hospital shouldn't have been charged for, as well," he replied. "Unfortunately, nothing that will get her thrown in jail. However, I can't say the same about her job."

"Do you think she'll get fired?"

Cam shrugged. "I guess it depends on who Catherine is buying lingerie for. If it's her boss..."

"Who happens to be the hospital administrator," Jessie groaned. "Nothing will come of it."

"If it's not, though," Cam continued. "That's something at least. After everything she's done, she needs to be knocked back a few steps. But..."

"We shouldn't dwell on her. We're happy and together. That's what's important."

"I know." Their eyes locked, and in his, she saw the same regrets she was sure were in hers. There was also desire simmering just below the surface. And since they couldn't explore how deep it went, Jessie circled back. "Whose idea was it to go looking for fancy lingerie?"

"Princess," he nuzzled his nose against hers, "there are just some things you don't discuss with your parents."

"I get that."

"Was there something else you needed to ask me?" Cam questioned. "Or did you miss me? Miss this?"

He kissed her, one of those open-mouth kisses that sucked out her soul and ratcheted up her desire as quickly as a heartbeat. It had her thinking about stripping him bare and seeing how far she could push him. Then, let him do the same to her. There was nothing she wanted more than to spend the night wrapped...

"Stop." Jessie pushed him back a step. "We can't."

Cam dropped his head against her shoulder, and gradually, his breathing slowed. When he glanced up, his eyes were dark moss green. Her lipstick was smeared across his mouth, and his body was primed and ready to go.

HE TOOK A DEEP BREATH. ON THE ONE HAND, HE DIDN'T WANT TO mention her hospital visit, but on the other, he knew he had to. Everything needed to be out in the open.

"You're right, we can't."

Jessie's turquoise eyes dug into him as if she was trying to read his mind. "Cam, why don't—?"

"Wait." He kissed her, a quick, hard one, and cut her off. "I need to say something first."

"It's about my going to talk to Catherine, right?" she sighed. "Are you going to yell at me?"

A corner of Cam's mouth curved. "Do you think you need to be yelled at?"

Her eyes flashed, and she took a step back. The woman before him was the one he'd only just met. She'd taken him by surprise, but the more he got to know her, the more she mesmerized him.

"I told you why I felt like I needed—"

"Jessie." Cam kissed her again. "Just listen."

She grinned. "If I don't listen, will you keep kissing me?"

He laced his fingers loosely behind her back and waited for their eyes to meet. "I'm proud of you. Initially, I had trouble processing the fact that you'd gone after her alone. Especially after you'd made a point of not wanting me to do the same."

"I know," Jessie sighed. "I just..."

"Let me finish, please. Then we can put it behind us, okay?"

"Okay."

"You were right on a couple of fronts regarding Catherine."

"Of course I was." She frowned. "But how do you think I was right?"

"It all started with you," Cam replied. "It all started when she arranged for you to leave Swan Harbor. From there, it snowballed. Catherine blamed you and Molly and wanted both of you out of the picture. But—"

"Molly wouldn't have been as easy to manipulate as I was," Jessie jumped in. "Like I said earlier, I inadvertently helped Catherine."

"*We* helped her," Cam emphasized. "Just no more. Our future is just that, *our* future."

"I love you, Cam."

"That's good to know, Princess." He leaned in to kiss her, and just as she'd done in June, she put her finger on his chin and stopped his descent.

"What have I told you about that?" she retorted, her princess voice on full display.

"About what?" he teased.

"When someone says they love you, what are you supposed to say?"

"Oh, that." Cam grinned. "I love you, Princess. Is that it?"

"That's it." She toyed with the button on his shirt for a heartbeat, then glanced up under her brows. "Is that it about Catherine? Can we put it behind us? Really?"

"Do I think Catherine will stay out of our lives?" he asked. "I think so. Her plan to take our happy ending failed. She'll move on."

"I hope you're right. Now that's all taken care of, there's something else I wanted to say." Jessie hesitated. "Or should we go inside and talk about it later?"

"We should probably go inside," Cam answered. "However, before we do, I want to run something by you."

Jessie held up her ring. "Does it have something to do with a wedding date? You know, as soon as we go inside, they'll want to know."

"Can we get married tomorrow?"

"Tomorrow!" Jessie exclaimed. "No."

"Next week? Next month?" When she said nothing, Cam's heart ticked up, "I'm not waiting until next year to marry you, Jessica Marie Prince!"

"I didn't say you had to," she assured him. "However, I do have an idea."

"When?"

"I'll tell you in a minute. Your turn first.

"If I move into an apartment, will you move in with me?" he asked, then held his breath, waiting to see what she'd say.

"You're not afraid Dylan will come after you with a loaded pistol, right?"

"He didn't come after me with one when I stole his cruiser," Cam reminded her. "And he didn't point one at me earlier. So, I think I'm safe. Yes, we have our entire lives ahead of us, but..."

"We need to make up for lost time." Jessie nuzzled the underside of his chin. "Don't you think so?"

"I do," he agreed. "But more importantly, I want you to be the first thing I see each morning and the last I see at night."

"I want that too." She slid her arms around his neck. "So, how fast do you think you can move out?"

"With any luck, soon. Now that I've had you, I don't want to wait years to love you again."

Jessie's eyes flared. "No, Cam, I don't want that either."

He pushed her hips against his and kissed her. Like always, the spark of desire burned bright and threatened to run away. When he didn't think he could control it any longer, Cam released her mouth and hugged her. Then he saw his mother holding the champagne bottle and tapping her watch. "I think we're being summoned."

Jessie giggled. "I knew it wouldn't be long. We're lucky we got this much time alone."

"That we are, Jess."

Cam kissed her once more and led the way into the noisy house. His father handed them champagne glasses, then tapped on his to get everyone's attention.

"Mary and I want to take this moment to congratulate Jessie and Cameron. It's taken you a while to get to this point, but as I always say, it's not how fast something happens, but the journey you take to get there. And now that you're here…"

"Love each other," Mary took over. "Listen to each other. And learn from each other. As long as you do, everything else will fall into place. Welcome to the family, Jessie."

Cam clinked his glass against Jessie's and took a sip, his eyes never leaving hers. "I love you," he whispered. "Yesterday, today, and forever."

"Good." Her eyes twinkled up at him. "That's very good."

"Have you set a date? I can't wait to help plan the wedding." Mary paused a beat. "You are going to let me help, aren't you?"

"Of course, Mary," Jessie exclaimed. "I don't think I could do it without you."

"And a date?"

"New Year's Eve." Jessie's eyes met his. "I thought it would be the perfect way to end one year and begin another."

"Oh, Jess," Mary murmured. "The date your parents were married. I think Ruth and Robert would approve."

"What about you, Cam?" she whispered. "Do you approve?"

"Try to keep me away," he barely got out before their family and friends surrounded them, and the well-wishes started.

You are cordially invited ...

TWENTY-SIX
WEDDING DAY

Key West, Florida
December 31
8:00 a.m.

Jessie's phone buzzed, and she couldn't stop the giggle when the text tone was the wedding march. Cam had '*borrowed*' her phone the night before. However, he hadn't been forthcoming with why he'd needed it.

> Cameron: Good morning, Princess. I missed holding you last night.

> Jessie: I missed being held. But it was only for one night.

> Cameron: One night is too long.

> Jessie: I didn't want to deal with any of those superstitions. We've had enough bad luck.

Cameron: Our bad luck is behind us, and in a few hours, you will become my wife.

Jessie: I can't wait.

Cameron: Me neither, Jessie. I love you.

Jessie: I love you too.

Cameron: Did you like your gift?

Jessie: My text tone? It was a nice way to wake up.

Cameron: I bet you'll like how I wake you tomorrow better.

Jessie: I bet I will. I'll see you at sunset.

Jessie tossed her phone aside and rolled over. They had decided on a small wedding with family and friends—just not in Swan Harbor but in Key West, Florida. She'd wanted something different and unique. Somehow, a wedding at sunset fit. Plus, they could keep the ceremony intimate—like they'd wanted. Once they were home, they'd have a large party.

Life had been a whirlwind since they'd gotten engaged. They'd moved into an apartment at Harbor Towers, Dylan had been elected Sheriff, and Catherine had finally gotten her comeuppance. While she hadn't been arrested, she'd been fired from her job at the hospital and pretty much dropped out of sight. The future seemed to be what they wanted it to be. If you were patient—and fought—dreams really could come true.

Jessie splayed her fingers and studied her engagement ring. Soon, it would be accompanied by a wedding band, bringing one more wish from the past to the present. She would be Jessica Marie Hunter, just as she'd been dreaming about since her fourteenth birthday.

The last few months had also given her new insight into her past. Two times in her life, her world had shattered. Both times, the darkness threatened to consume her, overwhelming her and making her feel lost and alone.

As an adult, she understood her darkness was depression. She could also admit there were times when she might have benefited from medication. However, she'd been fortunate. Her family had been there for her. Cam had been there for her. In her eyes, it had been their love that had saved her.

Clint's words, "*...it's not how fast something happens, but the journey you take to get there,*" resonated. The sentiment had merit. Over the last few years, she'd changed and grown. Her past hadn't been easy, but those experiences had turned her into the person she'd become. Someone who wouldn't run the next time life was hard.

Three sharp knocks on her door caused her heart rate to skyrocket. "You'd better not be Cam."

"Open the door, sis," Dylan replied. "I have something for you."

Curiosity had her inviting him inside. He was carrying a tray with coffee and some fresh fruit.

"You brought caffeine. Nice."

"That's very observant of you," Dylan teased.

"Well, I did come from a family of law enforcement officers, Sheriff," she tossed back. "Mom and Dad would have been proud."

"I like to think so. In fact," he handed her a wrinkled envelope, "Mom and Dad are who I wanted to talk to you about."

Jessie looked down at the envelope, and tears sprang to her eyes. Written on the front were the words...

For Jessie...
To be opened on your wedding day.

"That's mom's writing, isn't it?"

"Yeah. After Molly moved in, I found a box of letters in the closet."

"What kind of letters?"

"Letters our parents wrote to each other when they were in college. Plus, some cards we'd given her." Dylan shrugged. "Most of them I left in the box, but..."

"But what, Dylan?"

"There was that one," he indicated the envelope she was holding, "as well as one for me and one for James."

Jessie's breath caught. "Did you read James'?"

"No. It felt wrong. I just read mine."

"Should I read it now?"

"That's up to you, Sis." Dylan hugged her. "I'll see you downstairs."

Once he left, Jessie looked at the envelope. The seal hadn't lasted, and when she brought it close, she imagined she could still smell her mother's perfume. With trembling hands, she removed the letter and a blue feminine handkerchief.

She slowly unfolded the pages, and a million things flew through her mind.

Ruth had worn Estée Lauder perfume.

Her mother's handwriting was much neater than she remembered.

Why did the thought of reading the words scare her?

Jessie took the letter out onto the balcony. She stared at the blue sky and imagined her mother looking down at her. With the breeze blowing softly, she took a deep breath and read.

Dear Jessie,

You are only a few hours old as I write this. But with my pen hovering above the paper, I'm wondering what one should say to a newborn. Please remember as you read this, you were born a week after your due date, and I was in labor for twelve long hours. So, if I make little sense, it's because I'm tired but happier than you can imagine.

I love your brothers, but from the moment I knew I was expecting, I hoped you would be a little girl. On the day we found out my wish had come true, I cried tears of joy. I have so many hopes and dreams for you, really too many to name.

Except there is something essential for me to say, Princess. Please never doubt that I loved you.

Through the sleepless nights and the tantrums of toddler years, I loved you.

Through your sassy times and stubborn times, I loved you.

And through those teen years when I didn't like you very much, I still loved you.

Make the most of every day because no matter how much you may want to, you can't turn back time. Learn from your past, and look toward the future.

As you read this on your wedding day, I hope you've found a man worthy of your love. One who lifts you when you're down, celebrates your successes and allows you to be everything you are meant to be. (If not, I'm sure your daddy, Dylan, and James will have a word ... or two with him.)

I pray your husband makes you as happy as your father has made me. Marriage isn't easy. It takes hard work, lots of love, and laughter. Trust him with your secrets, and communicate your concerns. (Especially if you inherited your father's stubborn gene.) And never forget we are your family and will always be there to catch you when you fall.

Although I'm a little late to the party, I hope you'll carry the enclosed handkerchief if you've not chosen something old and blue. Your grandmother Roberts carried it at her wedding, and I carried it at mine. Now, it's your turn.

Enjoy the day. It's your time to shine. Your father and I will be with you every step of the way.

Love,

Mom

Jessie stared at the crumpled ball of blue cloth in her hand and tried to hold back the need to fall apart. How was she supposed to handle all the emotions racing through her body?

"Jessie?" Mary came out onto the balcony. "What's wrong?"

Jessie held up the crumpled envelope. "It's from my mom."

"Oh, sweet girl." Mary held out her arms, and Jessie fell into them, tears coming fast and free.

She lost track of how long she cried. More than once, she thought, she was done. But then, another fresh wave of despair would rush over her.

"I knew Ruth wrote these," Mary whispered. "I just didn't know what happened to them."

Jessie grabbed a napkin and blew her nose. "Dylan found them. She fingered the blue cloth. "Mom wanted me to carry this today."

"Perfect." Mary's smile turned melancholy. "You know that picture of Ruth and me in my office?"

"The one where you're eating ice cream?" Jessie grinned. "You two looked like you were conspiring."

"Oh, we were," Mary hummed. "That was just after she found out you were going to be a girl. She was over the moon. While we were enjoying our ice cream, Ruth said, '*Wouldn't it be wonderful if someday your Cameron and my Jessie fell in love?*'"

Jessie blinked rapidly several times. "Mom would have been happy."

"Ruth would have been ecstatic," Mary laughed. "Then she would have gloated.

"You're probably right."

"Are you feeling better?"

Jessie tilted her chin just enough for the warm breeze to dry her face. "I'm okay now. My face, though, is all puffy."

"Just a little." Mary ushered her inside to where Molly, Sadie, and Cassie waited. "We have some work to do, ladies."

Casa de la Esperanza
December 31
4:00 p.m.

CAM RACED UP THE CASA DE LA ESPERANZA STAIRS, THE BED & Breakfast where he and Jessie would spend the following week. When he'd discovered it and learned the meaning of its name, he'd decided it was meant to be. Hope was what had kept him pushing forward through the bleak times.

"Welcome," a bubbly brunette, who appeared ageless, greeted him. "I'm Vivi. And you must be Mr. Hunter."

"Cam, please. Your home is lovely."

"Thank you. We love it." She glanced behind her, where a wall of windows showcased her tropical paradise. "The view isn't so bad either."

Just beyond the walls, lush green foliage gave way to the beach and a small dock. Several boats were tied up, but the beach appeared empty and peaceful.

"It's beautiful. I think Jessie is going to love it."

"Congratulations on your marriage," Vivi grinned. "I recommend it. My husband and I are going strong, even after forty years."

"It sounds like I should be the one congratulating you."

"Marriage isn't always easy," Vivi replied. "However, it is very much worth it. Now, let's get the pesky paperwork out of the way."

Cam signed several forms, and Vivi led him upstairs to a corner room. It was furnished with a king-size bed and had a bathroom complete with an oversized tub and a water view.

"Does this work?"

"It's perfect."

"Good." Vivi smiled. "The champagne you ordered will be left next to the table. Would you like me to turn down the bed?"

"No," Cam said, "I've got that taken care of."

She gave him a secretive smile as if she could read his mind. "Just stop by the desk for your keys."

"Thanks, Vivi," he murmured. "I'll be right there."

As soon as she was gone, Cam left the suitcases in a corner and went to work. He spread rose petals on the bed, set candles in the bathroom and beside the bed, and left a Bluetooth speaker on the nightstand. The scene was set. Now, all he needed was the girl.

When he returned to the hotel, Gray was pacing in front of the lobby door.

"It's about damn time you made it back," he grumbled. "Mom has been fretting, and you know what that means."

"Dad's getting grumpy," Cam sighed. "Sorry, I had to take care of a few things."

"Did you forget something?"

"Forget something? Like what?"

"Protection?" Gray tossed out.

"Why the hell would you ask me that?" Cam grumbled.

"Well," snickered Gray. "It was the only reason I could think of that would cause you to run off so close to the ceremony time."

"If you must know. I had to check on the hotel."

"Where was it you said you were staying again?" Gray asked. "I don't remember the name."

"That's because I didn't say," Cam pointed out. "It's a secret—until we get back home."

Gray barked out a laugh. "Were you worried Dylan would follow?"

"Hardly," Cam scoffed. "I wanted to sweep Jessie away someplace that's just for us. Does that make sense?"

Gray's expression was contemplative. "Yeah, I'm beginning to see the beauty of that."

"Ready to ask Sadie to move home?"

"Thinking about it."

However, Gray didn't offer any more information. Then, once they reached his room, it was time to get dressed. Cam grabbed the bowtie and, for the first time, noticed it wasn't tied. Which meant he'd have to tie it. Except, how was that done with shaking hands?

"Hey," Cam grumbled. "Whose idea was it to get a bowtie that wasn't already tied?"

"I believe that was you, Cameron." His mother's eyes met his in the bathroom mirror. "Do you need some help?"

He glanced down at the offending garment, then held his hands up to see if they were still shaking. "I guess."

"It's not the end of the world," Mary assured him. "I've tied your bowtie plenty of times."

"Sure you have, mom. When I was a kid."

Mary turned him toward the mirror and straightened the tie a few times. Once again, their eyes met. This time, though, hers were glassy.

"You'll always be my '*kid*,' Cameron," she whispered. "Always."

"That's what you always say."

"Just wait. Someday, when you have a child, you'll understand."

"One step at a time," he replied. "One step at a time."

"Aren't you glad I stopped you from throwing that ring in the ocean," Mary teased. "That would have been such a waste."

"Damn straight." Cam shook his head at the close call. "It was the only good thing that came out of that night."

"You know how it is. Things happen when they're meant to happen in Swan Harbor."

"Is that your way of saying, '*I told you so*?'"

"Would I say that?" She hugged him, holding him a bit longer than she usually did. "Be happy, son. Take care of each other."

"You don't need to worry about that. I learned from the best."

Mary blinked several times, then put on her '*professional*' face, as he called it. "I don't want to have red eyes for the photos. We were able to help Jessie with her puffiness. But at my age…"

It took a minute for what she'd said to register. "Wait, what was that? Is Jessie okay?"

"Oh, I'm sorry. Jessie didn't want you to know about the tears."

"Let's get a move on." Clint stuck his head in the bathroom, holding Cam's jacket. "You don't want to be late to the altar."

"Wait, Mom."

"It's a non-worry." Mary pushed him out of the bathroom to fix her makeup. Unfortunately, it didn't answer his questions.

"Do you know what's going on with Jessie?" he asked his father.

"I know your bride-to-be is ready, beautiful, and waiting for you," Clint answered. "Isn't that enough?"

"Mom, what's going on?" Cam asked again when she opened the door.

"It's nothing," Mary assured him. "Ruth wrote Jessie a letter to be read today, and there were a few tears. But," she gave him a conspiratorial smile. "I told her Ruth, and I had planned for you and Jessie to fall in love before she was born."

"Huh," Cam hummed. Somehow, that fit. They danced to the song *I Knew I Loved You* at his graduation party. From that night on, *it* became their song. Finally, he understood why. Jessie was chosen for him from the very beginning.

He straightened his jacket once more, then patted his pockets to ensure he had everything. "Ring!" Cam looked wildly around the room. "Where's Jessie's ring?"

"Calm down, Cam." Gray held up the diamond and gold band. "I've got it right here."

"I'm okay. I'm okay," Cam mumbled. When he looked at his hands again, he realized he was. His happy ending was waiting. Nerves were not allowed.

They made their way to the first floor. Then, out onto the beach, where he would wait for his bride-to-be. With each step he took closer to the arch, he grew calmer. He was where he was meant to be.

The music started, and everything was so perfect, Cam felt as if he were living in a dream world. He wanted to take everything in at once but forced himself to focus on one thing at a time. Jessie's beauty as she walked toward him. The softness of her hand when she placed it in his and her radiant smile.

Surrounded by family and friends, their ceremony began. The rolling waves and calling birds serenaded them, and the sun shielded them from darkness. As it touched the top of the Atlantic Ocean and painted the world around them, they pledged their lives to each other.

"I now pronounce you husband and wife. You may kiss your bride."

Words he felt as if he'd waited his entire life to hear. Cam savored the moment, and instead of pouncing as he wanted, he slowly lowered his head. One inch at a time. Jessie's eyes flared, then drifted shut. Their mouths connected, and a surge of completeness rushed through him. At long last, he'd found his home.

EPILOGUE

Main Street
February 16
3:30 p.m.

Killian stepped out into the snowy, tree-lined main street of Swan Harbor. The low-rising shops and restaurants up and down each side were quaint and much different from what he'd expected. Just not as contrasting as the muted sounds. Horns, sirens, and the buzz of conversation were in short supply.

His attention was drawn to a woman as she stepped from the diner across the way.

"Bloody hell." He whistled. Her strawberry-gold hair and emerald coat stood out against the white of the snow, and he unconsciously turned in her direction.

She was speaking to someone on the phone, and based on the smile on her face, it was someone she knew well. He was surprised but pleased when she bypassed the parking lot and continued, her footfalls sure and steady.

With his black hair, bright blue eyes, and square jaw sporting a hint of scruff, he was used to drawing more than his share of female admiration. Perhaps the lovely lass would be interested in helping him celebrate his new job, quickened his feet. Before he could catch her, though, she turned a corner and disappeared.

It didn't take long for him to reach the last spot he'd seen her, and she was nowhere in sight. However, with luck from the snow and his investigative skills, she wasn't missing for long.

"Sonny's." He pulled open the door, and the loud music had him second-guessing his decision to enter.

That was when his attention was drawn to the large ice-skating rink in the middle of the barn-like structure. In the center of the ice stood the lass with the children gathered around. For a brief moment, he wondered what she was doing, but then she started skating.

"Bloody hell, she's beautiful."

"That's my wife you're referring to." The male voice brought Killian's head around quickly.

He studied the man, a blond, several inches taller, who didn't look happy someone had appreciated his wife.

"Sorry, Mate," Killian grinned. "Didn't mean to encroach."

The man stood a little taller, his goal to intimidate.

"You're not from around here, are you?"

With everything he'd been through the past year, Killian's radar fired. "What gave me away?" he snapped. "I bet it's the accent, right?"

"It's a small town." The man's eyes twinkled as if he were privy to a private joke. "It helps that Dylan is my brother-in-law."

Killian relaxed, somehow pleased with the town's gossip line. "He seems like a good guy."

"Dylan has his moments." He held out his hand, "Cameron Hunter. Welcome to Swan Harbor."

"Killian Reade, and thank you. Seems like a nice place to live." He looked back to the ice where the children were working to imitate the woman's movements. There was something about the way they watched her that caused his chest to tighten. However, before traveling too far down memory lane, he turned away and dropped onto a nearby bench. "I need to find a place to live. Any recommendations? I was going to ask Dylan, but…"

"Dylan and his wife just moved across the hall from us," Cam explained. "They have a leaky roof. Would you consider subletting a furnished place?"

"Whose?" The possibility aroused Killian's interest, as he'd only brought two bags and didn't relish having to furnish an apartment.

"Mine," Cam glanced toward the ice, "ours. My wife has this need to help others and wants to work with a not-for-profit outside of the country for a year or so."

"Commendable."

Cam shrugged. "I want her happy."

"You must be newlyweds." Killian laughed. In his experience, time wasn't always kind to marriages.

"Is it that obvious?" Cam's eyes once again sought his wife.

Killian grinned. "Your ring still has the new on it."

"We've only been married for a couple of months," Cam offered. "But I think I decided I was going to marry her twelve years ago."

"Amazing," Killian whistled. "That's a long time to love one person."

"Our happy ending wasn't without complications." A corner of Cam's mouth curved up. "But that's a long story. Anyway, since Jessie's almost done, let me introduce you, and we can show you the apartment. We're living at the Harbor Towers, just on the edge of town. You'll be doing us a favor."

"It sounds good." Killian winced. "But how is living across from family?"

"Timing stinks."

That Killian could imagine, as he wouldn't relish living so close to Liam. "When would you be leaving?"

"This weekend."

"I'll be okay at The Beachside Inn for a few days," Killian assured him.

"Good. Let me get my wife, but I should warn you, Dylan's wife, Molly, might feel the need to '*fix you up*.'"

"No need."

At Killian's brief reply, Cam quipped, "A woman back home?"

"No," Killian moved closer to the wall, "my heart's fine."

He wasn't sure he'd been heard as Cam took several steps onto the ice before turning back. "Beware, Killian Reade. This is Swan Harbor, where the heart wants what the heart wants."

Killian watched the lass, Jessie, skate into her husband's arms, and when they kissed, he found he needed to look away. Public displays rarely affected him, but watching the couple on the ice had him feeling—dare he say ... envious?

But envious of what? Cam — because he'd seen the beautiful woman first? Or was he envious of the obvious love and affection between them?

Had to be the first, as, after what he'd been through, his heart was immune to feelings.

"The heart wants what the heart wants," he scoffed. "Right."

"Killian," Cam slipped across the ice toward him, "I'd like you to meet my wife."

Jessie smiled, her face alight with happiness. "Welcome to Swan Harbor, Killian."

Sign up for my newsletter and download an extra Jessie & Cam scene.
Happy Anniversary
https://www.subscribepage.com/swan-harbor_bonus_scenes

Purchase a copy of **Kittens, Puppies & Love**
https://books2read.com/KittensPuppiesandLove

KITTENS, PUPPIES & LOVE
SWAN HARBOR'S HOPE BOOK 1

Would you expose your heart for love?

Veterinarian Emma Foster arrives in Swan Harbor with one thing on her mind, making business a success. But she didn't anticipate the lure of the small town or the pull of a man's magnetic blue eyes. Their potent combination threatens to derail her well-ordered plans.

Investigator Killian Reade has used his good looks to layer masks over his true self — until a flash of yellow peels off one. Then, the people of Swan Harbor add a crack in another. When Emma looks through him, though, he's forced to take a journey — one that has him searching for the man he's meant to be.

As their barriers fade, Emma makes an off-hand comment, leading Killian to uncover a disturbing behavior in their small town. When all is revealed, will they wrap the layers tighter or allow love in and set their hearts free?

Read an excerpt, watch the trailer, & download a copy.

Kittens, Puppies & Love
https://sophiebartow.com/book/kittens-puppies-love/

Hope & Hearts Series
Without hope, there would be no happy endings.

FROM DARKNESS INTO LOVE

KITTENS, PUPPIES & LOVE

BROTHERS, HOPE & HEARTS

KISSES, FAMILY & HOPE

A TREE, MISTLETOE & A SUNSET

HOPE, HEARTS & FOREVER

THE MEMORY OF LOVE

THE INNOCENCE OF LOVE

THE FORGIVENESS OF LOVE

THE POWER OF LOVE

THE CHRISTMAS LOVE SONG

THE KISS OF LOVE

THE LESSONS OF LOVE

THE HEART OF LOVE

THE JOURNEY TO LOVE

Bonus Hope & Hearts

CYGNETS & DREAMS

Hope & Hearts Historical Novellas

GUIDED BY LIGHT - 1952

GUIDED BY HEART - 1964

GUIDED BY LOVE - 1969

WELCOME TO SWAN HARBOR - 1979

FINDING HER LOST HEART - 1983/1990

GUIDED BY A KISS - 1995

Other books by Sophie

SWAN HARBOR

MYSTICAL WATERS CANYON

LOVE'S PROMISES
A Swan Harbor Spinoff

ABOUT THE AUTHOR

Sophie crafts small-town mystery romances that weave intricate plots with richly developed characters. Her female leads are intelligent, resourceful, and resilient, while her male characters, often stubborn, exude sexiness, wit, and a protective nature. She delights in building slow-burn romances, savoring the tension and delaying that first kiss for as long as possible. No matter the trope, every story she writes has a happy ending.

After a fulfilling 30-plus-year career as a speech-language pathologist, working with adult post-stroke and Parkinson's patients, she is enjoying her new journey. With their four children spread out, Sophie and her husband live in South Florida. They share their home with a pampered cat named Irma.

You can find her on her website: **https://sophiebartow.com/**   *Sophiexo*

facebook.com/SmallTownAuthorSophieBartow

x.com/SophieBartow

instagram.com/sophiebartow

goodreads.com/sophiebartow

bookbub.com/profile/sophie-bartow

pinterest.com/SophieBartow